Jack Addison vs. a Whole World of Hot Trouble

The complete series

K.A. Merikan

Acerbi & Villani Ltd.

This is a work of fiction. Any resemblance of characters to actual persons, living, dead, or undead, events, places or names is purely coincidental.

No part of this book may be reproduced or transferred in any form or by any means, without the written permission of the publisher. Uploading and distribution of this book via the Internet or via any other means without a permission of the publisher is illegal and punishable by law.

Text copyright © 2018-2019 K.A. Merikan
All Rights Reserved
http://kamerikan.com

Editing by No Stone Unturned
https://www.facebook.com/NoStoneUnturnedEditingServices/

Cover design by Natasha Snow
https://natashasnow.com

Table of contents

Jack Addison vs. Man-Ravishing Spider 9
Jack Addison vs. Nessie's Tentacles 35
Jack Addison vs. a Pack of Horny Werewolves 73
Jack Addison vs. Centaur Pimps 128
Jack Addison vs. Merman Seduction 177
Jack Addison vs. Asexual Vampires 234
Jack Addison vs. Foxy Lies 271
Jack Addison vs. Catnip Dealers 337
Jack Addison vs. Doing the Right Thing 374
NEWSLETTER 413
PATREON 415
About the author 417
Other books by K.A. Merikan 419

Foreword

This crazy story was first published on our Patreon. We would like to thank our 3$+ patrons for making some of the main character's choices for him. While we prepared a storyline for each of the choices, it was up to the patrons to blindly decide which of the events would end up happening on page.

In this serial, each episode encompasses a single event from Jack Addison's career, but while they are partially self-contained, some of the arcs (the romantic arc, Jack's personal journey) develop over time, so it's best to not read this story out of turn.

Many of our shorter or less commercial works are available on Patreon first, so if you would like to have access to them, please consider supporting us.

https://www.patreon.com/kamerikan

Kat and Agnes Merikan

Jack Addison vs. Man-Ravishing Spider

Jack Addison Vs a Whole World of Hot Trouble #1

K.A. Merikan

"Please write down my name. Jack Addison."

Jack Addison. Son of a famous monster hunter. Grandson of a celebrated inventor. He has a lot to live up to, but his ego is as big as the expectations of his family. At just nineteen, he's fresh out of a prestigious academy, set to make a name for himself in a world where people need protection from strange and dangerous creatures.

During the annual hunt for the Loch Ness monster, Jack finds a rival in Roux Chat-Bonnes, a cat-like being who recently joined the same profession and is set to steal the bounty—and fame—from under Jack's nose.

Jack won't let that happen. He sets out on the hunt alone, but the creature that he finds in the cave near Loch Ness doesn't have tentacles. Instead, it's got hairy legs, eight black eyes and a taste for human flesh.

Chapter 1

The damp cold soaked into Jack's clothes, biting his skin as he walked down the path spiraling between the trees. The coachman who had brought him here from the nearest train station had told him that all the other venators had already arrived at Loch Ness, but Jack wouldn't let that stop him from kick-starting his monster-hunting career with the most prestigious event worldwide.

So he might have boarded the ship for Europe a little bit too late. Big deal—what counted was that Halloween lasted for another twelve hours, which was more than enough time to collect the bounty for Nessie's head and become another bright star in the Addison family tree.

As he followed the winding track, his feet gradually sank into the clouds of vapor that obscured the undergrowth. The loch itself, visible in the dying sunlight, was also partially hidden by the thick fog, providing cover for the monster that only left the depths once a year.

The sound of music and voices ahead gradually became louder when Jack neared the shore, and the cheerfulness of it all started to drill its way under his skin. Could it be that someone already had got the bounty? Was he too late after all? But when Jack left the trees behind and saw the large inn by the dark waters of the lake, there was no carcass in sight—only empty carts, cages, and human silhouettes in lit windows.

He sped up, eager to step into warmth. He hadn't thought his outfit through all that well, and the short leather jacket meant that the wind kept licking his back through the shirt. Then again, life was meant for living, not dreading a pinch of cold. Most importantly, he had his pistols, his family sword, and the latest Addison device, which would give him an advantage over other venators and lead him to the hell hole Nessie had crawled out from.

He pushed the door of the Monster's Head open and stepped inside. He didn't expect the Scottish to recognize him, since he'd lived in New York most of his life, but he was sure there was no venator alive who wouldn't recognize his last name. After all, the device they all carried had been named after its inventor, Jack's late grandmother.

The music he'd heard on the way came from a gramophone in the corner, but a large contingent of the people gathered sang to the lively melody while sampling beer, as if this was an opportunity for socializing, not the annual hunt for the Loch Ness monster. Almost fifty years since its first appearance, Nessie had only been captured by photography and sketches, and there was no way to predict where exactly it would appear this time, but Jack was still disillusioned by the behavior he was witnessing.

Was no one even trying to stay in adequate shape for tonight's hunt?

And worst of all, with the commotion, hardly anyone noticed his presence. Quite tall and muscular, despite being just nineteen, he had the kind of charm that drew the attention of women and men alike. To top it all off, his wide smile full of even, white teeth, sunshine hair, and blue eyes in a lightly tanned handsome face ensured that even without his last name being mentioned, he never drank his beer alone.

The inn was filled mostly with other venators—something Jack could recognize by the emblems sewn on their clothing, but they all ate and drank in groups, talking in many languages he did not recognize.

"Hello, love. If you need someplace to sleep, we only have hay mattresses left," said a busty blonde woman with a thick Scottish accent. She approached him out of nowhere, dressed in civilian clothes and wearing a dress with a neckline slightly deeper than propriety would normally allow, she was likely a member of staff.

"What? You don't have rooms available? But the nearest town is an hour away!"

She sighed and patted his chest. "You must be new to this. There's only so much space available at the inn. I could accept a down payment for next year. Many choose to sleep in the barn."

Ha! Next year. There would be no hunt next year, because Jack Addison would catch and behead Nessie tonight. Especially since everyone else seemed to only be there for a good time over beers and whiskey.

This conversation did seem like a good opportunity to drop his name though. "Yes, please write down my name. Jack Addison."

No reaction, just a smile. How demotivating. But a man sitting by the nearby bar gave Jack a curious look and poked two of his friends, both of whom were also venators.

"Addison? Like 'The Kraken' Addison?" the guy asked in a polite accent that sounded exactly like Jack's only English professor at the American Institute of Interdimensional Studies.

Pride swelled in Jack's chest, and he approached the men with a smile. "I am his son."

The Englishman squeezed Jack's hand. "Hector Collins. And these are my former schoolmates, William Tucker and Drake Nguyen."

William tapped the bar counter, trying to draw the attention of the pretty young barman who had so many orders to complete that his cheeks were glistening and rosy despite the cold. "What are you drinking, Addison?"

Jack licked his lips, sliding his gaze off the barman's neck and to his new friends. "Oh, I'll have coffee."

All three English men laughed to the point of slapping their knees.

"Good one, Addison. Keeping your wits about you, eh?" asked Drake.

Hector gaped and touched the thick handle of Jack's two-handed sword. "Is this… is this the sword that ripped open the Kraken?"

Jack smirked and reached back, pulling Gouger out of the sheath on his back. "The very same. You can touch it, but be careful, it's extremely sharp."

"Can I have some butter, please?" someone asked in a strong French accent behind Jack's back, and he wouldn't have paid it any mind, if it wasn't for seeing his new friends exchange curious glances.

What could be more interesting than the legendary Gouger? Jack wanted to sneak a peek at the guy, but once he looked over his shoulder, everything else was forgotten. He put the sword back into the sheath.

A chat. A real-life chat!

He'd read about them in the first Monster Manual written by his dad. The textbook had since been redacted to call them 'creatures', but that didn't really change what these non-humans were.

About Jack's height, but much more slender, even in the long leather jacket, the chat was ginger with a few white stripes on his head. The massive ears that twitched in attention hid white tufts that would have been cute on a normal cat, not this man-sized critter. His paws were white, as if he were wearing gloves. A ridiculous notion for a creature that was more animal than human. Did the fluffy fingers really hide killer claws?

As the barman served the chat a freaking plate of butter cut into squares, Jack stole a glance at the chat's back, and there it was, sticking out from the folds of the leather coat—a long ginger tail as furry as the rest of the creature. More disturbingly though, on the back of his coat, the chat wore the crest of the Paris Academy for Interdimensional Matters, Europe's largest school dedicated to venator education. Had he won it in a game of cards? Because he sure as hell couldn't be a venator.

"Can I help you?" said the chat, and caught Jack's gaze with his massive green eyes. Wow, even his spiky canines were the enlarged version of what one would expect to see in the muzzle of a domestic cat. And the same could be said of the chat's face. It looked like a large feline head. A well-bred one, but still that of a cat. Though this one's features were somewhat elongated, with a pronounced dip above the pink nose.

Jack's father would have said that creatures had no place among humans. Jack did not agree with that statement nearly as strongly, and he'd seen glimpses of them in London and Birmingham, but they should've been kept from joining a profession that was all about keeping their kind in line. Besides, being a venator required not only physical prowess but also brains, something creatures were lacking when compared with humans.

"You shouldn't be wearing this," Jack said, pulling on the chat's coat.

The chat slapped away his hand, and despite the gesture being aggressive, Jack couldn't help a silly smile at how the inside of the creature's hand felt like a padded cat paw.

"Excuse me? Are you questioning my credentials?" The chat straightened on his strange legs that ended with large paws, not shoes. He supposed footwear was unnecessary when you were an animal.

Jack sensed people's eyes on him, and it fueled his confidence. He gestured at the chat. "That emblem you're wearing. The Paris Academy for Interdimensional Matters is a serious institution, and only a graduate should have the honor of representing it."

The chat squinted, and his whiskers bristled. "My name is Roux Chat-Bonnes, and you better remember it. I am most definitely a graduate of PAIM. Top of my class, in fact. What would make you think otherwise?"

Another young man approached them and pulled on Roux's sleeve. "Come on, Roux, it's not worth spoiling your night over," he said in heavily accented English. He too, sounded French.

Jack shook his head. Unbelievable. This thing actually had human acquaintances. It was a far cry from back home, where creatures and humans didn't intermingle. Even venators in training had rarely met a creature before they took the practical classes toward the end of their education. "No venator academy would accept a chat."

His new friends looked at him with somber expressions, but didn't join the conversation. What was up with that?

"You're years behind the rest of the world across the pond," said one of the few female venators present. "PAIM is currently educating two non-humans, and some other schools are considering opening their doors to them too. And good. What's the point of missing out on talent over prejudice?"

That statement elicited some groans, and the merry singing mostly stopped, leaving space for loud conversations.

Drake pulled on Jack's jacket. "Can't we just enjoy ourselves? No point in discussing this when the issue is so miniscule."

But Jack would not give it a rest. He was an Addison, and he would not back away from a rightful fight when everyone was watching! "It's a great shame that the Institute bowed to outside pressure instead of keeping to its principles."

The tiny, but still audible growl coming from the chat gave Jack the satisfaction he was craving. "Maybe you should go back to America then, so you don't have to endure looking at me."

Jack snarled. That was exactly the kind of entitlement creatures exhibited when allowed to integrate into human society. "Why would I? This is my world. You are only a guest."

Drake's hand tightened on Jack's shoulder in warning, but why was he keeping quiet? Father would have been embarrassed if he'd known Jack had spoken to a chat, because even that implied that they were equals. Maybe that was the reason for all the silence?

Roux dragged his claws over the counter. Was this meant to be a threat? The audacity! "We share this world now, and we're all responsible for keeping it stable."

"Oh! A pussycat will be teaching me about my world now?"

A few of the Frenchmen hissed, shaking their heads, and the fur on the chat's head bristled. "What did you call me?" He grabbed the rapier at his side and pulled it out of its sheath with a metallic sound that made the barman freeze.

Some of the venators stood, others just watched, but the music was now completely off, leaving a tense silence that did not belong in a room full of people.

Was no one going to intervene?

Behind Jack's back, Hector cleared his throat and slid off the stool. "All right, I'll be off. Need to tend to my horse," he said and rushed to the exit, followed by William. Drake stayed behind, but he backed away, standing closer to the table where all the French people sat.

Was there no one to step in and support Jack in this? He bet they were all too afraid to say what they were really thinking.

"Listen, Roux—"

The chat straightened up with the rapier in his massive paw-hand. "It's monsieur Chat-Bonnes to you!"

Jack snorted. "My mother's cat was called Mr. Paws. Is that what your name means?" He kept his gaze on the tip of the sword. Inhuman or not, chats were known for speed and acrobatics, and he would not be injured before he got his hands on Nessie!

"And you'll be called Mr. Emmental once I'm done with you!"

Jack squinted at Roux, unsure if he should be offended or not.

"It's a cheese, you bumpkin! With holes. Don't you have proper dairy where you're from?"

Enough was enough. Jack pushed the rapier aside and kicked at Roux's legs, attempting to knock him off his feet. But instead of dropping like a log, the chat gracefully caught himself mid-fall and skipped away, squaring his shoulders once he stood. "What a dirty move. So typical."

Fire burned in Jack's veins, and he scowled, squeezing his fist until it creaked. "What are you trying to say, huh? A diploma doesn't make you any less of a pussycat. Even the device you carry at your belt has my name on it!" he said, indicating the well-polished addison attached to Roux's hip.

The chat let out a hiss, and his whiskers bristled when he revealed his sharp canines. "Is there anything you worked for yourself? Did you even have to pass any exams at the academy with that last name, or did Daddy take care of it all for you?"

That was a blow below the belt, but it still had Jack still for a few moments. He wanted to deny it all, but words got stuck in his throat, because Roux was right. Were it not for Jack's name, he'd have probably failed before the first year was out. But the academy did not want "Kraken" Addison's kid out, so Jack had been repeatedly given opportunities no one else got.

"Spit that out, animal."

"Never!" Roux hissed, his ears flattening right before he pounced at Jack with his rapier and missed Jack's arm by half an inch, only thanks to

Jack's reflexes. So maybe his schooling was patchy at best, but he did excel at its physical aspects.

The people around them became a blur. Jack attempted to strike Roux's muzzle, but the chat skipped through the air and landed on the table, crouching amidst dirty plates. His large ears lay flat against his head, but the moment the barman approached him, ready to berate Roux for jumping on tables, Jack's opponent shot through the air as if his bones were hollow.

Jack swallowed, balling one hand into a fist and pulling out his hunting knife with the other. The Gouger was not meant for this kind of petty fights. After all, Jack didn't want the chat dead. "If you want to be a man, then fight like one, you coward!"

That worked, but Jack didn't expect the force with which Roux's rapier would meet his own blade, and he slipped on spilled liquor. The chat continued his assault even after Jack fell, so with blood pumping in his veins like mad, Jack was left deflecting. From the corner of his eye he spotted an opportunity.

When Roux thrust his rapier forward again, Jack rolled back, grabbed the legs of a nearby chair and swung it at Roux's feet, hitting his target. Satisfaction exploded in his heart at the sound of a panicked cat-like whine, and the chat fell without the earlier grace. Blood spilled from his pink nose when his chin hit the counter on the way, but Jack wasn't done yet. He rolled to his knees and pushed the chair, not only trapping Roux under it but also putting down more weight to teach the thing a lesson.

Nobody disrespected Jack Addison. Especially not some entitled creature.

"That's enough!" Drake said, trying to pull Jack back, but he was too caught up in his triumph to listen.

"Are we done here, pussycat?"

Someone burst in through the front door, huffing for breath. "Nessie's been spotted!"

Chapter 2

Nessie. His first job. A big one at that. A head for Jack's empty trophy wall. He could not let anyone get to the monster before him. He froze between the desire to hunt and his pride, but the moment his attention slipped, one of the furry paws pulled out of his grip. He instinctively recoiled when a flash of red appeared before his eyes, but he wasn't quick enough, and the nails tore through his cheek, leaving behind a violent sting.

"You fucking thing! Stay down," he snarled and jumped to his feet. He was an Addison. He wouldn't let some chat pull him away from his destiny.

With his hand against his aching face and blood dripping from between his fingers, he joined the crowd of venators leaving the inn. He didn't even spare the animal a glance. Greatness awaited him just outside the inn and he wouldn't waste another second.

He slammed into Drake, who moved the other way and offered Jack a frown. "The kitty got you?"

The question tore through Jack's mood like a blade. Just great. Now he'd be the laughing stock of all the venators. The stakes for catching Nessie couldn't have been any higher. "He did it after I already pulled away. Typical chat. They're not known for playing fair."

Drake nodded. "Backstabbers."

But there was no time to waste on petty conversation when his face hurt as if cut by razors, and the others wouldn't wait to check up on him or listen to his story. They all wanted a piece of Nessie, so Jack followed them into the night, running blindly down toward the lake.

Many venators were already ahead of them, following clues shouted by watchmen perched in trees, and Jack clenched his jaw, counting his fellow hunters. There were too many. If he stabbed Nessie in the heart, his achievement would inevitably remain unnoticed in the crowd of venators who would be credited with the kill by participation alone.

What a disgrace. He couldn't let that happen. But he had no clues other than the ones shouted from above, so he followed the procession of venators who were chatting as if this were a marketplace, not a hunt. Because what else could he do?

Instead of staying by the loch, they ventured into the woods, and Jack's enthusiasm dwindled until he was among those lagging behind. What a useless day. He should have planned this more carefully. He had burning wounds on his cheek, and little to no chance at finding glory tonight.

That was, until his new generation addison trembled against his thigh.

Jack stood still, startled, but there was no doubt that the device was giving him a signal.

He swallowed and looked at the others, but the venators paid him little attention, too busy wasting time on conversation as if none of them felt that Nessie was within reach.

Who had given them their diplomas?

He stepped aside, between the bushes, acting as if he were planning to relieve his bladder, and only once he was out of sight, he glanced at the device.

The little arrow point away from the path taken by the venators blindly roaming through the forest. None of their devices had picked up the faint magnetic waves emitted by a crack between dimensions, but Jack had the best of the best, and he now had the advantage he needed to get to the monster first.

The arrow indicated at a steep wall of rocks, and when Jack strained his eyes, he realized that the darker color, that at first glance seemed like just shadow, might be a discreet entrance to a cave.

Perhaps this undiscovered place was where the monster originally entered this world. The device vibrated against his hip, but he knew how elusive Nessie was and ended up switching it off to stop it from making any more noise. The crack in the rocks hadn't been an optical illusion, and when Jack approached, with his heart beating fast from the excitement of his very first real hunt, cool, damp air blew into his face. Jack's feet moved over the soft moss until he reached the entrance of the hidden cave and peeked inside.

The tunnel was narrow, but for all they knew, Nessie could be a shapeshifter, or a blob of goo that moulded its body to the cracks. Hairs stood on the back of his neck at the sound of a strange clicking noise that resonated all the way to his bones, but he pushed on.

From afar, the cave entrance had looked more like a trick of light, but once Jack pulled in his stomach and stood on his toes, getting through the cramped space became a possibility. He tried to breathe quietly, giving himself time to listen after each step forward, but once he could move freely, the dilemma presented by the absolute darkness inside the cave made him stop for a couple of moments. The hollowness of the space around Jack made his skin crawl, even though he couldn't hear anything encroaching. There was the rhythmic sound of water dropping at regular intervals, but other than that? Nothing.

He spread his arms and tried to touch the walls but only met air, which posed the question: how big was this cave?

He hesitated for a couple more heartbeats, but there was no point of going on a hunt if he couldn't see, even if the light might betray his presence to the monster. He pulled out his lamp and found the switch. The portable electric lights were still very new, so Jack assumed most venators at this hunt would have to rely on oil, but Jack Addison had all the latest technology. Nessie would become the first trophy on his wall.

Was his wall even big enough?

His thoughts were stopped short by another series of the clicking noises he'd heard before. They were unsettling enough to make him stop and stare into the darkness surrounding him.

A whisper followed with gusts of cold air. Jack turned, barely capable of controlling the sudden tension in his limbs. His brain kept telling him that it was just irrational fear, but his body wouldn't listen and shook gently, sending Jack's senses into overdrive.

Something scratched the stone floor right behind him, and he slowly, very slowly looked back, squeezing his sweaty hand on the lamp.

He switched it on.

The massive form above him flinched at the change in illumination, and Jack backed away so fast he almost fell over when the heel of his boot hit a rock. The creature moved on hairy stilts, but Jack didn't want to see any more. He turned away and ran deeper into the cave, practically flying down the irregular path between tall rock formations, forgetting even his name.

He'd faced captured monsters back at school, but none of them was this big. None of them had faced him one-on-one either, and the sense of absolute dread pushed him forward, as if there was no other option.

If only he could find a small crack that he could crawl into and wait until the thing was gone.

The clicking noise followed him, and when Jack realized it was getting louder, he screamed. He should have waited and gone with the others. He shouldn't have been such a fool. His heartbeat was out of control spurred on by a vision of the monster's jaws on his flesh, but he was too scared to glance over his shoulder and check what the creature actually looked like, other than having long hairy legs.

Then again, maybe he should face it? His imagination had surely provided images far worse than reality could be. So he gathered the courage and turned his head.

The single lamp created deep shadows, somehow making the creature chasing Jack even more impressive. It moved on stilt-like legs, dragging its massive body through the air as if it weighed close to nothing. Something small moved where he imagined its mouth to be, but with the illumination so unstable Jack wasn't even sure if he would hit its head, if he tried to shoot.

He collided with a strange, yielding surface. Jack sucked in air as his electric lamp dropped. He stepped back—or at least tried to, but the gluey threads pulled him back in. They stuck to his cheek, to his clothes, and the approaching monster slowed down. Did it know that Jack was trapped? Did it have the mental capacity to have set this up in advance?

He sure as fuck had no mental capacity for anything but screaming when the creature reached the threshold of light, and all eight black eyes glistened, staring at Jack with emptiness that could swallow even the surrounding darkness.

It was a spider.

A spider the size of an elephant.

Jack could barely breathe, stiff with fear as the giant arachnid approached its trap, moving the strange claws at the front of its face. Bristle-like fur covered all of its body, and when it sank low, hovering its fat abdomen above the cave floor, the movement was like a dance.

Did this creature play with its food?

Fuck… fuck… This couldn't possibly be Nessie, which was known to be a marine beast. This was something else, not yet known to science. Perhaps Jack should have paid more attention to his studies when he still had the chance.

He tried to reach one of his weapons, but with both his arms trapped by the sticky web, he had no chance of grabbing anything and remained at the mercy of the monster that was already making his guts turn inside-out with fear.

"Do… y-you speak?" he tried, and it came out with a pathetic whimper when the spider leaned forward and moved the bristles on its jaws to reveal two sharp fangs. Black and already dripping with some kind of slime, just the sight of them made Jack push back into the web and cry out.

He still tried to struggle, but it was no use. The web was too strong even for him.

He would end up poisoned and devoured—his liquidized insides consumed by this huge arachnid, and no one would ever speak of him fondly. Gone before he could even make a name for himself.

A scream tore out of his throat when something hard moved down his back. The spider was close. He could sense its musky smell, and hear the clicking noises it made with the jaws all too close. Was it trying to communicate?

Would it hurt to be eaten, or would he die quickly? Maybe the creature would tranquilize him first so he wouldn't have to suffer? Back at school, he'd heard the story of a venator found with holes in his body, his organs removed. Only much later had investigators found out that vultures had stuffed their heads into him and eaten the carcass from the inside. It had seemed a curious gory tale back then. Now—not so much.

One of the fangs touched Jack's lips, and when he turned his head away in panic, the creature followed, eventually pressing the slick black fang into his mouth, so that he couldn't even scream.

Too scared to do anything, he shuddered as the oddly sweet substance trickled into his mouth. It was like sugar syrup flavored with something slightly bitter, but he had no choice but to accept what was happening to him as the spider's large body pushed on him from behind. Its long legs spread over the web until Jack's miniscule size was completely hidden. The spider's saliva slowly dribbled into Jack's mouth, filling it until he was forced to repeatedly swallow, on the verge of hope that maybe if he stayed completely still, the monster would lose interest.

Or was he swallowing a solution that would melt his insides for the creature to suck out? Even Gouger wouldn't save Jack now. With no choice left but to stay still, he let more tears spill down his face. Why had he been so stupid? He wasn't ready to die. He should have started small, hunting down necrorats in London sewers, not trying to slay Nessie. There were still so many things he wanted to do, countries he craved to explore. Was he supposed to die a virgin?

So unfair.

He shrieked when the spider pulled back its fang, but it stayed close to Jack, as if it wanted to absorb his body heat. Its furry jaws kept moving against the back of his head, but the arachnid wasn't striking yet.

Jack cleared his throat when it became oddly hot. A couple of seconds later, so did his stomach, and after a bit more time, it felt as if there was a burning trail linking Jack's mouth with his innards.

A sob escaped his lips. It was coming. He would be melted from the inside, and this was only the beginning. Already, his head was starting to spin from the odd heat that would surely turn into pain.

But instead, he was only getting more erratic. From his ears, to his toes, he was engulfed in flames, yet no pain followed. He licked the sweat off his lip but became attentive once more when the spider dragged its terrifying leg along his back, ripping his jacket and shirt with its claw. Gouger fell with a dull clang, like the sign of ultimate defeat.

Jack wanted to beg for his life, understanding that the monster would now feast on him, and there was nothing he could do, no matter how much he pulled on the sticky cobweb. Only a babble he himself didn't understand came out of his mouth, accompanied by drool spilling down his chin. Was he losing motor functions already? His skin felt oddly sensitive, and when the spider's jaws twitched by his naked back, the sensation of its hair touching skin had Jack twitching with something that was oddly like pleasure, no matter how much that went against his rational thought.

The arachnid clicked loudly, sounding almost gleeful as it moved over Jack, pushing his legs wider apart. The pressure on the limbs grew, and despite the haze clouding Jack's overheated brain, he realized the monster was securing his legs in place with yet more cobweb.

Stay still, it seemed to say.

There was no point trying to reason with the thing, but Jack still tried, frustrated when his tongue wouldn't move as normal, which resulted in slurred speech.

A huffing noise came from the spider, but when it rubbed its abdomen up and down Jack's naked back, the touch no longer felt intrusive. The tickling sensation transformed into heat that relaxed all of Jack's muscles, leaving him absolutely defenceless, but also devoid of fear. Perhaps it was physically impossible for the human body to take so much stress at once, and it gave up?

That thought only lasted a couple of minutes, because when something blunt thrust between Jack's thighs, his entire body shook, struggling uselessly against the entrapment. The moment the spider ripped his pants in the middle, revealing his bare ass, he stopped moving altogether.

He was hit by the realization that the sounds, which before seemed random, had rhythm and sense. Could it be that the creature was in fact sentient?

Legs spread wide, clothes ripped, and sweating from the heat coming from inside him, there was nothing Jack could do when he realized that a slick appendage devoid of any hair was touching his inner thigh. Not a leg then.

He arched against the heat of the hairy body on top of him, and while one half of him was repulsed, the other yearned for the touch as if he were a mindless animal, thinking of only his current physical need.

And what was this physical need exactly?

Yes, human, open up to me, the monster communicated without words. It was as if they now had a connection and the creature spoke directly to Jack's mind.

Or he was going mad.

He understood the spider's meaning once the prick-like appendage slipped between his buttocks and rubbed his anus almost gently, leaving Jack shocked by his own reaction. He moaned and writhed in the cobweb—not to escape but desperately arching toward the touch. Was there even room left for shame at this point?

All he knew was that his whole body throbbed with the need to connect with the monster and get off.

A faint thought lingered that his feelings about penetration had always been somewhat ambivalent, but his brain was thoroughly soaked in the delicious anticipation at this point. The furry jaws slid to his shoulders and tightened on the sides of his neck, and as the huge form behind Jack shifted, two of the long legs rested on his hips, trapping them in the position the arachnid desired.

Jack couldn't tell if it was all instinct on the part of the monster, or if it knew what would be most convenient, but at this angle, the damp appendage pushed at Jack's anus. He gave a choked cry when his sphincter squeezed against the force, but the spider was insistent in its needs and wouldn't relent until Jack's body let it in. The pain of penetration was like a stab, but once the muscles were forced to relax, the spider cock slid in with no trouble at all.

Perhaps the tube was there to eat Jack from inside out? Trapped in the cobweb, he knew that he should be terrified out of his mind, but whatever the spider had drugged him with was working, and no matter what Jack's brain screamed at him, he couldn't wait to rock against the appendage. Hard and slippery, it moved inside slowly, so clearly the monster didn't wish to rip him apart. Jack's sphincter throbbed around it, gradually allowing the invasion. What should be beyond wrong couldn't have felt more right.

He moaned his pleasure, his tongue and lips so numb he dribbled saliva down his neck, focused solely on the spider's… cock? Was it a cock? He didn't even care anymore. He burned to have it deeper inside him.

The jaws tickled his neck lovingly, and he arched back, trying to rub against the massive body while the appendage thrust in deeper, until it hit something that made Jack squeal in surprise. Then came a pang of pain. Not too bad, but the sound Jack made was adverse to the spider, which started retracting the thick tube.

"N-no," Jack whimpered, squirming to stab himself on the worm-like appendage. The creature stopped, but it seemed to get the hint, as the cock-thing started pushing back in a constant movement that had Jack questioning the length of the thing. And his own sanity.

Every now and then, the penetration would cause cramps in Jack's insides, but then the appendage retracted before once more fighting its way in until Jack's back was curved into a bow, and his dick stiffer than it had ever been.

Jack did everything he could to grind it against the cobweb, and its sticky touch, as strange as it was, offered that bit of relief as he desperately thrashed in the bondage. No future or past mattered. It felt as if dying would be a better fate than not coming.

He became frustrated when his tormentor's dick stopped moving, but then the spider twitched against him, and something pushed at his sphincter again. At first, he thought the beast hadn't yet shoved its entire length in, but then it became clear that whatever was worming its way into him now was inside the tube.

Jack's lips felt dry even after he dampened them with his tongue, but he had no complaints when the bulge passed his entrance and moved deeper, making space for another one. It was as if the spider cock was gaining thickness, hardening, only to soften again. Jack couldn't take the intensity of the experience any longer.

Whatever moved inside him, stimulated a spot that caused pleasure to ripple through his body. Bound, spread open, with a hairy body on top, he couldn't think of anything but rubbing his cock against the sticky cobweb faster.

The spider made that clickety sound again as if to soothe Jack, tell him that all would be over soon.

The pumping continued as the appendage passed more and more objects, depositing them deep in Jack's gut. It made him frantic with need but also caused discomfort as his gut expanded, filling so thoroughly he was losing his mind. It was only when the spider cock slid out of Jack's hole, and something pushed at the sphincter from the inside, that the mountain of pleasure crumbled, making his entire body shudder in ecstasy that consumed everything—the spider, the web, and even Jack himself.

Chapter 3

Everything hurt.

His stomach, his legs, his muscles, his throat, and his wounded cheek. Hell, even his head, so he stubbornly kept his eyes shut despite the bright light shining onto his face. Something kept tickling him, but he didn't react, wanting to fall into merciful sleep again and no longer deal with the pain and nausea. Something buzzed and bumped into the side of his head, making Jack sit up, only to fall back into the pillows when a powerful cramp twisted through the entirety of his insides.

"F-fuck!"

"Just stay down," said a female voice. "Doctor Hunt! He's waking up!"

The yelling made Jack's head hurt even more, but when he growled, the burning in his throat made him gag.

The woman above him wore a dark brown dress, with a starched white apron and a headdress that immediately identified her as a nurse. Her mouth was pursed into a pitiful expression, and she was quick to pull Jack's head up and put a glass of cold water against his lips. The liquid soothed the soreness of Jack's throat, and he shuddered, falling back to the bed after a few swallows.

Only now did he realize there were other people around. He lay on a metal bed by the window, but to his right was a divider, and someone coughed loudly on its other side. The smell of iodine and alcohol penetrated his nose so violently it took all of his willpower to keep the water down.

"You're one lucky lad!" said a doctor, rushing in. "How are you feeling? Do you remember what happened?"

Judging by Jack's state, the spider hadn't been a nightmare. Did all these people know what—?

"Inside of me!" Jack yelled, sitting up again. "There's something inside of me!"

The nurse smiled at him while frowning, which created the weirdest expression of both pity and consolation. "It's all right, doctor Hunt had your innards emptied, and your fellow venators disposed of the eggs safely. You were very brave," she told him, but it sounded like something she would have said to a crying child after inoculation.

Jack's mouth was dry again, and he pulled the blanket all the way to his chin. "I... what..."

The doctor pulled on his gray beard and nodded at the nurse, who mercifully left, sparing Jack the embarrassment of listening to this in the presence of a lady.

"That tarantoid poisoned you, but you're getting stronger. In two days or so, you will be able to walk out of here on your own two legs," he said, taking some notes, which he then pinned to the footboard of Jack's bed. "You need to be more careful. If you hadn't been found on time and the eggs hatched inside you, the young would have eaten you alive."

With a somber expression, he reached into the pocket of his coat and placed a jar on the bedside table. Small, objects that looked very much like large raisins, floated in brine. Jack's mind took its time to put two and two together, and his stomach twisted when he realized it was the spider eggs.

He drowned in the mattress, trying not to think too much about the tarantoid dick moving inside him and filling him up. He shouldn't have liked it. "Does anyone… know?"

The doctor frowned. "Only the venator who found you, but I'm sure professional solidarity will keep his mouth shut. Then again, it's hard to say how much you can trust a chat."

Jack's mind went blank.

"A chat."

"Funny ginger fellow. Well behaved for a Frenchman."

Jack's heart might have as well stopped beating.

Saved by a chat. If his father found out, he'd disinherit Jack and never speak to him again. "Thank you."

The doctor glanced at his watch and adjusted his coat. "All right then. You will be fed a liquid diet for the next two days. The chat left a newspaper for you, in case you got bored. I'll see you during the afternoon rounds," he said, retreating behind the divider.

Jack cleared his throat. "Could I… keep one of the poisoned eggs? As a reminder that I should be more careful in the future?"

The doctor shrugged. "I don't see why not."

When he left, Jack looked under the comforter, wanting to make sure everything was fine with his junk. Did getting fucked by a tarantoid even count as losing one's virginity? He was probably on virgin territory with that question.

The moment he grabbed the newspaper from the bedside table, he understood why the chat had left it.

Roux Chat-Bonnes saves the night!

The Annual Nessie Hunt could have ended in tragedy if it wasn't for Roux Chat-Bonnes, the first non-human venator to graduate from the Paris Academy for Interdimensional Matters. Instead of chasing fame, he slayed a tarantoid that had tormented the local population for months, and saved a young man from becoming a spider incubator.

Good luck with Nessie next year, monsieur Chat-Bonnes!

Underneath the headline on the front page, Roux smiled at Jack from a photo where he held the giant spider's head in one paw and the leather sack containing bounty in the other.

Jack covered his face with the newspaper and breathed in the scent of ink, but it would not obscure his shame.

Maybe next year then.

Jack Addison vs. Nessie's Tentacles

Jack Addison Vs. A Whole World of Hot Trouble #2

K.A. Merikan

"I'm not here to make friends. I'm here to slay Nessie."

Jack Addison is on his way to becoming a famous monster hunter, but luck had been against him at the Annual Nessie Hunt the previous year. Now, he's back at Loch Ness to show everyone what he's made of.

He's got a lot to prove to Roux Chat-Bonnes, the snotty cat-like creature who saved his life last time, so Jack goes into the woods to hunt Nessie armed with a brand new detection device.

But the creature he finds is nothing like he expected. Where he thought he would slay a monster, he ends up learning a valuable lesson about opening his horizons to new lifeforms. The learning curve is made delightful with the help of tentacles, suckers, and lots of slippery slime.

Previously on Jack Addison vs. A Whole World of Hot Trouble:

In the world of monster hunters, Jack Addison's surname really means something. His father is a living legend of the profession, and his grandmother invented the essential equipment of a venator. Hungry for fame and eager to prove he is his own man, Jack joins the annual hunt for the Loch Ness monster.

Jack is delighted when his name immediately makes him the center of attention (even if everyone is most interested in touching his sword), but his mood drops when he realizes he is to compete for Nessie's head with a cat-like creature, who has recently become the first non-human venator in history. When Roux Chat-Bonnes refuses to acknowledge Jack's superiority, their argument is resolved with a fight that leaves Jack with a scarred face.

As the venators begin their hunt, Jack goes off alone, and enters the secret lair of a giant spider. Trapped in its web, Jack becomes the vessel for the monster's future offspring, but before the eggs can hatch, he is rescued by the despised Chat-Bonnes. He decides to keep one of the eggs removed from his body as a reminder to never again be so careless.

Chapter 1

A year was a massive chunk of time when you were twenty. Twelve months had passed since the unlucky Halloween night that had initiated Jack's career in monster hunting and proved to him that being a venator wasn't all fame and glory. Sometimes it was tarantoid eggs up your ass.

But that unlucky night felt like a lifetime ago, and Jack returned to Scotland as a new man. If the run-in with the giant spider had taught him anything, it was that even an Addison needed to start small, so he'd polished his skills killing necrorats for a couple of weeks after his release from hospital. He'd then progressed to bigger bounty, and had assisted his father in hunting down a rabid bigfoot a month back.

This year, Nessie's head would surely be his to hang on the trophy wall. The tarantoid egg he kept for good luck was safely tucked into the inside pocket of his shirt. What could go wrong?

But first, he'd enjoy himself in the company of friends, because as he now knew, venators started arriving at Loch Ness a couple of days before Halloween. Since it was an excellent opportunity for hunters from across the globe to meet, brag about their accomplishments, and get blackout drunk, Jack had arrived with his own jolly group the evening before the event.

The four of them unpacked their belongings from the coach. Drake Nguyen, who'd invited Jack to stay with him back in London, Alwyn Hughes, who claimed to have experience with large creatures since his encounter with a giant in Sweden, and Michael Gager who, despite his name, had no gag reflex.

Michael was Jack's latest conquest, and in the past two months had proved to be a fun person to be around. He'd arrived in London fresh-faced and ready to take on the world after graduation from the American Institute of Interdimensional Studies, just like Jack had last year. Jack had been happy to take him under his wing when asked to do so by his father, but was even happier to find out Michael was a hot piece of ass. Red-haired, freckled, and as curious about monster research as he was about finding new positions to have sex in.

Jack was more than happy to assist him with the latter. For science.

The pre-hunt party was in full swing, and with the weather relatively mild for this time of year, the yard in front of the inn had become a venue in its own right, attracting guests with the promise of cheap drinks served straight from barrels, and a bonfire. Jack and his friends opted for the comfort of the barn, where many of the participants of the Halloween events would spend the night. Despite last year's annoyance with the sparsity of accommodation, Jack had ultimately decided against booking a room in advance, having not known that he would be traveling with a lover. It was by sheer luck that someone had been late to pick up their keys, thus enabling Jack to get some privacy with Michael after all.

They would celebrate regardless of the result of this year's hunt.

Drake rubbed his hands together with a wide grin. "I'll get us some drinks."

Alwyn sat on a pile of hay and dropped his bag next to it, but Jack couldn't pay him much attention once he heard French spoken nearby. He discreetly glanced over his shoulder, searching for a glimpse of ginger fur, but Roux wasn't among the group of Frenchmen claiming a part of the barn for their use.

"Some suspect that the interdimensional crack that has released Nessie is actually at the bottom of Loch Ness," Michael said, opening one of his many notebooks. Jack wasn't generally a fan of nerds, but Michael looked sexy when naked and with his nose in a book, so he let it slide.

"Did they say anything about it back at the Academy?"

While all students at the American Institute of Interdimensional Studies received the same basic education, the focus of their studies diverged significantly in the third year, so while venators, like Jack, learned the practicalities of hunting beasts, researchers focused on theory, which most of the time was kind of irrelevant. But Jack would listen to Michael and nod, since it usually made him more eager in bed.

Michael adjusted his wire-framed glasses and leaned against Jack, pointing to a complicated diagram he'd sketched. "There's a group of scientists from Edinburgh who presented this theory at a conference last year. Apparently, the reason why Nessie can only be spotted once per annum is because it leaves its dimension at will. It opens the gap between worlds on Halloween, hunts for one night, and then leaves, closing the veil behind it."

Alwyn snorted, cutting a slice from a block of cheese they'd brought with them for snacking. "You're making it sound like a sentient creature."

Michael shrugged, shutting the notebook when Jack gently squeezed his thigh. "No one has conclusively proved it's not."

Alwyn rolled his eyes. "Here we go…"

"Why don't you ask Drake? He's had a run-in with it last year," Jack offered.

"He said he stabbed it, not talked to it," Alwyn said with his mouth full.

Michael gasped and pulled on Jack's sleeve. "Is that... a chat?" he whispered, and Jack turned to look.

He'd both dreaded meeting Roux again and anticipated it. He'd gone through a thousand witty retorts he could make in case the chat wanted to embarrass him over last year's fiasco, but now he couldn't remember a single one.

Roux walked up to his friends, without even noticing Jack. "They gave my room to someone else. Said they couldn't wait any longer. It's not my fault the boat was late!" He made a scowly face and his lip curled to show spiky canines.

Jack swallowed nervously. That must have been the room he'd been lucky to snatch. Considering that Roux had saved his life last year, the honorable thing would have been to come clean and offer Roux the room. But then Michael rubbed his hand down Jack's back, and all of his good intentions went out of the window. It wasn't as if Roux needed privacy with a partner. Or did he?

"They have this new gin. The landlady says its invigorating, if you know what I mean," Drake said, placing an entire tray of small copper cups on the makeshift table made of a barrel. He grinned and sat cross-legged at Alwyn's side, adjusting clothes which were entirely too nice to wear for a hunt. He was dressed as if he was about to court a lady, not take down a monster.

Alwyn snapped his fingers, finally making Jack tear his eyes away from Roux wrapping a long gray scarf around his neck. "Not again, Jack. Let it go."

Michael grabbed one of the cups all too eagerly. "Let what go?"

Drake lifted his eyebrows and pointed to Jack's face. "Jack got his scars in a brawl with the chat last year."

Michael opened his mouth and gently traced the lines left behind by claws. "That thing did this to you? How is it allowed back here?"

Jack scowled. This wasn't how he'd expected this conversation to go, considering that Michael had an overall positive view of sentient creatures, all things considered. "We got drunk and had a bit of a fight. Nothing anyone should worry about," he said, weirdly uncomfortable with Roux Chat-Bonnes being called an 'it'.

And not only because of the debt he now owed the chat, but also because he'd met many different creatures during the past year. Many of the European and African countries had significant creature minorities, and depending on local laws--some of said creatures lived among humans. While he'd been hunting necrorats in London, one of his lovers had even introduced him to a family of fae who had settled in Hyde Park. While Jack wasn't always comfortable with creatures, he was also curious about them, and he'd found out long ago that making a connection was close to impossible when you viewed them as animals.

Despite his fluffy fur and cat-like grace, Roux definitely wasn't an animal.

Drake exhaled, rubbing his knees as he watched the copper cups. "Can't believe we might see her again."

So it was back to Nessie. Drake hardly spoke of anything else since Jack and he had become close friends earlier this year.

"Are Collins and Tucker not participating in the hunt? I thought they were with you when you encountered the monster last year," Jack said, sampling the gin.

"No, we got into a fight, and split during the hunt."

Michael laughed. "Seems that all venators do is fight each other more than monsters. You'd think you guys would be tired of it once you're off the clock."

Jack grinned, discreetly squeezing Michael's buttock. "Maybe sometimes it's the other way around. Drake here fights humans, but he looooves Nessie. Do you have a ring on you at least? Can I be your best man?"

Drake's face flushed so fast for a moment it seemed he might faint from the abrupt change, but Drake snapped his teeth and quickly downed all his gin. "Oh, fuck you, Addison! It's you who's all too interested in creatures."

Michael laughed and rubbed his cheek against Jack's face, missing the sudden tension. "Maybe he's just curious about their strange behaviors."

Alwyn poured himself more alcohol from his personal stash. "I've heard he called that kitty there a 'pussycat' last year, so he must be very interested in their behaviors."

Drake choked on his gin, and this time the redness of his face was due to laughter.

Michael frowned. "What does that mean?"

But Jack didn't know. He'd referred to Roux's resemblance to a domestic animal. Was there anything more behind it?

Alwyn shook his head. "You really don't know? That's what chats call males who don't breed. Pussy. Cats. Get it?"

Jack's gaze briefly darted to Roux's silhouette, with the tall ears with cute tufts. He groaned, rubbing his face. "Like… fucking other male cats, or castrated, or… what?"

Alwyn put his tin bottle back and glanced Roux's way. "The kind who likes getting fucked."

Jack barely kept his tongue in because his lips went so dry he couldn't focus. He didn't know creatures could be gay. Was Roux really a 'pussycat'? Did he fuck people? Or had he been so offended because he was the kind of chat who did breed?

Michael laughed. "If you ask me, many chats look like girls. I hear guys can sometimes be fooled when they meet one after dark. I guess a tongue and whiskers are all the same anyway."

Drake rolled his eyes. "I heard their dicks have hooks all over, so I can't really imagine being drunk enough to try that."

Alwyn frowned. "I thought you only liked girls."

Drake shrugged and looked at them all with a sheepish smile. "Everyone experiments in school."

Jack remembered the steady glide of the tarantoid's appendage inside him, how good it had felt in the moment, and how painful its impact had been in the days that followed. The thought of hooks inside such a sensitive area made him shudder.

Michael giggled, already drunk. "Why don't we just go ask him? You know, for science?"

Alwyn sat straight with a silly smile. "Yeah, Jack, go ask him. I'd pay to see that."

Jack wanted to protest, but then Drake pointed at him with a serious expression. "Are you scared you'll get another set of scars from that kitty?"

This Jack couldn't take. Nobody accused Jack Addison of cowardice.

"Spit that out."

Drake shrugged and watched him with a self-satisfied expression. "Then go and ask him about chat cock."

Jack rolled his eyes. "Why would I do that?"

Michael moaned and rubbed Jack's thigh suggestively. "Because I'm asking you. Maybe we could one day publish a paper about it in a research journal. Pleeease?"

Jack rolled his eyes but lost his smile as soon as he turned his back on his friends and started walking toward the chat. Should he really ask Roux about something so private?

Chapter 2

Jack picked up two of the gin cups, and slowly approached the group of Frenchmen. Roux sat on the periphery, leaning toward the oil heater with his paw-feet close to the flame burning behind the grate. He'd replaced his coat with a fluffy turtleneck sweater that had a collar reaching all the way to the base of his head.

Could he smell Jack? Because he hadn't turned around, but still put his paw on the rapier attached to his belt. Jack sighed, entranced by the way the warm light played in the red fur.

"I didn't think we'd meet again so soon," he said in the end.

Roux took a deep breath and turned his huge green eyes on Jack. Was he smaller? Or did Jack gaining a few inches in this past year account for the difference? The chat's ears were up and attentive.

"Yes. Too soon."

Jack shook his head and sat on the edge of the bench next to him. The chat didn't move an inch, which left little room for Jack, but he wouldn't let that bother him and rested his arm against Roux's. Some of the red fur stuck out through the knit and tickled Jack's bare skin.

"I'm sorry I called you a pussycat. I literally just found out that it's a slur."

Roux's nose wrinkled. "No need to talk about it."

Jack licked his lips "You seemed pretty upset," he said, and tapped his scars.

Roux's ears twitched time and time again, and some of the fur on his head bristled. "You said it yourself. It's a slur."

"Yes, but it's for chats. Most people don't know." Jack tried smiling at Roux. In vain.

The feline face remained unmoved. "Do you want something?"

Jack cleared his throat and discreetly glanced at his friends before focusing on Roux. "How have you been?"

The huge green eyes squinted. They were pretty amazing, even if freaky. Roux actually had eyelashes. Very faint, but they were there. "What are you trying here, Addison?"

Jack rolled his eyes, frustrated by the standoffish behavior. He didn't encounter this very often. "Why do you have to be so difficult? Can't a man talk to you?"

"Last time we met you called me Mr. Paws. Excuse me for being apprehensive about your intentions."

"A lot has changed in the last year. You're not gonna make any friends if you keep grudges forever."

Roux's whiskers twitched from side to side. "I'm not here to make friends, Addison. I'm here to slay Nessie. Which I couldn't do last year because I had to save your sorry ass."

Jack frowned, increasingly agitated. "Oh, so you're in it only for the fame? You don't care about saving people? Or is it just me that you don't care about?"

"I think I've proved I care about saving people last year." Roux's face was hard to read. Furry all over and just... different, it didn't show emotion in the same ways human faces did. "Nessie is yet another threat to the world. It's said the creature is massive. Most of all, the crack between dimensions hasn't been closed, and if Nessie got through, then something much worse might, too."

"I hear it might be opened and closed by Nessie every time. Science says that," Jack quickly repeated what he'd heard just moments ago.

"Science hasn't been very effective in tracking Nessie down so far."

Pride swelled in Jack's chest, and he pulled up one side of his jacket, revealing the small oval device his older sister had invented recently. He was the first one to ever test it in the field. "Maybe it will this year." He was excited to see that he had caught Roux's attention.

"What are you saying? What is it?" The chat reached out, but caught himself halfway through the movement.

Jack smirked. "Go on, you can touch it. It's a prototype my sister made. It can track Nessie's cries, even those too quiet for the human ear."

Roux's tongue made a split-second movement all the way up to his nose. "Thanks, I'll be fine with my own two ears. We can't all have the advantages of wealth and fame."

"Maybe you should just be happy you saved Jack Addison, so he can do great things in the future."

Roux's jaw dropped, revealing a tongue with tiny nubs on it. "You should be happy you're not baby tarantoid feed. You haven't even thanked me for that. I could have left you there."

Jack let out a long exhale. "That's why I came over, but you can't be civil like a normal person."

"At least I'm a person to you now," Roux grumbled. His body language was so tense just looking at it made Jack tired and stiff. "I accept your gratitude."

Jack cleared his throat and offered Roux one of the cups. "How does that tongue feel?" Did chats give each other oral sex with them?

Roux took the cup in both paws, and Jack itched to touch their pads and check if they felt soft. "Huh? What do you mean?" His ears laid a bit flatter, and it had to be the cutest thing Jack had ever seen.

If they had been alone, he might have attempted to scratch them, but they were not alone, and he didn't want some weird gossip reaching his close friends and family. "I mean, your tongue has those nubs. Do they feel like a cat's or is it smooth, like mine?" he asked and tapped his bottom front teeth with one finger.

It was ridiculous how apprehensive Roux seemed, as if he believed Jack was about to pounce on him or something. In the end though, he stuck out his tongue, letting Jack look at it in detail before speaking again.

"Like a cat's. But not to scale, if that makes sense. If a cat was my size, the hooks on his tongue would be massive." Behind them, Roux's tail started slowly swaying in the air, and Jack found himself fantasizing about it discreetly making its way under the back of his shirt.

"So they're actually sharp? Would it hurt if you licked me?" Jack asked, oddly excited about this conversation. He was on a roll!

Roux moved an inch away, and Jack had to stop himself from catching Roux's tail. Civil. He was supposed to be civil.

"Why would I lick you?"

Jack raised his hand. "It was a figure of speech. I mean... unless you are... interested in human males? I've seen this erotic picture with chats, and they were licking each other," he said, suddenly acutely aware of every single twitch of the pretty white whiskers.

Roux's ears went flat once more, his eyes widened and he rose so fast some of his drink spilled to the wooden floor. "What are you insinuating?"

Jack just followed his instinct, grabbing Roux's paw and pulling him back down. It was soft. Like a baby kitten's. Roux didn't walk on those pads, so they hadn't hardened the way his feet surely had. But despite the distraction, Jack focused on Roux's eyes, on the fluffy mouth, and his pink nose. "It's academic curiosity, but if that means anything to you, I am into males. You know, like a pussycat," he said in a low voice, and winked.

Roux didn't even blink. In the dim light, his pupils were huge, breathtaking. He pulled his paw away when he noticed Jack was still holding it, but there was not a claw in sight. "Don't say that word."

Jack nodded, sitting close, with his thick thigh touching Roux's slender one. "Sorry. I just wanted to say that you're a very... attractive chat, if you were interested in knowing that I think that."

Roux's eyelids lowered, and he let out the softest purr.

Oh, fuck. He was into it. He was a pussycat.

Would Jack actually be into that though? He'd heard that some people ventured into sex with other sentient species, but Jack wasn't like that. He was just curious from an anthropological standpoint.

His fingers found Roux's gorgeously soft tail on their own accord, even though he had no idea what he wanted to do about it.

Someone whistled behind them.

Roux's eyes snapped open. "I know what this is! Your friends set you up to this! I'm so gullible! Stupidest chat ever! But not that stupid." He snatched his tail away.

"What? No. They wanted to know about chat cocks, but that's not the conversation we're having, right? Calm down," Jack said, once again squeezing Roux's forearm. He wished it wasn't covered with a sleeve.

Roux growled. "Of course they want to know about chat cocks. You're all the same. I refuse to calm down. You should have stayed with your people."

"What? What did I do this time? I came here in peace, so stop being so fucking sensitive."

Roux pulled away. "I don't need to be anything you tell me to. And my dick is none of your business! You really are the worst."

Jack rolled his eyes. "Just great. That's not the way to integrate."

"I'm done integrating. I'm here to do my job, and I can't even get a good night's sleep before tomorrow's hunt because my room's been given away to some human. You people always get all the preferential treatment, but I bet as an Addison, you barely even notice how the world just opens up to you."

Jack's room hadn't been given to him because he was human. Or had it? Impossible to tell, but as Roux leaped away from him and jumped onto a pile of sacks in a single move, he knew there would be no more talking. Roux didn't even look back at him and started gracefully climbing up the wall, towards the thick beams keeping the barn in one piece.

Loud meows erupted in the drunken crowd around Jack, mocking Roux as he settled on the beam, pretending to be unbothered. Something strange appeared at the back of Jack's mind. Was it guilt?

"Roux, no. Come on, I have a proposition for you," Jack said, mounting the sacks with far less grace than the chat had displayed.

Roux hissed at him. "Leave me alone!"

A choir of laughter echoed behind Jack but he was undeterred and reached out toward the tail dangling far above his head. "You could join us. We have a room at the inn."

Roux's eyes went as wide as never before. "I will not join in your debauchery!"

Michael pulled on Jack's arm. "There's no debauchery here, you prude chat! As if that was what Jack meant!

Jack scowled. "Suit yourself. Every time I see you, you're such a goddamn naysayer!"

Roux squinted at Jack from the beam with a dignified lift of his chin, despite the mockery. "For once. Jack Addison is getting to hear the word 'no'."

Anger burned Jack to the core, and he instantly spun around, pulling Michael in for a kiss. The applause and whistling wasn't quite enough to soothe the injury to his pride but it would do.

Chapter 3

In the right light, Michael's hair was the same shade as Roux's fur. Jack wondered if Michael would have been up for a threesome with a chat, had Roux stayed in the room with them. But they did have plenty of fun on their own. Michael was barely standing from the hangover.

"Stay safe," Michael said in a raspy voice, resting his hands on Jack's chest. "And if you can, bring me a piece of it. Could even be a single scale."

Jack put on his shirt. "I always land on my feet."

Michael's puffy eyes turned to slits. "Are you sure you don't want to wait for everyone else?"

Of course Jack didn't want to wait. Everyone else would be staying idle until one of the watchmen spotted Nessie, but he had a device that could lead him straight to monster, and he wouldn't share the glory of a successful hunt with anyone!

Michael's eyes went wide, and he lifted his hand, as if he was about to slap Jack's chest. Jack instantly looked down, and the hair at the back of his neck bristled when he spotted a spider on the front of his shirt, right next to the pocket where he kept the tarantoid egg for luck.

A flush overcame his body, and right away he was back in the cave, pumped full of tiny eggs. But when Michael was about to squash the little thing, Jack grabbed his hand. "N-no. That's my pet spider."

Michael frowned. "What? You don't have a pet spider. Kill it, or at least throw it out. You know I hate spiders."

Jack opened and closed his mouth before quickly rushing to his luggage, where he kept a jar that still contained bits of cooked meat. If this little bugger had survived the poison its egg had been treated with, then he did not deserve to die so thoughtlessly. "I do. I was... waiting for the egg to hatch in my pocket." He reached into the pocket, and when he pulled out the little, soft egg, his mouth dried when he saw that it had popped. This tiny spider really was the spawn of the tarantoid, and it had been inside him. Was it possible that he'd incubated it with his body heat?

Michael crossed his arms and sat up on the bed. "If he's your pet, what's his name?"

"Chad." It was the first thing that came to his mind but when he glanced into the shiny eight eyes, he couldn't feel disgusted or afraid.

"Chad? Your spider's called Chad?"

"Yeah, 'cause he's so handsome. Just look at him!" Jack grinned and approached Michael, but laughed out loud when Michael squealed.

"I don't want to look at him!"

The tiny spider must have gotten spooked by all that noise, because he—Jack chose to call it 'he' until proven otherwise—crawled up Jack's neck and settled there as Jack punctured the lid of the jar with one of his daggers a couple of times. "Yeah, yeah. Just make sure he's out of direct sunlight," he said and offered his fingertip to the tiny arachnid. In the mirror, he saw it tentatively touch the nail with one of its legs before eventually transferring to the digit.

Jack gently put it inside the jar, shocked when Chad jumped off halfway and crawled onto a piece of meat. "Poor thing. He was so hungry."

Michael raised his eyebrows. "I guess. As long as it's in the jar."

Jack playfully wagged his finger at Michael. "It's my child you're talking about, so watch it."

"What?"

Right. No one apart from Roux knew this. "Just kidding."

Michael gave him one more kiss before they parted, and Jack was pretty sure the guy would be falling back into bed to nurse his hangover. He, on the other hand, pulled out his brand new high-frequency sound detector, and turned it on as soon as he left the inn.

The air still smelled of yesterday's bonfire, but he was too excited to waste time on breakfast. As soon as the device activated and the cogs started moving, he followed the direction suggested by the little arrow, surprised when it led him away from the lake. Since no one had ever managed to capture Nessie or find the portal she came through, the general consensus was that both were likely hidden deep underwater.

Instead, the arrow pointed away from the water, toward the hills descending to Loch Ness. Jack's instincts told him to walk along the shore to find the lost signal, but his sister was a brilliant inventor, and he chose to trust her creation instead.

With his trusty sword on his back, and the pistols at his sides, he would accomplish what others hadn't been able to. Drake had never told anyone how the creature looked, so his boasting about having stabbed the monster were likely only that--boasting. In the worst case scenario, if the thing really was too large for Jack to handle, he'd retreat, but no one would witness him fleeing. But, as his father had proven by slaying the kraken, a well-aimed stab was sometimes all it took.

The instrument led Jack uphill, along an easy yet narrow path, and while he needed to button his jacket due to the cold, the crisp air made him aware of his surroundings. Whatever happened, thanks to the device, he would at least know where the danger was coming from.

Ten minutes into the hike, the path diverged from the direction indicated by the prototype, and Jack sighed, faced with thick bushes forming a new barrier between him and Nessie. He could follow the comfortable way and hope that the device would eventually adjust, but getting to places in forested mountains wasn't always straightforward.

He was still making up his mind when a bird flying high above squawked so loudly that Jack followed its rapid dive between the trees. The eagle's wings were spread wide, creating an imposing image as it plunged, only to lift again following a commotion in the bushes. A loud shriek echoed through the air, and no one other than Roux Chat-Bonnes bounced into the autumn leaves.

Jack, who'd instinctively closed his hand on the hilt of his sword, uttered a curse and let go of Gouger. "Are you following me?"

Roux jumped up from the leaves, brushing them off in a hasty manner. "Someone has to make sure you don't die."

Jack rolled his eyes. "No. You want to be recognized as the slayer of Nessie! How about you work for that yourself instead of trying to drink cream from my plate?"

Roux started walking his way, so Jack hid his device, just to be on the safe side. "Really? Milk puns? Shall I ask if you'd like to make an omelette with all that cream?"

Jack squinted at Roux, wondering if this was some French thing he was missing.

Roux waved his paws in the air. "Omelette. Because of the eggs? The spider eggs…?" He hissed in frustration.

Jack scowled. "Not funny. I offered you a truce last night, and you pushed it away. I can't see why I should allow you to hunt with me today."

Roux huffed and rubbed his paws over his cheeks a few times, slicking back the fur that looked out of place. "You did say I'm an attractive chat…" He glanced at Jack with those massive green eyes and smiled, showing his sharp teeth.

Was this… an attempt at seduction just so that he could get a better shot at Nessie? Unbelievable.

"I'm horny, not stupid. You think you're gonna make big cat eyes at me, and I'm just gonna go with whatever you want? And just so you know, I do not actually sleep with creatures, okay? I'm just a curious guy."

Roux's lip curled over his canines and he folded his arms across his chest. Why had Jack even propositioned him last night? Had it been the alcohol? He most definitely didn't want his dick between pointy teeth.

"Let's just hope curiosity doesn't get you pregnant again. I'm done here."

"That's right. Go hunt some mice and let men handle the monsters!" Jack yelled as soon as the chat turned on his heel, presenting that agile, soft tail.

Roux didn't walk, but sped up as if he wanted to show off how fast he could go.

Jack sighed and once again looked at the thick bushes ahead, then along the curve of the safe, comfortable path. He followed the arrow on his device.

It wasn't as if he wouldn't find his way back to the inn later. He did have a compass, after all.

His initial steps told him that he wasn't up for an easy hike. The undergrowth was so thick and tangled that it grabbed at his shoes, so he adjusted his gait to prevent getting stuck and wasting energy on ripping tall, tangled grass out with its roots. He could hack his way through the wall of greenery with his sword but decided against leaving such obvious tracks for the other venators. After all, if he was to get Nessie's head on his trophy wall—which at this point only contained a bundle of necrorat tails—he couldn't have anyone claiming the monster first.

He would do this on his own terms. Alone.

The woody stems of the shrubs gave him a hard time, but at least none were thorny. Yet.

After an exasperating few minutes of pushing his way through the thick flora, he was surprised to find himself on a carpet of damp moss, surrounded by trees that grew farther apart, thus making walking easier. He marked one of the trees with a JA cut into the bark and followed the arrow on the device again, delving deeper into the ancient woodland. It might have taken fifteen, maybe twenty minutes, but he saw a clearing ahead, only to realize he was approaching a narrow valley. Hoping to see something from higher ground, he continued until he reached the steep fall.

When he reached the top of the gorge and took in the view, he wasn't sure what he was looking at. In the freezing water of a stream heading toward Loch Ness, a man was taking a bath. And not just any man. Even from his spot far away, Jack recognized the beauty of wide shoulders, pale skin, and, most extraordinarily, blue hair. Long locks in different shades of blue went down the man's back, over his shoulders, and in the early morning sun, they glowed with an iridescent sheen.

Jack took a deep breath, his feet frozen to the ground, but as he leaned forward and a branch broke under his foot, the stranger glanced straight at him.

Chapter 4

Jack's feet moved down into the gorge on their own accord. Whatever this enticing man was, his eyes called out to Jack. For help maybe? Was he lost? What if he'd fallen through an interdimensional crack and was confused, didn't know what to do?

Jack would gladly offer him a hand.

Or another body part.

The slope was steep so Jack's feet ended up sliding over the mud too fast for his liking. He grabbed at small trees and vines, and with the penetrating gaze of the stranger watching his every move, he absolutely needed his descent to be graceful. By the time he reached the bottom of the ravine and stepped on the damp moss, his skin was flushed with heat, but he was proud that he'd managed to avoid embarrassing himself.

The sun barely reached the peaceful spot protected by thick woodland and steep walls, but its rays made the young man's skin glow as if it had been covered in morning dew. The cool air managed to penetrate Jack's clothes, but the stranger seemed unmoved and smiled at Jack from the little pool formed in the winding creek. He rested his elbow on the shore while keeping most of his lithe form submerged in the icy water, and while his body language didn't betray fear, his deep blue gaze didn't stray from Jack.

Its intensity burned Jack's flesh as he approached with careful footsteps, the addison trembling against his hip completely forgotten.

"Hi there. Can you understand me?" he asked softly, raising his hands to show that he didn't mean any harm. As he came closer it became clear that the man wasn't human. His features and body shape were roughly similar to a slim man's, but his irises consumed the entirety of his eyes, and his long iridescent hair moved in gentle waves despite there being no breeze.

Only then did Jack notice that he couldn't hear any birds or insects, just the gentle whisper of the flowing water. He tensed when a snake slithered out of the creek, but quickly realized the viper-like form was the stranger's tail.

"Yes, I can," said the man with a smile, surprising Jack with his French accent.

Jack would definitely not want him to be kicked back into his own dimension.

Was it a species that lived only around here, so deep in the woods it came in contact with humans too rarely to be discovered by the rest of the world, or had an interdimensional hole only just opened and spat out this single creature, putting Jack on the forefront of discovery?

Michael would suck his cock so hard if Jack let him in on this.

But that could come later, because right now Jack was way too intrigued to think about fame and glory. "How long have you been here? Are there more of you?" he asked, watching the smooth tail seductively glide its way along the stranger's thigh.

"No. Only one of me." The man stepped forward, moving that bit closer to Jack. "Don't be scared. I mean no harm."

The creature was hairless, and Jack tried not to stare where the tail moved, but it was a losing battle. He did see something under the surface of the water... A blue dick? That would be something else.

Jack licked his lips, feeling his addison tremble so hard it was starting to distract him from the tempting creature. When he moved, his wet body glinted in the sun, without even a trace of gooseflesh.

"Aren't you cold? Do you need help?" he asked, somewhat uneasy about the stranger's calm demeanor.

"I am a bit cold actually. Will you hold me?" The lapis lazuli eyes mesmerized Jack with their vivid color.

Fuck yes, he'd hold this creature. Whatever he was, in terms of shape, he was basically human. So he had a tail, big deal. "Sure, come over." He opened his coat and spread his arms.

The man had an irresistible smile. "Silly. I won't get warm with all that fabric between us." He walked Jack's way, revealing that his dick did indeed have a pale blue color. If it was even a dick. Its shape reminded Jack of an elongated cone, darkest at the tip. But who was he to judge? If the creature was otherwise human-ish, and craved warmth from Jack, it wouldn't hurt to give him what he wanted.

"Oh... yeah, I guess you might be right," he said, offering a toothy smile and already getting rid of his jacket and scarf. He was a big boy, and he could stand a bit of cold if he was to get a body this fine as a reward. As Jack undressed, he was puzzled when he noticed that the arrow on his addison twirled in circles instead of showing direction. Then again, it only was a prototype.

Nessie could wait.

It didn't escape his attention that marble-sized bumps appeared on the creature's cock. Was he into the hug? Jack sure hoped so. They seemed to understand each other without words, because the guy touched Jack's face with smooth, gentle fingers. They weren't cold at all, which was fortunate since Jack wouldn't have been able to get turned on if caressed by ice.

"Is it very hot where you're from?" he guessed, quickly removing his remaining clothing and stacking it all on top of the leather jacket, so nothing would soak up the moisture from the damp moss.

"Very much so. I find this place refreshing." Without shame or uncertainty, the creature slid his arms under Jack's and hugged him tightly, not even wet anymore. His cock was definitely growing against Jack's, making all his preconceptions of sex with non-humans melt.

Was it just because he was caught off-guard, or because no one would know what happened next? Or was it the way the stranger showed no inhibitions whatsoever, eager to touch and caress a human?

Jack licked his lips and slowly moved his hands to the creature's back before sliding them down, all the way to the base of the tail. The skin under his fingertips was incredibly smooth and delicate, even if cold, and he found himself completely entranced by the deep shade of the man's eyes. Something at the back of his mind reminded him of the events that had landed him in a hospital a year ago, but he chose to ignore that nagging voice, because what could a creature so friendly possibly do to him?

"What's your name?"

"Lavaan." And while saying his name, Lavaan kissed the side of Jack's neck. For the first time, Jack pondered that, to other creatures, humans could be strange and interesting. Would hands seem fascinating to someone who only had err... paws?

The hair at the back of Jack's nape bristled with excitement, and he rubbed the base of the tail with the utmost gentleness. Lavaan's eyelids fluttered shut, and the whole seductive body pressed against Jack, suddenly tense.

So that was a good spot to touch. "That's a... nice name."

"Yours is too. Very strong."

Wait. Had Jack introduced himself? Maybe he had. It was hard to think with Lavaan licking his way to Jack's jaw. For once, he'd met a creature who shared his dislike for wasting time. They could figure out where Lavaan was from and how to get him back once they were both sated.

Lavaan's hands glided up Jack's back, making him tremble with excitement. As a venator, wasn't he also an explorer in many ways? And what better way to explore the customs of different creatures than to communicate with them in the most primal way?

Or was he just seeking excuses to bang any male he came across?

Would he actually fuck the chat if given the chance?

Lavaan smirked and pressed closer to Jack, so close that their lips aligned. That was Jack's hint. He leaned in and pushed his tongue in, exploring the smooth insides of Lavaan's mouth. It was hot as a cup of tea on the verge of burning, but he couldn't bring himself to pull away when Lavaan's strange cock moved against Jack's balls. Stiff but somehow flexible, covered in the marble shapes, it made Jack desperate to look down.

Instead, Jack grew more comfortable petting the scaly tail. After all, what was it but just another body part? Touching Lavaan was nothing like the awful experience with the tarantoid. The creature in front of Jack was sentient, eager, and oh so fascinating in its differentness. Lavaan playfully rubbed his tail around Jack's wrist, making him chuckle into the warm mouth.

No one needed to know that Jack enjoyed the way Lavaan wrapped his arms around Jack's neck and petted his nape. He could explore in secret, indulge without making a big deal out of it. Didn't people do weirder things to each other than this completely consensual encounter with an alien being? It wasn't as if he was about to fuck a helpless goat, Lavaan was frank about how much he craved company.

Jack smiled into the deep, scorching kiss, unbothered that Lavaan's hair did in fact move on its own and now caressed Jack's arms. In fact, it felt great. Unusual. Delightful.

Lavaan's agile tail lifted, as if Jack's new strange lover was inviting him further into the heat of his body, but he took his time, teasingly kneading the tail while they kissed, the hunt and the reality beyond the ravine long forgotten. The silky hair that had fascinated Jack from the first glimpse now tickled his bare shoulders and arms, trailing over skin.

Lavaan's tongue seemed to swell, and Jack considered if it was possible for a creature to become erect in other places than just the cock. Why not after all? Different dimensions held endless possibilities.

I want to touch you everywhere, Jack, Lavaan said, but Jack wasn't sure where the voice came from, because Lavaan's tongue was now deep inside his mouth, massaging it, hot and covered in the same bumps as his cock.

Jack didn't have the brainpower to question any of it. The voice of reason was getting quieter by the second, shut down by the addictive scent of Lavaan's body and the taste of his hot, long, nub-covered tongue. Jack gave a choked gasp when Lavaan's dick wrapped around his and started pumping back and forth. Before he knew it, Lavaan's tongue forced his own down and dove deeper into him, pushing at the entrance to Jack's throat.

The sense of panic was only brief, and Jack sank into Lavaan's cozy arms, oddly calm despite the tongue blocking his air flow every time it sank inside him.

There was no violence in Lavaan's moves, but Jack was itching to look down between their bodies to understand what was happening, no matter how pleasant the slippery motion was.

Lavaan's arms were growing the little bubbles as well, but at this point Jack could only wonder what amazing pleasure he'd be getting out of that.

They were stroking his back in the same loving motion that mimicked the movement of Lavaan's tongue and his cock-thing.

Jack's mind stopped for half a second.

What arms?

Lavaan's arms were still around Jack's neck, but they were thicker now, and he seemed to have grown by at least two inches in height. This was getting much freakier than expected, but Jack couldn't make up his mind about leaving. His dick twitched in the grip of the long, muscled cock that randomly pinched his foreskin, as if Lavaan couldn't deny himself the teasing.

The world around Jack glowed in unusual colors for the late autumnal landscape, and when streaks of pink and red stretched across the sky, he shut his eyes, completely focused on the thick tongue fucking its way into his throat, past the gullet, until Jack's mouth was completely slack and pliant. Even his legs were slowly giving up under him, and when he tugged on the tail, to signal that he wasn't sure about this whole thing anymore, it wrapped around his wrists, keeping him bound to Lavaan's warm form.

But, as if Lavaan were sensing his distress, the flexible arms that still held Jack's back, supported him when Lavaan lowered them both to the warm moss. Even the air wasn't cold anymore when Jack found himself under Lavaan, his cock getting sucked into the heat of Lavaan's body.

How?

Frantic, Jack fought for a glimpse between their bodies, but once he managed, his muscles went slack. He had no idea what he was looking at. Lavaan's penis had expanded, opening wide enough to allow for Jack's cock to enter. It was halfway in already, and as it pushed up the strange cock, Lavaan's flesh clung to Jack's like a sleeve made of rubber.

It was hot.

And freaking terrifying.

What if the creature actually wanted to bite his dick off?

Jack writhed in the hold, bucking against Lavaan, following the instinct to flee from danger rather than the one that had pushed him to seek pleasure.

The tarantoid had also tricked Jack's body into longing for intrusion, why would this be any different?

I won't hurt you, Jack. I want only your pleasure, Lavaan sweet, calm voice communicated straight into Jack's brain. transcending his fear.

Had the creature poisoned him? He had no strength to fight, and when Lavaan rose over him, the thick, nubby tongue reaching past his graceful collarbones. Even Lavaan's face looked different, as if Jack's senses couldn't quite grasp what it was. The long hair glinted in the sun, parting into thick bundles that too had nubs, and when they extended from Lavaan's head, Jack realized they reminded him of tentacles--

Tentacles?!

And as if to mess with Jack further, there was a smile in Lavaan's eyes, hidden in the creases around the eyelids.

Only if you want this, Jack. I promise you a world you haven't even imagined existed.

What Lavaan actually meant was vague, but two tentacles, warm and smooth, slid down Jack's back and caressed him between the buttocks.

Jack's hips twitched, and he gasped in pleasure, on the verge of coming when Lavaan's penis-like appendage sucked on his dick harder. Should he just roll with it and see what happened? What if the creature ate him?

Lavaan chuckled. You are safe with me.

Another tentacle slid over Jack's chest like a giant snake, and its suckers teased his skin as if leaving a hundred kisses all at once. In some ways, Jack was still apprehensive, but Lavaan was friendly, eager to please, and had even given Jack a way out.

And no one needed to know that Jack agreed to this.

Was it so wrong to be curious?

The two arms prodded at Jack's ass, demanding entry. He moaned, stirring in the embrace of so many tentacles while the penis-like appendage twitched around his dick, sucking him more ferociously than a virgin would his first cock.

Humans are so fascinating, Lavaan said in Jack's mind, and his voice was a sexually-charged bomb exploding inside of his brain. Jack didn't even know when he opened his legs, but he must have, because one of the long arms was leaking a slippery substance and rubbing it all over his hole. He'd gained a lot of sexual experience throughout this past year, but he both feared and anticipated the girth of the tentacle, trembling with fright and pleasure.

Above him, Lavaan's lips curved into a smile, and the nub-covered tongue rolled back out, sliding up Jack's neck and leaving behind a damp trail. Jack opened his mouth without thinking.

It felt so hollow.

Lavaan filled Jack eagerly, slipping the long tongue back in with ease. Jack relaxed, moaning into Lavaan's lips, but his ecstatic sound turned into a shriek when the slick tentacle pushed into Jack's body. His sphincter tensed, sending a wave of pain down his thighs. His brain was back in the cave, under the tarantoid who'd have rather ripped Jack in two than stopped fucking him, but Lavaan wasn't so ruthless. He briefly froze, tightening his arms around Jack's chest, as if wanting to offer comfort. It was only then that Jack truly believed Lavaan would not violate him.

Thoughts sped through Jack's brain, coming up with questions that, if answered, might change everything. He'd been taught all his life that humans needed to separate themselves from creatures, but was it really so wrong to enjoy the company of a being so magnificent? If he said yes now, what would stop him from keeping his hands off non-humans next time?

Lavaan kneeled between Jack's legs, but even as he moved, the appendage between his legs sucked on Jack's cock, kissing it with a dozen suckers from the inside. The one in Jack's mouth left him slobbering, but its slow movement was like another cock fucking his mouth while his ass was being treated to something completely different--a sensation he'd never experienced even though he'd considered himself an adventurous guy, and once had even had a cucumber up there.

The tentacle wasn't merely stiff and large though. Like a living being, it crawled into him insistently, pushing slightly deeper after each time it withdrew. And while Jack's ass was gradually relaxing, the appendage felt thicker with each thrust. It would have likely hurt if not for the copious amount of the slippery fluid exuded by the nubs covering the surface of the tentacles. Soon enough, all discomfort subsided, leaving only the ecstatic sensation of pure hard muscle nestling deep inside him. The suckers teased his sphincter as they passed in and out, making delightful popping noises, and when Lavaan got bolder and applied more pressure to Jack's prostate, Jack ended up raising to his toes in an awkward position where he tried to both push into the stimulation and avoid it.

This was insane. No human could have ever given him an experience so completely mind-blowing.

Jack was a whimpering mess, caressed by Lavaan's many tentacle arms. The one that had earlier slid along his chest, was now wrapped around his middle, giving him support in the new position. Jack murmured around the slippery meat in his mouth, communicating just how good he felt, despite knowing that Lavaan could read him anyway.

Jack wasn't even frightened when the tip of another tentacle inched between his buttocks and wormed its way to his ass alongside the first one that was already deep inside and fucking him faster by the second. How had he not come yet was a mystery he would never uncover.

Lavaan must have overheard Jack's thoughts, because he chuckled, and the strangest thing was that Jack didn't mind being listened to at all. He was an open book anyway at this point—both physically and mentally.

When the tip of the other tentacle trailed around his buttocks before prodding at the already-filled hole, Jack's mind screamed with indecision. He could say no, but he didn't know whether he wanted to. Lavaan's touch, and his surprising strength were too delicious to deny, and when the many narrow tentacles growing on Lavaan's head descended to Jack's neck and chest, gently sucking his sensitive skin, he pushed out his ass, wordlessly begging for this new intense experience.

The other tentacle pushed in through the sphincter, and Jack might have passed out from the transcendental nature of this moment. He'd never felt so blissfully filled. Covered in warm goo and kissed by suckers all over, he was floating in ecstasy that was about to tip him over the edge of orgasm.

The new tentacle penetrated him gently at first, carefully pushing its way next to the thick girth of its predecessor, but time and time again, it teased Jack's sphincter, while the thicker arm massaged Jack's insides in a spot that emptied his brain, leaving space for pleasure and nothing else.

He moaned loudly around Lavaan's tongue and jerked his entire body when he came, shooting his cum deep into the appendage that had been milking him for what felt like ages.

A blaze of heat coursed through Jack's body, and at the very peak of pleasure, the other tentacle pushed all the way inside him, opening him up so rapidly he could barely believe it possible.

He had two fat, long dicks inside him, and it didn't even hurt. It was fucking hot, and the sensation of being stretched so wide alone sent giddy shivers all over his flesh.

Violent shudders ran up his spine, his bones filled with liquid joy, and as ecstasy stretched into an endless sequence of thrusts and caresses, it felt as if Jack's orgasm would only end if his muscles tore and his bones broke.

You are so beautiful, Jack. So wild, Lavaan spoke straight to his insides.

Jack didn't have the brain space left to offer the same to his lover. The tentacles kept moving inside him, going deep each time, first at once and then out of sync, rolling in his hole like two snakes desperate to find their pleasure in his ass.

No longer afraid, he let Lavaan worship him, completely resigned to his glorious fate.

Time wasn't even something he recognized anymore, and Jack lost track of it. When Lavaan's tentacles began to recede, he was exhausted beyond belief and knew there would be no more hunting today.

When the sucking appendage slipped off his cock, it instantly folded, without spilling even a drop of his spunk.

Jack shut his eyes. He was too hot to notice the cold of the moss, yet welcomed the warmth of Lavaan's smooth body when he rested next to him, lifting him into his arms with the tentacles.

Jack could have sworn he drooled all over when the tongue pulled out of him.

He lay trembling in Lavaan's arms, and the gentle kisses of the one tentacle that hadn't pulled back into Lavaan's body continued endlessly, soothing him, and licking him clean.

Jack exhaled, finally finding the energy to stare at Lavaan, who once again looked like he had when they'd met, with wavy blue strands for hair and human features. He smiled at Jack and tapped his spent cock. Even if Jack hadn't been so painfully tired, with balls so dry, he wouldn't get hard today again. Not a chance.

"I think it's time to say goodbye," Lavaan said before slowly sitting up at Jack's side.

Jack blinked and quickly grabbed the smooth tail, turning the attention of the deep blue eyes back on him. "Already? Wait…"

"I think you've had enough, sweet Jack." Lavaan laughed and his tail became oily, slipping easily from Jack's grip.

Jack wasn't sure what to say, pumped out and shocked by what had happened, so he stared at the creature walking back to the stream. Naked, glorious, with a tail, tentacles, and ways to communicate beyond what any human could comprehend. Since he'd become a man, it had never occurred to him that he might find creatures worthy of his lust. Accepting Lavaan had opened doors in Jack's mind that he'd never even considered approaching.

"C-can I see you again?" he asked, sitting there in the grass as Lavaan stepped into the water.

Lavaan turned his head and winked at Jack. "Maybe next year."

Something clicked in Jack's mind, and he scrambled to grab the addison he'd earlier placed with his clothes. As Lavaan slowly followed the stream, Jack could barely breathe, watching the tiny arrow on the device point straight at the beautiful creature. "N-Nessie?" he uttered, looking around for his sword.

But when he finally found it and glanced at the slender form walking along the ravine, he realized that not only did he not want to raise his sword against a creature that had given him so much pleasure, but that Lavaan… Nessie was not a monster. He was sentient and only deserved good things.

Just before Lavaan left the gorge, he smirked, staring back at Jack, and his sweet voice echoed through Jack's skull. Whose hunt is it every year? Human? Or mine?

He disappeared from sight before Jack could bring his mouth to move.

The birds were singing again. The creek whispered all too loudly, and Jack stood there, stark naked in the gorge that had heated up from their fucking. The sun had moved over the sky since Jack had last looked at it. Hours must have passed, but Jack was as profoundly changed, as if years had passed instead.

It was so clear to him now.

What else was out there for him to fuck? His family wouldn't approve, but what dad didn't know couldn't hurt him.

"Jack! Jack!" Drake ran down the gorge wall so fast he tumbled and landed headfirst in the nearby bushes.

Jack didn't even try to hide his nakedness. It was nothing Drake hadn't seen before. "H-hey." His voice was raspy from the ferocious thrusts of Lavaan's tongue, so he cleared his throat.

Drake ran up to him, grabbed Jack's shoulders and shook him. "You've met her. Where is she?"

Jack blinked. "Who?"

Drake was having none of it. He bared his teeth and pushed Jack back so hard Jack barely kept himself standing on noodle-soft legs. "Don't play dumb with me. Lavaan! I know you've met her," he said, indicating Jack's sweaty, naked state.

Jack frowned. "Lavaan's a guy."

"Most definitely not. She has the most beautiful set of breasts I've ever seen. And well, she can actually suck with her down-there."

Jack looked into Drake's eyes and for a while they stayed silent, until they both said at the same time:

"Shapeshifter."

*

Next time on Jack Addison vs. A Whole World of Hot Trouble:

Will Jack meet Roux Chat-Bonnes again?
Will Jack follow his heart and indulge in monster lovin'?
Or will he bite off more than he can chew?

Jack Addison vs. a Pack of Horny Werewolves

Jack Addison Vs. A Whole World of Hot Trouble #3

K.A. Merikan

"Apparently, black market werewolf pheromones were readily available if one knew who to ask."

Two years on from his first assignment, Jack Addison is a seasoned monster hunter, as hungry for fame and glory as he'd been when he first saw his rival, Roux Chat-Bonnes. They meet again when Jack is trapped by seven polyamorous gnomes, but what Roux doesn't know is that Jack has developed a taste for unusual creatures and got himself captured on purpose.

Roux himself, with his furry body and graceful tail, is just the kind of man Jack would like to get to know intimately, if he only wasn't so uncertain about flirting.

Opportunity for time together comes when the two of them are asked to hunt down a rogue werewolf pack. But with Roux being his usual uptight self, Jack turns his attention to the possibility of charming a werewolf. To increase his chances, he purchases a vial of pheromones, but once Jack and Roux are alone in the woods during the full moon, the line between hunter and hunted gets blurry.

Previously on Jack Addison vs. A Whole World of Hot Trouble:

Jack Addison might come from a line of legendary monster hunters and scientists, but he is only just starting out as a venator. After encountering the alluring Nessie during the annual hunt, he's opened up to the idea of dating nonhumans.

Away from the strict segregation of his country, he meets all kinds of creatures, each more interesting than the last. But, while Jack's thoughts keep drifting to his rival, Roux Chat-Bonnes, Roux doesn't share the sentiment. But does Jack have a chance to change the feline venator's mind when the two of them team up for a dangerous job in Bohemia?

Chapter 1

If Jack were to pick the most transformative moment of his young life so far, he would have to pick the day he'd met Lavaan—or Nessie—and lived to tell the tale to precisely no one. He did share the unbelievable secret (without details) with Drake Nguyen and a number of unidentified venators who'd stumbled upon the beautiful creature during the annual hunt, but for the most part he felt alone in his newfound affinity for non-human bodies.

It was an indulgence he needed to keep to himself, so only he and his lovers knew the truth about Jake Addison, and not a single word about his escapades could ever reach his father's ear. But away from the predominantly human population of his hometown, the world was rich in the weird and wonderful, and Jack's appetite grew with each exotic conquest.

There had been a giant far North, whom Jack had to jerk off using his entire body, and who had come so much Jack could have lost his life drowning in spunk. A few weeks later, he'd been sucked off by a male veela, and fooled around with a poltergeist who refused to leave its former home due to unfinished business. Thankfully, he was more agreeable after getting a good fucking from Jack.

But not all of Jack's attempts at broadening his sexual horizons had been as successful. Two months prior, he'd attempted to seduce a swarm of sentient bees, only to end up trapped and begging for mercy when their teasing turned into torture. Weeks had passed until all the ugly stings were gone, and his dick once again worked as normal.

But failure had never stopped an Addison from exploration, which had brought Jack to the beautiful valleys of Bavaria. And a group of seven polyamorous gnomes, all eager to get a piece of him.

Technically, his job had been to subdue them, trap them, and bring them to justice at the local interspecies negotiator's office, but when Jack had first read about their scandalous, obscene behaviors scaring away venators, he took a coach all the way from Berlin to try and get himself some action.

He let them entrap him and pin him to the ground with his own rope—naked—but what they didn't know was that the rope had been created by Jack's ingenious sister and would loosen if he pressed hard in a sequence only Jack knew. If he needed to, he could free himself from peril at any second.

One of the gnomes, a thick-limbed fellow with a salt-and-pepper beard and large feet, slapped his small hand against Jack's face, leaving behind a sting, before barking something in German.

Jack moaned into the gag made of the tiniest of comforters and a gnome-sized bedsheet, and jerked his hips, aroused by the prospect of getting intimately acquainted with this depraved septet. Were he anyone else—he'd have been trapped for good.

Packe, the youngest of the gnomes, still beardless and with a high-pitched voice, was the only one to know English. He gleefully crawled up Jack's chest on his hands and knees, offering a toothy smile. His teeth were so ungodly small in comparison to the size of his mouth!

"You will be sorry you walked into our territory, human," Packe said, before rapidly unfastening his pants to present his cock, which already seemed unnaturally large for his size, and still growing.

The one with the annoying giggle rubbed a feather along Jack's cheek, then all the way down his neck. He was saying something in German, but it sounded as if he were laughing at his own jokes. The glide of the feather down his body made Jack wriggle helplessly in the binds.

Another gnome pulled his cock out and had to use two of his tiny hands to stroke himself. No one would ever believe Jack if he told them about this.

Their cocks were small in comparison to that of an average human male's, but those gnomes were known to play rough, and just thinking about them parting his buttocks, two, maybe even three pricks pushing into Jack's hole at once, set his skin aflame and made him rock against the teasing touch.

That was exactly what he wanted—the kind of illicit experience most of his friends wouldn't have been able to get their heads around. He was about to get fucked into oblivion by seven gnomes, and do his actual job of bringing them to justice once he was satisfied. What a fantastic way of killing two birds with one stone!

Jack gasped when a rock fell to the side of his head. He hadn't imagined they'd be playing *that* rough. But the gnomes seemed confused as well, and when Jack turned to look where the rock fell, he frowned at the smoke coming out of the round object.

He knew the scent—a Slumber Smoke Bomb! He writhed in his binds in panic.

No!

Not yet!

But Packe's eyes closed, and he fell headfirst to Jack's chest, still holding his engorged cock. Jack fought the sudden tiredness, but it was no use. Soon enough, he dozed off as well.

*

Jack woke with a herby aftertaste at the back of his tongue. The world still rocked when he opened his eyes, but the first thing he saw made him sit up so rapidly the blanket covering his chest pooled in his lap.

The seven gnomes reached toward him from between thick iron bars of a wheeled cage, their little faces red, and their voices reaching a pitch so high his ears were starting to hurt.

He froze when someone spoke behind him.

"At least you wouldn't have gotten pregnant this time, Addison."

Roux Chat-Bonnes. Jack would've recognized that French accent anywhere.

A hot flush spread over Jack's face like wildfire, but there was no point hiding when Roux had already seen it all. At least he wasn't aware Jack had allowed the gnomes to capture him on purpose.

"You win some, you lose some. These things happen," Jack said, glancing over his shoulder at Roux, who watched him, while consuming dried fish and cream from a can.

He perched on a fallen tree trunk, and wasn't wearing a shirt, showing off the white streaks on his belly. "They happen to reckless venators."

So typical. Jack and Roux hadn't actually met in person in the six months since last Halloween, but a rivalry of sorts had still developed between them after Roux had reached Warsaw before Jack, ridding its people of the menacing basilisk that haunted the sewers. Jack had supposedly missed Roux by ten minutes, only to find the chat's mocking letter by the headless basilisk body. The note said only, *Got to it first.*

The chat was such a vengeful, sexy creature.

"Not everyone can reach the roof of a small cottage in a single jump."

Roux smirked and licked his paws once he was done eating. "Am I supposed to feel guilty over being good at my job?"

"You have an unfair advantage," Jack said and stood, letting the blanket drop. Would Roux look at him? Was he a *pussycat*?

"Says the man with more gadgets than anyone else, a last name that opens doors, and no worries over money. You really want to talk about unfair advantages?"

He did glance at his body, Jack was sure he did. If it wasn't for chats being such distrustful creatures, he would have banged one by now, but the opportunity just hadn't arisen, and the only chats that he'd found offering favors for money in Paris were female.

Jack chewed on his lip and started pulling on his leather pants. So he wouldn't exactly put it into words like Roux had, but the Addison name did make some things easier for Jack. But it wasn't as if he'd chosen who his family were. Was he supposed to shed his identity in order to appease his rival? Anyone would have made use of connections and opportunities.

"You're really blowing it out of proportion. None of the humans complain."

"And you shouldn't be complaining either, because if it wasn't for me, your 'not sleeping with creatures' count would grow to minus two. Or eight, for that matter." He got off the tree trunk and slicked his ear back with his paw. How was he both so cute and infuriating at the same time?

Something about his attitude and that mean way he was flicking his tail made Jack's blood move faster. "Do you sleep with creatures?"

Roux's ears popped right back up, and his pupils widened. "Excuse me? Aren't we all creatures? Or do you go by the outdated definition that singles out humans and lumps the rest of us together?"

"He's asking if you fuck other species, you dumb moggy!" Packe yelled from the behind the bars, waving his hand in frustration. "Just open this cage and I'll show you how good it can be!"

Roux shook his head. "With that toothpick of yours? I don't think so."

"So narrow-minded! Wouldn't want your spiky dick anyway!"

There it was—Jack's new favorite topic. "Oh, is it really spiky?" he asked, slowly completing his look by putting on the white shirt.

Roux took a step back. Always so skittish when it came to things that mattered. "That is none of your business. We're not just overgrown cats. Unless you are an overgrown baboon."

Jack grinned. "My ass doesn't look like a baboon's, I can tell you that with no shame. And I bet you've seen my cock twice already."—there, he'd put himself in a vulnerable position to entice the chat to speak—"Why don't you just tell me about yours? It's not like it's some terrible secret."

"It's a private matter, so I don't think it's any of your business. For someone not wanting to sleep with creatures, you are awfully interested in my genitalia." Roux walked past Jack and grabbed the rope with which he would pull the wheeled cage full of gnomes. At least he wasn't making a dig at Jack's cock, so maybe he *did* like it. Jack certainly did like Roux's tail. It was so soft and flexible. He wondered if chats used them for jerking off, and if that felt like being touched by someone else.

Like when you used your left hand.

"You know my family has academic traditions. I'm a curious man," Jack said and watched Roux send a pink flare into the air, to signal his position to the local authorities.

Jack ignored Packe's swearing and all the German curse words the rest of the gnomes were undoubtedly throwing their way.

"I have more important things to do than satisfy your curiosity, Addison."

Jack snorted. "So far, you've been wasting time deflecting my questions, Chat-Bonnes. Might be easier and faster if you revealed your secrets," he said, approaching Roux with his gaze focused on the soft-looking fur at the back of his neck. He was on the verge of burying his face in it but didn't want to cause a scene when the local negotiator could appear at any moment.

And if they were caught in the act, Roux would surely have no qualms about telling everyone that Jack Addison was, in fact, interested in touching creatures. Scandalous information like this would inevitably reach Jack's father all the way in New York, and Jack's adventures would be cut short. Jack didn't need more conflict in his life. He wasn't doing himself any favors by lusting for his enemy. Was Roux his *enemy,* though? Did Jack actually *lust* for him or was it just curiosity? He hadn't been with a furry creature yet, and perhaps Roux seemed available enough to draw Jack's interest.

Roux opened his mouth, but then meowed loudly, spinning around while all the hair on his body bristled. "Leave it! Leave it!" He hissed at Packe, who grinned at them with Roux's tail between his teeth.

As if on cue, the other gnomes grabbed at the vulnerable tail, and when they pulled Roux barely kept himself upright.

Jack hurried to the cart and twisted Packe's nose so hard the cartilage inside it might have been permanently deformed. He then grabbed Roux's tail at the base, to stabilize him, and proceeded to punch the sneaky creatures with his fist. "Let him go!"

Packe screamed, but at least he let go, and Roux managed to pull the tail to himself protectively. The fur was damp and stained red where Packe had bitten him.

"Always the easy target, huh?" He glanced at Jack with his green big-pupiled eyes. "Humans once attacked my dad and hurt his tail so bad most of it needed to be amputated."

Jack stilled, staring at him in horror. That had escalated quickly.

"I—I'm sorry, that's horrible. Let me take a look at that."

Roux stilled, as if assessing whether he wasn't in any danger, but he eventually extended the tail to Jack. "Cuts can be hard to deal with, too. Whenever I need stitches, they shave off some fur, and then I've got this stupid bald patch," he groaned. This had to be the first time Jack heard him open up about a problem.

He led an unresisting Roux to his backpack. "For moments like that, do you have like... toupees?" he asked, but his mind was already somewhere else. The tail felt so alive in his hand—warm, slim, and kind of bony under all that pretty fluff.

Roux shook his head. "Don't be ridiculous. A chat wears his scars proudly."

Jack spilled some of his water over the nasty bite before drying it with one of his spare undershirts. "Nobody knows about it, because you chats act so standoffish."

Roux's ears flattened, and he grabbed Jack's arm when Jack touched the bite. For an experienced venator, he seemed really sensitive. "Well, now you know."

Jack shrugged and took out his special wound and abrasion salve. The stuff was incredibly expensive due to some of its ingredients being so rare, like the pricy ambergris, but it was so effective the investment definitely paid for itself. He applied a generous amount to the wound. "Why don't we just forget our past arguments and start with a clean slate, huh? It's much more practical than leaving each other passive-aggressive notes."

Roux took a deep breath and looked up at Jack. "I suppose I *was* following you back at the Nessie hunt to try and get an advantage."

"*Kuss, kuss, kuss!*" the gnomes started chanting, and Roux instantly backed away, hissing at the cage.

Jack massaged the hurt tail, scowling at the pesky gnomes. He needed to rope Roux back in and see for himself how it felt to kiss a chat. Would the whiskers be a nuisance or arouse him by gently tickling his skin? Were chat lips even suitable for the kind of kissing Jack was used to?

"I know, and I forgive you. If you were straightforward about it, then maybe we could have hunted it down together," he said, even though there was not a chance Nessie could have fucked them both. If Roux had been with Jack that past October, he wouldn't have had that life-changing experience.

"I work alone," Roux said, slipping his tail out of Jack's reach.

Several voices approached them from the nearby path through the woods, so Jack gave up on the flirting... for now.

"Over here!" he yelled, and soon enough, the negotiator arrived with four men to help her escort the gnomes back to their own dimension. The locals knew where the crack between worlds was, but thanks to the negotiator insisting on not killing the gnomes, it had been left open. Guards had been put next to it, but it was far better to get rid of sentient creatures this way instead of killing them, or leaving them orphaned in a new dimension.

Roux stood on his toes, most likely to seem taller than he actually was, and held his paw out for the reward money. Jack joined him immediately, even though he preferred to remain subtle about payments, and usually waited for the officer of law to broach the subject.

The negotiator, a tall woman with hair wrapped around her head in a neat braid crown, frowned as she approached on a graceful horse. In heavily accented English, she spoke, not even touching the purse resting against her hip. "Monsieur Chat-Bonnes? Mr. Addison, I presume?"

They must have been the only venators who registered for this hunt, then. This, or the negotiator had seen a picture of Jack in a newspaper. His face was not one to be forgotten.

Roux made a courteous bow. "Roux Chat-Bonnes, at your service, Frau Gauch. I report successfully apprehending the gnomes."

"We've done it together," Jack said, offering Gauch his best smile.

Roux turned to him. "Excuse me? If anything, I saved you from molestation."

One of the women in the negotiator's party snorted.

Jack frowned, already cooking on the inside. He would not be mocked! "I don't know what you mean. I set a trap and was just about to apprehend them when you showed up to reap the rewards."

Gauch raised her eyebrows at Roux, who clenched his fists. "I refuse to argue about this. The reward is mine."

"I can't really process this claim, but I'm happy for the two of you to share the reward. After all, half is better than nothing."

Jack smiled at the negotiator, before turning toward Roux with a proud smile. "It was a special rope. I could have freed myself at any time. I can demonstrate this to you, so why don't we share and celebrate the bounty with some nice German beer?"

Roux's whiskers twitched, but he agreed, despite shaking his head, so it was hard to say where he stood.

"There's another urgent job if you two are up for it," Gauch said as she paid them both. "It's a matter of some discretion as well, so we haven't advertised it nationally. The last thing we want is more bad press for werewolves."

One of the men who'd accompanied her shook his head. "Maybe they should get what they deserve for breaking the laws and breaching their borders."

Gauch snarled but ignored her entourage and spoke directly to Jack and Roux. "Most werewolves are ordinary citizens who live their lives among us. They shouldn't all be punished for the crimes of the few."

Jack licked his lips. This was juicy. Central Europe had a large werewolf population. Most of the creatures lived on reservations created as means to offer them lots of land to roam while not encroaching on the rights of the human population. But some of the larger cities in the area also boasted werewolf districts, where people like Jack could sample their culture, and where illegal wolf pheromones were readily available if one knew who to ask.

Jack had been very excited to visit Prague, purchase a bottle, and meet some werewolves.

"Yes," he said, without much thinking.

Gauch blinked at him. "I haven't even said what the job was yet."

Jack smiled. "I'm not afraid of anything."

Roux's ears twitched. "Me neither."

Chapter 2

The little vial of werewolf pheromones was hot in Jack's chest pocket, and he kept touching it as he watched the monumental landscape pass by. He was alone in the train compartment, so he rested his feet on the seat opposite and ate warm pastries from a basket brought in by the on-board service. But while the sweet, flaky crust melted on his tongue, he kept thinking about the metal bottle that held the key to this hunt.

The werewolf district of Prague had been a bit of a disappointment, since the only fur he'd spotted there had been already stripped off the animal that had originally worn it. A helpful barman in one of the local inns whose forearms were covered by a thick pelt of fur, and whose teeth seemed rather sharp and large for a human, told Jack that city werewolves didn't want to stand out too much. Most of them only shifted away from human settlements, and Jack was too let down to look for werewolf fun in that place.

He wanted something authentic.

That reminded him of the letter he'd picked up from the local venator office before boarding, and he pulled it out of his coat pocket. A smile stretched his lips when he recognized Drake Nguyen's tidy cursive on the envelope, and he extracted the single piece of paper.

Dear Friend,

How are things on the Continent? Ruslana Ratayeva recently visited London on her way to Ireland, and she told me you two briefly met in Berlin. Good job with that bear shifter!

You'll want to know that Chad is growing fast. I inquired at my old college, and if he is indeed a male, he shouldn't grow to such enormous proportions as the female you encountered. He is very trainable, but it's not commands like sit and fetch that I'm talking about! The little bugger can count to ten, and I'm happy to tell you that we won't be alone in the exciting endeavor of raising him any longer.

I will start by saying that all is well, but little Chad gave me quite a scare a month ago or so. He's very active and growing bolder every day. I am trying to make the house as safe for him as possible, but I don't want to restrain him too much either, so he is generally allowed everywhere. One evening, he snuck into my office while the window was open and ended up falling to the front yard. I was alarmed by a horrific cry and immediately looked outside, only to find Chad curled into a ball, with one of his legs twisted.

The poor thing was so scared, and I have no background in veterinary sciences. Desperate, since he was in too much pain to let me see what exactly happened, I put him into a box and drove to the clinic for the treatment of small animals. I expected disgust or fright, and demanded a promise in writing that nothing about our boy would be revealed. The doctor was quite wonderful, and as it turns out, she breeds tropical spiders herself, so instead of fearing Chad, she demanded I allow her to visit him.

His leg is now mended, and Miss Constantine is most interested in helping us care for him. I initially thought she was only motivated by academic curiosity, but she's been incredibly tender with him. I believe her presence will be an asset to our co-parenting endeavour.

Please, do write us of your current whereabouts and visit soon. Not a day goes by without Chad napping on your pillow.

Sincerely,

Drake Nguyen

Next to the signature was a fuzzy spot with two claw-like shapes stamped onto the paper—the imprint of Chad's front leg. Drake knew how to tickle Jack's longing for a few weeks of stability.

Jack was about to doze off, since there was two hours left until the train arrived in Tarheim, but then he spotted a dash of ginger fur passing the door and sat up in alarm. Roux triggered a Pavlovian response in him, and Jack hadn't even worked out if the Chat really was gay. Or interested in humans, for that matter.

But there was no other way than to seek an answer through experimentation, so Jack stood and quickly left his compartment. Since the little argument about the reward, Roux had once again become obtuse, eluding Jack, despite them heading to the same place. He could only hope that a week was enough for Roux to calm down about this whole thing, because Jack really wanted to get his hands on his wiggling tail.

He sped up when the chat's red head disappeared behind a door at the end of the car. He entered the train's restaurant car in time to see Roux exit it at the other end. Maneuvering between waiters and customers dining in the bright, elegant space, Jack then passed the second-class eatery before entering what looked like a waiting room on wheels. People of all ages sat on hard wooden benches, their luggage resting on shelves overhead or blocking the floor. Almost everyone was engaged in loud conversation, which was further embellished by the clucking of a chicken and the distant sound of a fiddle.

It was all fun and games until one had to travel in this noise and squalor for several hours at a time. Which apparently Roux was doing, because he reached the end of the wagon and jumped up to a top bunk with the agility Jack had learned to expect from him. Two men were already sitting underneath, so Roux pulled up his legs, and then closed his eyes, leaning his head against the wall.

Jack licked his lips and approached his fellow venator through the obstacle course presented by luggage and toddlers playing in the middle of the aisle. "Roux Chat-Bonnes? What a pleasant surprise. I thought you took yesterday's train," he said, even though really he had no idea. But the full moon was tonight, and in his experience, Roux always tried to give himself time to spare.

Roux's eyes snapped open, pupils so wide they covered almost all the green. "Jack Addison. I've been busy."

Jack grinned at him and stood in front of the bunk, stealing a glance at Roux's big, fluffy feet. Were they alone, he might have touched them under some pretense. "Since we're working together tonight, how about discussing this over food?"

Roux's whiskers bristled, and he cocked his head. "I don't think we should do that amongst so many ears eager for gossip."

The man next to him snorted. "Go on, chat. I've seen it all."

Whatever that meant, Jack didn't want to know. "We could order to my compartment. I hear they have cream from some rare local breed."

"I suppose this is a business matter," Roux said with a deep sigh, as if Jack had asked him to dig ditches with him. He grabbed his bag and jumped off the bunk, landing inches away. Sadly, he was wearing the jacket with the venator emblem at the back, so there wasn't much opportunity for a sneaky touch.

Jack still marveled at the grace of his movements. "You might as well take all your things. We should arrive at Tarheim station in less than two hours."

Roux looked back, and his ears flattened. "This is all I've got. I like to travel light, as one never knows when one might need to leave for a job."

Jack briefly pressed his lips together. He wondered what possessed Roux to travel second class in the first place. He did enough jobs to afford better conditions—something very important in their line of work.

"Wise. I only have one backpack on me too," he said, acutely aware of the big green eyes following his every misstep. Fortunately, he managed to avoid stepping on a chicken.

When they finally reached his compartment, he sat down with relief and pressed the button that summoned a member of staff. "Make yourself comfortable."

Roux scrutinized the place and eventually took off his coat before sitting down opposite Jack. He pulled up his feet and leaned against the wall. His rapier was attached to his belt, as if to threaten anyone who might approach.

"I've heard that during the full moon, werewolves go rabid, so that is when the local population needs most protection. But it's also when we strike, because the werewolves will be least tactical about their actions," Roux said, all work, no play.

He could be such a bore sometimes.

Jack pursed his lips. "That's why the governments created the reservations. So that they could have space to hunt and live as they wish without putting humans in danger. If this pack decided to shift beyond the reservation, and so close to the full moon at that, then they deserve what's coming. They might be werewolves, but they are sentient. They know what they're doing."

Roux sat up straighter, and it tickled something in Jack's stomach to see him so interested. "Exactly. We will apprehend them only if they really are leaving their territory during the full moon. But I doubt the negotiator would be lying about it. Unless she was given the wrong information. We will find out."

Jack loved all this *we* business. Roux must have understood that this was a job for at least two venators, and that half the reward was better than none.

Jack shrugged. "The werewolves in Prague heard about it too. They're really worried about their reputation as a species. If something happens tonight, it reflects on them all. And there are always those people who spread false rumors about minority groups. Nothing new. If they're not breaking the law, we might be leaving Tarheim with empty hands," he said, even though he really hoped they would not. Then again, if the pack was just the victim of vicious rumors, then Jack might pay them a visit once Roux was on his way.

"You've visited their district? I've been too busy with a rat the size of a horse. It wasn't even all that hard to kill, but really ugly, and none of the villagers wanted to approach it."

"So they called a chat?" Jack snorted, but Roux wasn't laughing. *Oops.*

"Maybe let's just stick to the job at hand. Anything you found out about the werewolves that we wouldn't have learned at the Academy?"

The knocking at the compartment door stopped their conversation, and while the food was the hook Jack had pulled Roux in with, he was still frustrated by the disturbance. But once the waiter left, Jack wasn't even sure if he wanted to reveal his secret weapon. Too bad Roux had too good of a memory to forget where they'd been interrupted.

"City werewolves believe those who still choose to live in the wild resent the fact that they are bound to one place. By nature, they are a traveling species, so the reservations are restrictive, even if most are quite vast. That's why the temptation to break the contract with humans is so strong. That and, you know, that whole alpha predator thing," Jack said with a wide smile.

Roux squinted at him. "What alpha predator thing? You mean that they think they're better than everyone else?"

Jack shrugged and offered Roux a bottle of beer. "Yes. I hear they're keen to assert their dominance over sentient creatures, if you know what I mean," he said, feeling a pleasant warmth spreading down his thighs and abdomen. Just like the gnomes, a werewolf wouldn't have to know Jack wasn't defenseless against him.

Roux declined the beer, but leaned forward, his fur bristled. "You mean…" he cleared his throat. "Physically? That's repulsive. We need to make sure the locals have adequate protection."

Jack tried to keep his smile in check. *Oh, Roux, always the prude.* "I'm assuming they're locking their houses well at night, but the truth is that tensions have been high around the reservations for a long time. Even with the truce in place, no one can predict if a single werewolf doesn't go running wild and hunts where he shouldn't. When the full moon is up, they lose it and look for creatures to mate with." Jack leaned over the table and lowered his voice. "But then again, apparently, the werewolves don't need to attack anyone for that purpose. There were even hybrid babies born to some of the local women. It's all hush-hush, but people have different tastes."

"I understand that there might be an appeal—" Roux stumbled over words, but the door opened and a waiter came in with their food, saving him from the babble. It was too bad, because Jack was more than interested in finding out if Roux himself saw the *appeal* of intimate interspecies relations.

So he decided to lay everything on the line, and spoke as soon as they were alone. "I decided to bait them," he said, producing the little vial he'd gotten at an ungodly price.

Roux hissed so loudly cream sprayed over his whiskers. "Don't be ridiculous and put that away. They go mad for it. If you put even a drop of that anywhere near me, I promise you we will be working separately!"

Jack rolled his eyes. "I am not putting this on you. We could sprinkle it over a piece of fabric. You know, find a convenient spot to entrap them and wait until they come."

"No. Categorically *no*." Roux wouldn't sit still, shifting from side to side with his chalice of sweet cream. "Also, that is, as you said, *entrapment*. We are supposed to see if they truly leave the reservation. and apprehend them if they do, not lure them out!"

Jack raised his hands. "Whoa! If you think I want to lure them out for the bounty, you're mistaken." Now that he thought about it, were any other venators doing just that? Luring werewolves beyond their borders for monetary gain? It definitely was against the code of conduct but... would people actually do it? Jack's sexcapades weren't exactly clean business, either.

"Good. Because I wouldn't stand for that, no matter how much I resent werewolves. As long as they respect the law, we will let them be. It's just so frustrating that one species can spoil so much for everyone else."

Jack frowned and quickly pushed a praline into his mouth. "What? Do other creatures hate werewolves? That's the first time I'm hearing about it."

Roux sighed deeply, glancing out the window. He had a lovely profile. Was his pink nose actually cold? "They're often violent. And because of them, new laws have been set in place that affect other creatures. Fortunately, chats are recognized to be peaceful communities, but we still got slammed with the flea-check law. It's degrading. Chats are always clean, and we take great pride in our grooming."

Jack stared at the graceful curve of Roux's forehead and the puffy muzzle that looked so soft he wanted to pet it. "I get it. Everyone always assumes I'm a monstrophobe, because of my father."

Roux turned to him with a huff. "Poor you. What kind of persecution do you go through because of that?"

The persecution of not everyone wanting to fuck him, but Jack couldn't exactly share that. "In Berlin I went to this restaurant that employs creatures who accidentally crossed into our realm from their own--so basically interdimensional orphans--and when they found out my name, all the waiters started suddenly avoiding my table. I felt like a pariah through no fault of my own!"

"Oh no. Must have been *awful.*" Roux yawned, as if his sarcasm wasn't clear enough.

Jack leaned back. "What the hell does that mean? It's discrimination! You're going to just laugh at all my problems, because you think yours are worse?"

"Yes! I will actually. You are ridiculous. When we first met, you told me I'm only a guest in *your* world. And now you're playing the victim?"

Had he said that? He didn't remember.

"It was a long time ago," Jack said but knew it came out flat. Would Roux never really open up to him because of a misstep two years back? So unreasonable.

Thankfully, he didn't have to solve this issue right away, because their train started rolling into the station, and they needed to quickly gather their belongings.

Soon enough, Jack would meet a pack of werewolves and wouldn't have to deal with a snotty chat.

Chapter 3

Tarheim was a small town, and apart from a woman and her child, Roux and Jack were the only passengers getting off the train. The sun was still peeking through the clouds, casting its glow on the hillsides around them, but werewolves would be hiding in the woods, way beyond town borders, which meant that the traveling wasn't over for the day.

After the way their conversation had ended, Jack didn't feel like having another one, so instead they dealt with all that was necessary—registered with the local authorities, who gave them further information on the rogue pack, bought some provisions, and paid a local man to drive them to the place where the pack had last been seen.

"It's 'bout time they sent in some venators. The people here will be grateful if you get rid of those dirty fur sacks. A moon ago, they left some traps around the perimeter, but nothing came of it," their driver said. He was a middle-aged man with silver hair and skin that had been made leathery after years of working outdoors. As he said this, his gaze inevitably swiped over Roux, and Jack couldn't help the stab of anger in his gut.

"You are in luck. Roux Chat-Bonnes here is the first non-human venator in history. He is the top tier."

Roux glanced at him with a hint of smile that made Jack's heart beat faster. If only Roux let him on all that fur, Jack would cuddle him into oblivion.

"I guess it takes one to know one," said the driver.

Roux shook his head. "Werewolves don't even come from the same dimension as chats."

Even Jack hadn't known that, so it was hard to imagine the villager in the driver seat would.

The man sighed. "The way I see it, all creatures are the same. They invade our land and want special treatment. No offense, but that's what it looks like from here," he said, nodding at Roux.

Jack watched the houses as they passed by. He couldn't avoid noticing iron shutters or bars that could be locked in front of doors. A group of children played on the porch of their house, but they were gone the moment they spotted Roux.

Jack wondered how it was for a chat to travel on their own.

Roux didn't grant the driver an answer, focusing on the beautiful alpine vistas. Did his senses allow him to hear more? Would he be able to smell the werewolves from far away? Did he even see color? Some creatures were colorblind... and Jack had so many questions.

Why did Roux even go through all the hurdles to become a venator if he could have thrived in his own community?

Roux's nostrils flared. "They've been in close proximity. But it's hard to say how far away. Wind can carry aromas."

Jack inhaled deeply, but could smell nothing other than pine, grass, and fresh air. He understood the reasons behind the man's prejudice, but Roux had done nothing to deserve having to listen to this. Jack was glad when they reached their destination at the edge of the forest. The light had become warmer as the sun started its descent toward the horizon, casting a golden glow on the monumental hills covered by woodland.

He cleared his throat and pointed toward the glistening river nearby. "Let's freshen up before this all starts."

Roux nodded and got off the cart without even saying goodbye to the driver. To be fair, Jack could see where Roux was coming from. With his bag flung over one arm, he walked with such grace Jack forgot to follow for a moment, and had to catch up with him.

At the bank of the narrow river, Roux took off his jacket, and then the shirt, revealing all the fur Jack wanted to slide his fingers into. Would he take his pants off as well? They were both male after all. On the other hand, Jack might have asked Roux about his junk one time too many.

Roux sat in the grass and pulled a brush out of his backpack. The bristles seemed stiff but bent a bit when Roux began brushing his arm.

Jack decided he'd set an example and took off all of his clothes, stretching in the warm sun. "Are you not getting into the water?" he asked, stepping off the grassy shore and into the stream that didn't look nearly as icy as it was. But Jack made his expression stay neutral and only scowled when he faced away from the chat.

Roux inched closer and dipped his brush in the water but shook his head. "Not exactly my idea of fun."

"Yeah but you said chats liked to be clean so..."

"I'm cleaning myself now."

Jack turned around and faced Roux in all his naked glory. The shallow stream was slowly numbing his feet and calves, but that was fine as long as Roux got the chance to appreciate what he might have, if he only reached out. "So you only brush? Like a Golden Retriever?"

Roux stilled. "And you only wash? Like cups?"

"Huh?"

"Cups. Dishes. You wash them, they're smooth— never mind!" Roux hid his face in his paws.

Jack laughed and pointed at Roux. "Oh, I get it. You want to touch something smooth? Is that right?" he asked, approaching the shore slowly, so that he didn't end up slipping on one of the stones covering the riverbed.

Roux's ears went right up, and he curled his shoulders. "What? I never said that!"

A child's squeal made both of them more aware of their surroundings. The girl yelled something and ran toward two women approaching the riverbank. One of them dropped her basket to hug the girl, but when she looked up, Jack had no other choice, if he wanted to follow the rules of decency—he dropped into the icy water. He bit his tongue as his balls shriveled from the cold.

"Er... can you turn around so that I can dress?" he called out, but wasn't sure if the woman heard him over the cries of her lamenting daughter.

"Wolf, mommy! A wolf!"

Roux stood up with his hands in the air. "I'm a chat, it's okay. Me and my friend, Jack, are venators."

Jack's teeth clattered, but it still hit him. Roux had called him a *friend*. His balls weren't as cold anymore.

"Why don't you throw me a towel, friend?" he asked, reaching out until Roux did as asked. With his modesty saved, Jack finally extracted himself from the stream and looked to the other side, where the woman was still consoling her child.

"You don't have to worry, ma'am. Tomorrow this same time, there will be no werewolves to worry about."

The two women came closer with baskets full of laundry, but still eyed Roux suspiciously. "A Godsend. I hope you don't get hurt. They get feral in the full moon," said one.

Jack gave a small laugh and quickly put on his shirt. It clung to his damp body, but he chose to ignore it and sat next to Roux, who was still in the process of combing his coat. Would Roux need help with the brushing of his back? Jack imagined him shivering with pleasure like Mr. Paws had when Jack stroked the cat's spine.

"We've come all the way from Bavaria. It was a special assignment. Not everyone has the necessary skill do deal with those monsters," he boasted, even though he'd never met a werewolf out of his human form. But building trust was more important than precision in terms of truth.

"It's only been getting worse in the last months. There was this girl, Blanka. Never listened, stubborn thing," said the girl's mother. The other woman nodded. "She ventured into the werewolf territory time and time again. Then, following the full moon, she just never came back. Terrible business."

Jack licked his lips. Did Blanka stay with the werewolves out of her free will, or had she been taken? "We will look into it. If she is still out there, we will find her."

"Make sure all the houses are locked, and the children remain indoors," Roux said.

Jack was finding it hard to decide whether Roux was cuter scared, or when he was authoritative, like now.

The women told them some other horror stories about the local werewolves, but they left for their homes as soon as they were done with a small load of laundry. It was getting dark by the time Jack and Roux entered the woods, lighting their way with Jack's electric lamp. In order to easily find their way back if needed, they decided to follow the river, but two hours on, in near-complete darkness beneath the thick tree tops, Jack was starting to feel the strain on his nerves. Fantasizing about werewolves was all fine and good when you weren't so close to their territory. Especially considering that the village women had claimed some people had been eaten by the creatures in the past.

When Roux climbed one of the tall pine trees to get a better idea of their position, Jack backed away against the trunk, feeling his stomach twist at every sound. He took deep breaths and tried to convince himself that as a venator, he was more than equipped to deal with this situation, but when Roux suddenly landed right next to him, Jack barely kept in a scream.

"Uh... so, can you see the border of the reservation?"

"Yes, it's not far away, but we need to stay within our jurisdiction. Things can get messy if they try to defend themselves by claiming we've gone inside."

Jack nodded and moved along the water, which glinted whenever he directed the lamp at it. "You think they can smell us?"

"Probably, if they're close enough. But we're armed." Roux poked Jack. "Is the one and only Jack Addison scared of a few werewolves?"

Jack snorted, even though he most definitely was. Having Roux at his side made the dark forest much less intimidating. "No. I was just jealous that you could actually see stuff in the moonlight from up there."

Roux smiled, presenting his sharp teeth. "You? Jealous of me? Do you know that in Paris, they print trading cards with portraits of venators and creatures they are famous for slaying? And they come with ranks. Do you think you're above or under me?"

Jack stared at the green eyes, at the pretty canines and grinned, stepping that bit closer. "I'd be happy with both."

Roux blinked. "Really? I thought you were making it your thing to find the most unusual or dangerous creatures in all of Europe, just so that everyone knew your name."

Jack rolled his eyes. He couldn't believe this shit. "I obviously wasn't speaking about trading cards."

"What about then?"

Jack sighed and stepped so close Roux moved back to maintain physical distance. He was such a confusing creature. "About us maybe getting closer after this is over? We could rent out a room in a nice inn."

Roux stared. He couldn't be a virgin, could he? "I don't understand why you would suggest that." He turned around and started vigorously walking ahead.

Enough was enough. Jack needed to show his intentions instead of talking. He rushed behind Roux and pulled him closer by the tail, but Roux must have not been expecting it at all, because the screech that came out of his mouth was high-pitched and abrupt.

And resonated through the trees.

The sound was both distressing and cute at the same time. Jack let go. "Did that hurt? I'm sorry."

"Yes, it hurt!" When Roux spun around, he rubbed one of his eyes. "It's still tender where the gnome bit me, you ass. Wait. Did you hear that?" He stilled, holding on to his own tail, and this time Jack heard it too. A shuffling in the bushes approaching awfully fast.

No way.

No fucking way.

Jack couldn't help the tremble in his hands when the noise became louder, as if whatever was coming their way was much larger than he'd anticipated.

"Fuck, fuck, fuck! Run!" Roux yelled and took off, leaving his bag behind.

Jack's head was completely empty, but he ran faster than ever, faster than at his final exams, when the physical prowess score had to make up for his poor academic performance. His feet practically flew through the air, but the noise, the creaking, the loud, throaty gasps were not going away.

The lamp he still held swayed as he ran, casting its light at random things, but he switched it off and rushed forward, hoping to lose the pursuing werewolves.

Something crashed into his face so rapidly his brain rocked in his skull as if it were a rattle, and the whole world rolled around Jack until he landed in the grass, tasting blood on his tongue.

The stampede of heavy paws was followed by a howl, and when other werewolves joined in, Jack shut his eyes, still as a mouse as the werewolves passed him. Their paws stomped so close to him that dirt and moss hit his face, but not one of the massive creatures noticed his presence.

Roux's screech followed a clang of metal, and Jack's heart stopped beating altogether, because the chat screams wouldn't stop.

He didn't dare switch on his lamp, and for several terrifying seconds he just stayed still, listening to Roux's distressed cries. The werewolf growls sounded playful rather than aggressive, but when Jack's eyes got used to the darkness, he saw the pack standing in a circle in the middle of a small clearing. Pale moonlight revealed just how perilous Roux's situation was. With eyes wide as dinner plates, he struggled against a chain that was somehow attached to his leg, keeping him in place for the wolves. One of them, a tall creature with a streak of white fur down his back, pulled on Roux's tail so hard it cut his legs from under him. The cat-like cry of distress pierced Jack's chest, but he was too terrified to move. He was never terrified, so what the fuck was going on?

And the worst thing was that while the werewolves were busy with their new toy, he could attempt an escape.

He could later pretend that they went in different directions, and that would be that.

No one would know.

The werewolves were huge creatures, at least eight feet tall, with furry ape-like bodies and heads that weren't quite human nor canine. They had huge claws, and one of the creatures scratched Roux's jacket, ripping it open at the back.

Roux meowed in a way Jack had never heard before. Animalistic and desperate, with a high pitch that hurt Jack's ears.

"Here kitty, kitty, kitty…" The streaked werewolf laughed in a low tone that resembled a growl.

"Never seen one like him," said another, pulling on Roux's pants so hard they ripped as well, and it was only then that Jack realized what the pack wanted to do.

Roux squealed, twisting from one werewolf to the other, but with the cuff around his ankle, he wasn't going anywhere, no matter how hard he tried. The werewolves were just playing with him for now, but it would get worse, and Roux was terrified already. With that prudish nature of his, he might as well have been a virgin, so how was he to deal with five werewolves twice his size? He might be seriously hurt, and since he was different than any other venator, news of his humiliation would surely spread, no doubt ending his career.

Jack would not let that happen!

On trembling legs, he got up and stared at Roux, who was suddenly dragged over the ground by two thick arms. Jack needed to act. Now or never.

Before the creatures spotted him, he unscrewed the bottle of pheromones and doused its contents all over his body. The musky oil was warm in his hair, and pleasantly slick when it drizzled down his neck.

"Hey, fleabags! How about you try with someone closer to your own size?" he shouted, even though his voice came out in an uneven pitch.

Five sets of bright yellow eyes shone in the darkness, their gaze inevitably drawn to his presence. Jack dropped the bottle and reached back for his sword.

Chapter 4

Five sets of clapping jaws full of sharp teeth descended on Jack, but with the Gouger in his hand, he stood a chance. The werewolves went so frantic they bumped into trees and trampled bushes, but Jack stood his ground, ready for impact.

The first werewolf to clash with his sword howled in pain the moment the blade sank into his arm, but Jack realized what a grave mistake he'd made, favoring the sword over his guns, once a wall of fur draped over pure muscle crashed into him from the side. A jolt of pain shot through Jack's arm, rendering it numb, and his hand opened, dropping the precious weapon as if it were a stick not worthy of anyone's attention.

He gulped down cool night air, reaching out for the sword, but the werewolf pushed him down onto the moss, far away from the sword. Jack couldn't breathe. Above him, the five silhouettes morphed into a single beast with five heads, twisting and jerking against the background of the brightly lit night sky.

"I smelled him first!" growled one, and pulled on Jack's leg, while another tugged on his arm. He'd be torn into pieces before these monsters could come to an agreement.

A cold-nosed sniffed his pheromone-doused hair, and he wasn't sure if opening that bottle had been a good idea.

Streak looked into Jack's eyes with a long growl that was akin to a purr yet nothing like it. Somewhere deep out of that massive hairy chest came a sound that communicated pleasure, even though Jack couldn't speak wolf.

"Look, guys—" he tried, but when one of the werewolves squeezed his jaws on Jack's jacket and started shaking his head ferociously, fear squeezed Jack's throat and refused to let go. His plea turned into a scream when the other werewolf tugged on his leg, lifting his entire body in the process. "No! Stop! You're gonna fucking kill me!"

The werewolves became more frantic by the second. When one let go of him, another used the opportunity to grab Jack, and his jacket ripped at the sleeve. For a moment, Jack thought he was close enough to the sword, but as soon as he reached out, the monster bleeding from his arm where he'd been stabbed, tugged Jack away from it, shoving down Jack's pants in the process.

"Oh, no you don't..." the werewolf growled while another started pulling on Jack's jacket to get it off, but when the garment covered Jack's head, his world became so chaotic that he couldn't even say how many paws were grabbing him at once.

He could sense the sharpness of their claws, the cool roughness of leathery pads, and the coarse fur. Tossed between many pairs of arms, he was like a rag doll in the hands of those creatures, and by the time he landed on the ground again, and the jacket finally got ripped off, the night air froze his sweaty skin.

His eyes must have gotten more used to the dark, because when he looked up the massive brown legs, he saw the huge wolfman bristling and baring his teeth, as if he were protecting his rights to a meal.

Was this the end of Jack Addison? Eaten alive by a pack of werewolves, before he could make a name for himself? He flinched when the brown wolf with a pale streak hunched down and rested his front paws on either side of Jack's head, growling in a way that sent shudders down his spine. "It's my right as the alpha!"

All but one of the werewolves backed off. The one still bleeding from his arm, with a nasty set of long fangs, butted his head against Streak's. "I deserve to go first. I was wounded!"

Jack trembled under the mountains of coarse fur, his skin exposed to scratches and bites. He was sure it would only take a single bite to his stomach to open him up like a slaughtered pig. Though he likely wouldn't get to die quick, since the beasts were fighting over who'd get to bite him *first*.

Streak exhaled so deeply hot vapor hit Jack's face. "But I get to knot."

Jack was breathless. So they didn't intend to eat him... yet. Because werewolves weren't in the habit of fucking dead flesh. Allegedly. He was safe. He could get the werewolf experience right here and now, and he'd heard all about knotting from an underground pamphlet for werewolf aficionados.

"Listen, guys, I—"

The werewolf with long fangs leaned over him and pressed Jack's head into the damp moss. The sound of his frantic breathing filled Jack's consciousness, closely followed by the coppery scent of blood and the glide of coarse fur against his vulnerable ass. When the soft pelt was suddenly replaced by a piece of hot, throbbing flesh, Jack might have squealed at the size of that thing.

Fang's hot muzzle rubbed against Jack's defenceless back, all the way to his neck and hair. He could hardly breathe against the moss, terrified yet excited at the same time. Fang's nose was cold, but not his tongue. When he licked the back of Jack's head, his thick cock twitched against Jack's ass.

"That scent..." Fang let out a low growl. Despite Jack's fears, he didn't just shove his dick in raw, but lifted himself, and once more rubbed his muzzle down Jack's back, this time, all the way to his ass. He pushed his nose between Jack's buttocks, making him squeal at the thought of all those teeth so close to the delicate skin of his balls.

He'd wanted the 'authentic' werewolf experience, yet now that he was getting it, his heart, dick, and brain all had different opinions on the matter. It was almost as if those three organs pulled him in different directions, like the werewolves had. But once the huge muzzle opened, and a long, lava-hot tongue rolled out before sliding between Jack's buttocks, his brain stopped working altogether, and followed the lead of Jack's dick.

The scratching of sharp teeth against sensitive flesh added spice to the way the werewolf's slick tongue glided along Jack's crack, leaving behind a sticky, slick residue of saliva. Fang was no longer holding Jack's head down, too busy opening his ass with both padded hands, but Jack wasn't to have peace.

The alpha's claws sank into dirt right in front of Jack's face, and when the huge werewolf squatted down, Jack wasn't even surprised by the tug on his hair.

"Never met a man that smells like you." Streak grunted, and without much more introduction, he pressed Jack's sweaty face to his hard cock.

Red and thick above a set of heavy furry balls, it was already dripping fluid, so Jack licked it without thinking. Jack's cock was already rock hard against the wet moss, twitching every time Fang pressed his flat tongue against Jack's ass. As long as the werewolves didn't want a snack after fucking, he could handle them.

The smallest of the werewolves pressed his nose against Jack's ribs with a whimper, only to be shoved away by Streak. Jack hummed around the pointy tip of the alpha's penis, tasting the sourness of his pre-cum. There was so much of it that some of the slick liquid ended up dribbling down Jack's chin. Eager to please the boss of the pack, he carefully sucked on the smooth flesh, causing the wolf to ball his huge fingers into his hair.

But hearing the pack's omega whimper again, Jack reached toward him. If he was to survive this, he needed a friend. The smallest werewolf was still much bigger than him, but he arched to Jack's hand like an eager puppy, yearning for attention, and nudging Jack with his nose time and time again until Jack's fingers reached the ears of the beast.

Back in the day when Jack only fucked humans, he'd participated in several orgies, but while his partners had been so much smaller and weaker than the pack, one thing did not change—it was damn hard to focus on three things at once. Fang wasn't about foreplay, so when his cock invaded the slickened hole, Jack wasn't adequately relaxed. He arched his hips in hope of keeping some of the length out, but when Fang held Jack's buttocks apart, digging his claws into skin, there was nothing to relieve the discomfort of the sudden penetration.

Despite the lubrication provided by slick saliva, the dick was massive, and as it pushed into Jack with little preparation, his body resisted, clamping down on the cock as his sphincter pulsed with pain. Fang gave an impatient grunt and retreated somewhat, only to thrust back in before Jack was ready. Jack's cry was muffled by the alpha's dick, which moved deeper into his mouth, providing a welcome distraction until the narrow tip tickled the back of Jack's throat, making him cough.

This wasn't quite how he'd imagined sex with a werewolf.

The pup licked his outstretched hand before shifting his body and placing Jack's hand on the thick, throbbing flesh of his dick. At first, Jack had no focus to spare the omega, but when Fang stormed past the natural defenses of Jack's body, pushing all the way inside, Jack squeezed the pup's cock even as he gagged on the one in his mouth.

He was losing sense of space when Fang started pumping his cock in short thrusts that were all about getting off. He panted, rubbing his furry thighs against Jack's skin, and despite fear still coursing through his veins, Jack smiled around the dick in his mouth. Finally, he was getting to experience fur, even if its texture was nothing like the silky coat of a chat.

The alpha pulled out of Jack's mouth unexpectedly, only to make room for another eager werewolf, this one black as the night around them. The beast didn't wait even a second, and pushed the cock at Jack, closing his thighs around Jack's head and barely letting him breathe.

The joints of Jack's jaw squealed at the force that made them stretch even wider, but the omega humping Jack's fist provided a welcome distraction. His breathless gasps were slowly turning into tiny, cute yelps, and his hips worked overtime, moving so rapidly the wolfboy's hairy balls slapped against Jack's fist.

Black wasn't as patient as the alpha had been, and he wouldn't be sated by sucking only. The fur on the inside of his thighs was soft and smooth, and when he thrust his groin forward, the tip entered Jack's throat while the thick middle pushed down his tongue. He moaned, which in turn made Black gasp in ecstasy and move deeper into Jack's relaxed gullet.

He was too distracted to gag at this point. Fang was entering him so furiously Jack's ass felt as if it was being roasted, but at the same time, the inner massage felt so good he wouldn't dream of finishing just yet.

Fang pulled out right before coming, and with a low growl against Jack's back, he spurted his cum between Jack's buttocks. His claws eased their pressure on Jack's skin, but just as Fang started licking his shoulder blade, the fifth werewolf shoved him aside.

"My turn!"

Jack's head was trapped, serving Black, so he wasn't able to look back, but from the sound of the snarling behind him, Fang wasn't happy with the development. He might have been afraid of the wolfman's anger if Pup hadn't distracted him with a spurt of hot cum shot into Jack's fist and along his forearm, all the way to his elbow. The wolf came so much Jack couldn't believe the volume, so he praised his lover with a gentle squeeze around the knot at the base of the cock.

Before he could think, another cock entered his relaxed ass, and Fifth had as little patience as his predecessor. He grabbed Jack's hips hard and pistoned in and out with long, reckless strokes. His dick was much longer, which caused cramps that had Jack mewling helplessly into the dick that was stopping him from breathing. With his head spinning from the lack of oxygen, he barely registered that Black briefly withdrew, but as soon as he inhaled, the werewolf stuffed his mouth once more.

The omega slid his warm body under Jack's arm, and put one padded hand on Jack's back. His tongue lapped at Jack's neck and ear without a care about Black's dick continuously pumping into Jack's throat. The fur rubbing against Jack was getting him hornier by the second. Despite his arousal spiking and falling alongside his levels of fear or discomfort, he appreciated the chance to curl his fist into the omega's soft belly fur. The fucking was a wild ride, yet cuddling up to a furry body provided the kind of comfort he'd never experienced before.

He hugged the omega just before a stream of hot cum cascaded down his throat. Black held Jack close, face buried in the musk-scented fur while his cock throbbed in Jack's mouth hole. The knot pushed at Jack's teeth, but he wouldn't have been able to accommodate it unless it dislocated his jaw.

It was only when Black retreated, leaving Jack with a sore mouth and the taste of werewolf cum on his tongue, that he noticed the base of the cock fucking his ass thicken. His sphincter was relaxed, so the still-small knot pumped in and out, causing yet more pleasure, but Jack didn't get to experience it growing to its full potential.

A vicious barking fight started behind him, and when he looked back, Streak's teeth were bared at the fifth werewolf in a standoff between Jack's spread legs. That was the last place where he wanted beastly claws and fangs.

"No knot!" Streak grabbed Fifth's neck, and when the claws bit into skin, Fifth finally gave in. He whimpered, flattening his ears, and with Streak's hand around his neck, he pumped his hand up and down his slippery cock between Jack's buttocks until he came.

Since there was no one left to use Jack's mouth, he rested his cheek against the cool undergrowth, completely in tune with his abused body. Everything ached—from his jaw muscles, through his throat, the scratched skin, to the near-numbness of his ass. His insides felt fantastic, though. They were hot, and relaxed, and receptive, and in need of another cock, so Jack glanced over his shoulder and spread his thighs wider, whimpering when Streak captured his gaze, big red cock ready for action.

Jack dragged himself up to all fours, and Streak gave him a toothy grin that belonged in nightmares, yet didn't scare Jack anymore. Streak's yellow eyes shone when he shoved Fifth off Jack's back.

"I wish you were female so I could breed you," the alpha said in a raspy voice, thrusting between Jack's aching thighs. By now even the touch of those padded hands was enough to send Jack's arousal into overdrive.

Jack's mouth felt dry, and he shyly looked at the alpha, letting go of the pup in favor of squeezing his own cock, which was so slick from pre-cum, so hard, and so hot he just might come too soon. But before Streak pushed in, the furry presence at Jack's side shifted and crawled under Jack's body, providing not only support but also caressing him again with that coarse, long pelt.

For a moment, Jack imagined fucking the omega while Streak fucked him, but the werewolf wasn't in the right position for it, just rubbing his head against Jack's stomach.

The thick fingers ending in claws crawled up Jack's back, and the alpha grabbed Jack's shoulders before shoving his stiff cock in. He already had a hint of a thickness growing at the base, and Jack curled his fists on the moss every time that thing drove in, leaving him breathless.

He didn't expect a cold nose pushing against his balls, but then the omega licked up Jack's cock, sending a shock of excitement all over Jack's flesh. The moment he reacted with a moan, the omega let out a little woof, and kept licking with yet more eagerness.

Jack breathlessly petted the young werewolf's long tail, which was fluffy enough to create an illusion of thickness. He was no longer scared of sharp canines so close to his dick. All he cared about was the exotic pleasure of that long tongue rolling up and down his dick, the fur, and the strong, dominant presence behind him. The alpha wasn't impatient, like some members of his pack had been. He held Jack down without excessive force and fucked him in even thrusts, which got faster as the knot grew, plucked out of Jack when Streak withdrew, and plunged back in when he thrust. Fear once again penetrated Jack's brain when the huge ball of flesh pushed on and wouldn't go in, for some reason. He shrieked, trying to shove the werewolf off him, but the alpha growled in warning and lodged himself back inside Jack's tortured body.

This time, he stopped moving altogether, but the omega's tongue worked its magic and Jack came with the thick thing lodged inside him.

Jack's hole spasmed around the cock, and he couldn't stop moaning as wet, hot ecstasy overcame his brain.

"That's it, little one, milk me," Streak growled into Jack's nape.

In the end, Jack had to push the omega away, because his muscles were giving in, and when he lay spent in the moss, Streak followed, with his cock nestled in Jack's ass and still throbbing with heat. For a while, Streak licked Jack's hair, but then settled with his head next to Jack's and… fell asleep.

Still heaving, still spread open by the alpha werewolf, Jack looked around to find that all the other beasts had fallen into a slumber around them. Which would have been the perfect opportunity to make his escape.

If he wasn't pinned to the ground by three hundred pounds of flesh and a knot.

Chapter 5

Jack had no idea how much time had passed, but the knot at the base of Streak's dick disappeared, releasing his ass. But even with the soft cock out, it wouldn't have been easy to crawl from under the alpha werewolf, so Jack resigned himself to a little nap as well.

It was still dark when he woke up, but the weight on top of him had eased, the fur had been replaced by regular hairy skin, and when Jack opened his eyes, he saw that the other werewolves had also shifted back to their human forms. A slender young man, who had to be the omega, was snoring, curled up by Jack's side.

He was cute. Jack would've fucked him in either form. He felt bad about having to hand him over to the authorities, but that was the life of a venator. While he'd ended up enjoying himself, the pack had gotten to Roux first, and they could have attacked anyone who ventured into the woods at the wrong time. It was time to teach this pack a lesson.

Jack rolled from under Streak as gently as possible, and while he'd felt seemed fine before, the moment he moved, soreness and exertion blasted into him like a quintuplet of werewolf dicks. Fighting through the discomfort, Jack crawled to his backpack and swiftly took out the silver cuffs that would keep the werewolves in place. His skin was crusty from the dried cum, and his ass still felt damp from the alpha's giant release, but as he stretched, his body started feeling more normal. The sky was already overcome by a pink glow, and he didn't want to risk any of the men escaping justice.

All in all, this had been a good night. Maybe his means weren't orthodox, but he did manage to subdue five massive werewolves. He grinned to himself as he stared at the sleeping bodies trapped with silver cuffs, but stopped the moment a flash of pain went through his jaw. Maybe smiling needed to wait a while.

He spotted a figure behind the far-off trees and grabbed his fallen sword, ready to fight tooth and nail for his victory. Or was it Roux? Had he managed to escape the snares?

But as he stood, despite the pain in his pulled thigh muscle, the lithe figure emerged from between the bushes.

It was a naked woman with long blonde hair, and judging by the size of her stomach, she was nearing the end of a pregnancy. Jack's hands flinched, and he slowly lowered his weapon, not wanting to scare her. "Wh— are you okay? What are you doing here?" He asked, but her lips revealed clenched teeth, and she rushed forward like a rabid wolverine.

"Free them right now!" she said with the local accent, frantically looking around the cuffed men.

Jack had seen many things during his travels, but this was a first. "Absolutely not. I've arrested them, in the name of the law."

She pushed him back, and only then looked his naked form up and down. "They can get a bit rowdy in the full moon, but it's no reason to take them away. Please." She knelt by Streak and shook his arm. "Ota! Wake up, right now!" When the werewolf just snored in reply, she scratched his arm so hard she drew blood, and that did the trick.

The alpha's eyes went wide, and he let out a howl, trying to jerk his body up. His toes dug into the moss, his strong thigh and buttock muscles flexed, but he couldn't move. Not with the silver cuffs on.

Jack licked his lips, staring at the pregnant belly, and then at the werewolf. "Shit.... you've made a hybrid," he said, rubbing his face. This was huge— physical proof that werewolves were capable of interbreeding with humans.

The woman frowned at him and stroked her belly. "My children will be no hybrids! How do you think new werewolves are created? With a bite? What a joke. And have you ever met a werewolf woman?"

"Blanka... What are you doing here?" Ota grumbled as if he were waking up with a bad hangover, and managed to twist himself to his back.

She slapped him. "Me? What are all of *you* doing here, huh? I can't have these children on my own! Are you insane? You promised!"

Oh. So this was what happened to *Blanka*. Maybe she wasn't so reckless and stupid after all. Having all that wolf dick to herself sounded like an exciting break from farm life.

Ota curled his upper lip and snarled at Jack. "He's the one who caused all this. He smells like a female!"

Jack scowled and smelled his armpit, only to find the usual odor of morning sweat. But Blanka wasn't having any of it, and slapped Ota's face again, showing her small fangs as if she were a real wolf bitch.

"No, he caught you because you broke the law. Again. I don't care what you think your destiny is. You should have thought about it before you put your pups inside me!"

Jack stood still. He'd never been the kind of person who lived for drama, but anyone would have found this unexpected peek into pack life juicy.

Ota groaned and rubbed his head against the moss. "What am I supposed to say, cuddlepie? There was also some wild cat creature I think. We thought we'd only venture out to grab it."

Blanka rubbed her face and took a deep breath, before turning to Jack. "Please spare this idiot? I need him. I don't know what I would do without him."

Ota gave Jack a toothy grin. "Pretty please? I know they'll just tag them this time. They'll hate it, but they'll be fine. But I can't leave Blanka. Not when she's almost due."

Jack grunted and approached Ota with hurried footsteps, only to kick his thigh. "That was a sentient creature that you attacked. There is nothing to excuse your unauthorized venture. And during the full moon at that! If you keep this up, you will end up dead, and your bitch alone with the children. Is that what you want?" he asked, gesturing at Blanka, who frowned at him.

Maybe he shouldn't have used the b-word after all. He looked toward the clearing, but he couldn't see much. Was Roux safe?

Ota's smile was gone. "What can I say? Full moon can get a bit wild, if you know what I mean."

A hardened criminal, then.

Blanka growled at him and slapped his hairy pec. "What he means is that he is sorry beyond words, and he will make amends, and he will make sure the pack stays put next time."

Jack glanced at the pregnant woman again. At the end of the day, nothing bad had happened. He wouldn't let it all slide, but maybe he could let the father go this time.

"If you ever leave the borders on the full moon again without a permit, I will personally come here and castrate you," he said sternly.

"You wouldn't really want that though, would you?" Ota winked at Jack. Unbelievable. He did have a nice dick, though.

"There are plenty of werewolves in Bohemia."

Blanka huffed. "If you don't obey the law, I will cut you myself," she said before once again glancing at Jack, her eyes pleading. "Please, kind sir? I will personally make sure he's good."

Jack nodded, picking up what was left of his clothes. "Fine. Maybe you can make new arrangements with the local negotiator, if you actually bother paying him a visit in human form."

He took the cuffs off Ota, conscious of his every move in case the werewolf still wanted to attack, but the alpha turned to his bride instead, and pulled her under his thick arm. "If any of my wolves is harmed in custody, the deal will be off," he said, baring his teeth, but he was already directing his footsteps toward the reservation.

Jack sighed, resting his hands on his hips. He was kind of digging the werewolf's poise. No wonder Blanka had been swept off her feet. "Do yourself a favor and speak to the negotiator before the next full moon. And take Blanka with you. Everyone around these parts thinks she's been eaten."

Jack got no answer, which left him with four snoring, apprehended werewolves and a desperate itch to find out if Roux was all right. He grabbed his sword and turned on the portable lamp. Once he started walking, the aches in his body reminded him of the wild night with beasts, but Roux was more important.

He didn't have to walk far, and found the chat with a snare around his leg. The fur around the clamp had been rubbed raw, but Roux still got up as soon as he spotted Jack. His eyes were half-closed, the fur on his face matted, and he limped toward Jack as far as the snare allowed him.

"Jack! Are they gone? I'm sorry, I'm so sorry!" His words were difficult to understand, as they sounded more like meowing, but Jack easily got the gist.

He tried to move quicker, and finally reached Roux, diving to his knees right away. "It's fine. We need to get this off you."

The soft furry arms closed around Jack's neck, and Roux pulled him close, hiding his muzzle in Jack's neck. "It's not fine. I should have done… something. But I was too scared. I'm such a coward."

Oh. Ooh. Roux's fur was soft and warm, and Jack definitely didn't mind the hug. The snares could wait.

"It's not your fault you got entrapped. There was nothing you could have done. But it's all right. They're cuffed," Jack said, gently rubbing his hands up and down the slender back.

So. Fucking. Soft.

"I could have at least made noise, but I panicked after they attacked me." Roux sobbed against Jack's neck and tightened the hug. "Jack, I will never forgive myself. They violated you and I… I just sat there!"

Jack licked his lips and petted the back of Roux's fluffy head, enjoying its weight on his shoulder. He wouldn't mind being held like this more often. "That's okay. I used the pheromones to lure them away. I'm a big guy. Jack Addison can take it, and all that."

Roux pulled away to look at Jack, and his eyes were so big, glossy and green Jack's heart stopped at the cuteness. "Why are you putting on such a brave face? Those monsters deserve to rot for what they did to you. I can't wait to report them to the negotiators."

No. Jack Addison could not be known as the guy who got fucked by five werewolves and lived to tell the tale. "Yeah, please, don't. I appreciate that you haven't mentioned the spider egg thing to anyone, but this might be even more embarrassing," Jack said and put his hand across Roux's mouth to make the point, and the chat's ears fell. The pillow-like lips were just adorable.

Roux shook off Jack's fingers. "But this will mean they remain unpunished! Do you really want them to get out of this with a slap on the wrist for crossing the border?

Jack moved his hands up through the furry coat covering Roux's entire body, until he cupped his pretty face. "Look, Roux. It really wasn't all bad. I mean, the five of them were a bit of a stretch, pun unintended, but it kinda felt nice at times," he said, licking his lips. Would Roux understand what he wanted to say? That he was fine with fucking creatures now?

Roux cocked his head and blinked a few times. "Wait. What? But... but werewolves."

Jack took a deep breath and rubbed his thumbs across Roux's cheeks. "I've never told this to anyone, but being away from my family really broadened my horizons. I like experiencing all kinds of new things, and I really, really like fur," he told Roux, combing his fingers through his thick hair. "And I am sore now, but I wanted to have sex with a werewolf anyway, so I guess... no harm done?"

Roux just stared. "Y-you like fur? As in... sexually?" He ran his padded hands over Jack's neck. Their touch was aggravating to Jack's skin, and while he was too pumped out to want sex just yet, it did give him a tingle in his balls.

"Roux, I've been thinking about you for a long time. I imagine your fur tickling my skin, and your tail wrapping around my thigh as I press my dick to your soft stomach," he said, breathless from the excitement of finally saying all this out loud.

The whiskers, and even the few long strands above Roux's eyes bristled. "What? Why? When?"

"I guess I've had a thing for chats since I met you. You're so graceful, and elegant, and your fur is much softer than any other creature's I've touched." He growled, pulling Roux closer until their bodies were aligned.

"I've met other chats, but all of you are so skittish. Especially the men. You don't want to get to know any humans, and I'm trying my best."

Roux hissed. "Trying your best to what? Fuck a chat? Seriously? I thought you've been raped and mauled, and now I'm finding out that it's fine because you're so into fur? What else? Did you have fantasies of being jerked off with padded hands? You are unbelievable!" He moved away, but could only go so far with the snare around his ankle, so he meowed in helpless frustration. "I will not be objectified."

Jack definitely had fantasies about being jerked off with chat pads, but who wouldn't have? They were so fucking cute it was obscene! "What? Don't say that. It's a preference. When men say they like blondes that doesn't mean they are objectifying the hair, right?"

"Unless they're specifically looking for blondes to fuck because of their hair. I've met humans like you, Addison. I am *not* a novelty. And stop keeping me prisoner. Get me out!" He whined, increasingly agitated and twisting into positions that obscured his crotch. Only now it struck Jack that, despite the fur, Roux was technically naked, and while his dick was hidden, Jack caught a glimpse of the fuzzy ball sac, and his lips went dry.

"I... I'm not. I'll set you free, and we can talk. Don't get so defensive," he said and picked up the sword, which felt unusually heavy. He pressed the button that made the blade vibrate and slammed it down, breaking the mechanism that kept the snare shut.

Roux scrambled for his clothes with his tail between his legs. "Is that why I found you with the gnomes? Thrill-seeking?"

Yes.

"No, come on, Roux. It was just a way to sneak up on them, okay? This is different. You are completely sentient, and we have a lot of in common. It's not like you have anyone."

Roux bristled even more as he put on his ripped pants and pulled his tail through the hole at the back. "Oh, thank you for acknowledging I am, in fact, sentient. You've got some nerve, Addison. And why do you assume I've got no one? Am I desirable, then, or not?"

Jack followed him, not sure how to deal with all this anger. And why were they back to surnames? "You would have said. We talked a lot all day. I don't have anyone right now either. We could... explore together."

"No way! I am done here. I don't even care about the prize. I can't believe this is why you pretended to like me." The last word came out as a whimpery meow. Roux picked up his bag.

"Prete—no, Roux. I *do* like you. I like you, *and* your fur. I like both, okay?" Jack tried, grabbing Roux's shoulder, weirdly hurt. "I literally saved your ass tonight."

Roux stepped Jack's way with a hiss. "So what? I should put out for my savior? I *owe* you a fuck? How much do you value that at? I'll pay you back."

Jack clutched at his hair. "Oh, Gods! This is unreasonable. When I lured them away from you, I didn't know if they weren't going to eat me for dinner, did I? I was afraid for you, don't you understand that?"

Roux took out the flare pistol and shot it into the sky. "They wouldn't have attacked me in the first place if you hadn't pulled my tail." The red smoke burst above them, signalling to the negotiator where they were.

Jack hissed, losing his patience. "Oh, so everything is always the fault of the human, whether he had good intentions or not. Maybe we should be sent away from our own dimension, because we hurt you all so much!"

Roux threw the pistol to the ground and grabbed the last piece of his scattered clothes, the jacket. "Maybe you should!" He hissed so viciously his gums showed, and turned around, walking off in quick strides, despite his limp.

Jack could've followed the stubborn creature, but that would've meant deserting his bounty of werewolves. He'd won that fair and square, and not without effort.

"Come on, Roux! Don't go! There were five of them, all big. We don't know yet, I might as well have internal bleeding," Jack called out, but when Roux wouldn't answer, he went on, "Don't you need this bounty more than me?" he said, dragging his sword over the ground as he approached the spot where the werewolves all lay cuffed.

No answer came from where the chat had disappeared, so there was no point wasting his breath. How had they gone from the cuddles to this mess? Why was everything always supposed to be his fault?

Since the werewolves were still sleeping, he put on his spare pants. He wasn't about to make a handover to the negotiator butt naked. He glanced over the thousand bruises and scratches on his body. No one needed to know they weren't the outcome of a fight. Definitely not the negotiator, who might or might not pass on this story as juicy gossip. It would only take so much time for this to reach Father's ears, and he'd then go on to start some crazy anti-werewolf crusade.

Jack gathered his things and waited, watching the pink dye glinting in the sky above. He couldn't believe Roux bailed on him like this. Typical chat, too focused on his own reality to notice someone else's. And skittish, too.

Jack considered eating his breakfast when a low whine tore through the air, sounding like the most painful of complaints. Jack saw the pup stir, attempting to rise, despite the silver on his wrists.

Jack sighed. "It's not gonna happen. Be still or you'll hurt yourself."

The young werewolf rolled over to face Jack, his yellow eyes wide. "No, no, no! Don't take me! What's going on?"

He couldn't have been more than twenty with that smooth face, and relatively narrow limbs. "You are not allowed to leave the reservation without permits. Your kind attacks others, as evidenced by last night. You should have stayed home."

The werepup wriggled uselessly in the cuffs like a fish on sand. "I didn't mean to! Ota said I was old enough to roam. Please let me go, I don't want tagging. I'm scared," he whined, and the tears rolling down his cheeks reminded Jack of Roux's sobbing and desperate hugs.

Roux did care about Jack, no matter what he said as he was leaving.

Jack rubbed his face. "You should all know the law. There is no excuse for what you did last night. Let it be a lesson," he said, slowly approaching the pup.

The omega nodded. "It will be, I promise."

Jack hesitated, standing over the trembling young man, who'd likely come here following his elders, perhaps not even aware that he'd crossed the border. Did he deserve the punishment of being tracked for the next ten years?

"Will you promise me you'll never do this again? If you want to roam, do so in human form, during the day," he said, and when the guy frantically nodded, Jack freed his hands. He supposed he could make it an exception.

As soon as the guy jumped to his feet, he hugged Jack and gave his ear a lick. "Thank you. I won't forget this," he said, and ran off into the woods.

Jack looked around, standing above three sleeping werewolves who'd all come because of him at night. He shifted his weight, enjoying the slight burn in his ass. He'd repeat this someday. Maybe. In different circumstances.

And as for Roux? They were bound to cross paths again.

Next time on Jack Addison vs. A Whole World of Hot Trouble:

Will Jack finally flirt his way into a chat's bed?
Will Roux keep the truth about the werewolf incident to himself?
And where do venators go on vacation anyway?

Jack Addison vs. Centaur Pimps
Jack Addison Vs. A Whole World of Hot Trouble #4

K.A. Merikan

"Can I get a ride on your back?"
"Only if you get me a drink first."

Jack Addison's career as a monster hunter is blossoming, and so is his experience in dealing with all kinds of interesting species. But one creature still remains a mystery to Jack—the feline-like Roux Chat-Bonnes. His fellow venator has been avoiding Jack since their successful werewolf hunt in Bohemia, but a man can only pine for so long, which is why Jack decides to vacation on a Greek island famous for its centaur population.

Eager to get intimately acquainted with one of the hooved beauties, Jack instead uncovers a cruel plot that will change his view of human-centaur relations for good.

Previously on Jack Addison vs. A Whole World of Hot Trouble:

Jack Addison might come from a line of legendary monster hunters and scientists, but real life taught him that the world isn't what he'd been told all his life. After encountering the alluring Nessie during the annual hunt, he's opened up to the idea of dating nonhumans.

Away from the strict segregation of his country, he meets all kinds of creatures, each more interesting than the last. Jack's thoughts keep drifting to his rival, but since Jack got gangbanged by a pack of werewolves and admitted to having liked it, Roux has been avoiding him. Perhaps a vacation among centaurs could improve Jack's mood?

Chapter 1

"My Dear Son,

I hope your voyages are treating you well. Your mother and I have recently returned from our annual vacation in Florida, and with great sadness I must admit we might have to choose a different destination next year. The beaches that used to be our refuge from daily struggles have been overtaken by deep sea creatures who are in the process of building a large underwater city in international waters! A man can't even go to the beach anymore without being submitted to the sight of tentacles freely wiggling in the sand.

Those abominations don't know language, as they lack tongues, and even fingers. Instead, they communicate with crude gestures and by drawing pictures in the sand. For whatever reason, the local pactors refuse to use force, since it's a new species that we can't yet form quasi-intelligent dialogue with. If you ask me, the authorities have left their balls in their mommas' homes. They just let those illegals on shore and hide their heads in the sand. The world has gone mad."

Jack sighed, stretching in his sunbed as the nearby waves gently touched the shore. Maybe he should visit Florida next time he was back in

America? He wouldn't mind getting acquainted with more tentacled creatures. After all, Father didn't need to know everything. Shaking his head, he read on.

"I am working on these issues though, because somebody has to. Humans have gotten so complacent they forgot that we need to master our world, not crack open more inter-dimensional holes and invite creatures who will never integrate. I am lobbying for the training of more venators so any cracks between worlds may be promptly sealed. I am convinced that it's the lack of sufficient manpower that causes the issue of new species invading our resorts en masse. And, as numbers of venators rise, so will the sales of Addisons, but I digress.

Most of all, I wish you a good time on vacation in Greece. You sure need it after the feat of slaying the gorgon of Athens. I couldn't be prouder of you, son. Please, stay safe. I've been to Greece before, and those centaurs they have there can be quite a rowdy bunch. Watch out for them.

Sincerely,

Your father"

Jack folded the letter before stuffing it into the pocket of his backpack. He would definitely be mindful of centaurs, considering this was an integrated beach, and there were lush tails swinging everywhere.

Hidden in the shade of a large green parasol, Jack slurped his cocktail and lowered his shades, taking in all the large, muscular asses on show. This was his first day here, and he was overwhelmed by the relaxed atmosphere. Granted, he hadn't met that many centaurs in the old town, where his hotel was located, but there was plenty of them parading along the promenade, their lean legs rising high with each step they took.

One female centaur winked at him, but he made a point of not staring at her naked breasts when he smiled back, because he'd specifically come to the beach to spot the males. In town, the creatures wore poncho-like cloaks to avoid offending the human populace with the sight of their private parts, but at the beach, rules were much looser, and Jack was ready to spot some centaur cock. Would they be more human or horse-like? A mix of both? No one wrote about this in textbooks!

He was momentarily distracted by the sight of a huge male centaur with thick, furry legs approaching two human women, with colorful cocktails in hand. His organ wasn't visible in its entirety, but the sheath and balls were definitely there. Jack felt himself salivating when one of the women petted the stallion's calf, urging him to rest between them. It wasn't something people advertised, but Jack had heard rumors that the Greek towns with large populations of centaurs were a destination for adventurous pleasure-seekers, and that centaurs were keen to meet humans of all shapes and sizes.

Jack sat up in his sunbed at the sight of a centaur with a sleek golden coat and a white tail. Most of all, the human side of him was lovely too—all blond locks and blue eyes. Jack wasn't even specifically attracted to centaurs, but wasn't it all just so marvelously curious? Species intermingling, fur under his fingers, cocks of all types, creatures with such a variety of preferences. He was truly in a wonderful, wonderful place.

He was so entranced by the golden centaur that he hadn't noticed another one sneak up on him. If a centaur the size of a shire horse could even sneak up on anyone. This guy didn't make Jack smile as widely as his brethren. With a stern face and bushy eyebrows, he didn't make an amazing first impression. Then again, maybe the centaur wasn't here to make amorous connections but was selling something? Jack wouldn't mind some feel-good herbs for the evening.

"Hey there. Travelled from afar? I'm Dru."

Jack stretched his body lazily and had some more of the milky cocktail. "America."

Dru smiled wider. "Oooh! First time in Greece? Admiring the views?"

Jack wasn't sure whether Dru meant the coastline or centaurs, so he chose to stay vague and nodded. "I've never seen anything quite like it."

Dru crossed his arms, discreetly pointing out the centaur with the golden coat. Sadly, he was walking away down the beach with a human. "He really likes spending time with your kind, if you know what I mean."

Jack snorted, already feeling the effects of this second alcoholic drink. "Yeah? Is he broken in?"

Dru smirked. "Ha! A connoisseur then. Would you like to meet one that isn't? I could arrange that."

Jack frowned. "Like... a human-virgin?"

"Yep. One that's never had a human. Centaurs are such a curious bunch, it can be hard to find one like that here."

Jack sat up, more curious by the minute. "And you know who to ask? You must be the guy everyone knows, right?"

Dru nodded, looking pretty happy with himself. "I'm a local. If you're up for something really special, I even know a pony up for a good time. But he's only staying on the island until midnight."

Jack gave a little chuckle, but his booze-soaked brain jarred at the P-word. "No... I'm here to meet stallions. I want someone large, tall, ideally with a long tail."

Dru grinned, the pony forgotten, and wagged his finger at Jack. "Oooh! I know just the type. Tan, and I mean skin and coat, and a lush black tail as long as the hair on his head. You up for that?"

Jack's heart beat faster, urged on by the sight of two centaurs running along the beach, their manes and tails floating with the wind, their hooves splashing through the salty water. So glorious. "If he also has a pretty face."

"Believe me, he does. And he's one of those rare centaurs that has a darker stripe of hair down their spine, from the nape. Magnificent beast. You have to meet him."

Jack's face flushed, and he sat cross-legged. "Should I... prepare somehow? Will he show me places to go?" he asked, even though he wasn't entirely sure what this... date would entail.

Dru smirked and adjusted the collar of his short-sleeved button-up that left most of his chest uncovered. "He will know how to show you a good time. But there's a little catch," he said, lowering his voice. "If I go get him, I will miss time at work. So if you could compensate me for that..."

Jack blinked and reached for his purse. He wasn't stupid. It was obvious this was a fee for matching tourists with local centaurs, but he was ready to pay up if he was to get some quality tail.

Dru walked off, waving his bushy dark mane, and leaving Jack with the promise that one Calix would approach him in about an hour's time. Which meant one more hour of drinks. Did centaurs drink alcohol? Jack wasn't sure, but he couldn't wait to ask.

Did chats drink alcohol?

Jack's mood instantly plummeted. It wasn't as if he would meet a chat at the beach. Probably. It was nice and sunny, and he imagined chats loving the heat. Maybe if he could get a hold of that stubborn Roux Chat-Bonnes, he would actually have someone to answer those questions. But no, Roux most was most definitely avoiding Jack. Even the teasing notes he used to leave Jack at places frequented by venators had gone.

Jack enjoyed the sun, but now that he knew he was waiting for someone, he couldn't stay still. Would Calix be pleasant? Stubborn? Wild? Gentle? Was he broken in? He surely was.

From the corner of his eye, he noticed a centaur enter the beach through the gate, but he didn't want to stare, so he drank his cocktail and pretended he wasn't bothered by any of this.

But once the long legs covered with sleek tan fur stopped right next to him, it became impossible not to look up.

Calix was stunning.

His facial features had gorgeous symmetry, lavish, straight black hair cascaded down his shoulders and all the way to his taut stomach. He cocked his head with a smile, making all sensible thoughts disappear from Jack's head. If Jack were to get those lips around his cock, would he have to climb up somewhere? Or would the centaur sit in the sand?

Jack smiled, squeezing his glass with an odd sense of nervous apprehension. Jack Addison wasn't the kind of man who got nervous very often, yet here he was—wondering how one could get that bit closer to a beautiful creature like Calix. The centaur was naked, with the exception of a long shell necklace, which wiggled against the smooth skin of his chest like bait for Jack's eyes. Should he go straight to business? Should he pretend this meeting was accidental? Should he ask for Calix's name, even though he already knew it?

"I love this weather. I spend way too much time in colder climates."

Calix leaned down and stroked Jack's shoulder, giving him instant goosebumps. The centaur was so… big. "Oh, no! How do you manage without fur?" He laughed, making a snorting sound which was too cute for words, despite this man definitely being a stallion.

Jack chewed his lips. The touch was pleasant, not too forward yet steady. He already liked Calix. "That's a sacrifice I must make. Maybe I should make sure I have a reason to return to these parts as often as possible."

"You will love it here. I could show you around. There are some beautiful spots down the beach."

Jack cleared his throat. "Where are my manners? My name is Jack," he said, leaving out his surname, because Calix likely didn't want to hear that he was on a date with the son of that Bradley Addison, the face of the Make the World Human Again campaign.

Calix reached out to shake Jack's hand and then pulled him up with surprising strength. "Where did you get those scars? Somewhere thrilling, I'm sure." He ran his fingers over Jack's face, but then startled. "I'm sorry, I shouldn't have asked."

Jack instantly grabbed the opportunity to touch Calix as well, and gently squeezed his wrist. "Oh, it's an old combat wound. I'm not ashamed of my scars. Each one taught me something." Calix did not need to know that the ones on Jack's face stood for 'Don't tease the chat.'

Calix smiled widely. "Ha! I knew you were a thrill seeker. But how much so? Would you like to ride on my back?"

Jack's nerves lit up like fairy lights, and he wasn't even sure if the trail started in his brain or in his balls. "That is so nice of you. Can I hug you for stability?" he asked, already overwhelmed by the impression the centaur had made on him. Out of all the creatures he'd bedded, Calix was by far the most impressive... and Jack hadn't even gotten off with him yet!

Calix winked at him. "Only if you get me a drink."

Chapter 2

Calix asked for a very particular cocktail called Nymph's Dream, and while Jack's heart bled at its price, he decided to not be cheap with his new friend. After all, he needed to make an impression.

Jack couldn't believe he was spending quality time with a real-life centaur. Calix was far too large to sit in any chair, but there were rugs and pillows conveniently laid out next to the beach bar, and the gorgeous creature rested in a secluded spot close to the fence dividing the waterfront from the town. By the time Jack returned with their drinks, Calix was leaning against a pile of plush, watching Jack's every move as if he were eyeing his next meal. Jack rather liked that.

His face brightened when he saw the huge bowl-like goblet Jack needed to carry in both hands. "Thank you."

Jack scooted down and looked at the handsome face with a sense of achievement. "What's so special about this one? Is it sweet? Bitter?"

"Oh, it has this special grass that only grows once every five years. The flavor is incomparable to anything you've ever tried!"

So Jack did try, and then did his best to keep from scowling at the odd, hay-like tang that would surely cling to his tongue for minutes. But at least his new friend seemed content.

"Did you come to Greece just for the nudist beaches?" Calix asked, with an intoxicating smile that Jack already recognized as the centaur's signature expression.

Jack had never been with a human as handsome from the waist up. Calix was like a work of art. Like one of those classical sculptures one could see in museums. And yet he was seated across from Jack, his strong lower body on show, with its muscles and shiny coat, and his eyes never once strayed.

Jack licked his lips. What was it that made him so tense? Was Calix's magnificence actually making him shy? It wasn't like him at all, but perhaps centaurs had that kind of effect on people. "No. I was here for a job and decided to take a break. Loving it here so far. So many... pretty things to see."

"Looks like today is my lucky day. Sit with me." Calix reached out and stroked the side of Jack's head. When he pulled back, Jack followed the movement of his hand, already missing the touch. It felt like being graced by the attention of some half-god.

The bowl obscured Calix's face when he started drinking again.

Jack's brain hesitated, but his body was already shifting until he sat next to the centaur and aligned his side with the hard horse body. The duality of the creature's form kept messing with Jack's head, and he petted the smooth flesh, uninvited. "I was hunting down a rogue slime monster. It was choking people who came to bathe in this stream," Jack said, wanting to make sure Calix knew he was in the presence of someone distinguished.

Calix turned to him with his eyes full of awe. "You're a venator? I don't think I've actually ever met one!" He swished his tail playfully. Jack so wished to feel that soft lash on him.

Calix's words filled his chest with pride so immense he found himself straightening up like a peacock about to fold out its tail. "Really? Well, maybe it is your lucky day, then. If anything threatens you, I'll be there to help," he said, and scratched the large thigh.

"I wouldn't want to fall prey to some slime monster, that's for sure. I bet you've got admirers wherever you go. It's a big commitment to put your life on the line for others. Deserves all the rewards that come with it."

Jack laughed. "Well, I admit the non-financial rewards are way closer to my heart. I like helping people." It wasn't completely true, but he would definitely enjoy helping someone like Calix in time of need. And then reap the rewards, or course.

"How did you decide to take on such a dangerous career?" Calix bumped his massive rump against Jack's side, making it difficult for him to focus on anything else but the centaur's shiny coat.

Jack let out a laugh and leaned against the large bulk even more boldly. After all, this was an integrated area, and he didn't have to be self-conscious about being spotted or recognized. His hand rested close to where the centaur's main heart was—the one that supplied blood all over his lower part—and felt it beating. "To be honest, I never even considered a different career. It's a family tradition at this point. I'm the fourth generation."

"Oh my! Am I in the presence of a celebrity? I would have combed my hair if I knew," Calix said as if his black hair could get any shinier. He grinned and put away the bowl. "I hope I didn't cause offense by not recognizing you. We don't get that much news here in the islands."

Jack shrugged, but his ego had still been pleasantly tickled. "I'm hardly a celebrity, but some older members of my family--that's another matter. I hope to outfame them some day."

"I bet you were a child prodigy with a pedigree like that. Were you slaying giant moths at five years old?" This time, when Calix swished his tail, the soft hair reached Jack's back, making it ripple with gooseflesh.

He was doing it. He'd be fucking a centaur today.

If Father knew... it didn't matter, because Father would never find out what Jack did in his free time.

"Father took me with him, so that I could witness real life hunts. Times have changed since then. Our methods are now much more... humanitarian. But I remember all the lessons," Jack said, slowly lowering his head to Calix's side. Despite the slowly-burning arousal, he was enjoying the peace of lying against a body as powerful as this one. He could see himself sleeping on Calix's back, with his face buried in the fragrant coat.

"I always say a little love can go a long way." Calix stroked Jack's hair.

It was such a relief to speak with a like-minded creature, and Jack didn't stop himself from humming in pleasure. "It's not easy being me in my family. They... my father especially, are extremely specist. I dream of a day when he can look at the world with a different set of eyes, the kind of eyes I have, and see that we can all live in harmony. There's so many things different species can teach one another."

He sure hoped Calix would teach him how to handle a centaur's dick.

"Oh, no... It must be hard not seeing eye to eye with your father." Calix nodded, and the sense of fast-growing connection was already heating Jack's veins. It wasn't just because Calix was an attractive guy. He listened and understood Jack as well!

"I am envious of my friends who can be completely honest with their parents, but if mine knew I was here... well, let's say our relationship might never be mended."

Calix sighed and extended his arm. "Come here. You should enjoy yourself on our beautiful island, not succumb to this torment. You have to do what makes you happy, Jack."

Jack's mouth stretched into a smile, and he slid his arm around Calix's waist, shamelessly rubbing his face against the toned muscles of the human stomach, right above where it connected with the equine part of his body. "You are such a gem. See? We come from different places in the world, and our bodies are different, but we understand one another so well. Right now, I wish to never have to leave this paradise."

Here, no one judged him for wanting to ride a creature as magnificent as Calix.

"Keep the drinks coming, and you can stay," Calix teased, rubbing his fingers through Jack's hair. "I feel like stretching my legs. Do you want to explore the coast?"

That meant riding on Calix's back, which was a *yes*, and possibly heading off to a more secluded spot, which was an even bigger *yes*.

"I get it. You're embarrassed that another drink might cut the legs from under you," Jack teased, discreetly moving his fingertips across the centaur's taut stomach. Soon, he would get to explore more.

"Is that a challenge?" Calix snorted, but was already shifting. He raised his rump while keeping his front lower. "Hop on and see how stable I am."

Jack's salivated. He was so, so fucking horny just seeing Calix in that position, but this wasn't the right place for an amorous session, so he climbed onto his centaur's back and slid his hands to the trim waist, certain Calix could sense the hard dick against his spine.

"Impressive," Jack said when Calix rose, carrying him high above the ground.

Calix murmured. "I could say the same."

Jack snickered and emptied his cup in one gulp, before rocking his hips against the centaur's flesh. "And still so much to discover. I shall follow your guidance."

"No need to be this official. Hold on." Calix pulled Jack's arms tighter around his waist.

At first, he walked between the blankets on the beach, but as soon as they reached beyond the busy area of the shore, he sped up, rocking Jack on top of him.

Calix carried Jack along the coastline, and with the sun on his skin, light glistening in the crystal-clear waters, the warm body between his legs, Jack could forget all about his father's letters, or that he didn't know where his next assignment would take him.

While it didn't feel right to treat Calix like he would a horse, Jack eventually settled into the familiar rhythm of riding, hugging his future lover tighter and resting his head on the broad back. As the sun lowered toward the sea, its color changed the beach, the water, and the mountains, turning everything into a golden paradise that Jack didn't want to leave.

They eventually left shore behind, and Jack could still feel Calix's heart beating fast after the exhilarating gallop. The shade of tall olive trees was a welcome change, but while in other circumstances Jack might have wanted to cool off, now he couldn't wait to get even hotter and sweatier. They were alone, and he had no doubt that was Calix's reason for bringing him here, because they certainly wouldn't be learning how to make artisanal olive oil. Though oil could probably come in handy for what Jack wanted to do with Calix.

In the cove surrounded by bush and rock from one side and sea from the other, there was no one to witness what was about to happen. Perfectly safe with this beautiful creature, Jack could let his fantasies run wild.

"Is it a favorite spot of yours?" he asked, shifting his hips so that they rested on the place where the centaur's fur turned into smooth skin, and rubbed his chin along the muscular shoulder.

"Definitely. Centaurs hate clothes. But we're forced to wear them in human towns. Here, I can be free." Calix squeezed Jack's hand, but then lifted it to his lips for a kiss.

Jack gasped, moving the fingers of his other hand up the lovely flesh. Images of Calix resting in the sand, his hair scattered in post-coital bliss filled his head. "You shouldn't have to hide all that magnificence."

Calix sniggered. "I think some men are just intimidated, if you know what I mean. But it's not a competition. Apples and oranges. Snakes and bananas?"

Jack kissed Calix's nape and briefly cupped his pecs, feeling heat gather inside him at a rapid pace. "I would gladly compare. Not intimidated."

Calix arched his head back. "Well, I've been feeling it on my back for quite a while. Can't say I'm not curious…"

Jack licked his lips and carefully dismounted without taking his hands off Calix. His erection was an insistent presence in his pants, but he wasn't about to just whip it out like some brute. "Feel free to unpack it when you're ready."

Calix leaned down, and it was only then that Jack realized that having sex with a centaur might be more complicated than he'd imagined. The difference in size could make even reaching down for Jack's pants a challenge for Calix. But before things could get awkward, Calix grabbed Jack under his arms and lifted him with surprising ease. Jack wasn't a small guy, yet Calix managed to pick him up and set him on a thick branch of the olive tree.

Calix knew *exactly* what he was doing.

With his feet dangling in the air, Jack was at the right height for Calix to unbutton Jack's pants. He pulled in his stomach, breathless when he realized that centaurs were only inferior to humans in numbers. Were they determined to overthrow the current system and make Father's nightmares come true, they might well succeed.

But any worries melted away at the touch of soft, capable fingers. Jack exhaled and lifted his thighs slightly to allow Calix to pull down his pants and underwear. "Maybe I should adapt to your habits and get rid of those for good."

Calix snorted and dropped the clothes to the ground under Jack's feet. "I think that would be a service to all of humanity." He ran his big hands up the insides of Jack's thighs.

"And beyond humanity," Jack reminded him, spreading his legs slightly. Heat floated up inside him when Calix cupped his balls, then traced his cock with those nimble fingers.

Calix took a step closer, pushing his chest between Jack's legs and leaning in for a kiss as his hand wrapped around Jack's cock. "Definitely."

Jack exhaled and opened his lips, feeling unusually pliant. "How do you usually do this? I can't reach you from here."

Calix's tongue slipped under Jack's lip, making his cock throb in the thick fingers. "That depends what you would like to do. You could stay here and I could suck you off. Or you could get down and have a look at my tool. I know it's not as straightforward as with humans, but it'll be worth the effort."

A deep shudder went down Jack's spine, and he pressed his knees to either side of Calix's waist. "As lovely as your face is, I can't help but wonder what you're hiding down there." With that, he slid off the branch, not caring about the wood scratching his buttocks.

"Go on, see for yourself." Calix crossed his arms on his chest, his eyes half-lidded, and a lovely flush already coloring his cheeks. "I want to feel you touch me."

Oh. That made sense. Were centaurs considered such flirts because they couldn't jerk off on their own? Jack would have probably also developed some impressive seduction skills if his only way to get off were to include another person.

Jack grinned, but his excitement wouldn't let him wait any longer, and he moved toward the back of Calix's body, almost stumbling when he saw the impressive dick that was already out of its sheath. Wide, long, and with a flattened head weighing the whole thing down toward the ground, it was a magnificent piece of flesh. Jack's brain was instantly overcome with noise that tickled at the pleasure centers inside his skull, leading his mindless self closer, then to his knees.

"Beautiful," he whispered, not yet daring to touch the huge tool, and petting Calix's thigh instead. The centaur was tall enough to easily accommodate Jack underneath him in a kneeling position, and as Jack crawled farther under the taut belly, the scent of arousal—muskier than any human's—penetrated his nostrils like an arrow poisoned with lust.

His breath was barely a tremble when he leaned forward, wrapped both of his hands around the thick cock and licked the tip with a groan of satisfaction.

His venator senses broke past the lusty haze and drew his attention to fumbling in a nearby tree, and to his absolute shock and dread, he spotted a furry ginger body climbing the trunk. He would've recognized its markings anywhere. From the white stripes on the tail to the tufted ears and white furry paws, there was no doubt that this was no one other but Roux Chat-Bonnes, and if Jack didn't move now, he would be spotted.

Chapter 3

Jack's brain was a moist sponge that could no longer absorb any other information. So he stupidly looked back at the handsome chat, who'd purposefully ignored him for so long. The judgmental prude didn't even know what he was missing.

And for once, Jack had a way to show him. Without thinking, he licked the flared head of Calix's cock again, before delving his tongue into the slit. The firm thighs of his lover tensed, and one of the hooves lifted, only to loudly thump against the ground.

"Oh, yesss," Calix hissed in that accented voice, unaware that they had an audience. Or was he just as shameless as Jack?

The cockhead barely fit into Jack's mouth, but he sucked on it with eagerness, ready to show Roux that he was uninhibited, adventurous, and unafraid of tasting new pleasures. He reached for the heavy balls, wondering if centaurs groomed each other to be so clean. He could just imagine a whole courtyard of centaurs, getting water from a well, brushing each other's tails, and giving each other favors that went beyond a wash.

Calix's dick was long and thicker than any human male's Jack had ever serviced this way, so he had to rely on his hands to give his partner pleasure. With his lips stretched wide and hands tight on the girth, he couldn't deny himself a glance toward the tree where he'd last seen Roux. His insides burned with excitement, and his cock was rock-hard when he thought of the standoffish chat seeing him like this.

Roux hid behind the tree trunk, but his tail was visible, and when Jack caught him taking a peek, Roux hid as if his fur had been set on fire. Would he give in to lust and jerk off while watching Jack suck the centaur?

Jack reached to his own cock at the lewdness of it all.

"That's it, Jack. You're doing so good," Calix moaned, dragging his back hoof over the ground and rocking his cock into Jack's mouth. How much cum would this beast even have?

Plenty. Jack was sure he'd have his fill by the end of this. So he gave it his all, slobbering around the length, sucking, licking and mouthing it while his hands wandered all over his lover's groin area. His own dick was left neglected out of necessity, but whenever he thought about the third participant, hidden away yet listening and watching, his hungry cock twitched.

The centaur was a magnificent beast, and his hairy legs kept rubbing Jack's exposed skin whenever he moved. Jack playfully touched the top of his head against Calix's belly, making the centaur moan again. He was no longer conscious of propriety, so when the thick length exploded down his throat, he swallowed as if he were trying to down a whole bottle of water at once.

He stabbed his tongue into the slit at the tip as he undid his pants and grabbed his starved dick. It took only seconds for pleasure to wash over him like the warm waves of the sea.

He still moaned around the cockhead as he slowed his strokes down but kept his eyes half open, wishing to see Roux peeking out again. And there he was. Ears and whiskers twitching, Roux stole a glance at Jack kneeling under Calix with his mouth overflowing with cum and his cock in his hand.

The satisfaction of it was undeniable.

Jack gave Calix's leg a brief hug, but eventually tucked his cock back in and stood, resting some of his weight on his beautiful partner. "That was lovely," he said softly, petting the centaur along the back.

Calix turned to him with a blissful smile. "Not everyone is as skilled as you," he said, but lifted his front hooves off the ground with a yelp, at the sound of a branch snapping.

It had to be Roux's way of trying to warn them he was coming, because he was never this sloppy in his approach. Jack stroked Calix's back and even leaned down to kiss the dark coat that smelled of sun and sweat. In the corner of his eye, he could already see red fur.

Roux put up his paws, and the pink pads underneath were too precious for words. Jack had to bite his lip to stop himself from saying that out loud. Roux just needed to ask for it, and he'd kiss them all over. They could then go back to hating each other, or whatever.

For now, Jack would have the pleasure of enjoying the view, because with the weather so hot, Roux had opted for wearing only a pair of loose linen pants, inviting Jack's roaming stare.

"I don't want to hear it, I'm not here to find out about your freaky sex life."

Calix wrapped his arms on his chest with a frown. "And who are *you*? Freaky? Well, *excuse* me. Don't you chats have spikes in your dicks?"

Roux hissed. "This is none of your business!"

Jack stretched and stood in front of Calix, determined to be on his lover's side. "You of all people should not be judgmental. We are all the same. You want to be a part of what humans built, so you became a venator. What exactly is offending you so much about a human and a centaur spending time together?"

"Maybe the fact that you're using someone of lesser means to get off and move on. I've been on this island for a while now, and I've found out how things work around here."

Calix stomped his hoof against the ground so hard Roux flinched. "This chat better mind his own business if he doesn't want to end up trampled."

Jack protectively rested his arm on Calix's back. "That's right, Chat-Bonnes. You have no right to judge anyone based on your prejudice. Why did you disturb us in the first place?"

Roux kept his chin high, but Jack still noticed the green eyes dart down every now and then. *That's it, look at what you're missing out on.*

"I... I'm here on an assignment. I've had information that this is an area where a centaur foal has been abducted, and it's not the first disappearance of this kind. This is all a joke, a vacation to you, but you don't care that their little ones are being taken from under your nose."

Jack frowned. "Oh... I'm sad to hear that, but isn't that kind of stuff a matter for the police? Why did they call on you?"

Roux made a wide gesture with his arm. "Because the police are sluggish, and the family is desperate to find their son. They suspect the police don't care enough about the disappearance, and I wouldn't be surprised if that was the case. Do you think a centaur's life is all sand, hay, and sunshine?"

Calix groaned. "Great pun, chat. What cattery have they taught you that at?"

Jack laughed and patted Calix's back. "Good one. Who abducted the foal anyway? Isn't it family members in most cases?"

Roux's fur bristled, and he took off his backpack to pull out a notebook. "If I knew who'd done it, I would have handed them over to the authorities. Now stop wasting my time, and tell me if you've seen this youngling anywhere."

He pulled out a tattered photo of a young centaur with long black hair and a ball in his hands.

Jack sighed. He felt sorry for the kid and his family, but at the end of the day it was none of his bus—

"This can't be," Calix cried, snatching the photo out of Roux's paws. His proud form slouched, and a grimace twisted his previously serene features.

Jack's heart skipped a beat. "Calix?"

"It's my brother, Ezio. He… they were supposed to keep him away from the town!"

Roux's face went slack. "I'm so sorry that you had to find out this way."

Calix was breathing harder by the second. "I need to go to my family. I… I'm not always allowed to see them. I'm sorry, Jack, I need to go." He took a step closer to Roux, and leaned down to grab Roux's hand. "I'm sorry for any offence, Mr. Chat. Please find him, and I will be forever in your debt."

Jack grabbed Calix's forearm. His pleasure trip was rapidly turning into something sinister. "I want to help, too!"

"Meet me at the fountain in town in two hours. We can go search together, but I need to talk to my parents first."

Roux nodded. "We will do anything we can to find your brother."

Calix didn't even wait for an answer, and galloped past the olive grove, along the beach.

Jack's heart sank, and he looked at Roux, feeling his earlier relaxed enthusiasm fizzle out at a rapid pace. "Fuck. This is a kid. Shouldn't all the citizens be notified? Somebody must have seen something!"

Roux shook his head. "How about you go back to your drinks," he hissed, and to Jack's disbelief, he started walking back along the trail.

So Jack wouldn't be fucking a chat anytime soon.

"How about you take your head out of your ass for once? Wait for me."

Roux did stop, but even with his back to Jack, it was clear he'd crossed his arms over his chest. The tip of his tail shifted back and forth above the ground.

"How many species have you ticked off your bucket list by now, huh?"

Jack grinned at the thought of his notebook filled with observations. "Well, I haven't had a chat..."

Roux bristled. "We don't need to do this together. You are clearly busy with other endeavours."

Jack rolled his eyes. "Of course. You of all people know I have no heart and that I don't care for anyone but myself. Maybe I should have let you have a taste of the wolves."

Jack regretted his words the moment Roux whimpered and glanced over his shoulder with ears flat against his head. "I... um." It was a rare sight to see the stubborn chat speechless.

Jack scowled, joining Roux on the path. "Look... that didn't come out right. Point is, we didn't start off on the right foot, but I'm not a bad guy. I became a venator to serve humanity." And to become as famous as his Father. Or more, preferably.

"Of course you did. So why do you care about an abducted foal? He's not really *humanity*, is he?" At least Roux's tone wasn't as harsh as before.

Jack clenched his teeth and scratched his nape. "I meant it as a universal word... in the sense of all sentient creatures," he said, even though that hadn't been the case. When he'd started out in the profession, humans had been the only ones he'd found of interest and value. But things had changed. He was no longer that same man. "And besides, anyone would join the search for an abducted child. It's in our collective nature."

They walked side by side, and his mind went blank when he stole a glance at Roux's stomach where in the sparse hair, he spotted nipples. Were they sensitive to the touch?

"Not many venators think that way. I... I actually decided to become a venator to get involved in things like this. I'm always proud to slay a tarantoid, but too few venators want to help creatures, too. Most are just on the lookout for the next thing they can kill. Pactors don't actively work the way we do, and the police often neglect the problems creatures face."

Jack licked his lips, looking at the sand under their feet. There was a lot of truth to what Roux was saying. Most venators he knew were in if for the thrill, fame, and a job that wasn't in an office or factory. A venator could earn a decent living with only a couple of jobs per month, depending on the bounty. It was very rare that venators spoke fondly of creatures, or explicitly declared the will to protect them.

"That sucks."

They walked along the beach where not so long ago, he'd been pressing his boner against the spine of a centaur. Was it really so selfish to wish Roux's appearance had come that bit later? He'd barely began exploring Calix's body.

Roux let out a low grumble. "It does suck, Jack. Just like you." He paused. "Wait. Not because I'm trying to shame you for literally *sucking*. I—What I mean is—"

Jack groaned. "Really? What did I do, huh? What don't you like about me this time?"

"You're... You're using that poor centaur. You don't care." Roux hissed and backed away when a wave washed over his feet. "All you care about is indulging in your fetish."

Jack frowned, but his lips stretched into a smile full of disbelief. Had he even heard that right? "*Using* him? He got the head of his life. Who'd say no to that?"

"He's a prostitute, Jack. You think I don't know that? Why do you think his brother was abducted? Because people like you don't treat them as creatures with their own dreams and goals."

Jack rested his hands on his hips, trying to swallow the bitter aftertaste in his mouth. "Prostitution is as old as the world itself. And besides, we both know centaurs don't have all that many work opportunities here. This pays well, and it's not like I'm making weird demands. I just think he's very attractive." And a centaur.

As if to slap Jack in the face, on the other side of the beach, two giggly women were riding one centaur and patting his rump, even though he was telling them to stop it.

Roux sped up, so Jack had to as well. "Right. And you haven't wondered why they don't have that many opportunities. Because, who cares, sexy centaurs, right?"

Jack spread his arms. "I don't make the local politics. So many of those centaurs see this as an opportunity to give their families a decent life, and that's a choice they are making. I want my lovers to enjoy themselves, and they are getting cash on top of that. What's so wrong in helping each other out?"

"Helping? You don't know what his situation is!" Roux's fur got all bristly. "All you're thinking about is your own pleasure. I can't imagine being pushed to do a job like that."

Jack gestured in the vague direction of the town. "And not all centaurs do it. But some enjoy it. Calix definitely does. They're not like chats, so what's the point of comparing yourself to them?"

Roux put his hands up and stopped by the beach bar. "Pay for sex if you wish. I can't tell you what to do." He took off his backpack and pulled out some posters featuring the foal's photos.

He was adorable. And had features so similar to Calix's it made Jack's feet freeze to the sand. "I don't… usually do it. I don't have to. It's just that I've been approached, and he seemed nice."

He must have said something right, because Roux's tense expression softened. "Will you help me put up the posters?"

Jack took half of them from Roux's paws and looked around the beach, at the people who enjoyed the afternoon sun without a care in the world while a child was missing. "Do you have a plan? Should I ask around? Maybe I could try to intervene with the police? You might not like it, but my surname opens many doors."

"I guess it does make sense." Roux scratched his ear. "Can you go and put up the posters in town, too? And I will meet you at the fountain."

Jack glanced at the smiling face of the centaur foal, sighing when his insides twisted in sympathy. *Poor Calix.* "Will do. See you soon," he said and raised his hand.

Roux frowned and very slowly lifted his paw for an apprehensive high-five. It gave Jack a secret thrill to touch him. Would it be inappropriate to try to flirt again? Probably.

"Thank you. I wasn't expecting this of you."

Jack smirked and tapped Roux's paw again, just to touch the soft, cute pads of skin again. "If there are women, children, or men to save, Jack Addison will always be your man, Chat-Bonnes!"

Roux looked to the sand with a little smile. "You may call me Roux."

Jack stared at him, perhaps for a bit too long. "Jack. See you soon, Roux," he said, stepping away from him without turning around.

When Roux moved, his tail rubbed Jack's hand, and Jack had to bite his lip not to groan. He only released his breath when Roux walked off.

Jack stared after him for a couple of heartbeats, but the thick wad of paper in his hands reminded him what he'd promised to do. He left the beach behind and proceeded to staple the posters to energy posts, wooden fences, and even asked shopkeepers to put them up in their windows. Jack didn't have as much success as he'd hoped for at that.

Some of the salespeople suddenly forgot English when he told them his request, others outright said that things like that were bad for business, and that he should put up the posters somewhere else.

There were, of course, many places that accepted, at least verbally, but the sheer percentage of the businesses that denied their help left Jack with a sinking feeling in his gut. In this beautiful place on the shore of a warm, shimmering sea, people did not care for their neighbors enough to put minimum effort into finding a child. He could not understand that kind of attitude.

He was glad to finally see the local police station and marched in with purpose, headed straight for the front desk, where two members of the force sat hunched over an open newspaper.

"Good afternoon."

A policewoman with a tight black ponytail and looked up at him with a smile. "Is everything okay?"

Jack gave her a polite nod. "Nice to meet you. I'm Jack Addison," he said, making sure the male officer got an equal share of his attention. He didn't want to neglect either if he was to win something here.

The policeman put down his paper and raised his eyebrows. "Like that venator device."

Jack nodded but kept his gaze lowered, as if he were embarrassed. "Yes, my grandmother was the inventor. But I am here about a personal matter," he said, now that the importance of his person has been established. He whipped out one of the posters and put it on the desk. "The young brother of a close friend of mine is missing. They suspect he'd been abducted. I wanted to offer my will to cooperate in any police searches and enquiries," he said, knowing they couldn't just sit still on their asses once he put the matter in front of them. Shaming into action wasn't the perfect way to motivate people, but it was *something*.

The policeman's brows twitched, and for a moment he said nothing. "We already searched, and there's no proof of abduction. He most likely ran away from home."

The woman sighed. "Terrible business, but centaurs can be so wild when they're on the cusp of adulthood. I think watching his older brother has had a detrimental effect on the boy."

Jack frowned. "Excuse me?"

The policeman opened his palms. "He is family of Calix Equus, right? That centaur is well known to the police and everyone who looks for a good time here. If you know what I mean," he said, and his gaze told Jack that the policeman knew Jack understood too.

The policewoman pushed the poster Jack's way until it almost rolled off the edge of the desk. "A young centaur doesn't have many perspectives in these parts. He likely believes he could be as successful as his brother. A witness told us he's been seen at the train station."

Jack's stomach clenched unpleasantly. Could this be true?

"So you won't be looking anymore?"

The policeman shrugged, with a smile that didn't reach his eyes. "I've heard centaurs take care of their own. I'm sure he'll be back soon."

Jack left the police station stunned, unsure where to turn. He hadn't even seen a search for the foal advertised as a job for venators. What would he say to Calix? Where else to search?

He dragged his feet toward the fountain and managed to leave some leaflets with a bunch of foreigners enjoying late night drinks, but he still felt ineffective. And Jack Addison always succeeded, damn it!

He sat on the edge of the fountain, watching the water glint in the lamplight when he noticed the sound of hooves. He knew it was Calix before he even looked up. He realized he'd talked so much about himself he hardly knew anything about him. It had made sense at the time, yet felt depressingly selfish now.

"Jack, any news?" Calix asked. His hair was tied back and he wore a cape over the horse part of his body.

Jack stood, approaching him with the remaining posters. While still beautiful, Calix was no longer a glamorous creature that existed only for Jack's pleasure, and just thinking that was how Jack saw him before left him guilty. There was a tension to his features, and his gaze darted to various points around them, as if he hoped to see his little brother somewhere.

Jack didn't feel comfortable sharing that he'd had no success, but he restrained the urge to hug Calix, because maybe he wouldn't have appreciated it without money involved. "I asked around, distributed leaflets. I even talked to the police. They tell me Ezio was seen boarding a train."

Calix made a broken sound and took a deep breath. "Ezio wouldn't run away. He's a good boy. He wants to go to art school. My parents are devastated and don't know where to look anymore. They've organized the other centaurs, but we're not allowed in town in large groups. Jack, please, there must be a way to find him. I've been saving money so that he can go to Athens. He would have told me if he changed his mind."

Jack licked his lips and gently squeezed Calix's forearm. He couldn't get over the injustice of this. Someone *had* to do something. And that someone would be him. "If we're to investigate, I think it's best to ask the people who have seen him last. Your family? Friends?"

"Anything?" Roux asked, and Jack had to stop himself from a yelp, because the chat had sneaked up on them without alarming any of Jack's superior venator senses. Then again, Roux was no ordinary man.

He shrugged. "The police don't want to get involved. They claim Ezio ran away, but Calix says that's impossible."

Calix took a deep, laboriously-sounding breath and briefly hid his face in his hands.

Jack cleared his throat, meeting Roux's gaze, angry with himself that he hadn't asked about the other matter while he was alone with Calix. It was an embarrassing topic for them both, but with the foal's safety at stake, there was no point stalling. "They also suggested he might have decided to try the same kind of work you do. What do you think?"

Calix went silent, watching Jack with a blank expression that was nothing like the seductive smiles he'd given Jack at the beach. "Ezio… I didn't exactly advertise to him what I do. I wanted him to follow his dream, not my lead."

Roux stepped closer to the centaur who towered over him. "Do your parents know? I know this is hard, but anything could be helpful now."

Jack lowered his gaze, noting how Calix was so clearly distancing himself from his job. He wouldn't even call it by name, as if out of the context of pleasure, he found the whole business nothing to be proud of.

"I'm sorry people are making any assumption about you or your brother. We just want to help."

Calix reached to Jack's shoulder. "I know, Jack. You seem like a genuine person."

Roux's whiskers twitched. "Is it possible that he's already been taken off the island?"

Off the land. A pony.

A foal. A pony. Tourists might not even grasp the difference.

Jack's brain lit up with fireworks of realization, and he dropped the posters, staring at Calix while his heart beat so hard it would have been frightening in any other situation. "Oh fuck... this guy I met at the beach, Dru... he told me there was a pony who could keep me company. I assumed he meant... like a small guy, not a kid, but maybe—"

Calix grabbed Jack's shoulder harder. "Dru is a piece of shit! What did he say? I'll fucking rip him apart if this is his doing!"

Jack swallowed, not even daring to look Roux's way, because beautiful Calix was terrifying in his anger, his hooves clicking against the cobbles, muscled body twitching. "He said the pony will be leaving the island at midnight."

Calix stomped his hoof on the cobblestones so hard Jack was afraid for his foot for a second. "Port. Now. Get on my back!"

Chapter 4

Jack's blood pumped through his body as if his heart had absorbed all of his energy and was now using it to work like an industrial piston. There was nothing comfortable about being on Calix's back when he was speeding breathlessly through the cobbled streets toward the port, and the hard bones of the centaur kept punching Jack's groin and thighs as he struggled to stay on without a saddle. His arms wrapped around Calix's torso were the only thing keeping him in place, and he was glad that the long mane obscured his view, keeping him from noticing the sheer abruptness of this run.

Behind him, Roux held on for dear life, his slender limbs—and surely his tail—clung to both Calix and Jack, with two of his upper paws digging into Jack's chest and his furry head resting on Jack's nape. So maybe there was *something* nice about this hellish journey.

Jack's comfort wasn't a priority when Calix's brother could be leaving the marina in a matter of minutes. Dru had said the pony was only 'available' until midnight, and Jack hated himself a little bit that he'd chosen pleasure over investigating what that meant.

They could already see the water, and a fishing boat was setting off as Calix galloped onto the long wooden pier, his hooves creating thunder and sounding so hollow, that for a moment Jack believed the wooden planks would break under their combined weight. But they did not, and Calix practically flew down the pier, toward the boat, where Jack caught a glimpse of centaurs and humans moving in haste.

"Ezio!" tore out of Calix's throat, and when a loud, frightened whinny answered, all questions were put to rest.

Fighting through his fear, Jack dug his knees into Calix's flesh and shouted at full volume, "In the name of the law, stop!"

Calix slowed at the edge of the pier so rapidly Jack hit his head against the centaur's back. Roux let go of him, and before they could coordinate any plan, Roux crouched on Calix's back. With the amazing strength of his legs, he pushed himself forward and floated through the air, onto the boat that was already out of Jack's reach.

Calix yelled his brother's name again, his hooves on the edge of the pier, but he was unable to do anything. Jack could only dream of jumping as far as Roux, but he didn't think much more about it when he saw the chat brawling with the people on deck.

He jumped off Calix's back and straight into the water.

Even through the shouting, he could hear the engine working once his body submerged. The sparse light coming from lamps on the pier offered him little guidance, but the water was warm, so he quickly swam back to the surface, blinking away the salt stinging his eyes. There was no time to waste. He had no idea how many Roux was up against, and poor Calix couldn't possibly board without a gangplank. All was in Jack's hands now, and he furiously rowed with his arms, intent on catching up with the boat, which was already gaining speed.

Behind him, Calix was calling for help, and drumming alarm with his hooves. Each noise he made was like a boost to Jack's efforts. Jack could barely catch his breath by the time he reached the boat and grabbed the metal ladder on the side, but he still used all the energy left in his muscles to haul himself up. His shoes slipped on the damp hull of the boat, but a moment later, he crawled onto the deck, looking for weapons.

He stalled for half a second at the sight of Roux taking on three opponents at once. Kicking, clawing, hissing, he was a sight to behold, but without his rapier, danger was just a whisker away. A fourth man approached Roux, not noticing Jack.

This was his moment.

He forgot all about being unarmed, and tackled the backstabbing fucker all the way to the deck, smashing his elbow into the guy's temple and when the head rose, eyes glancing at him without focus, Jack smashed it down with his fist.

One down.

Without thinking, he searched the unconscious opponent, and when he found the familiar shape of a knife, he swiftly took hold of it and rose. "Give up the foal or be ready to bleed out into the sea!"

His words distracted Roux's opponent. He pounced the man, who was already bleeding from his side, and toppled him to the deck as well. "We are both venators and have the right to arrest you!"

It was then that Jack spotted Ezio behind a huge bundle of rope—inside a cage far too small for his size.

The remaining men looked at one another before jumping into the sea at the same time.

Jack put his hands into a tube. "Two are swimming to shore! Don't let them get away," he shouted, before dropping to his knees and using some of the thick rope on the deck to restrain the unconscious thug. Roux was dealing with the other across from him, and when their eyes met for the briefest moment, Jack almost felt as if the feline mouth was smiling at him in the dark.

Roux tied the man's hands proficiently, and attached the bindings to the railing of the boat. "You're going nowhere."

"I didn't even know what the job was until tonight!" The man's face darkened with every passing second. He knew he wouldn't be getting away with this. "It was this massive centaur, Dru, he arranged it all. Told me this was his cousin or some shit!"

Jack's frown deepened, and he shook his head. "The keys."

The thug didn't hesitate telling them where they were, and soon enough, Jack approached the cage where the pretty long-haired pony was cowering, with his hands squeezing the bars. Jack tried to be as gentle as possible when he opened the lock and offered the boy his hand. "It's all okay now. We will return you to your family."

Roux approached them once he'd turned off the engine. "You're safe." He smiled and put his bloodied paw on Jack's shoulder.

Jack glanced at the stained fur before tapping Roux's chest. There was a lot of commotion going on at the pier, but Jack's attention was on Roux gently hugging Ezio. The foal crawled into the furry arms, wordlessly asking for reassurance.

People with lanterns ran down to the shore, including several centaurs, who galloped into the water, splashing about as they chased the two runaway thugs. A powerful-looking female whinnied, standing on her hind legs, and the stance shocked one of the abductors to the point where he dropped into the sea like a log.

Jack left the boy in Roux's care, before going off toward the helm. "Time to go home."

His heart pounded, and he'd never felt prouder. Not when he'd slayed the gorgon, or when he'd chased away a herd of giant flesh-eating worms. This was different. And the sense of contentment didn't just come from holding his chin high and weighing a sack of gold in his palm. It came from looking at Roux stroking Ezio's hair and knowing that the child would be safe.

It was the type of pride that didn't need to be seen, and he didn't expect praise, even though he knew it was coming. The satisfaction of knowing that he'd protected someone whose safety had been neglected made his heart full, regardless of the cheers erupting from the shore.

For once, he really felt like a hero, not just a celebrated hunter.

Calix was at the end of the pier, among a group of policemen, who were arresting the two captured men. His eyes were focused on his baby brother, his arms stretched toward him while his hooves tapped the planks of the pier with anticipation. He was too large to board the boat, but as soon as Roux and Jack secured the vessel and helped Ezio onto the pier, the two brothers fell into one another's arms in the most perfect moment of Jack's entire existence. He actually had to rub a speck of dust from his eye.

With the police swarming around the victim and perpetrators, Jack and Roux were left on their own at the edge of the pier, and Jack rather liked it.

Roux pulled out the little brush he never parted with. He dipped it into the water and started combing away the blood and dirt left on his paw. Jack watched, mesmerized by how someone who'd fought so viciously could also be so gentle.

"You're not so bad Jack," Roux said, looking up at him.

Jack snorted and leaned against the railing next to Roux. "Oh really. You hate me a little bit less now? Who'd have thought," he said, stroking the scars left behind by the very paw Roux was holding the brush with.

Roux stilled, eyes going wider. "I'm sorry about that. I just find it hard to trust, but your heart's in the right place. And thank you for saving me from werewolves, even if you enjoyed it, you perv." His words sounded good-natured, and he leaned closer, rubbing the top of his furry head against Jack's neck, right under the jaw.

The soft hairs tickled Jack, making him stiffen and dig his nails into the other hand to stop himself from shivering. Okay, this was getting interesting. "I did walk funny for two days after, so I guess I learned my lesson."

Roux snorted and pushed at Jack's wet chest with his padded hand, but wasn't moving away. "What's that lesson? Don't *moon* werewolves?"

"Huh? I don't get it..."

Roux whined and once more pushed his head under Jack's jaw, which was getting dangerously arousing. "You never get my puns! Mooning is when you show someone your ass. But that joke's lost now."

"You know me, all muscle, little brain. You need to talk straight," Jack said, chuckling, but when Roux stilled, pushing against him like a loving cat would, Jack cleared his throat. "Sometimes, I went to the same places as you, applied for the same jobs, but each time people would tell me you already left. Are you avoiding me?"

The long silence made Jack swallow hard.

"I freaked out after the werewolf thing. I figured you're a fur junkie." Roux's hand on Jack's chest made his heart pound quicker by the second.

Jack sighed. "I mean... some people like blondes, some people like red fur," he said, grinning, even though his body was already boiling hot. Would Roux rise to his bait?

Roux arched his head up and dragged his cold nose under Jack's chin, but it was the barely-there touch of claw tips against his skin that made his balls heavy.

"Watch it, Addison," Roux warned, even though he laughed.

The stomping of hooves was like a hammer breaking the bubble around them, and Roux instantly pulled back when Calix stopped in front of them.

"Jack, Roux, I can't thank you enough." Calix said both their names, but stared into Jack's eyes with such awe, it was impossible to look away.

Jack still missed the touch of Roux's soft fur, but he was nevertheless entranced by Calix's hands squeezing his.

"Oh, it was nothing, really. Anyone would— I, we just did what we thought was right. Is Ezio fine?"

Calix grinned, teeth brighter than moonlight. "He hasn't been hurt, he's just a little rattled. My parents are inviting you for dinner, but I'm so riled up, I can't wait to finish what we started." He winked at Jack.

Jack's face flushed, but Roux was already leaving the pier, his red tail twirling behind him like a wave goodbye. He was once again reminded of the things Roux had said about the centaurs living on the island, and he was ashamed that Calix might feel the obligation to repay Jack the favor with his attention. "I'm flattered, but you don't have to. I mean, your family had such a terrible time recently. You must want to spend time with them."

Calix stroked Jack's cheek, and in truth, Jack would've loved that hand on his cock. "I don't have to, but I *want* to. To be honest, I thought you were a bit of an ass when we met, but a really hot one." He bowed down to catch Jack's lips in a kiss.

Jack's eyes fluttered shut, and he gasped into the tempting lips, putting his hands on the centaur's shoulders. "I must be an ass. Chat-Bonnes thinks so too."

Calix picked Jack up like he had in the forest, and lifted him so that Jack stood on the railing and could put his arms around Calix's neck for balance.

"I could help you with that if you decide to stick around for a while."

Jack swallowed and rested his hands on the centaur's bare shoulders, squeezing them gently. His heart rate picked up, and he didn't even care that there were people here who could see them. "You sure you want that?"

Calix's smile left no doubt about his sincerity. "Do I want to date a hero venator who saved my little brother and can't wait to suck me off? That would be a *yes*." He kissed Jack again.

Date? Calix wanted to date him? Jack hadn't exactly made any plans like that, but he supposed he could stay longer. Calix was a magnificent man, so kind, and so straightforward. Why wouldn't Jack give it a go?

"I'm glad to be your hero," Jack said and entwined his fingers with Calix's.

Chapter 5

For a couple of days after Ezio had been recovered, Jack felt regretful over not asking Roux to stay a bit longer, but once the emotions died down and the town (rightfully) expressed how awful Dru's scheme had been, life went back to normal. The centaur pimp and his thugs were behind bars, and Calix did everything in his power to convince Jack that staying on the paradise-like island was the best course of action.

So Jack wasn't in a hurry. There were plenty of low-key jobs for venators on the Greek mainland and the islands to keep him busy, and the climate really did agree with him. As did Calix's beautiful body and pleasant personality.

Once Jack had arrived at the home of Calix's parents in the centaur village near town, he was stunned by just how little he knew about those creatures. Researching details of their lifestyle had never seemed very important, so he didn't know what they ate or even how they lived.

He was baffled to find that they didn't have conventional houses and instead slept in roofed buildings without permanent walls, and only used wooden screens or curtains when they wanted privacy. Not much could be hidden in the centaur village, so Jack was kind of glad Calix didn't mind moving into town with him, and Jack made sure to find a house on the outskirts, which had a small garden and a space that was big enough for a centaur.

Father hadn't been exactly thrilled by the news of Jack settling in one place so early into his venatorial career, but as long as he didn't know about Jack's new relationship, he wouldn't protest, so Jack decided to follow his gut and Calix's lead, living in the moment somewhere between the human world and that of centaurs.

Calix's old job didn't agree with Jack because he was much too greedy about his new lover to share him. Not to mention that Calix was more than a lover. He was a friend, a *boy*friend, he was fun to be around, an awful flirt, and was a great cook, even if Jack needed to deal with his carnivorous needs himself. Discovering all the little quirks of centaurs was just as exciting as getting to know Calix as a person.

All that boiled down to Jack doing the honorable thing and providing for them both until Calix could find some job he'd rather do. Jack didn't mind. He didn't live off his family money, but he made enough as a venator to afford paying their expenses. Especially on the tiny island where living was laid-back and inexpensive.

Days passed by in happiness and without urgency. And every time Jack came back from a job, Calix was there to greet him with open arms, always interested in Jack's day. It was pretty damn perfect, and his boyfriend's family—even the whole village—accepted him as their own after what he'd done for Ezio.

For the past few days, Jack had been away hunting down a harpy that had been attacking small animals on a nearby island, so once he was back it was a pleasure to just enjoy Calix's company.

Since Calix and other centaurs didn't like being restricted by clothes, Jack also took everything off as soon as they were alone in the centaur part of the island. Riding naked on Calix's back was a dichotomy of discomfort and arousal, since he got to rub his junk over the sleek coat of the centaur. The novelty of it was slowly passing, but he still enjoyed the touch of the flesh and the sheer size of his lover. Calix was magnificent in every way.

Hence Jack had a rubber plug in his ass, knowing well that like all centaurs, Calix liked to get frisky in the wild, and due to his lover's size, Jack couldn't take his cock without a lot of preparation. He was still a bit self-conscious over his own dick being so small in comparison, but Calix seemed to enjoy it inside him, so Jack chose to not let it bother him too much.

"What about this one?" Jack asked, shifting closer to Calix's human back and pressing another grape into his mouth. He'd gotten a mix of several varieties during this morning's trip to the marketplace, and he was eager to indulge his partner with their sweetness.

Calix chewed for a second, swishing his long black hair to tickle Jack. "Love it. New favorite."

Jack's lips stretched into a smile, and he shifted closer, until his groin pressed to Calix's spine. Hugging the naked body from behind, he rubbed his chin against the strong shoulder. "You need energy."

Calix bucked his hind legs, making Jack hold on tighter. "Oh yes! I've been missing you, Jack."

Calix was an eager lover and required lots of attention. Jack had only realized as he met more centaurs that they lived very close to each other because they needed help with grooming, which also explained a lot about them not having much shame in front of members of their own species. But Jack had soon found out that he wasn't as unbothered by other people seeing him with a partner as he'd thought. He'd had group sex, but even with many partners there was a degree of intimacy to the act, since everyone was participating. He didn't, however, want witnesses who were hanging their laundry or gossiping while watching Jack fuck as if it were background noise. So he always preferred to do it in his little home. Or here, in the woods, where Calix's powerful body had all the freedom it needed.

"Well, you know me. I've been dreaming of you every night I was gone." It wasn't the entire truth, but one couldn't control their dreams.

"Of course you have!" Calix snorted. "I can just hope you haven't managed to break any hearts." He reached back and stroked Jack's thigh. "You feel like running a bit?"

Jack exhaled, staring at the strong fingers caressing his flesh. He knew what that question meant. In fact, he'd found out very soon after he and Calix had gotten together that centaurs had a whole ritual for sexual play. It involved play-chasing each other between the trees until the hunter caught his willing victim.

He trembled, remembering the first time Calix had chased him down. It had been so, so hot.

"Do you even need to ask?" He nipped Calix's shoulder and gingerly slipped off.

Calix stomped his hooves on the grass in excitement, and Jack could only hope that he'd be able to accommodate his lover. Calix's cock wasn't as massive as those of some other centaurs', but definitely much bigger than an average human's.

"Go on." Calix grinned and gently pushed Jack.

The key to not losing this game within seconds was choosing routes that weren't easy for a centaur, so as soon as Jack's bare feet hit the ground, he sped uphill, where the olive trees were their densest. The branches scratched his skin, but he was determined to offer Calix a worthy chase. His dick, already engorged from the excitement, moved erratically as he ran, supporting himself with his arms during the steep climb. The large plug he'd been wearing for the past hour now pushed against his sphincter, its tip teasing Jack's prostate and making his erection grow with each step.

The warm sun tickled his bare flesh when he darted onto the path and sped away from where he'd left his lover, the fragrant air already burning his lungs. The distant sound of hooves hitting the dirt made Jack's brain scatter, and he jumped over a fallen tree, once again rushing into the dense woodland.

Every now and again, the sound of hooves stopped, only to quickly resume. Jack could feel like a kid again doing this. Well, maybe apart from the fact that the endgame was fucking a centaur. Or, in this case, a centaur fucking him.

The sound of galloping intensified until Jack could have sworn the ground under his feet trembled, and he could almost hear Calix's gasps. He tried to go faster, and the toy in his hole shifted from side to side, distracting him so much he didn't notice a large root in his way. His toes pushed against it, and the unexpected impact shifted Jack's direction, sending him into the dirt.

Gravel scraped against his hands and knees, but Calix was near, and Jack was not yet ready to give up. Breathless, and with hay for brains, he shot up despite the ache in his limbs, aiming for the nearest bushes, but Calix descended on him like a flash of golden brown, and hauled Jack off his feet as if he weighed close to nothing.

The centaur laughed triumphantly, and before Jack knew it, he ended up bent over a fallen tree trunk. With his feet swinging in the air, he didn't even try to escape. He was tired, horny, and ready to enjoy himself.

"Never gets old," Calix said breathlessly.

Jack whined when his dick rubbed against the bark a bit too hard, but the hot presence behind him and the sheer size of his lover were enough of a distraction. With a throat thick with arousal, he whispered, "I surrender."

"Do you now? And how shall I claim my bounty?" Calix rubbed his hands up and down Jack's chest, but when the front of his horse body nudged

Jack's buttocks, Jack couldn't help but spread his thighs, knowing that at this point Calix would be aroused by the hunt, his long, thick dick out of its sheath, prepared to enter his prey.

"Please, don't kill me," Jack said, and squeezed his ass around the toy.

"Shouldn't have come to centaur territory..." Calix reached to Jack's ass and squeezed the buttocks, pulling them apart.

Every time this was about to happen, Jack was torn between wanting to be filled by his magnificent stud, and the fear of discomfort, which was always present to some degree when he bottomed. Maybe it was this dichotomy that made sex with Calix so addictive.

He moaned, holding onto the fallen tree and eventually finding some support for his toes, so that he could brace himself with more ease. Sweat was already beading on his skin, and he trembled when Calix licked along Jack's spine.

Calix pulled at the toy a few times until it slipped out with ease. "So ripe for me." He let out a low rumble that made Jack curl his toes. The horse part of his body was so massive it could squash him if they weren't careful. That was not a way in which Jack Addison wanted to go down in history.

He'd used so much lube during his morning preparation that even Calix should've been able to enter him, but he was still tensing up, and his mind couldn't provide an answer to this dilemma. Calix rested both his hands on Jack's shoulder blades, but moments later the firm horse legs rested on a branch of the tree that hung above Jack's head, and the long dick swung against Jack's ass. A yelp tore out of Jack's mouth when Calix hummed, letting his length rest at the seam of Jack's ass, against his balls.

He felt so vulnerable. So powerless against what was about to happen, and he both loved and hated it. The thick cockhead kept pressing at his lubed-up hole, but he knew from experience that no matter how rigid the erection was, Jack's hole was so tight the cock couldn't enter without aid.

"Come on, I want to be inside you," Calix huffed, dragging his hoof over the top branch. His body exuded heat far greater than a human's, and Jack practically melted when Calix impatiently pushed against him. Without thinking, he reached back, grabbed the snake-like dick and pulled his hand over it, all the way to the head.

"You won. Fair and square," Jack whispered, so hot he could barely think, once the blunt tip was against his well-lubed opening.

Jack was glad that they were alone because he wasn't proud of the high pitched whimper he made when the broad thing pushed through his sphincter, stretching it beyond its normal size.

"How does that feel, huh?" Calix was breathing hard and no doubt watching him from above, his cock drilling in farther, sinking deep until Jack could've sworn it might've just pushed right through and spit-roasted him. The girth filled Jack until he could barely breathe, completely focused on the sense of helpless ecstasy that came with being opened so wide. He dug his fingers into the bark, unable to speak, so a mumble escaped him instead. The pleasure came at the price of pain, but it was dim at this point, a perfect complement to the play-violence of this act.

Calix did take care to not thrust too hard, but the back and forth movement of his cock was quick and consistent, hitting all the pleasure spots inside of Jack and making him sweat. He was lucky to have the tree under him, even if it scratched his flesh, because his legs were shaky every time that long tool went in.

He moaned his lover's name and frantically raised one hand when Calix pushed a bit deeper, his horse hips powering the thrusts that were both brutal and delightful. Jack felt like he was floating, even though—pressed flat against the tree—he was anything but. The movement inside him was unstoppable. With each thrust, Jack's innards relaxed until all of his body was numb from the intrusion, and he felt like a plaything, like spoils of war that his centaur could use as he pleased.

He knew Calix would be coming any moment when he actually pulled out, and with just a few inches inside, thrust faster, grunting in excitement. It never got any less surreal to be under his half-human half-equine body.

The heat of Calix's orgasm flooded Jack, and it always felt like balancing on the edge of a cliff when fucking Calix this way, because one hasty move could mean a world of pain. Yet Jack still kept coming back for more, addicted to the rush of danger and the heat of his lover's muscular body. The cum shot deep into him and filled him like warm liquor that both caressed and burned his insides.

He screamed out, so close to coming himself the emptiness in his hole angered him. He needed to come. Right. The fuck. Now.

"I know, I know," Calix said, between one deep breath and another. With a grunt, Calix dropped his front hooves to the ground and turned Jack around, back to the tree trunk.

Jack whimpered, spreading his limbs to wordlessly beg for attention, but relief came fast when his centaur dove right in and sucked his cock into his mouth, pressing the head to his palate with that soft tongue. Jack twitched in the embrace when four fingers entered him all the way to the knuckles, and the chalice of lust overflowed, sending the contents of Jack's balls down Calix's throat.

He didn't even know he was whining until he heard his own voice through a veil of pleasure. Calix took his time licking Jack's softening dick and removed his fingers, petting Jack's stomach with his other hand.

Jack stroked Calix's smooth black hair mindlessly, never less amazed by its beauty. And Jack had spent some time around centaurs now, so it wasn't just the novelty. Calix was a stunner.

"Oh Gods, so good," he whispered, hugging Calix, still obscenely spread out on the tree. He didn't care. "Can't believe I can take this monster."

Calix licked his lips with a smile. "It's an achievement, Jack. Come closer to me. I want to feel you." He pulled on Jack's arm, urging him to mount his back.

Jack's limbs were like overcooked noodles, and as soon as he was on the strong bulk, he let himself rest, hugging Calix while his body adjusted to the new reality of not having a piston made of flesh pushing back and forth inside him.

Calix reached back and stroked Jack's arm, strolling back through the forest. His body was as hot as sand on a summer beach, and Jack put his cheek against it. He shut his eyes, just enjoying the closeness, the sun on his skin, and the gentle whisper of branches and leaves.

He was exhausted, yet his blood flowed fast as his man carried him back home.

Next time on Jack Addison vs. A Whole World of Hot Trouble:

Will Jack and Calix's love last?
Will Jack find out whether Roux is still a virgin?
Will Jack's father finally realize who his son is sleeping with?

Jack Addison vs. Merman Seduction

Jack Addison Vs. A Whole World of Hot Trouble #5

K.A. Merikan

"Mermaids had a bit of a reputation for accidentally drowning partners who got frisky with them in the open sea. As a gay man, Jack was immune to their charms."

It turns out that by staying with Calix, Jack had bet on the wrong centaur. A year on, he is broke and heartbroken after his boyfriend left him for someone with a thicker wallet. Salvation comes in the form of a message from Roux, Jack's rival and crush all in one. Jack is willing to do whatever it takes to prove he's a changed man.

As the only non-human in their profession, the humanoid feline Roux not only hunts down creatures but also understands their unique needs. Can Jack help him save the beautiful merman Lauro from the claws and teeth of jealous mermaids? And can he resist the seductive merman in the process?

Previously on Jack Addison vs. A Whole World of Hot Trouble:

Jack Addison might come from a line of legendary monster hunters and scientists, but real life has taught him that the world isn't what he'd been told all his life. After encountering the alluring Nessie during the annual hunt, he's opened up to the idea of dating nonhumans.

Away from the strict segregation of his country, he meets all kinds of creatures, each more interesting than the last. Jack's amorous thoughts keep drifting to his rival, but since Jack got gangbanged by a pack of werewolves and admitted to having liked it, Roux has been avoiding him. They met again while Jack was on vacation in Greece, in the act of romancing the beautiful centaur Calix.

The mood instantly changed when Calix realized that a missing centaur foal Roux was attempting to track down was his little brother. The three saved the boy from the clutches of centaur traffickers, and while Jack did want to reconnect with Roux, the temptation of Calix's lips lured him back to the centaur. When the two of them moved in together, life became a fairytale. What could possibly go wrong?

Chapter 1

Jack rolled out of bed sticky, slimy, and unsatisfied. Last night was supposed to have been his grand rebound. He'd sulked over his breakup with Calix for two weeks, and had decided that it wasn't like him to get so hung up on relationships. So he'd put all his effort into finding the most outrageous creature in all of Venice, and ended up taking a slug-like creature with gorgeous blue eyes and a sticky mouth to his hotel room. The thing was a bit strange, and Jack couldn't exactly work out its gender at first, but that didn't matter. He was Jack Addison, and he needed to remind himself what it was like to freely roam the world.

But things had gone downhill as soon as he'd ended up alone with the creature. Instead of a night full of pleasure, he'd ended up listening to the slug-man's life story, and comforting his lover-to-be over him being the only one of his kind in this realm. Jack had tried to be understanding but felt offended instead when Grall'ogg—or whatever the creature's name was in his own language—had started complaining about humans treating him as a novelty.

He'd mentioned a stream of lovers who never wanted to stay for his lovely breakfast consisting of a variety of lettuce—which he supplemented for the humans with croutons—and who refused to treat him as anything more than a fleeting fancy. A serious issue, considering his kind lived for hundreds of years and bonded for life.

But despite his annoyance, Jack had tried to do the right thing, still hoping that his dick would eventually find its way into Grall'ogg's sticky mouth-hole. But with each passing word, each deep inhale—Grall'ogg didn't have a nose—he'd felt the chances for a positive resolution of this night dwindle.

In the end, Grall'ogg had a bit too much herb liquor and had fallen asleep after crying for half an hour. His heavy, pillow-like body had slumped on top of Jack, leaving him horny, upset and destined to ponder his breakup with Calix.

At first, all had been great with the centaur. Exciting. New. Jack had grown to see glorious creatures like Calix as much more than a sexual curiosity. But in the end, Calix had proved to be more human than Jack could have ever imagined. After sucking Jack dry of his money, he'd moved on to a rich centaur from Athens.

Jack had been warned about Calix being a gold-digger, but whenever he'd looked into Calix's beautiful face, he just couldn't make himself believe those rumors. But where he'd seen his partner as a noble, graceful creature, Calix must have taken him for a fool. It didn't help Jack's confidence that when they were breaking up, Calix had rubbed his face in the fact that a human could never rival a centaur in the size department.

So in a way, he and Grall'ogg were in the same boat. Only Jack was a handsome young man with a glamorous profession, whereas Grall'ogg was a giant, sticky slug who worked as a children's entertainer and occasional grass mower. But at least Grall'ogg hadn't had his heart ripped out and thrown into his face, nor would he ever feel the humiliation of having his dick mocked, because he didn't have one.

Throughout the night, Jack fell in and out of sleep, and when he eventually opened his eyes to bright light around the curtains, relief overcame his body. So maybe Grall'ogg had been breathing loudly into his ear all night, maybe the slime he was covered in would soil the bed to the point of Jack having to cover the cost of repairs—or flee the hotel—but at least Grall'ogg would soon have to return to his miserable life and leave him be.

A knock was the perfect excuse to move farther away from his lover-not-to-be. Jack half-opened the door to spare Grall'ogg's modesty, but the maid slipped a letter into Jack's hand, curtsied, and left with her cheeks red.

Ha! Could it be Calix had come to his senses and was begging Jack to come back? Tough luck, because Jack was over him, and on his rebound sex-fest trip. Calix would need to do much more grovelling than a letter could possibly convey. A serenade maybe?

Jack ripped the envelope open, but the writing was nothing like Calix's graceful calligraphy. The letters were round and simple, even if very easy to read. Could it be a letter from a fan?

Dear Jack,

I wouldn't have bothered you, but I've heard you're in the area, and I hope that out of respect to our acquaintance you would aid me in a task. I will tell you all the details in person, but your unique set of skills—"

Ha. Unique set of skills. Jack Addison, known and valued already at twenty-two. For his unique skills. He read on.

"and the array of modern devices in your possession might make or break the task given to me. I usually work alone, but this matter needs immediate attention, and I am ashamed to admit I cannot manage on my own. Please respond via telegram at your earliest convenience to the address provided. If you choose to accept, please bring something that will help you stay underwater for a longer period of time.

Kind regards,

Roux Chat-Bonnes"

Up until the signature, Jack had intended to dismiss the letter, since it didn't mention a prize, but when that name brought back soft red fur, large tufted ears, and the long, wiggly tail, dismissal was soon replaced by pride.

"So, you need my help after all," Jack said, scowling when the letter stuck to his fingers.

Behind him, Grall'ogg shifted on the bed and spoke. "Jack, I didn't dare ask…"

No.

No way. No fucking way.

With a wide smile glued to his face, Jack turned around. "Did you say something? I'm sorry, but I just received a call to action. I need to shower and hurry to the train station."

Grall'ogg's wide mouth opened with clear disappointment, so Jack decided he could do with a visit to the local bathhouse instead of staying there another minute. He could even grab a snack on the way, and the last thing he wanted was salad with croutons.

Jack grabbed yesterday's clothes and quickly pulled on his pants. "Sorry, Grall'ogg. It's really urgent. Don't believe those people who say that the life of a venator is all fame and glory."

Grall'ogg's elongated, slimy body expanded as he took a deep breath, and then slimmed down as he exhaled with a miserable look in his blue eyes. "Sure. I understand," he said in a tone which revealed that Jack would now join the ranks of the people Grall'ogg had complained about last night. Well, the moment Jack left this room, it would no longer be his problem, so he stuffed his backpack at record speed.

Behind him, Grall'ogg was saying something about adding a bucket of salt to his next bath, but Jack didn't really get any of that chatter and shut his luggage as soon as it contained everything he owned. "Bye."

"Farewell," Grall'ogg hummed, but Jack wouldn't turn back to the needy creature.

In fact, he did everything he could to forget the night with Grall'ogg as soon as he stepped out of the room. When his feet carried him down the stairs, so much closer to the whereabouts of Roux, the memory of the soft fur sliding against his skin became so visceral he could smell it already.

He remembered the *moment* he'd had with Roux on the pier. Was there a chance to rekindle that exact state in the chat? If only Jack hadn't chosen the easy way of falling into Calix's embrace and had worked harder on his connection with Roux, he might have—what? Was he actually considering a relationship with Roux? He didn't even know what orientation Roux was— even though he did have his suspicions—or whether he even wanted to be with anyone so soon after Calix's betrayal in the first place.

Whatever the answers were, an adventure at Roux's side was way more preferable to sulking in Grall'ogg's company.

He should start on a high note and bring Roux a snack from Venice. Maybe that would make that tail swirl between Jack's legs?

Chapter 2

The sea glistened in the afternoon sun as if it had been sprinkled with pearl powder. Nothing could ever rival the beauty of the Italian coast, and when Jack saw the town emerge into view, his heart skipped a beat. Only this time it wasn't about the glory of nature, or the wonders of architecture.

His hands felt weirdly sweaty as the train rolled into the station, but he wiped them on the front of his shirt. It had been a year, and the prospect of seeing Roux again was oddly stimulating. Maybe Roux could be his rebound? Then again, that seemed to cheapen what they had. Whatever it was.

Jack grabbed his luggage and couldn't wait in his seat anymore. He needed to be the first one out, the first one to see the platform. He unbuttoned the collar of his shirt, adjusted the sword on his back, but couldn't stand still. The fact that it was Roux who'd reached out to him made his chest swell with pride. Anticipation send tingles down to his fingers. The letter had been the first thing to really move Jack into any sensible action after the breakup with Calix had sent him on a drinking rampage all the way to Italy.

Jack watched benches and lamps slowly come to a halt on the other side of the window, and he unlocked the door immediately after, jumping onto the platform without worrying about pesky things like stairs or handles. He was a man of only twenty-two, and his joints could withstand the impact, despite being weighed down by both his body and the luggage.

He spotted the ginger fur in an instant, and for a split second the sight of it took his breath away. The light bouncing off the water made everything somehow grander, more beautiful, but the backlight of the setting sun hitting Roux's fur with its golden glow made the chat look otherworldly. His ears perked up as soon as he saw Jack, but he waited, calling Jack over with his big green eyes.

And of course, Jack responded, walking steadily toward the fellow venator while other passengers took their time disembarking the train. Roux wore a new, fancy scarf with a seagull print, and its deep, emerald color complemented his lush fur. Was it just Jack, or had it become thicker and shinier since they'd last met? He must have been eating well.

"Roux Chat-Bonnes! It's been a while."

"Hello, Jack." Roux extended his paw. "Thank you for coming. I wasn't sure who to ask, and then I heard you were in Venice. I wouldn't have pulled you into this, but I know you've… changed since we first met. You care about creatures other than humans, and then there's your centaur boyfriend, so I thought I'd give it a shot."

Shit. Shit, shit shit. As much as Jack was glad Calix was out of the picture, given his intentions, it still stung to hear his name.

He squeezed Roux's paw, gasping when the soft beans rubbed his palm. "I'm done with him."

There, it was out of the way, at least.

Roux stalled with his paw in Jack's hand and his ears lowered. "Oh. Have I misjudged things then? You're back to your old ways? What I've called you for isn't exactly a hunting trip."

Jack scowled and took his hand away, looking around to see if there was anyone close enough to overhear their conversation. A year back, he might have lied that it was him who'd ended the relationship, but he didn't want Roux's opinion of him tainted.

It didn't make him any less embarrassed over being made a fool of.

"Calix is happily settled in Athens. With his billionaire centaur boyfriend."

Roux stared, and his whiskers rose. "Oh. I'm sorry. I didn't know. I thought you were in Italy for work. Was your father angry when he found out about the whole affair?"

Jack sighed, already moving toward the exit. "If my father knew, I wouldn't be here. All I can say is that my intentions were pure while Calix's were not. There isn't much to talk about anymore."

They walked in silence for a while, but once they left the train station, Roux gently patted his back. "Not the only centaur in the sea?" he tried, but it made no sense whatsoever, and Jack had to snort.

"Such a bad joke, Roux. Gotta say I might have missed you a little bit."

Roux smiled, showing off his canines. "It's been a while, hasn't it?"

Over a year actually, and Jack had no real idea anymore if they were still rivals, work colleagues, or friends. He wouldn't dare flirt just yet since the stakes felt much higher than ever before, and the fear of ruining their strange new camaraderie was much more insistent than his urge to pull Roux's pants down, grab his tail and bury his face in the soft fur.

"I'm happy you learned to value my skills. I've brought them all, even the unique ones," he said, winking at Roux as they left the station and walked all the way to a pier.

Roux watched him more intently, and the smile was gone. "If I told you something embarrassing, could you keep a secret?"

Embarrassing? Jack was dying to hear any dumb stories Roux had to tell. Maybe they could share more, once they'd purchased some good local red. "Of course."

Roux sat on the edge of the stone pier and swung his big feet over the glimmering water. He pulled on Jack's pants to encourage him to sit nearby. "There's many stereotypes about us chats, you know?"

Oh, Jack knew. He'd heard a few at school, and had then learned many more since arriving in Europe. Chats were idle, slept all day, had more offspring than they could afford to feed, and often used their natural skills to become proficient thieves, yet even then, were too lazy to make big money and settled for stealing boatloads of tuna.

Har. Har.

And maybe he would have believed Roux to be an exception, if it wasn't for the many times he'd witnessed people acting in ways that defied expectations. Take Calix, for instance. Weren't centaurs supposed to be noble?

"I am aware, yes," Jack told Roux, watching the fur on his cat feet gain a new dimension as the light changed.

"I try to prove to people that they're not true by the way I live. I'm a venator, I do my best to fit in. But I really don't like water." Roux hid his face in his paws as if he'd uncovered a shameful secret on par with getting herpes from a Minotaur. And Jack wouldn't share that one with Roux in a million years.

He snorted and squeezed Roux's paw, just to feel that soft fur give under his touch again "That's it? Really? There I was thinking you were going to tell me you have a secret harem hidden away somewhere."

Roux groaned and waved his paw dismissively. "I don't have time for such things. But this is very shameful to me. At the last meeting of JUSTICE I was dismissed from a job because they assumed I couldn't handle water. So like the dumbest chat out there, I said I was nothing like that, and that I'd do what was necessary, but then I arrived here, I tried it a few times, and I just can't do it. My fur gets heavy and I feel like I'm going to die."

The smile died on Jack's lips, and he stretched his neck. "My sister's like that about spiders. One time, she actually fainted when she saw one crawl from under her pillow. Hit her head and all that," he said, trying to comfort Roux, even though he couldn't help but imagine Roux cutely fretting about waves while he stood on the beach. "What's JUSTICE?"

Roux sighed. "The Jolly Union for Sovereignty, Truth and Interdimensional Creature Equality."

Jack gave a short laugh, but when Roux's eyes narrowed, he recognized the chat wasn't joking. "That's quite a mouthful. Jolly?"

Roux groaned and reached to the water with just his toes. "That was this stupid leprechaun's idea. We don't love it, but he's funding most of our work, so nothing can be done about it, really."

Jack smirked, even though what he was about to voice made Roux's request feel much less special. "Must be nice to be a leprechaun. Is that why you called me? You need someone who can enter water without getting a panic attack?"

Roux's big eyes and flattened ears expressed such sadness Jack wanted to pet his head and soothe him in an instant. "I will pay, but I do ask you to keep this to yourself."

Wait.

Pay? Pay?

Jack shot to his feet with fire raging in his chest so ferociously its heat reached his face. "So that's how it is," he said through clenched teeth. Of course Roux didn't consider them friends. Why would he after getting ditched for a centaur gold digger?

Roux looked up with a frown. "What? Not enough glory for Jack Addison? You have to get credit for everything?"

Jack hissed and poked Roux's chest. "I was under the impression you asked me for help, not offered employment!"

Roux cocked his head. "So you'd do it for free…? Do you want to join JUSTICE?"

Jack sat back down and crossed his arms. "I'm not joining an organization with a name so stupid." Not to mention that becoming an official member of an organization would have been proof of his sympathy for non-humans. And he couldn't afford to have that out there. "But I can do it as a favor. You know, for old times' sake."

Roux gave Jack a playful nudge without a hint of claws. "That time when I saved you from becoming a mommy?"

A daddy. Definitely a daddy. Drake had recently sent Jack a letter in which he insisted Chad missed him. Maybe he should head for a vacation in London after this was over?

"More or less. You're good at catching insects, and I can swim. Fair exchange. What's the job?"

Roux pointed at the horizon. "There's an island with a cove not far from here. Merfolk territory starts there. Usually, they keep to themselves, but a merman had lately sent a signal of distress, and word got to JUSTICE eventually. The merman, he… doesn't fit in with his kind, and he's at risk of being cannibalized."

Jack frowned. "Doesn't fit in? What do you mean?"

Roux scratched his ear, avoiding Jack's gaze. "He's more like a mermaid than a merman. Instead of hunting, he tries to attract the attention of fishermen and sings beautifully. He's different. This kind of behavior's not exactly accepted in his species, and it's really important to me to save him, because I know how it is to be different from your own kind."

A shiver went down Jack's spine. The metaphor was all too clear, because there was only one reason mermaids sang to fishermen. They were hunting, but not for meat.

"What do you plan to do? Move him to a different group of merfolk somewhere down the coast?"

"We don't yet know of any group that would take him in, but we've put together a team, and he is welcome to stay at a natural pool by this seaside inn. He will be allowed to sing for guests all he likes. It's all been arranged. His immediate safety is crucial first. You, Jack… um, you must understand it can be hard for him, right?" Roux glanced at Jack, searching for answers to questions other than the one he'd asked. Jack had been pretty blunt in the past about his preference for males. It had never been a problem, since his sister already had two children to carry on the family name.

"Is this about me dating a centaur?" he asked in the end. Because that would have been a problem for the whole Addison clan, and Jack hadn't been very open about it to anyone, for fear that news would travel across the pond, or ruin his reputation as a venator.

"Yes, it's hard to be looked down on because of your preferences." Roux stared at his own feet touching the water, and no matter how much Jack itched to ask him if he was in fact a pussycat, if they were flirting, or if Jack had been reading it wrong all this time, the moment didn't feel right. Jack had been pushy in the past and it had gotten him nowhere.

So he took a deep breath and looked at Roux's feline profile. "What do you want me to do?"

"Once the sun sets, you will take a boat to the cove and dive there to find where Lauro is hiding. The other merfolk roam in the open waters at night, so it's safer to go once it gets dark. Then, bring him here, and I will have a carriage waiting for him."

Jack glanced at the sun, which pleasantly caressed his skin. "There's still plenty of time. How about dinner?" he asked, and pulled out the little yellow can of sardines with a lot of French words written on the package. It was quite fancy, and not the least expensive product in its category, so Jack wasn't embarrassed to offer it to Roux as a gift.

His heart stilled at Roux's blank stare, afraid he'd made a misstep, but then Roux's smile became so wide his canines showed.

"Where did you get these? They're my favorites! With thyme." Roux smelled the can and made a purr that had blood drain down to Jack's dick. Oh yes. He'd done well. Another score for Jack Addison! He wished he had two right hands so he could congratulate himself.

Chapter 3

The full moon reminded Jack of that glorious night when he'd saved Roux's ass and had gotten fucked by four werewolves. Time had blurred the pain he'd felt in his muscles the day after, and the nasty argument he'd had with Roux. When the moon shone so brightly, he looked back fondly on his first night with furry creatures.

He'd been rowing for almost an hour now, but he could see the tall shape of the island where, according to Roux, the merman took refuge. He was now deep in merfolk territory, and was glad that the calls of the females did nothing for him, because he could hear the melodic voices of the sea maids from every direction, sometimes getting louder, as if the creatures were trying to fight for his attention, synchronizing into a unified melody.

He was a bit confused about his sleeping arrangements for tonight. Roux had his belongings, so perhaps Jack would be invited to stay with him? After this mission proved successful, Roux would surely be grateful to Jack for saving his good name. And who knew what could happen if they stayed together for the night, with no werewolves to disturb them?

Jack watched more closely when a long, graceful tail passed right under his boat. The water was crystal clear, so he could see what was under the surface, even though it was night-time. Mermaids had a bit of a reputation for accidentally drowning partners who got frisky with them in the open sea. As a gay man, Jack was immune to their charms, and the perfect venator for the job.

But as he approached the small, bare island, watching the moonlight create interesting shapes on the rock, another kind of voice reached his ears. Rich yet subtle, it was the most beautiful tenor that had ever graced Jack's ears. He looked around, breathless as his skin tingled in response to the high notes coming from the island.

Jack anchored the boat and took off his shoes, his mind oddly frantic. The last time he'd felt like this, a witch had given him a green potion, and he'd woken up the following day naked and with a mushroom head stuck on his dick. That had been a weird one.

He couldn't recognize the words, because they were blurred by the hum of waves, yet they spoke straight to his soul. Had he really become such a sap after his breakup with Calix? Just last year, he'd considered himself unbothered by all that romantic nonsense, but Calix had been his first real relationship, so unlike the flings, long and short, he'd had before. The betrayal had hit him hard. To find out that all the months they'd spent together were a lie had been much more devastating than he could have ever imagined.

Jack shook his head to chase away the wave of memories, and sat on the edge of the boat. He'd gotten so lightheaded he'd almost forgotten to put the breathing device into his mouth. In only a tight set of undergarments, he jumped, and the water sucked him into its warm depths. When he first opened his eyes, the salt stung, but the gentle voice was like a drug he wanted a bigger dose of. And he needed it *now*.

Without thinking, Jack swam against the buoyancy of his body, toward the seabed, which glistened with the reflection of moonlight and stars. His dark shadow passed over scattered stones and patches of seaweed. Never before had he swam with such ease. His arms moved in perfect harmony, just to reach his goal faster.

Urgent in his need to find the source of the heavenly voice, he scraped his fingers against the coarse wall of volcanic stone that made up the island. The melody called out to him, but the stone was unforgiving and left Jack slapping his palms against it time and time again until he came to his senses.

He was being ridiculous, just splashing in the water uselessly. The buzz in his brain became more insistent when he submerged his head, and only then did he notice a bright blue glow on the ocean bed, right by the rock. He breathed in air from his handy apparatus and dove deeper, toward the reflection in the sand, and the voice that became louder with each passing second. A warm stream touched his body, so he followed it, straight to the light coming through a narrow crack in the submerged rock.

He'd thought the voice was enticing, but now that his ears were under water, the melody hit him with a new force. It spoke of longing and sorrow, yet had an underpinning of lust. As Jack swam through the crack in the rock, he could even close his eyes because the sound guided him with promises that soothed his broken heart.

Sharp stones scratched his skin, but he was numb to it, completely entranced by the song. Once out of the narrow passage, he entered a natural pool in the middle of the island, but when he looked around, trying to spot the merman between the colorful underwater plants, it was only fish he could see.

Until a graceful, large fin moved close to the shore.

Jack drew in more air and stopped resisting the push of salty water, letting it carry him all the way to the surface.

The merman gasped at the sight of him and curled his tail away, but it was Jack's jaw that dropped. He had no doubts that this was Lauro. Jack had seen handsome, muscular mermen on his way from Greece to Italy, but Lauro was nothing like them.

Lithe, with narrow shoulders dusted emerald green, and a face that drew all of Jack's attention, no matter how pretty the blue nipples on Lauro's chest were.

Lauro wasn't just handsome. He was stunning, pretty from his long red locks to the tip of his tiny nose. His big green eyes had lashes for days, and despite the pearl blue color of his full mouth, they seemed warm and inviting.

Jack raised his hands above water, licking the salt from his lips as soon as he removed the breathing apparatus from his mouth. "It's all right. You're safe. I'm from JUSTICE, and I came here to take you to safety. Are you Lauro?" he asked, just to be polite.

The glorious creature's eyes widened, and he dipped his tail back into the water. The green-blue scales that started at his hips had a pearlescent shimmer, just like his lips. "I thought you'd never come, and I would be stranded here for eternity until only my bones were left to sing with the wind." He reached out to Jack and grabbed his hand.

His nails were longish but thick as animal claws, and could have surely been an efficient weapon on hands less gentle than Lauro's. His touch was unexpectedly warm, and Jack found himself shivering in response, even before his gaze met Lauro's. "I... you shouldn't be singing at all. What if the other merfolk found you?" he uttered, when everything beyond the pretty face turned blurry.

Lauro slipped farther into the water and ran his hands up Jack's chest and to his neck, while the warm tail wrapped itself around Jack's legs. "There was nothing left for me to do. It was the only way for me to find a hero brave enough to fight the tide and save me. The song inside of me cannot be silenced."

Jack wanted to answer him, but instead remained mute, like an idiot while this ethereally beautiful creature slowly leaned back, until the gentle waves of the pond made his locks rise to the surface.

"Well, I-I'm here now. Whatever happens, I'll protect you, but why does your tribe reject you? Your song… is so beautiful."

Lauro slipped his fingers into Jack's hair. "They don't understand me. They think that just because I'm a merman I should be the fighter, the protector, when all I yearn for is to bring others pleasure. With my song, and with all I've got to give. I refuse to be tamed by their rules. The sea doesn't yield, so why would I?" He hugged Jack tightly, and even his speaking voice was like the murmur of waves against the shore.

Its sound was so soothing and sweet he hugged Lauro back, burying his face in the merman's damp hair. "You're right. You shouldn't have to. We all… we just want you safe and happy."

"That's so sweet of you, my savior. What is your name?" The lips against Jack's ear were as smooth as mother of pearl.

"Jack. I come from a line of venators. And I'm good at what I do," Jack whispered, hoping to impress Lauro, though the bragging sounded childish even to his own ears.

"You must be if you managed to reach me. But… when we connected in song," Lauro pulled back to look into Jack's eyes, and his beauty was so pristine it made Jack's eyes well up, "Your heart resonated with sorrow. I need to know what troubles you."

Jack froze, and the blur around them suddenly became that bit sharper, but Lauro petted his cheek. Was Jack imagining things, or did his skin start glowing with an otherworldly shimmer? Jack's throat tightened, and he covered his mouth, fighting the sob rising in his chest.

What the hell was happening to him?

"I—"

Lauro kissed Jack's lips. "You had your heart broken," he said, as if he could taste it on Jack's skin.

Jack bit the tip of his tongue, nervously swallowing when his mind went back to the image of his hand gently petting the flesh above Calix's hooves as they rested in their huge bed. Back then, there had been moments when he believed their happiness would last forever. "He left me for someone else."

"Oh, sweet soul…" Lauro cooed and kissed him again, the tail sliding up and down Jack's legs in a soothing fashion. The scales were smooth and soft, creating a massage-like sensation when they moved across his skin. "It is a terrible thing for trust to be broken."

Jack inhaled and slowly rested his head on Lauro's chest, feeling strangely peaceful the moment the steady rhythm of the merman's heart overpowered the sound of his own. "He lied to me all along. He wanted to meet someone better through me, and I thought we really had something good. People warned me, but I refused to believe he was anything but angelic. I'm such an idiot," he said, before letting out a pathetic sob.

Lauro stroked Jack's shoulders, but cocked his head. His coral-red hair flowed to the side. "Was it something other than your heart that guided your decisions?" He winked, reading Jack like an open book.

Jack took a deep breath, eviscerated without a knife. So maybe he was not immune to merfolk charms after all, but the relief of telling someone what had happened was too good to fight against. "I overlooked the red flags, because of his beauty, and because of the way he always appreciated me. He knew exactly what to say every time, and I didn't question any of it, like the biggest idiot. Because I'm not perfect. I know this. Roux always says it like he sees it…"

Lauro pressed against Jack and trailed his tongue up Jack's neck. "So much more to love than beauty, isn't there, Jack?"

Jack hugged Lauro tightly, shutting his eyes and getting on top of the sweet merman, eager to feel him with the entirety of his body. Without thinking, he pulled off his undershirt, moaning when his nipples, which at this point felt unnaturally sensitive, brushed against the lithe chest. "I don't know... next time... I'll be more careful next time."

"You don't need to be careful with me. It's not in my nature to wound." Lauro pulled Jack in for another kiss, and they toppled into the shallow water. "Do you believe in connection that transcends the passing of time? That can happen even if one has only just met the other?"

"Huh?" Jack asked, entranced by the soothing tone of Lauro's voice. He found it hard to remember the reason for his visit here, but all he wanted now was to kiss those shimmering lips and rub against the lithe body.

The smooth fingers brushed over Jack's forehead and hair, and Lauro entwined their hands. "I see you for who you are, and I need you close, even if just this once. Please don't tell me it revolts you." The pretty green eyes glistened, and Jack was instantly desperate to weed out any sadness that might have set root in Lauro's heart.

"N-no. Of course not," he said, rolling back into the waves and pulling Lauro close. The long tail flapped in the water, sprinkling them with warm droplets. "What do you need? Remember? I'm here to give you whatever you need," he said, somewhat aware that this particular service was not included in the job description. But to hell with it. He was Jack Addison, and he did what he thought was right!

"I want to be close, Jack. To connect. It's been so long since I've been treated with kindness. It would make me so, so happy." Lauro sighed in a way that brought back many erotic encounters in Jack's mind. He guided Jack's hand to his stomach, then lower, to the scales around where his hips were.

Heat bloomed on Jack's face, and he gave a short laugh, touching his forehead to Lauro's as if they were lovers. "How does that work with your kind?"

Lauro's tiny smile revealed needle-sharp teeth that weirdly reminded Jack of Roux's. "Over here," he whispered and guided Jack's hand a bit lower, leaving Jack confused, since he hadn't seen anything resembling genitals there.

All became clear when his fingers dipped into a slit between the scales. It was pulsing with heat, and sensitive too, judging by Lauro's moan. As a venator, Jack learned something new almost every day, but this was the kind of discovery he appreciated most.

Without thinking, he rolled on top of Lauro and watched his hand move against the slit. In and out, then caressing the edges. It was a new kind of organ for him, and the way it felt teased his sense of adventure. "How deep can I go?" he asked, trailing his lips up the slender neck while Lauro writhed, splashing the water with his fin.

Lauro rubbed his hand up and down Jack's arm. "I want you to slide yours in there," he whispered breathlessly, and the gills on his neck trembled. But despite the invitation that made Jack dizzy with lust, he still recognized a hard shape growing against his fingers and pushing at his hand. Was this… where mermen had their cocks tucked into when they weren't fucking?

"Does that feel good?" he asked, slowly pushing his hand deeper. Lauro's muscles refused to give at first, but the slick fluid that kept the inside of the slit damp eased the way. Once Jack's knuckles were in, he was able to cup the oddly smooth length inside.

Lauro's pretty lips trembled, and he nodded vigorously. "Yesss… Your hand is so big. I love your touch." He leaned in for another kiss, and this time he deepened it, adding his sleek, long tongue to the mix while his insides throbbed against Jack's hand.

Lauro slid his fingers down Jack's chest and all the way into his underwear. When he gripped Jack's cock, the smooth sensation of his touch had Jack seeing stars.

"Have you done this before? I don't want to scare you," Jack whispered, even though the firm grip on his dick spoke of experience. Still, it felt like asking was the right thing, even if he had his entire hand inside Lauro by now, and the slit expanded slightly when he started rubbing the merman cock.

"Sailors have always been my vice." Lauro stroked Jack's cock in a lazy manner. He gently slapped Jack's thigh with his fin, triggering a pleasant rush in Jack as the prickle left by the strike receded.

Jack smirked. "So that's why the mermaids don't want you around. You're stealing the men," he said, gently slipping his hand out of the slit. His cock was as hard as the rocks around them, and he knew that for the duration of his time with Lauro, Calix would no longer be on his mind.

Maybe destiny had brought him to the rebound he needed.

Lauro giggled, tossing his red hair in the water. He was a most charming creature, and Jack leaned down to kiss his blue nipple.

"Might just be the case, Jack."

His words were so melodic even this simple conversation felt like a duet, and Jack found himself firmly on top, cock in hand and nudging the hidden entrance to that tight, wonderful hole. "Well, they won't get me. That's for sure," he uttered, rubbing against the scales until it felt like they existed only for adding pleasure.

The slippery hole opened up, and heat surged through him when his dick rubbed against Lauro's inside the pouch. The merman arched his tail, parting Jack's legs and pulling him closer.

"No, only mine," Lauro whimpered, hugging Jack tightly and rocking against him like a wave.

He was stunning, but what really mattered was that he made Jack feel welcome in his arms. When Jack's dick was in almost entirely, their mouths met in a breath-taking kiss that pulled Jack's mind into a spin through the memories of all the lovers he'd had, only to land him back on top of the sweetest and most understanding of them all. He grabbed the back of Lauro's neck and glanced into his eyes, slowly dragging his cock in and out of the tight slit. The connection was unmistakable. Without words, Lauro was right there with him.

When they were together, everything else melted away like a bad dream.

The little moans Lauro let out were music of their own, and Jack licked them off the pearly lips. Water splashed around them with each of Jack's thrusts, echoing off the surrounding walls. Jack could think of nothing but the gorgeous face contorting in ecstasy, and his own cock pounding into a hot mouth where it got to rub against another dick.

It was perfection, and as they moved together in the water, creating waves that spread throughout the pool, time stood still until Lauro's claws gently scraped his back, and he came inside the pouch, imagining his partner's cock covered in his cum.

"Oh, Jack..." Lauro whimpered. "Your seed is so hot."

Jack trailed fervent kisses along Lauro's jaw line, and as the cum slowly drizzled out of the hole and over his balls, he whispered into the beauty's ear, "Will you show me your dick?"

He was spent, but the temptation was too great. He slid off Lauro, only to see a tentacle-like appendage emerge from the slit, pushing out yet more of Jack's spunk.

Lauro bit on his knuckle, looking shy with the blush on his cheeks. "It's been such a long time since I've had a man pleasure me, Jack."

Jack frowned, trying to focus on the beautiful face and not on the hard, unusual cock covered by his own release. "Well, that's just a crime. You deserve to be pleasured. It should be an exchange, don't you think?" he whispered before finally taking in the gloriously indecent sight in front of him. The pink, smooth cock stood out from the background of scales, and Jack closed his lips around the narrow tip.

"Yes, yes, an exchange!" Lauro gasped, rubbing the bottom of his tail against Jack's hip and rocking his cock deeper into Jack's mouth. It was so smooth, the skin felt like the most untouched flesh on the inside of Jack's mouth, and as it moved, the musky, salty flavor of Jack's cum spread down his tongue, mixed with a hint of a seaweedy aroma. He would have laughed over that taste if he wasn't throat-deep full of merman cock.

Lauro's fin flapped about wildly, splashing warm water over them time and time again, but then he moaned, rocking his hips a few more times, and as his cum filled Jack's lips, he went limp in Jack's embrace.

The island became silent, disturbed only by their gasps for air.

Jack gave Lauro's cock a few gentle suckles before letting it out of his mouth and lying alongside him, one leg resting on top of the tail. He couldn't remember the last time he had felt so at peace, but in the safety of the pool, in the arms of the sweet, pliant creature and with taste of cum on his tongue, he felt free.

"Thank you."

Lauro giggled and poked Jack's pec. "Silly. It was my pleasure."

It was as if connecting with Lauro, talking to him, loving him this one time, pulled all the pain of the breakup out of Jack's heart. He didn't know if it was catharsis, or some merman magic, but he was glad for it.

"Jack? Can you hear that?" Lauro whispered and clutched Jack's shoulder.

At first Jack wanted to say 'no', but he spotted the commotion in the water and swallowed.

Chapter 4

Jack shot to his feet despite the postcoital tiredness dragging him down. His top was a ball of fabric in the sand, so he quickly tucked his cock into his underpants and reached back to grab the Gouger.

Only the sword wasn't there, because he wasn't an idiot who went swimming with a sword.

Fuck.

Fucking hell!

A head emerged from the waves, then another, and many more behind it. He recognized the mermaids in an instant. Hissing, their eyes glinting with anger, they looked nothing like the beauties of legends. Perhaps he saw them differently than straight men? When the water became too shallow for them to swim in, they crawled toward the beach, so Jack did the first thing that came to his mind.

He grabbed the terrified Lauro into his arms and backed away to give himself time to think.

"Hang on!" he yelled, running as far away from the shore as possible, all the way to where rocks formed a shelf broad enough to accommodate

Lauro's tail. "Don't come any closer," he called out, as soon as he put his lover down.

Lauro curled up his tail, already a shivering mess.

"Move aside, these are merfolk matters," growled the mermaid at the front with hair like seaweed, and black eyes.

Jack offered Lauro a brief nod. Now that his lust had been satisfied, the stunning face appeared different. The angular lines of his face were almost too sharp, reminiscent of a predator, but that changed nothing about Jack's mission, or the time they'd spent together. With conviction forming invisible armor on his wet body, Jack approached the crawling mermaids, whose muscular tails pushed sand around, leaving behind deep lines that expressed their anger.

"It is not. I am a venator, here on behalf of the law, I command you to stop right now."

Technically, he was more of a mercenary than an officer of law, but he doubted the underwater creatures spent enough time with humans to know the difference.

A few growls came from the water, but the mermaid at the front stopped inching his way. "We are beyond human jurisdiction…"

She'd caught the bait, so he quickly continued, stepping closer. "No, you're not. The water belongs to you, but this island is Italian, as is the vessel over there." He pointed to where his boat was anchored beyond the rocks. "Lauro has been granted asylum by Italy, and you have no right to interfere!" And to make all he said even more believable, he added, "Paragraph XB 29.6"

No such paragraph existed, but he'd found out long ago that introducing rows of letters and numbers into one's argument helped the cause, whether one was lying or not.

The mermaid hissed, showing off strangely sharp teeth, and slapped her reddish tail hard against the sand. "He still owes us flesh"

"Flesssh," the other women repeated through their teeth in a way that made Jack's balls pull closer to his body.

"He no longer owes you anything. If you don't comply, we will be forced to strip you of this secured reserve. You'd have to move, perhaps somewhere where you won't have the chance to encounter any fishing boats."

The mermaid huffed and clawed her fingers through the sand. "You leave tonight. And if he ever comes near these waters again, we will rip his scales off one by one!"

A threat like this still meant that they would let him pass. Or so Jack hoped.

The mermaids inched back, their heads disappearing under the water.

Lauro was still scared, but once he was back in Jack's arms, his worries dissipated, though he still feared to leave the little island despite it being necessary. Jack went first, to make sure the mermaids stayed away, and while they continued hissing at them from a distance, they did not interfere when Jack and Lauro climbed into the boat.

So that had been an adventure.

Lauro watched him with shiny green eyes, and Jack smiled back at him. He was always proud of a job well done, but somehow saving the merman or Calix's brother felt more fulfilling than bringing another trophy head to the home he shared with Drake in London.

As Jack rowed, he told Lauro more about JUSTICE and Roux, who'd arranged everything in the first place. Jack had almost told the merman about Roux's fear of deep water, but then remembered it was a secret and bit his tongue. Once he was done talking, Lauro sang for him again, and there was no sorrow in the melody this time.

That late at night, the pier was empty, so they could easily make their approach. Roux's silhouette was obvious because of the tail. He walked up and down the pier, looking out toward the boat, and waved from afar as soon as he spotted them.

Jack smiled and waved back. "That's Roux Chat-Bonnes. Make sure to thank him, and if anyone asks you, he was the one who saved you," he said, rowing with even more vigor. There, he was a hero. Someone worth being friends with, even to a standoffish chat.

Lauro smiled, much more at ease now that they'd left the merfolk waters. "I shall thank him in song!" He opened his mouth to sing, and the wordless melody conveyed so much emotion Jack sighed in awe.

Roux's shoulders fell, and he scooted at the edge of the pier like a curious cat. Jack's lips stretched, because he knew exactly how his fellow venator felt. "Throw us the rope!" he called out, when they were just meters away.

Roux looked up at Jack with dazed eyes. The oil lamp next to his feet gave his fur a golden glow, and his ears perked up. "Huh?"

Jack's heart beat faster when Lauro extended his hand toward Roux, who patted it in a catlike gesture, as if Jack hadn't just asked him for help. And if a mer*man* could put Roux under his spell the way he had Jack, it could only mean one thing.

Jack licked his lips watching Roux succumb to the smiling merman's charm. But moments later, Roux's head snapped up, and he let go of Lauro's hand. "Yes. Rope."

It didn't take long for them to tie the boat once Lauro's song ended, and Jack carefully lifted him onto the wooden pier. In the warm light of the oil lamp, Roux's pupils were huge whenever he glanced at the merman. Jack joined them on the polished planks and touched Lauro's hip. "Safe and sound. What now, Roux?"

Roux pointed to the town. "There's a carriage waiting to take us to the inn." He started walking, but then tripped when he looked over his shoulder.

Lauro sent him a kiss, but the moment Roux averted his eyes, Jack gave the tail a gentle pinch. "There are many others for you to seduce. Not him," he said in the quietest whisper. He could see Roux was embarrassed enough already.

Also, if he was here, he wanted Roux to appreciate *him*, not the merman he'd just met.

Lauro giggled and wrapped his slender arms tighter around Jack's neck. "I cannot wait."

About the time when Lauro was becoming a bit heavy in Jack's arms, the carriage emerged in the glow of the lantern Roux guided them with. Jack wondered how heavy Roux was. The fluidity of his movements made Jack assume he didn't weigh much, but then again, Roux had been ferocious and hard to beat during their fight.

He would just have to find out some time.

What Jack didn't expect was that the creature who jumped down from the wagon bench would also be a chat. Much taller than Roux, with black fur, a leather vest and a pair of harem pants, he made a completely different impression on Jack than the nervous Roux. As if to add to his roguish charm, he was missing half an ear, and had long canines that touched his bottom lip when he smiled.

"Finally! I thought it all went to shit," he said, and assessed them before opening the carriage door.

"Not at all. In fact, it went quite well," Roux said, and it didn't escape Jack's attention that he tensed.

"Roux destroyed those mermaids, am I right?" Jack asked, winking at Lauro with the eye the carriage driver couldn't see.

"He was so fierce out there," Lauro added.

Roux's ears lowered. "It was teamwork," he said softly. "Jack made it work."

Jack stilled, for a moment staring back into the beautiful eyes. "I was just assisting you. I don't need any credit for what I did," he said, eventually approaching the opened door of the carriage and gently depositing Lauro inside. The merman struggled out of the water, but put on a brave face about it, and was glad to see a large wooden basin filled with water waiting for him.

"Either way, good job, you two. Can't wait to get to the inn and warm my bones. I'm Antoine." The chat held his paw out to Jack, and when they touched, Jack couldn't stop comparing him to Roux. Antoine's fingers were longer, more slender, while Roux's much shorter and cuter. Jack had seen other chats before, but hadn't had much opportunity for interaction.

"Jack. It's good to know Roux had someone helping him with this... initiative," he said, unsure what to do now that the job was complete. It seemed Roux and Antoine would be the ones to take Lauro to his new home, but where did that leave him?

Antoine snorted. "He smelled so nice, I couldn't help but give him a discount." As if to add offence to injury, he rubbed his paw over Roux's ruffling his hair.

Roux huffed and pushed it away, but Antoine just laughed and returned to his seat.

Jack stuffed his hands down his pockets and reluctantly met Roux's gaze. "It was a good job. I'm glad you contacted me."

"You're the one who offered their time." Roux looked around, scratched his ear, but finally met Jack's gaze. "If you're not too busy, maybe you would like to come with us? Meet some of the others? It could be an opportunity to make valuable connections. You know, for work."

When Jack stared into those wide chat eyes, he knew there was only one connection he wanted to make tonight.

"No. No, I was supposed to go on vacation with Calix, but that's not happening. I'm available," he said, taking that one step closer to Roux's feet.

Roux smiled and when he urged Jack into the carriage, their hands touched for the briefest of moments.

Chapter 5

"What are you doing so far away from home, Antoine?" Jack asked, wanting to somehow rope the driver into conversation. After all, he was an outsider here, and the journey to the inn might take a while.

The black chat glanced over his shoulder. "I've got eleven kids to support, and they're all under fifteen. Not much work prospects out there in Bonnes, right Roux?"

How well do these two know each other?

Roux groaned, watching the sea to their right. "The scenery is nice."

Eleven? *Eleven*? Jack kept his shock to himself and went the polite route. After all, the past years had taught him that many problems between species could be avoided if everyone remained civil. "That must be tough on Mrs. Antoine. Taking care of them all."

Antoine waved his paw dismissively. "Nah, they roam around a lot. It's what's nice about the countryside."

Jack laughed. "I wish I could have *roamed around* at that age. What about you, Roux?"

Roux made little whimper. "I was busy studying."

Antoine snorted. "Studying the local studs."

"I refuse to acknowledge that accusation!"

"Just calling a spade a spade. Can't fake the way you smell."

Jack looked between the two chats, his head still ringing with the bit about studying studs. That sounded just like him. "What's wrong with the way he smells?"

Roux hissed. "Nothing."

"*Oui*, nothing is exactly wrong with it. It's more that… at certain times of the year, he smells like a girl."

"Antoine, shut your face, or I will throw you off there and drive this carriage myself! I was eager to leave Bonnes because of chats like you."

Jack wanted to chip in, because Roux was clearly upset by the notion. Jack guessed he'd be too if someone accused him of using floral perfumes. "That's right, he smells nothing like a girl. He has this clean scent to his fur!"

Roux's head whipped right back to Jack with his lips parted, but Antoine kept talking.

"You're human, you wouldn't know. But as far as I recall, Roux left Bonnes because he was the twentieth kid in his family, and his brothers aren't exactly doing much to help out. Hasn't your sister had three more babies this past summer?"

Jack was embarrassed. For himself, for Antoine, and most of all for Roux. He'd prided himself on representing the best in chats, and now here they were, talking about how his family was a chat stereotype.

"Oh, you have nephews? Congratulations," he said, gently nudging Roux with his elbow.

Roux sighed deeply, and his ears lowered. "Thank you. I'm planning to visit them next year."

Antoine seemed to be enjoying the torment too much to stop. "By then you might have more, because Jeanne had her first heat a few months back. Then again, I've heard she's made some human friends, so you might be safe."

Roux's feet tapped the floor, his shoulders hunched. Jack had enough of this. "Dude, what's your problem?"

Antoine's tail twitched. "We're just having a conversation."

Jack frowned. "No. You're talking about someone else's business. What's the point of this?"

Antoine looked back with his eyelids lowered. "Is this embarrassing, Roux? Do you take issue with what I'm saying?"

"There's just no need for any of it," Roux said.

"Why? You've left Bonnes, and that makes you think you're so much better than us?"

"He wasn't the one to say that," Jack said curtly. "You're the one who talks about his personal life to a work colleague of his you've barely just met."

But Antoine wouldn't let it go. "It's not so personal if all of Bonnes knows it. Or are you ashamed of your own family, Roux?"

The expression on Roux's face reminded Jack of the one right before Roux had left scars on his face years ago. "I'm not ashamed. But I also don't think all chats need to produce a litter every few months."

Antoine shook his head. "*You* would say that, since you don't—"

Roux hissed and stabbed his claws into Antoine's thigh.

Shit.

"I mean... family planning isn't a bad thing," Jack tried, but Antoine ignored him and bared his teeth, hissing and bristling his fur at Roux.

"You're jealous of the females. That's all there is to it!"

Roux pulled away his paw and crossed his arms on his chest. "Let's just end this charade! Yes, Antoine, I'm a pussycat. Are we done here?"

Jack bit the inside of his cheek when those offensive words, the same he'd asked Jack not to use, fell from Roux's lips. A part of him was glad to finally know that he hadn't been attracted to someone who couldn't reciprocate his interest, but that left him even more disgusted by Antoine's behavior.

"There's no need for this language. What's the big deal, Antoine? He's not the only one attracted to his own sex."

Antoine did a double take at Jack with his eyes wide, but Jack could only focus on Roux's flattened ears and lowered gaze. If this was how other chats treated Roux, who was an accomplished venator, no wonder he wasn't keen on visiting home often.

Jack hated this god-awful homophobic chat for making Roux feel like shit on a day of such triumph. "Not to mention that Roux Chat-Bonnes is a known venator, a great ambassador for your species. He is a success story. Everyone in the field has heard of him, and you should all be grateful for the kind of respect he commands."

So maybe Jack was overdoing it a little bit, but this was Roux's moment to shine, and he didn't deserve to have it spoiled by a coach driver who felt so much better than him just because he was making babies.

His heart did a backflip when Roux looked up at him with those pretty green eyes.

Lauro opened a little window between the bench and the inside of the carriage, and his fin sent a splash of water Antoine's way. "I would like you to know—Antoine—that you are in the minority in this carriage."

Antoine rubbed the water off with his sleeve, and they all fell silent.

Jack grinned Lauro's way and gently patted Roux's back. "I'm guessing he won't be invited to the inn?" he whispered, but judging by Antoine's hiss, he hadn't spoken quietly enough.

It wasn't like he cared.

Roux rubbed his head against Jack's shoulder. Only once, but it still sent warmth all through Jack's heart.

Soon after all the nastiness was silenced, they not only spotted the inn, perched on a cliff, and with a large sea pool not far below, but also *heard* it. Music, singing, yelling, all reached their ears as they approached.

Jack's mood instantly lifted, and he scratched Roux's back once more before jumping off the wagon to stretch his legs. "Damn, Roux, how many people should I expect? This sounds like a serious party."

"The organisation counts over twenty members, but... they have friends, and I imagine the innkeeper has invited half the village to reveal his new star attraction." He seemed to purposefully ignore Antoine, and rightfully so.

Lauro extended his arms to Jack through the window. "Oh! Oh! I cannot wait to sing for everyone!"

Jack laughed, glancing at Antoine from the corner of his eye as he helped Lauro out of the bath. "Oh, so it's *singing* you want. What a nice euphemism."

Lauro giggled and slapped Jack's shoulder. "What else could I possibly mean?"

Once they stopped, Roux paid Antoine in silence, but people—or rather, creatures of all sorts—poured out of the inn to greet them, and those who had hands held drinks.

Jack grinned, spinning in place to show off Lauro's attributes. "Ladies, gentlemen, and everyone in-between, meet Lauro. And be nice to him, since he's been through a lot of hardship recently," he said, before passing the merman into the waiting arms of a huge creature, who looked as if he was made of stone. Another interdimensional orphan, perhaps.

"We're so happy to see him safe and sound!" said an older man with a round belly and a bald head. He wore an apron, so he was likely the innkeeper.

Jack was too busy gawking at the variety of creatures gathered along with humans to engage with him, though. They all followed the stone-man down the steps to the sea pool where dozens of chairs and tables awaited guests. Colorful lights hung from the roof, and trees growing out of huge clay pots created a cozy atmosphere that went hand in hand with the live music produced by a creature with so many arms it was playing four instruments at the same time.

Jack didn't even mind seeing a centaur among the crowd, because tonight he'd gotten Calix out of his system for good.

Lauro dove straight from the arms of the stone man into the pool, to a round of applause. Jack was so enchanted with the sight of the merman's joy he hadn't even noticed when Roux had left him.

Fortunately, there was only one chat in attendance, and his fur had an eye-catching color. Jack found Roux receiving a cocktail of vodka shaken with ice and sweet cream, and he made his presence known by snatching himself a glass of whisky. "There you are."

Roux stilled with the glass at his lips. "H-hello. I know you like to make friends, I didn't want to be the fifth wheel."

Or he was embarrassed by what had been said in the carriage and fled. So Jack decided to act as if that hadn't happened at all and clinked his glass against Roux's. "I'd rather catch up with someone I haven't seen in a while," he said, even though they'd talked a lot throughout dinner already.

Roux downed his drink after a moment of hesitation and lapped up some that had spilled on his chin. It didn't help Jack's imagination that the drink was white. No matter how much he tried to be decent, he still imagined cum on Roux's fur.

"That's nice of you," Roux said, and Jack had to laugh at how stiff that sounded. Roux definitely needed another drink, so Jack poured him one.

"Go on. Just relax. Antoine's a jerk who doesn't have much to offer the world. No point thinking about it."

After a moment of hesitation, Roux ordered two more cocktails from the passing barmaid. He rubbed his ear with a groan. "I guess... I just didn't want you to hear any of that."

Jack swallowed some of the whisky and leaned against the wall, watching Roux's cute, furry fingers twitch against a glass. "Why?"

Roux sighed deeply, avoiding Jack's gaze by looking toward the singing merman. "It's such an embarrassment. My family—I love them—but they fit the stereotypes to a T, and then... I know you're into men yourself, but I'm not used to being open about it. It's not our way of doing things." He eagerly grabbed the cocktails as soon as the barmaid brought them.

Jack stretched his neck, and a small smile tugged at his lips. "To be fair, you found me getting impregnated by a tarantoid. Your family can't be any more embarrassing than that."

Roux snorted and poured another shot into his mouth, once more licking around his lips. "I won't say I hadn't felt a tingle of satisfaction back then."

"I hope it was because you saw me half naked," Jack tried, discreetly watching Roux's reactions.

Roux's ears lowered, as did his eyelids, and he pushed at Jack's arm. "You just can't help yourself, can you? You'll fuck anyone or anything that comes your way."

Jack hesitated whether he should be honest or not, but in the end he met Roux's gaze. "I've been faithful to Calix while we were together, but I see no reason to deny myself pleasure when I'm not attached. And sometimes being in another man's arms is the only way to scratch an itch. Even with a broken heart."

Roux's gaze drifted off to Lauro, but then snapped back to Jack. "Wait. No! You didn't! ... Did you?"

Jack cleared his throat, only slightly embarrassed. "You may not believe me, but it really helped. You must see how lovely he is."

Roux's ears flattened and he sighed. "He is irresistible when he wants to be, but I find it hard to see those scales and not think of food."

Jack stilled, shocked that not only was Roux not judgmental, but he'd actually made a joke. Jack grinned, slowly sipping his liquor. He was used to drinking alcohol since school, but judging by the gradual slowing of Roux's movements, the chat's head wasn't as strong. Jack could bet his skin was rosy red under all that fluff. "You're relaxed for once. Who'd have thought you're even capable of it?"

"You get burnt a few times, and you don't want to let go as much," Roux said, but he slurred slightly, his head lolling from side to side.

Jack laughed and nudged him with his foot. "Are your hangovers so bad then?"

"I just... don't want to be judged, you know? It's so, *so* exhausting." Roux sighed deeply and leaned against one of the clay flowerpots. Or rather intended to, but missed the mark and leaned against air.

Only Jack's intervention saved him from falling. Though Jack wouldn't have been himself if he hadn't used this opportunity to his advantage. He pulled Roux closer.

"I get it. A lot of the time, when I meet new venators, I don't know how sincere I can be. You know, some of them are horribly specist," he said with a sigh.

Roux shook his head and used Jack to help his balance, but pinched Jack's cheek as if he were a baby. "Oh, no!" He gasped. "How do you possibly deal with such a horrific problem?"

Jack's lips twitched, but the truth was he didn't really find it amusing. Still, he led the way farther from the pool, where shadows provided more privacy. "It's not that I'm embarrassed. I'm sure you heard about my father."

"Who hasn't?" Roux groaned, but let Jack lead him because his legs wouldn't have gotten him far.

"He can't know. That's why I have to censor myself sometimes."

"Of course. You wouldn't want him to cut off the funds because you fell for a centaur." Roux sounded bitter, but Jack couldn't exactly blame him. And he *was* drunk.

He still rolled his eyes and let go of Roux, finishing his drink. "Would you want your family to never speak to you again? So maybe you're embarrassed of them. Me too. But I still want to go home for Thanksgiving or Christmas and just spend time together, even if I can't tell them everything about my life. Is that really such a crime?"

Roux sat on a stone step after losing his balance again. "I guess I'm just jealous. I can't hide like that. The other chats can smell it on me."

Jack helped him up. Perhaps it was time to take Roux to his room. "Wouldn't that make finding partners easier?"

Roux meowed so desperately it pulled on Jack's heart strings. "No! They all want one thing, and then go find themselves lady chats."

When Roux to his feet ended up with the chat slumping again, Jack went ahead and hauled him up into his arms. And he found out that Roux wasn't too heavy, nor was he too light. His weight sat so comfortably against Jack's chest he would have gladly carried him during a challenging run.

"You can't be serious. There must be other chats like you. And also..." He took a deep breath when the liquor he'd had messed with his balance. "You're interesting. Your fur is so nice, and your profile has this elongated shape. It's graceful," he said in the end, somewhat embarrassed.

Roux rested his fluffy chin on Jack's shoulder and wrapped his arms around Jack's neck, but the only answer he had for Jack was a deep, continuous purr. It was as surprising as it was erotic, and Jack hugged Roux tighter.

How had they even gotten to this point? This had to be the first time Roux had truly let loose around Jack, and he would cherish it like the memory of finding a pearl on the beach. Even if Roux's state meant there was no chance of taking their connection any further, Jack loved knowing Roux felt so comfortable around him.

"I think I should take you upstairs now," he said softly, looking into the huge, sleepy eyes while his heart beat ever faster.

"It's room eleven," Roux mumbled. So pliant and limp in Jack's arms, Roux seemed even cuter.

Jack bit his lip when Roux's tail found its way under the back of his shirt, but he didn't hesitate, and started climbing the stairs. "Um... I forgot to talk to you about this but, is your room big?" he asked, unable to stop himself from massaging Roux through his fur. It was so wonderfully smooth he wished he were allowed to really *pet* it.

Roux purred against Jack's ear in answer, for once so close to Jack it was difficult to believe what was happening. He smelled the fresh aroma of Roux's fur, and couldn't help but bury his nose in it by Roux's ear. All perfectly justified, since he was carrying the chat, so he couldn't exactly help it.

When he finally reached the room in the attic, he found it was only big enough to accommodate a double bed and a washing cupboard, and far below the standard he was used to. But if Roux really sent a large portion of his money home, maybe this was the reality of his travels. It made Jack feel guilty for having demanded half the payment for catching the gnomes back in Bavaria. He swallowed, but moved the comforter with his knee before placing Roux on the mattress.

The chat wouldn't let go of his neck though, and kept pulling him into the bed, making tiny sleepy whimpers that melted Jack's heart. He could hardly believe what an idiot, what a mean bully he'd been to this lovely creature when they had first met.

He'd been so ignorant. So stupid.

And now? Was he being stupid now by letting this happen?

His brain no longer provided answers. He kicked off his shoes, dropped his jacket and tack, before rolling into bed next to his friend. Roux was small enough to leave room between them to keep things decent.

An additional blanket would serve as a barrier, but when Roux cuddled up to him, pressing his pink nose against Jack's neck, and wrapping his furry arm over Jack's chest, its functionality was put into question.

Heat shot to Jack's face, and he cleared his throat, wanting to remind Roux he wasn't in bed with a plush toy but with a man who could— potentially—be interested in him. In fact, this man was very much interested. So interested that, knowing their history and Roux's personality, he didn't want to accidentally fuck things up by taking advantage of Roux's drunkenness. "So..."

All he got was a nudge to his ear and a purr that resonated through Roux's chest and against Jack's side. It was both cute and unbearably sexy.

He took a deep breath when the tickle of soft fur triggered a hot jolt of electricity that ran all the way to the tips of Jack's toes. With his heart beating rapidly, Jack dared to rub the side of Roux's head with his hand, and his entire body reacted when the chat purred, sleepily leaning into the touch.

Was this it? His chance?

No, it wasn't. He needed to stay here and make sure Roux didn't puke all over himself after all that vodka cream.

Roux covered one half of Jack's body with his own, making him heat up by the second. He'd never imagined his night would take such a turn. And yet, no matter how pure of an angel he craved to be, Roux did smell like catnip, his fur was soft to the touch, and Jack did imagine what it would be like to feel the touch of a chat's body against his naked skin.

Fortunately, there was a blanket between them.

This was fine.

Outside, Lauro started singing again, and Jack could feel the beautiful notes physically pulling on his dick. He groaned.

Why? Why was this happening to him now of all times?

Because he was in bed with Roux, who for once was pliant and had no mean words for him.

Licking his lips, he turned his head to look at the pretty face. Roux's chin was covered by the cutest fuzz, and the whisker pillows? Oh, what Jack wouldn't do to for a chance to nip on them. Was this what he could have had a year ago if he hadn't been so hasty to choose Calix?

Then again, everything was a step forward in life, an experience. There was no point in wondering what if when Roux was in bed with him right now, even if half-asleep. He'd been much more sober when first wrapping his arms around Jack's neck.

The party outside had to be rowdy, because Lauro's song spoke to Jack on a visceral level, and the warm body on him wasn't helping him to focus on anything other than caressing Roux's fur and the hope he'd finally find out more about chat dicks.

But not tonight. Tonight he just needed to take care of his own stiffening dick. Only how was he to do that when Roux lay on him? Jack didn't want to disturb his sleep.

He could hear the soft purr even through the melody sung outside, and when Roux sleepily moved his head, tickling Jack with his whiskers, keeping his hands on top of the comforter was no longer possible.

Jack dove one under the covers and grabbed his rock-hard cock.

He moaned in relief, but had to bite his lip to keep his voice low. He could only hope Roux didn't actually wake up and find him dick-handed, but pressing a boner against Roux could have been even worse, so he closed his eyes and hoped for the best.

He stroked his cock quickly, but his mind still drifted off to a fantasy where the soft fur pressed against his cheek was actually touching his balls. He could just imagine those desperate, horny meows as he drilled his cock into Roux's slender body.

His hips twitched, his toes curled, and he had to bite his lips so that Roux remained undisturbed. But once waves of pleasure crashed over him, he was left with a beautiful chat hugging him from the side—unaware of what just happened—and a mess in his underwear.

What a prize for the hero.

Chapter 6

The smooth flavor of strong coffee awakened Jack's brain, sip by sip. The bright sun didn't reach him under the cloth roofing above the terrace, but he still felt heat flush the back of his neck every time he glanced at Roux, who sat next to him on the rattan sofa, having a glass of cold milk.

Every now and then, he rubbed his eyes with the inner pads of his palms, and one of his ears got folded back. Jack itched to reach over and straighten it, but didn't want it to look like he was making a move on Roux, so he sat there, in the conundrum of decency.

Waking up together had been surprisingly not-awkward, mostly because Roux acted as if nothing happened. Because nothing *had* in fact happened. Just two buds getting drunk and sharing a bed. Nothing out of the ordinary. If it wasn't for the fact that he and Roux had never been so physically close before, and that Roux had confirmed he was in fact interested in males.

And the quick jerkoff while Roux lay right next to him, which could have ended in disastrous consequences, had he awakened while Jack was at it. Just thinking about it had Jack's head hurting.

"I could stay here forever," Jack said, hiding behind the cup.

Roux opened his big eyes and looked out to the sea. With the sun so bright his pupils were barely slits, the green color of the iris flooded the whole inside of the eye. The short, pale eyelashes were visible as well, making Jack sigh with the urgent need to pet Roux's face, even though he knew chats weren't *cats*.

"I go where work takes me."

Jack sighed. "I know, me too, but... as disastrously as my relationship with Calix ended, I realized how nice it is to have a home of my own. Among people I choose and who I don't have to tiptoe around."

"You mean in London? You go there quite often, don't you?"

Jack licked his lips, smiling when he thought about little Chad. Maybe he should visit soon instead of sulking all alone. "Yes, that, but also my home in the centaur village."

Roux stayed silent for a while, just watching the waves and sipping his milk. "I like to visit my family, but I never feel at peace there."

"Where do you feel at home, then?"

Roux stared into his empty cup. "Nowhere."

It had to be one of the saddest things Jack had heard in a while, and he gently squeezed Roux's forearm. "What do you mean? Are all the chats there like Antoine?"

For once, Roux didn't pull his arm away. "No, but a lot of them. They all go about their own lives and we can't really connect. But I like to travel and see new places, so that's all good."

Jack sipped more of his coffee. As someone who's been popular all his life, he couldn't understand how Roux felt, because he always had someone to talk to. It had to be a miserable existence. "I like that too. And I am... grateful to our profession that it allowed me to step out of my comfort zone and meet people who I would have never encountered home."

Roux snorted. *"People."*

"What's with that sarcasm?"

"You seem to be exploring much more than people."

Jack no longer felt only humans were *people*, but his brain could only focus on the cute way Roux's whiskers moved after he had another sip of the milk. He gently unfolded the crooked ear on Roux's head, astonished by how delicate and thin its flesh was. "I still haven't explored a chat."

Roux didn't roll his eyes, didn't hiss, but just watched Jack with widening pupils. "Is that something—?"

"Jack Addison? I was sure I recognized you!" spoke someone in an American accent.

Jack's heart might have stopped for a second, and he frantically turned his head, taking his hand away from Roux as if he'd been burnt. Only a handful of other guests sat on the terrace at this early hour, but the two men in neat suits approaching were like a cloud of deadly disease. Jack rose the moment he spotted a camera.

"I'm sorry. Do I know you?"

One of the men laughed. "Of course not. I'm hardly a celebrity, unlike you, sir. My name is Felipe Elbert, and I write for *The New York Hound*. I'm doing a piece on the inn and its merman, but when I heard you're staying here, sir, I was hoping for some commentary."

Jack stiffened and moved away from Roux, conscious of the camera. He didn't want his father to see him with a chat, all cozy on a terrace in Italy! "Oh, it's not me who should be interviewed. Roux Chat-Bonnes here brought the merman to safety," he said, gesturing toward Roux, despite his stomach cramping so aggressively he wished he could run off to the hotel room.

Roux's ears perked up. "Yes, the merman has been viciously hounded by his own kind, and as a member of JUSTICE, which is the Jolly Union—"

Felipe waved at Roux dismissively. "That's fascinating, but we'd love some juicy details from Mr. Addison. Our readers will be more acquainted with a member of the Addison family. So, Jack, is it possible that even a man like you, a venator, could find a merman attractive? I've heard they can be seductive creatures."

Jack's face remained blank. "I'm regretful, but I have nothing to say. I've never met a merman in my life," he said, lying through his teeth. "I'm sure Mr. Chat-Bonnes can tell you something about it."

Roux put down his cup and got up. "Mr. Elbert is clearly interested in an interview with you. Take your time, Jack. I need to go pack anyway."

Jack gave a short laugh and looked at the journalists. "Maybe another time. I have another job lined up, and it's time-sensitive. Good day, gentlemen," he said, following Roux into the hotel. The sway of the red tail was like a light in the fog of his brain.

Fuckers ruined his moment with Roux. He couldn't believe it.

The journalist tried to get a word in, but they were out of sight fast.

"This interview could have moved you up in the venator popularity rank," Roux said. He didn't sound mean. Maybe a bit bitter.

Jack huffed. "I don't like being disturbed. And I'm not making his job easy for him after the way he treated you. This was your night, not mine."

Roux's shoulders lost their tension, and his eyes softened. "Thank you. It's just that no one wants to listen about what matters. Everyone just wants 'the juicy bits'."

Jack swallowed, stepping closer to Roux. The world wasn't fair, but if it got that bit fairer thanks to Jack, maybe that was more important than gouging the eye of the Kraken? "They're hyenas. Don't worry about it."

As they were about to go upstairs, the innkeeper ran out of an open room and stopped them. "Mr. Addison? A friend of yours has arrived. Drake Nguyen. He's asked me to inform you that he's staying in room number two."

Roux put his hands in his pockets. "So popular, Jack."

But Jack's heart skipped a beat. "Have you actually met Drake? Come, let's say hello."

Roux's pink nose twitched. "I'm not sure… He's your venator friend, isn't he? I don't want to impose."

Jack rolled his eyes and pushed Roux along the corridor. "I'm telling you it's fine. He's on the same side as we are. You know, creature-positive?"

"Oh, that's nice to know. I suppose I can spare a minute or two."

Roux could be so formal at times it bordered on silly. Jack knocked loudly on the door and announced himself.

They popped open, and the slit revealed Drake's smiling face, but his expression faded somewhat when he spotted Roux. Not this again. If there was something Drake wanted to talk about in private, they could do that later. So Jack pushed the door open and walked Roux inside.

"Can't believe you missed me this m—" he stilled when his gaze met the eyes of a tall, slender woman in casual clothes. Before Jack could have questioned her presence, something tapped against the wooden floor, and then a brown tarantoid the size of a German shepherd jumped onto one of the two beds so abruptly its small sailor hat tilted, covering two of his eight eyes. Chad wore a matching shirt, complete with a blue scarf, and he raised his front legs, clicking gleefully the moment he saw Jack.

Roux let out a high-pitched yelp and jumped on the window sill, but still grabbed his rapier. "What is this?!"

Drake stood between him and Chad with his hands raised. "Calm down! This is Chad, he's very friendly."

Roux's wide eyes settled on Jack with a silent question as Chad rushed over to Jack and hugged his leg with all eight of his.

Jack's thoughts became a whirlwind, but before he could ask Drake who the woman was or why had be brought Chad here, or even answer Roux's question, he picked up Chad and looked into his eyes. "Oh. My. God. You've grown so much! I've been gone way too long."

Roux hissed. "Jack! What is the meaning of this! Please don't tell me your new lover is a tarantoid. They're not even sentient!"

The woman shook her head. "Lover? Chad is still a baby."

Jack pulled Chad into a hug, and the thick legs squeezed him back, to the tune of chaotic clicking noises. He turned to look at Roux, feeling like a bug about to be crushed. "No... this is my... uh, my foster kid."

Roux put his rapier back and spread his arms. "This is insanity. You can't foster a tarantoid. They're monstrous and eat people, for fuck's sake! Excuse me, madam."

The woman adjusted Chad's hat. "Maybe they eat people in the wild because they don't know any better. There's no magical quality to human meat. Chad lives on fowl and insects, and he's perfectly fine."

Jack rubbed his chin against Chad's head. "That's really unfair, Roux. He can count to ten."

Drake stepped closer, with a flush coloring his cheeks. "Jack, just listen to him, okay? *Listen!*"

At first, Jack was confused about Drake's meaning, but then he noticed that the frantic clicks formed patterns, and his heart beat faster.

<Daddy. Daddy, I miss you,> Chad told him in Morse code, shaking his backside, as if he had a tail to wag.

The woman's smile was wide and toothy, but when Jack turned to glance at Roux, he immediately knew that the chat knew Morse code too by the look of dread in his eyes.

"Jack. You did not. Please tell me you didn't!"

Jack exhaled and rubbed Chad's back, approaching Roux. "Look at him. There's not an evil bone in his body."

"Because there is no bone in his body! He's a spider!" Roux backed up, flattening himself against the window.

Jack exhaled and came even closer, itching for understanding. "But he speaks! You must have heard him! You of all people should understand."

Roux let out an unhappy meow, his lip curling. "Teaching him tricks doesn't make him sentient. Or harmless."

Drake stepped closer. "No, no, he really communicates. He's learned Morse code so fast!"

Roux went silent, watching Chad apprehensively and leaning away when the child reached out to him. "How did you survive his… err… birth?"

Jack offered Chad an encouraging smile and stepped even closer, so Roux and he could get acquainted. "That's the thing! Turns out they don't have to be parasitic and eat humans from the inside. This one hatched in my pocket."

The woman nodded. "Warmth is enough. The female would usually abandon the eggs, hence the need for warmth and food from an outside source, but since Jack fed Chad, the problem was non-existent."

Roux shuddered. "I would prefer not to touch it."

Chad recoiled against Jack's chest and hugged Jack, clicking, <sad.>

Jack scowled at Roux and mouthed, *"Really?"*

Roux took a deep breath, rubbed his cheek and got down from the window sill. "Fine. I'm sorry," he muttered and it took him a while, but finally, he patted Chad's back a few times.

The tarantoid seemed hesitant at first, but in the end, he extended its arm and let Roux shake it.

Jack grinned. "Happy family." He slowly turned around to Drake and his tall companion. "I assume, this is Miss Constantine."

Rachel Constantine smiled. "I'm happy to hear Drake's written about me."

"But what brings you all the way to Italy? *And* with Chad?"

Drake smiled sheepishly. "Honeymoon."

Jack inhaled a big gulp of air. "No way!"

There was no end to congratulations, but before Roux could have managed to excuse himself and leave, the happy couple decided to have a look at Lauro and left Jack with Chad, who'd gotten tired out by all the excitement and fell asleep in the middle of the bed.

Jack smiled and nudged Roux's side. "Isn't he the cutest baby you've ever seen?"

Roux scowled. "Jack... He's revolting," he whispered.

Jack frowned at him. "That is not true. He's got beautiful eyes, and a really nice shape, and those cute bristles all over."

"So I suppose the future of creature-human relations is very important to you now that he's in your care."

Jack glanced at the little ball of eyes and limbs. "I want him to have the same chances as anyone else."

"I know you said you don't want to join JUSTICE, but... if you're not too busy, would you join me for a trip to Transylvania? There is some business with the vampires that I need to handle on behalf of the union, and a human companion could prove useful."

Jack's mouth stretched into a smile as a giddy feeling settled in his stomach. So they were friends now. Finally. "Sounds like a plan. Aren't they celebrating Dracula's undead birthday this month?"

"Yes, the Blood Moon. It's a big thing in their social calendar. Have you met any vampires before?"

"Only in passing. Why?"

Roux snorted. "I just figured they'd be on your checklist of creatures to bed."

Jack hadn't actually thought much about it before, since they were so much like humans, but... there was no harm finding out, was there?

Next time on Jack Addison vs. A Whole World of Hot Trouble:

Will Jack get into Roux's pants?
Will they uncover a secret satanic plot on the way to Transylvania?
Will Jack meet Roux family?

Jack Addison vs. Asexual Vampires

Jack Addison Vs. A Whole World of Hot Trouble #6

K.A. Merikan

"Are you planning to sleep with every creature you encounter?"

The popular monster hunter Jack Addison is on his way to Transylvania to participate in a vampire festival and meet up with the coven elders. But no matter how thrilled he is to see the elusive creatures of the night in the flesh, he is far more excited about traveling alongside his frenemy/crush Roux. When the pretty chat invited him on the trip, Jack had hoped that perhaps the skittish creature would finally yield to his charm, but Roux is even more irritable than usual.

There are plenty of vampires to go around at the festival, and Jack had never been close enough to an undead creature to consider his curiosity satisfied. But when Roux's behavior changes from annoying to alarming, it will be up to Jack to help his friend, no matter how many pairs of glinting canines beckon him closer.

Previously on Jack Addison vs. A Whole World of Hot Trouble:

Jack Addison might come from a line of legendary monster hunters and scientists, but real life has taught him that the world isn't what he'd been told all his life. After encountering the alluring Nessie during the annual hunt, he's opened up to the idea of dating nonhumans.

Away from the strict segregation of his country, he meets all kinds of creatures, each more interesting than the last. Jack's amorous thoughts keep drifting to his rival, the catlike creature Roux. After a period of mistrust, Roux learned to appreciate Jack for his good heart and invited him on a joint mission to Transylvania. Will Jack succeed at getting into Roux's pants, or will he become vampire prey?

Chapter 1

Jack needed to focus on something else. Anything. The seat was somewhat uncomfortable, and the movement of the train only made it worse, but the night outside was quite spectacular with bright stars, and a huge full moon casting its glow on high mountains in the distance.

But he couldn't focus on anything so wholesome when the tufts on Roux's ear kept tickling his neck. Roux had fallen asleep a while ago, leaning on Jack's shoulder more with each minute. It wasn't unpleasant. I was way too pleasant for Jack's comfort.

"Oh. Oh no," Jack whispered to himself when Roux's silky soft head slid off his shoulder and then lower. He swallowed, watching the fluffy fur dip even farther as the train rattled, yet Roux couldn't have been more peaceful.

Worse still, Roux's state only reminded Jack of the night they'd spent in one bed, when what happened in Italy should have stayed in Italy. But it didn't. It was stuck in his mind like the dumbest recording that his brain found worth remembering.

Roux's fur was silky, and seen up close, it glistened as if Jack's fellow venator had treated it with oil. Perhaps it was that oil that made Roux's scent so goo—

The train came to an abrupt stop, and Roux's head rolled straight into Jack's lap, sending sparks of arousal all the way to the tips of Jack's fingers. This was not how he'd imagined the two of them traveling together. He hesitated for a second or two, but was unable to resist the temptation of petting the soft cheek.

The tufted ears twitched again as if Roux were having a bad dream, so it was only fair that Jack offered comfort. Anyone would have, really. When Roux let out a strange whimper from the back of his throat, Jack's cock twitched. He couldn't help it.

It wasn't his fault Roux had curled up next to him, and he wondered what it would be like to have his cock licked with that nubbed tongue as long whiskers tickled his thighs.

So he kept on petting, and when Roux's hands and feet started trembling as if he were running in his sleep, the motion made Jack yearn for relief. Yet he couldn't just go to the restroom and leave Roux on his own—vulnerable and adorable.

Roux rubbed his head against Jack's hand in his sleep, making him imagine what it would be like to have Roux in his bed. Long gone were the days when Jack wanted an experience with any chat. What he wanted with Roux was about so much more that satisfying curiosity. They shared the same profession, they knew parts of each other no one else did, and Jack would not only get off with Roux. They could cuddle until morning and do it all over again.

Roux sneezed.

Then looked up at Jack with his big eyes, still confused and sleepy.

Shit.

Holy fuck.

A silly smile emerged on Jack's face. "Hello. You fell asleep."

"Hn?" Roux covered his mouth and yawned, only to still. "Are you?" He jumped to his feet, his fur bristled. He pointed to Jack's crotch with a hiss. "What are you doing, you pervert?"

Jack quickly covered his growing bulge with the jacket he'd placed on the seat next to him earlier. "I did nothing. It was you who fell into my lap and started vibrating!"

Roux's eyes grew wider. "I do not *vibrate*."

Jack attempted to imitate the purring sound he'd heard from Roux.

"That is *not* how I sound."

"That is exactly how you sound! Besides, you were shaking in your sleep, and you slept with your head in here," he said, pointing to his crotch. "Show me one man who wouldn't have reacted!"

Roux huffed and crossed his arms on his chest, looking away from Jack. "This is a work trip. Your thoughts should be on ways of liaising with vampires."

Jack couldn't believe Roux's hypocrisy! They might have just laughed it off if he weren't such a prima donna, but no, he had to make a big deal out of something as natural as an erection. "Oh really? Was that what you were thinking about in your sleep?"

Roux stalled. "I don't remember my dream."

"There you go! Maybe there was a reason you fell into my lap like that."

"You just can't keep things professional, can you?" Roux shook his head.

Jack used to feel guilty about his 'unprofessional' behavior sometimes, but realizing that Roux was a bit of a hypocrite in that department relaxed him greatly. Roux had been the one to get blind drunk back in Italy.

"Maybe not. What counts is that I'm successful at my job."

"Shall I remind you that our job there isn't to have sex with as many vampires as humanly possible, but to propose an alliance."

Jack crooked his head, watching Roux with a sly smile. "I didn't actually think about it, but now that you said it... it is going to be their largest gathering, right?"

Roux hissed and sat opposite Jack, which was disappointing after the closeness they'd just enjoyed. "Are you planning to have sex with every type of creature you ever encounter?"

Jack's gaze didn't flinch. "What is there to stop me? I'm not attached."

There. A challenge for the stubborn chat. Let's see how that goes down.

Roux's pink nose twitched. "Oh really? Shall I just go around and fuck every other human I meet like some tomcat?"

Jack shrugged, because he knew Roux wouldn't follow up on that threat. "Is that a rhetorical question? I'm sure the humans would have been ecstatic if you allowed them anywhere close."

His answer confused Roux so much he just sat there, watching Jack. "I refuse to be a novelty," he said in the end.

"You are not a novelty. You're too difficult to be around to become anyone's disposable fling," Jack shook his head and briefly moved his fingertips over the silky fur.

Roux looked away, but the held-back smile was there. Too cute. Did he pride himself on being hard to get? "But you're on the train with me anyway. I must be persuasive."

"Too persuasive. But you should consider that when I write my memoir, you might not be a part of that grand work," Jack said, thinking back to his collection of memorabilia. The folder contained items taken from his various lovers, and created a wonderful palette of creatures— different yet all sensual and interesting. Maybe apart from the slug guy, Grall'ogg.

Roux's ears stood to attention and his eyes grew wider, which only made his features cuter. "You? A memoir? What would you possibly put in there?"

Jack spread his arms. "Oh, you know, exploration of love in a world we all share."

"Wait. Are you planning to write about your sexual exploits? Unbelievable!"

Jack spread his arms. "Someone has to do it. How else are we all to *integrate*?"

"We can integrate without the use of our penises."

Jack snorted. "And what's the fun in that?"

"Jack Addison, you are unbelievable."

"I'll get something to drink. And perhaps start working on my memoir," he teased, ignoring Roux's scowl.

He'd said it as a joke, but the farther he went down the train car, the more sense the idea made to him. The book would have to be anonymous, of course, but would allow for all manner of creature lovers to gain knowledge from his exploits. He could explain the best way to entice an ogre, or where a merman's privates were. Who wouldn't want to know such details once the idea of pursuing a member of a different species crossed their mind?

He was closing in on the restaurant car when he heard commotion ahead. And when he looked inside through the glass door, what he saw was a fight between four vampires, or rather—three ganging up on one that looked most frail.

Maybe they were jealous, because the vamp was a looker. He wore a cape, his long black hair resembled silk, and his skin couldn't have been any clearer.

"Let go of me at once!" he yelled. "You do not know the wrath of a vampire! If you do not let go, I will have no mercy!"

One of the others patted his cheek. "Oh no, I'm already shivering. Are you going to meet your correspondence vampire boyfriend? It might just be me."

The pretty one snarled and stared back at his tormentor. "What a joke! I can do much better than you."

Okay, that was it.

Jack stepped inside. "Is there a problem?"

The blond man holding their victim's arms back rolled his eyes. "Not *your* problem, move along."

Jack sighed. So that's how it would be. Fine. He'd taken on a pack of werewolves into his holes one after another, so he could surely handle a group of vampires having an altercation on public transport. "I believe it is my problem, given that you are all vampires!"

One man who'd stayed back with his cigar frowned. "Are you a hunter? We're all just humans messing around."

Jack couldn't have been any less impressed.

The blond nodded. "Yeah, look." He was wearing a silver claw ring, which he pressed against the small man's cheek.

The sudden sizzle and burn to his skin made Jack's eyes widen, and everyone went silent once the vampire was done screaming his lungs out.

This one clearly was the real thing. Shit on a stick, how did had he got himself into this mess?

Jack pulled out a pistol. Fun and games were over. "Drop the silver, impostors. Lie on the floor, with your hands on the backs of your necks. I am Jack Addison, and this is an arrest."

The blond guy pushed the vampire at Jack, and all three of the bullies fled, leaving behind burning cigars and beer. *What a bunch of lowlifes.* The poor vampire seemed frail, as if he'd been weakened somehow, and Jack struggled to find a reason for his disposition. Too bad Roux wasn't there. He would have known what made vampires lose steam.

"Tough night?" he asked, placing his pistol back into the holster.

The vampire choked, his face showing tension caused by the lingering pain, but there was true beauty hiding beyond the scowl. If Roux didn't want Jack in the compartment, perhaps he should find a more eager companion for the remainder of the journey?

"Aren't you going to chase them?" the vampire asked.

Jack smirked. "The train won't stop until morning. Plenty of time to make the arrest once my partner wakes up."

The vampire watched him with wariness. "You do know there are laws to protect us vampires, right? Hunting was outlawed years ago, during the Third European Night-Day Summit in Cracow."

Jack frowned. "I am a lawman. Why do you think I've pulled out my gun on those three?"

The vamp's shoulders slouched. "Oh. I could have handled them myself." He cleared his throat and pushed back his long black hair. "Since I'm a vampire."

Jack snorted. Something was off about this one, and he knew it, despite never having the pleasure of talking to a member of his kind before. "I'm sure. Maybe you're just having a bad night. Jack Addison," he introduced himself yet again, charming a smile out of the vampire with one of his own. "It's both my job and pleasure to regulate interspecies relationships. If humans give you any trouble, you'll know who to look for."

"Vasyl Gorgonov. You say it's a pleasure?"

Jack stepped closer, eager to test the waters with the vampire. Was his body cold? Would it take forever for Vasyl to get it up, or would it be the opposite if he could control his blood flow? "Of course. It is my job to ensure everyone's safety. Especially a handsome vampire's," he said with a wink.

Vasyl swallowed, his eyes paler than a normal humans, with an odd, reddish sheen that Jack found exotic and attractive. "Are you heading for the Blood Moon Festival then?"

Jack rested one of his gloved hands on his hip and picked up the beer left behind by one of the impostors. No need for it to go to waste. "Yes. I'm an envoy for an interspecies organization. We want to go into talks with the vampire covens. Perhaps you know someone who could get me in touch with the elders of your race?"

So maybe he'd overinflated his importance, since Roux was the actual envoy, but wasn't this an innocent lie?

Vasyl tried to stand taller, as if he too strove for Jack's attention. "I do know a vampire older than some of the villages around here, but what do I get in return?"

The question was like dynamite about to explode in a flood of pleasure and cum. Trying to play it cool, Jack leaned against the table, never looking away. "Impertinent. Are you bargaining with the man who might have saved you the pain of your body having to repair itself from more than a minor burn?"

"Hmm… Maybe you deserve all sorts of rewards then." Vasyl took a step closer, and when his gaze inevitably drifted to the side of Jack's neck, it triggered a rain of shudders down Jack's spine.

"How old are you?" Jack asked, wanting to sample more vampires soon. He was curious how their needs and performance changed with age.

"Does it matter with a vampire?" Vasyl asked with haste. Young then. Fair enough. Jack could work with an inexperienced vampire. If a vampire was a virgin, would it mean he'd be deflowered each time he had sex again?

Jack smirked and pulled on Vasyl's belt, to make his intentions even clearer. "I guess not. Is it true that your bodies permanently harden as you age?"

Vasyl grinned. "I wouldn't know. Depends on which parts we're talking about."

Jack looked back, then toward the other end of the carriage, to make sure they wouldn't be interrupted, and he pressed his body more boldly to Vasyl's. "Maybe we could find out."

Jack couldn't wait. He felt safe enough in the packed train to just go with the flow, and he couldn't help a little shiver when Vasyl's cold fingers touched his neck in search of the artery. He was about to offer up his throat to this beautiful creature of the night when he spotted a dark figure soundlessly enter the train behind Vasyl. The man was like a sculpture of wire and clay, with gray skin and bony hands, but when he opened his mouth, the voice that came out was nothing short of booming.

"Stop that right now!"

Vasyl opened his lips, but the man in black robes released a purple smoke from his palm and the pretty vampire... disappeared.

Or so Jack thought, until he spotted a tiny bat wriggling and screeching on the floor.

He looked between the bat and the newcomer. "You attacked him, you dried-out coffin!" he choked out in shock, and quickly retrieved a high-end stake he'd purchased for occasions like this one. The other vampire stepped back with a loud hiss, and his rapid movement sent a cloud of dust into the air.

"I have the right to transform him, for as per vampire law he is mine to govern!"

Jack's almost-lover thrashed around at his feet, briefly jumping up as if he intended to fly, but it was in vain.

"And… you have proof of that?" Jack asked, still uncertain. He should have been a better student when they'd gone through inter-species laws at the academy.

The vampire scowled and showed him a small metal plate that confirmed a Magnus of Rome was Vasyl Gorgonov's maker and was therefore responsible for him. "He's not even been initiated into the coven yet."

Vasyl flapped his wings and clawed at Jack's boot, trying to climb his leg. It was cute and pathetic in equal measure.

Jack let out a soft sigh and picked up the tiny ball of fur, leather, and squeaks. Vasyl was… a bat. He didn't want to have relations with a bat. "You were prettier in your human form."

Magnus's fingers were icy when they shook hands. "Ridiculous. We do not adhere to human beauty standards."

"Sure, sure," Jack whispered, though he only cared about his own standards when it came to those matters.

The law was the law though, and he handed the bat over to his guardian, wincing then Vasyl sank his claws into Jack's hand. What a vengeful creature. Still, Jack felt sorry for him and petted his little head between the ears. "Take care of yourself, little one. I'll take care of those bullies for you when my partner awakes."

Jack watched them leave, hoping he hadn't wasted his one and only chance for fucking a vampire.

Chapter 2

Roux had been prickly throughout their whole journey to the Transylvanian vampire festival, Covenalia, but his attitude reached new heights of absurdity once they reached the inn where they'd booked rooms via telegraph message.

"What do you mean you only have one room left? We booked two rooms, so I *demand* two rooms." Roux's fur bristled, whiskers twitching at a rising speed.

The clerk, a frail little girl who looked like the picture of meekness would not budge. She adjusted her tiny spectacles and offered them a professionally sad smile. "I'm sorry to hear that. The person who took the booking must have made a mistake, because I only have one room booked for Chat-Bonnes."

Jack sighed, mentally rolling his eyes, but there was no point in forcing his presence on Roux. "Maybe we could just go somewhere else."

The girl crooked her head. "Oh, Sir, I don't think you're going to find a place anywhere. This is the world's largest gathering of vampires, and there is plenty of other creatures coming to witness the celebrations, too. The whole town is packed. You could try asking locals if they wouldn't spare a room in their own house, but I'm afraid you might end up having to sleep on a park bench."

And again, that flawless smile.

Bitch.

"I am not sleeping on a bench!" Roux raised his voice, which ended in a screech.

Jack shrugged. "I guess we'll have to take the one room, then."

Roux growled and ran his claws over her desk as he took the keys off it.

The clerk frowned. "I will add any damage to the bill."

Roux didn't answer and swooshed his fluffy tail when he faced the stairs, leaving Jack to take his bag.

"You're in a mood…" Jack muttered, following his feline friend.

Roux's shoulders were set, and he hissed at the door when the lock wouldn't open right away. "Is it really so much to expect? Two rooms when one requests that number? I don't think so! All I ask is to be treated with respect. I bet they gave one of our rooms to a bunch of vampirophiles who wouldn't be back for the night anyway."

Jack raised his brows when the key dropped from Roux's fingers. Was he nervous about them staying together? Because he'd surely slept in much worse conditions before. What bothered him so much?

"Calm down. I'm not gonna do anything you don't want," Jack said, as he entered the room and placed their luggage in the middle of the floor. The space was small, with a sloped ceiling on one side and, predictably, only one double bed.

Of course. He could anticipate Roux's further complaining already, as if sleeping next to a hot guy was such a terrible fate.

Roux's eyes grew wider, and instead of thanking Jack for bringing over his luggage, he waved his arms in the air. "What? You think I'm scared of you? I just don't care for sharing a room! Is that so hard to understand?"

Jack was slowly losing his patience. "Are you a chat or a porcupine?"

Roux spread his fingers, releasing sharp claws. "Do not test me, Jack. Not tonight, not ever."

Jack pushed Roux's bag his way with a kick. "What is up with you? Did someone give you fleas or something?"

"Fleas? Seriously?" Roux paced around the room as if he were trying to measure its area. "All I wanted was a quiet night on my own. Is that so much to ask?"

Jack spread his arms. "Yes. You picked the wrong place and time for luxurious demands. I don't understand why you expect me to just take your shit because something spoiled your mood."

Roux sat on the bed and made an impatient whine. Did the blood moon affect chats too? This was beyond ridiculous. "Didn't you want to go out and party with the vampires anyway?"

Jack exhaled, watching his partner's hunched shoulders. Perhaps it would be better to remove himself for a bit and let Roux deal with whatever he needed to deal with. "Do you want something?"

Roux huffed and hugged himself. "Butter."

Maybe he'd gotten a letter about some family stuff and didn't want to talk about it. Fair enough. Jack could give him some space.

And get some tail!

He wondered if chats could become vampires too, but he decided not to ask, and unpacked his backpack to retrieve a few essentials.

Like lube.

"Okay, see you later then."

Roux nodded absentmindedly. "Take your time, I don't mind," was his polite way of saying: *give me the whole room because I'm the prince of chats and need the whole bed to myself. But don't forget to buy me some butter.*

Yet Jack still liked the bastard, so maybe he was a secret masochist. Was this something to try with vampires? After all, they did want to drink people's blood, and he was an open-minded guy.

It was already getting dark when he left the hotel and ventured through the streets of the cute medieval town, which seemed unusually lively for its size. Locals and non-vampiric guests alike added finishing touches to decorations, but by the time Jack had eaten a meal of goulash, red and orange lanterns lit up the darkness, and the people of the night left their lightproof hideouts to celebrate Covenalia.

Jack had left his jacket with the venator emblem at the inn, because tonight he would be a civilian looking for fun. Roux could sulk on his own, if that was his idea of pleasure. They weren't scheduled to talk to any coven leaders until the day after tomorrow, anyway.

Despite the chill in the air, Jack had a stomach full of warm food and was ready to search the town for a vampire willing to get frisky. He knew he'd hit the nail on the head when he walked out of the narrow alleyway onto a square filled with... creatures, because not all of them were human.

In the middle, a band played traditional music on pipes and violins, enchanting Jack with a glimpse into a world he knew nothing about. A group of younger men and women danced with their hands stretched to the sky. They wiggled in place like a sea of hypnotized snakes, moving in tune with the melody, while their feet ignored any rhythm played by the band, staying immobile. It was an odd way to dance, but Jack appreciated the exaggerated hip rolling, even though it was mostly the women who performed this strange local dance move.

The festivities continued down the main street, where visitors in dark clothes, cloaks, and beautiful gowns paraded over cobblestones, sampling scented candles, looking at artisanal coffins, and other vampire-oriented products presented in market stalls. The actual coven meeting was a day away, and it seemed that on this first day of the Covenalia even old vampires wanted to let their hair down, as evidenced by a dried-out lady in early-medieval clothes riding a mechanical pony, to the delight of her companions.

Jack was just about to walk on when right there, over the stall filled with moon-shaped necklaces his eyes met a familiar gaze.

Vasyl.

No longer a cute bat, he was back in his alluring form, all long black hair and porcelain skin. They smiled at each other from afar, and Jack could bet their thoughts were heading in the same direction.

He checked his teeth with his tongue, to make sure there wasn't a piece of salad to spoil his image, and walked confidently toward the beautiful vampire. Vasyl exchanged a few words with a jewellery seller and met Jack halfway, his face somehow even more charming than on the train.

"I'm one lucky bastard," Jack said, shaking Vasyl's hand, just to have an excuse to rub his cool, silky skin.

"Quick, let's go before Magnus comes back," Vasyl said, and pulled the hood of his cloak over his head. He squeezed Jack's hand with surprising strength.

Jack grinned and followed him with a silly smile. "I wouldn't want him to interrupt us again. Do you have a place?"

Vasyl looked back at Jack, and the rising blood moon gave his eyes a reddish glow. "I know of a spot. I wished to see you again, Jack."

Yes. Perhaps he wouldn't get *tail*-tail tonight, but he *would* get tail.

"Me too. You're such a beauty," Jack whispered as they ran farther from the noise and into the labyrinth of narrow cobbled streets.

Vasyl grinned, showing off his canines. "I've been initiated, awoken to the night."

"That's great," Jack said, even though he had no idea what that meant.

Vasyl must have thought it was self-explanatory, and Jack didn't ask, unwilling to spoil the mood as they left the city walls behind and walked up the gentle slope of a hill leading to a small church. In the moonlight, its pale walls had a reddish shade, but Jack was too surprised by being let to the cemetery next door to marvel at the sights.

Okay. He supposed he *could* do that.

Vasyl quieted Jack's worries with a kiss of his cool lips. "The blood moon shines brightly here. For us vampires, it's almost like experiencing sunrise."

Jack looked up. "Oh, but it happens like... only a few times per century," he said before realizing his mistake. Here was to hoping Vasyl was too horny to care.

"Yes, apparently drinking blood at a time like this feels like consuming sunshine itself."

Vasyl led Jack on a stroll between the tombstones. The moment he turned away, Jack decided to seize his chance and put his hands on Vasyl's hips. "This glow is romantic. Red. Like a heart. Like lust." *Or a brothel*, but he'd leave that thought to himself since Vasyl seemed to be the spiritual type.

Vasyl sat on the grass by a tombstone and patted the ground next to him. "Like blood. I promise to be gentle."

Jack pulled his teeth over his lips, and instead kneeled between Vasyl's legs. "I'm not sure how blood loss will work on my manly prowess. Maybe let's start with something else?" he suggested, rubbing Vasyl's thigh.

The vampire blinked. "Oh, Jack..." He cupped Jack's face with those incredibly smooth fingers. "Now that I understand vampire ways, those needs are foreign to me."

What?

What?

Jack pulled back with an awkward smile. "So you just want my blood? I don't even know if I'd like that…"

Vasyl offered Jack a tempting smile. "Only one way to find out."

Jack scowled. First Roux, and now Vasyl? Was his dick cursed tonight? "But I'm so horny…"

Vasyl cocked his head, gently massaging Jack's jaw. "Hm. I mean… I guess we could do some stuff you, like if you promised to offer your blood later."

Jack's smile instantly widened. "Yes. You can have some if you give me some," he whispered, pressing his mouth to the white column of Vasyl's neck. The vampire was such a graceful, statuesque creature.

Vasyl took his time mulling it over, and his skin turned the prettiest shade of pink in the moonlight. "I guess that does sound like a fair agreement." He leaned over for a kiss, and when their lips met, he pulled Jack down to the grass.

The sturdiness of the vampire's body felt good under Jack, and the cold chill of it was such a novelty he forgot there were dead bodies underground all around them. It was best not to ponder any of that anyway. But when, after a lot of necking, he reached between Vasyl's legs and found little to grab onto, reality called him back.

"You're really not into it, are you?"

Vasyl sighed, entwining their legs. "I mean… there is enough pleasure in touching so that I enjoy myself."

Chapter 3

Jack couldn't believe it. Vasyl still was as pretty as when they'd first met, but the idea of having sex with someone who didn't really want to participate was distasteful, and he pulled away, clearing his throat. The gravestones peppered around in the reddish moonlight were suddenly like a bad omen, and he wanted to leave the cemetery as soon as possible.

"You know, maybe we should both find someone else after all."

Vasyl stared at Jack's neck with longing that was becoming uncomfortable. "You don't even want to try the ecstasy of being bitten?"

Jack tried to smile. "It's not really my kink."

Vasyl groaned and laid back in the grass. "Seriously? Why are you at the Covenalia then?"

Jack shrugged. "I'm on venator business. I'm not… into vampires in particular," he said, already thinking about the slender, furry body he'd left at the hotel. As fascinating as vampires seemed, their cold, hard bodies were not Jack's type. But a tail sliding between his legs? Yes, please.

If only a certain someone wasn't so irritable all the time.

After a long, awkward silence, Jack got up. "So... yeah, I'll be going."

Vasyl waved him off with a princely gesture and a pout. Maybe Jack had dodged a bullet.

The encounter with Vasyl left Jack dissatisfied and disillusioned about vampires as sexual partners. At least he had a button accidentally torn off Vasyl's cloak to put into his trophy journal. He remembered that he'd promised Roux butter, and it was only by sheer luck that he'd managed to get some from a market stall right before it closed for the night.

Following a quick shower in the hotel's communal bathrooms downstairs, Jack was clean for bed and knocked on the door to their room.

"No service needed!" Roux said from the inside.

So at least he was awake, and Jack wouldn't have to break into his own lodgings.

"It's me, Roux! I have your butter."

The prolonged silence made Jack roll his eyes. Had he disturbed Roux's licking session or something?

"You can bring it in the morning!"

"Are you kidding me? Open the door," Jack demanded and knocked that bit louder.

"Go away!" Roux actually hissed on top of the vicious words.

Jack took two deep breaths. His first instinct was to try to break the lock, but he decided to play dirty if Roux couldn't be fair toward him. "I've been attacked by a vampire. I don't feel so well. Come on..."

"What?" came in an instant.

"I'm telling you. I was with this vampire, and I think he drank too much. My head is spinning. Please, open the door!"

The lock clicked, and Roux's eye appeared in the tiniest gap when the door moved Jack grabbed the handle and pushed his way in, pointedly putting the wrapped butter on the table. "Are you shitting me? You heard it yourself, there are no more rooms available in town. I paid for this room too!"

Roux was wearing... a blanket. A thick blue blanket that covered even his head, so he looked like the Virgin Mary of chats, and he stared at Jack with wide eyes.

"But..."

Jack locked the door and started tossing off his clothes. "I've had a shitty evening, and now you're trying to kick be out of my own bed? What's wrong with you?"

Roux suddenly shuddered, as if the accusation pulled him out of the stupor. "No! Go away! How could you use my good heart like that?" He pushed at Jack, and a hot water bottle fell to the floor from under the blanket, which he struggled to keep closed around him during the struggle.

At this point, Jack was ready to try kicking *Roux* out of the room to give him a taste of his own medicine.

He poked Roux's chest through the blanket. "You were the one to invite me here, and you've been acting like a prima donna when I didn't do anything to you. Or maybe I did, because one can never know with you!"

Roux whined and turned his back on Jack. "I needed alone time."

So Jack was supposed to sleep in streets full of intoxicated people and vampires because Roux felt like pampering himself?

He massaged his forehead. "Look, I know everyone has bad days. Maybe something happened with your family, but you can tell me you're in a bad mood instead of pushing me out of my own goddamn hotel room!"

Roux whimpered and pulled the blanket tighter around himself. He was having some sort of meltdown, and despite Jack's frustration with tonight, he still tried to meet Roux halfway and face him. He put his hands on Roux's shoulders and looked into his eyes.

"You can tell me, whatever it is."

Roux stroked his cheek, and his ears flattened. "It's hard to explain," he said, as he put his other hand against Jack's chest. It was an oddly intimate gesture, especially coming from the standoffish chat, but Jack tried to keep cool.

"Do you need help with anything? If there's some strings I could pull, I will."

Roux closed his eyes and gave a raspy laugh. "I'm sure you could." He massaged Jack's chest with his furry fingers, but then took a step forward and pushed his head under Jack's jaw.

Jack's brain might have rolled around in his skull, but before he could have understood what was happening, Roux's warmth and the tickle of fur against skin pulled at his balls. "Okay, that's new."

"I told you not to come in..." Roux groaned, wrapping his arm around Jack's waist and insistently rubbing his head against Jack's neck. It was as if his mouth was saying one thing, but his body another.

The blanket slid to the floor, leaving Roux without a thread to cover him. He was naked. He'd actually disrobed for Jack, and it was so shocking Jack didn't immediately react. Was this it? Did Roux finally get to a point when he could no longer tame his lust for Jack?

He mindlessly caressed the soft hairs on Roux's cheek, hypnotized by the way his ears perked up. "You are so pretty..."

Roux groaned, pressing into the touch. The soft pillows of his fingers ran up Jack's back, making him shiver. He wished to be as naked as Roux and press his whole body to the silk-like fur.

"I'm in heat, Jack. It's embarrassing," he said, and punctuated it with a desperate meow.

Jack cupped Roux's face, for the first time touching him the way he'd wanted to for so long. "Oh... but you're..."

Roux hugged Jack more tightly, already setting Jack's skin on fire. His pupils were so big they made his eyes black. "Hn?"

Lust and tenderness alike were already intoxicating Jack, but he shook his head. "I thought it was only the girls."

"Unless you're a pussycat," Roux whispered and let out another meow, running his pads up and down Jack's back. "We're... anomalies."

Jack sighed. That again.

"Don't say that word. Haven't you told me yourself that it's a slur?" he asked, pulling Roux to bed and helping him sit. At first he wanted to kneel between the long furry legs, but realized that Roux's genitals might be too much of a distraction, so he parked his ass next to him instead.

Roux wasn't making things any easier for Jack and climbed into his lap as if it wasn't comfort he needed, but something else altogether. He was so light in comparison to a human man. And so fluffy. And naked.

"I don't know anymore. It's not like I can get pregnant, but twice a year, I get this unbearable urge to mate, and it hurts all over. It feels like I'm losing my mind, and any male chat around me can smell it."

Jack knew he shouldn't voice his immediate thoughts, but this might have been one of the hottest things he'd ever heard. In theory, because it seemed that Roux wasn't thinking of heat in terms of fantastic orgasm material. He'd never considered Roux a sexual being, since he was always so buttoned-up and prudish, but what if there was more to his chastity?

"So, you're in pain, and you'll get better once you have sex?" he asked, overwhelmed by the beauty of the elegant creature already grinding his cock against Jack's covered crotch.

Roux wrapped his arms around Jack's neck. "Yes, but I don't want to just go and fuck a stranger. That's not me, you know? And now I'm telling you all these things you don't want to hear and making them your problem, too."

Jack's palms slid down the slender body, feeling the meat under the silky coat. "Roux, I'm sure you know I'm attracted to you. If that's what you want from me, it's really not much of a sacrifice."

Roux watched him with those giant, beautiful eyes. "I just… don't want it to feel like an oblig—"

Jack kissed Roux's cheek, overwhelmed by the intensity of Roux's glorious scent. He was all musk, and cream, and the grassy cologne that clung to him sometimes. "But… like… do you get those needs only during heat?" he asked, needing to know if he was to treat this as a one-time thing. A man needed to put things in order in his brain sometimes, so that said brain wouldn't get any stupid ideas.

Roux chuckled, his slinky body like putty in Jack's hands. "I may not express it much, but I have needs. Often. Intensely. I got badly burned a long time ago, so I'd usually rather wait them out than live with regret. But in heat… Gah. It gets unbearable." He moved his teeth over Jack's shoulder without biting.

Jack licked his lips and rubbed Roux's back before gently sliding his face against the puffy lips, which tickled him with fur and whiskers. He wasn't sure what to think about Roux's revelation, but the fact that Roux did in fact want sex made it all good in his book. "So… is there something I shouldn't do?" he asked in the end, because the last thing he wanted was to aggravate Roux again with some dumb misstep.

Roux licked Jack's skin with that nubbed tongue, sending goosebumps down his arm. "It's happening, isn't it? Just don't make it weird, Jack."

It was hard to make it much weirder.

Jack groaned and pulled on Roux's face, bringing their lips together so he could finally taste him. The whiskers were hard where they pressed against his skin, but the pads at the front of the mouth were like velvet, and that strange tongue against his? He was practically feeling its teasing touch on his dick already.

"Buckle up. It's going to be a wild ride."

Roux nuzzled Jack's cheek with his cold nose and rocked against Jack. It was time to find out if chat cocks had hooks, but now that Jack knew Roux, having him in his arms was so much more personal than the excitement and curiosity that had guided his actions when he first started sleeping with non-humans.

As the kiss continued, mostly between their tongues since chat lips weren't as flexible as those of a human, Jack let his hands explore the body he'd wanted to touch for so long. Sides. Back. Thighs. Ass. All so firm under all that silky fluff. The tail was a separate limb, and when he touched the base, it slowly wound itself around his arm.

Being with Roux was nothing like experiencing the violent lust of werewolves. Where werewolves had been all sharp teeth and growls, Roux was pliant under his touch, accepting and gentle even though his hands hid claws.

"Do you want me?" Jack whispered as he rolled them over, pressing Roux to the bed with the weight of his own body. It shouldn't have mattered, because he was finally getting what he wanted, but if the only reason they were doing this was Roux's heat, then he might end up with a bitter taste in his mouth.

Roux's pupils were that bit smaller when his eyes met Jack's. "Yes," he whispered and lifted his hips, pressing his erection against Jack's stomach.

It was out of the sheath too—hard, smooth, surrounded by soft fur. Jack smiled, nuzzling Roux's small nose as he trailed his hand down the muscular chest. He wanted to touch the mysterious cock, but when his fingertips discovered a trail of little nubs hidden in the soft hair, he was too fascinated to ignore them. There was eight of them in total, and Jack's breath became shallow when he moved his hand in circles, drawing lines between the sensitive nipples, until Roux purred, spreading out on the bed, his tail swinging in the air.

Jack pressed a final kiss to his lover's mouth and moved lower, replacing his hand with his lips as it went even lower. And there it was. Warm, hard and narrow at the tip, Roux's dick got broader at the base, and the hooks didn't feel like hooks at all. They were blunt nubs, very much like those on Roux's tongue.

The stifled moan Roux uttered was music to Jack's ears. Roux's claws pressed on his back when he gave the chat cock a gentle tug while pulling on one nipple with his lips. The fur got stuck to his tongue, so he squeezed the tender flesh with his lips instead, gently twisting. His heart beat fast, as if he were a virgin again. Whether it was because he finally got to bed a chat, or simply because *Roux* was here with him, he wasn't sure, but he was already addicted to the silky touch of fur against his skin.

"I really like you, Jack," Roux confessed, and few things could've been sweeter than that.

Jack groaned and once again pressed their mouths together. He grabbed one of Roux's hands and led it down, to the front of his own pants. "Yes. Me too," he found himself saying, and it was true.

People usually weren't worthy pining for, so Jack tended to swap the object of his desire when there was no reciprocated interest, but Roux was like an itch at the back of his mind that he could neither ignore nor replace with another object of desire. Even when Jack had been with Calix, the memory of the fiercely proud chat had remained a guilty thought he wouldn't have dared to share with his partner.

And now that he finally had Roux in his arms? Few things could've been sweeter than chat pupils widening when Roux rubbed the soft pads of his fingers around Jack's cock.

"It's... been a while for me," Roux whispered.

"Have you been with a human before?" Jack asked, leaving small kisses along the feline face as he slowly worked Roux's cock.

Roux's breath was irregular, his eyes glued to Jack's face. He'd dreamed of such attention from Roux, and he'd do everything in his power to not blow this one chance.

"I've had this… boyfriend back at the academy."

Jack smirked. "Of course. Such a catch," he whispered, slowly leaning back to look at the prick in his hand. He could feel its unusual shape, and the nubs caressing his palm. Now he wanted to see.

A dark pink color, it was a proud presence, smooth at the top and with pale nubs closer to its base, but no hooks whatsoever. Jack would be losing the bet he'd made with Drake over chat genitals, but it wasn't like he wanted to share that new piece of knowledge, suddenly protective of this intimacy with Roux.

The chat moved his padded foot down Jack's calf.

"I wanna suck it," Jack said, staring into the huge green eyes and gently twisting his hand on the cock.

"Oh," sounded like a meow. "Yes…" The claws on Roux's feet must have pushed out, because they scratched along Jack's leg. Roux wiggled under him like a horny eel, and Jack grabbed his wrists, playfully pinning him to the mattress. When their eyes met again, the heat of arousal became somehow fuller and more overwhelming. He didn't know what to say, stuck without wit, so instead, he buried his face in the soft fur and moved lower until the narrow tip of the cock poked at the underside of his chin.

A rasp left his mouth, and he allowed the hot manhood to move up his cheek. Roux smelled so good—musky yet almost sweet, and his fur was sparser on the inner thighs.

"I can't believe you're here," Roux said, as if Jack hadn't been declaring his interest every time they met, but the intensity in Roux's gaze carried so much honesty Jack was confident it wasn't just the heat talking..

They looked at one another above the hard cock, and Jack wouldn't stop even when he slowly teased the underside with his tongue. He tasted the hot flesh, and each lick was fuel to the arousal burning deep in his loins. Without thinking, he teased Roux's furry balls with his hand and slowly lapped at the tip of his cock.

Roux whimpered and rose on his elbows, bringing his thighs closer to Jack's face.

"I need you," he muttered between one shallow breath and another. Seeing this new sexual side of him was more arousing than any aphrodisiac could have been. After years of only having claws, fangs, and sharp words for Jack, Roux was finally letting him in.

Jack grabbed Roux's thighs harder than he would have someone whose skin lacked the protection of fur and leaned down, feeling the nubs move up his tongue until his lips squeezed around the wide base. He was shaking slightly by the time he started sucking, every part of him hot as if someone pressed burning coals to his skin.

"Enough," Roux whimpered and pulled on Jack's arm, his gaze unfocused, frantic. "Inside. I need you inside. I need you to come inside me."

Okay, wow, that was intense.

Jack absolutely fucking loved it.

"Yeah, you won't be satisfied until I cream you?" he rasped as soon as the chat cock dropped out of his mouth. His senses sharpened as if Roux's dick had been covered with cocaine powder, and he could remember everything in the tiniest detail—from the tremors shaking his lover's flesh to the texture of his fur.

Roux nodded. "It's... a h-hormone thing," he muttered as if he needed to explain himself. Jack definitely wasn't complaining, but things got even better when Roux turned around under him, and pushed his ass up.

Jack was left speechless for a second, overwhelmed by finally getting to ogle Roux in such obscene detail. More white markings dotted Roux high on the thighs, but when he curled his tail up to reveal all that had still been left to the imagination, Jack moaned.

His hole looked so tight. It was pink, and so smooth in comparison to the thick pelt around it. Jack couldn't help himself. He squeezed the base of the tail and teased the anus with the tip of his tongue.

Roux let out a high-pitched whine and spread his thighs wider, moving his tail aside. He was so eager Jack almost laughed from the joy of it all. In this moment, Roux was anything but frigid, and Jack couldn't wait to make him meow until morning.

His ass was round and well-muscled under the short fur, flexing every time Jack teased the hole with his tongue.

"Ready when you are," he said, hastily ripping off his clothes. This was happening, and he would be naked to experience the whole deal.

Roux glanced over his shoulder with eyes half-closed and ears flattened. He looked so vulnerable Jack wanted to both cuddle him and fuck him hard. He supposed these two possibilities didn't exclude each other.

"Go on," Roux pushed back, rubbing himself against Jack's cock, legs spread in invitation.

Jack grabbed Roux's narrow hips, but when he saw his cock closing in on Roux's hole, he remembered that he had lube in his clothes and dove for his pants. Going through pockets meant endless frustration, only doubled by Roux's reaction.

"Come on, Jack..." Roux groaned writhing on the bed and wiggling his ass as if he truly didn't care for his comfort anymore.

When the small pot was finally in Jack's hands, he felt like he'd just gotten a medal. Caressing Roux's lower back, just above the tail, he dropped a dollop of the salve around the hole before carefully pushing in the tip of his finger.

It slipped in with ease, as if Roux's whole body was inviting it in. The needy gasps weren't helping Jack focus either. He leaned over his lover and pulled his hand back, making it curl around his cock as he worked another finger into the tightness of Roux's body, coating it with lubricant. Urgency was thick in the air, but he didn't want to hurt Roux by accident. The chat was smaller than him, so Jack needed to test the waters first, no matter how greedy Roux was for cock.

The padded fingers working his dick made thinking excruciatingly hard. If it wasn't for Roux's urgency, Jack would have taken his time and asked to feel the nubbed tongue on his cock, but oral pleasures could wait.

Roux pushed back against the fingers, his body swallowing them to the knuckle. He writhed with impatience, and Jack understood why his chat chose to hide during his heat. Roux took pride in his detached demeanor and would likely feel embarrassed once the effect of hormones wore off, but the fact that Roux chose to let him in after all made this experience even sweeter.

When Roux's insides spasmed around his fingers, accompanied by yet another glorious meow, Jack could no longer wait. He breathlessly coated his cock with yet more salve and pushed it at the entrance to Roux's body.

Roux arched his spine, clawing at the covers. He was the definition of 'horny', and Jack couldn't get enough of this lusty version of him. Even when he put his hands on Roux's waist, the chat reached back, pulling on Jack's arm to get him closer. Jack's balls nestled against soft fur within the blink of an eye, and Jack leaned over, moulding himself to the heat of Roux's slender shape. He ran his hands up his thighs, his sides, across the stomach. Every single movement triggered so much sensation he was already flying, and the tight grip Roux's ass had on his dick promised him this wouldn't last very long.

"You're like a vise..." Jack whispered, capturing the tip of the cool ear with his mouth.

Roux growled, wiggling his ass impatiently. "Fuck. Jack. Stop talking and fuck me. *Please.*"

Jack didn't need to be told twice. He held Roux tightly against him, loving the touch of the fur against his chest, and started fucking Roux in earnest. He couldn't wait to leave his cum in the needy chat. If this was what Roux needed during heat, Jack was happy to comply every single time.

Maybe he could become Roux's go-to fucker during heat? Lock themselves in a remote cabin every few months so that Roux could be free to scream his pleasure out as loudly as he wanted. Jack wouldn't mind sticking around and filling Roux with cum any time he asked. During heat or otherwise.

He would very much love to stick around.

He'd feared that Roux would be a frail lover, but the chat wouldn't stop begging for more as he twisted in the sheets, scratching the comforter and making those strange yet delicious noises as Jack drilled him at an increasing speed. Pleasure was overflowing Jack's brain fast, like a river of gold the color of Roux's reddish pelt. He nipped on one of the ears as he slammed home, keeping Roux pinned with his weight.

Sweat dripped down his nose as he came, inhaling the delicious aroma of Roux's fur. The tail ended up squashed between them, but slipped out just enough to tease Jack's side. He was too far gone to care. He closed his eyes, emptying his balls into that sweet, tight ass.

From there, things only got better. Roux went wild under him, as if the cum infused him with fresh arousal, and he must have come too, because he let out these tiny rasps and moans as his ass clenched on Jack's cock time and time again.

Jack struggled for breath, but once he managed to take a gulp of air, he collapsed on his side and pulled Roux with him. They were a mess of damp skin and matted fur, the room smelled of sweat and cum, and it was absolutely glorious.

Roux relaxed, gasping for breath as he smiled sheepishly, pressing his nose under Jack's chin. "I feel so much… better."

Jack pulled him closer and kissed the ear he'd earlier bitten. He loved how it gently flinched against his lips, so thin and cool to the touch. "So… is this it, or do you need another go?"

Roux chuckled. "We'll talk in half an hour."

Chapter 4

Jack awoke to a serene warmth and sunlight caressing the side of his head. The pillow still smelled of Roux's fur, and he hugged it before slowly opening his eyes. This morning was bliss.

Roux being already dressed wasn't what he'd hoped for, but what was dressed, could be undressed. "Mornin'," he muttered with a smile, admiring the chat, who sat cross-legged on the table by the window.

Instead of purring at the sight of him, Roux squinted and continued licking his stick of butter. "Good morning."

Jack smirked, stretching so the covers would go lower, revealing his bare pecs. "Why don't you come here and greet me properly?"

"I don't think that's necessary. We have more urgent matters to attend to." Roux wouldn't even meet Jack's eyes. Was he shy about what they'd done? This too could be amended.

Jack rolled out of bed, enjoying the rays of light hitting his naked body with warmth. "What could be so important this early in the morning?"

Roux didn't even check him out and pushed a letter Jack's way instead. "There's a call for venators to go to Siberia." With the icy attitude Roux was like Siberia himself.

But Jack would not be rebuffed after the intense night they'd shared, and he buried his face in the soft fur at the back of Roux's head before nipping at his lovely ear. The tuft tickled his skin, and he groaned, closing his arms around the chat. "Weren't we supposed to negotiate with the coven elders?"

"Get off me!" Roux pushed Jack away so fast he dropped his butter. "We might get to talk to the coven elders at another time, but this letter states the job in Siberia is of the highest priority, due to the extreme danger to the local population."

Jack looked at his chest, half-expecting to see blood, because he had felt the claws scratch him. "Why are you being like this? Just last night, you were all over me!"

Roux jumped to the floor with his face scrunched into a scowl and tail waving aggressively from side to side. "I accidentally saw your journal when I was looking for the butter. I don't know what more you could want from me. Last night's encounter should have been enough to fill the two pages you left blank and entitled 'chat'."

Shit.

Shit.

Shiiiiit!

Jack opened his mouth. "Why did you look through my things?" he asked in a desperate attempt to direct this conversation elsewhere. Those two pages have been left empty since he first started having relations with creatures, so why would they be the reason for such discontent?

Roux stomped his foot, but his claws were already out. "I told you I was looking for butter! You can add to your notes that chats in heat are wanton sluts up for taking anyone's cock!" He screeched the last few words.

Jack frowned and grasped Roux's hand. "You're not like that at all. Why don't you sit down?"

Roux pulled his hand away so abruptly the razor-sharp claws left slashes in Jack's palm. "No! *You* sit down. You did help me yesterday, so I thank you for that, and let's move on. We are adults, and there is no reason we can't stay colleagues. When you publish your so-called memoir, I only ask you to keep me anonymous."

Jack looked at the shallow scratches before focusing on Roux again. "The journal has nothing to do with you! It's been obvious for a while that there's something buzzing between us."

"I don't know what you're talking about. Heat can cause lapses of judgement like the one I made last night." Roux raised his chin in the infuriating way that made Jack want to tackle him to the sheets and fuck the snotty attitude out of him until he spoke the truth.

Instead, he bit the inside of his cheek and balled his hands into fists. The words were like a slap and still stung not only his face, but also the balls he'd drained into Roux thrice last night.

"You don't really believe that."

The way the tufted ears lowered at that comment almost made Jack feel sorry for Roux. Almost, because the chat brought it on himself with his own attitude. "I believe I've misjudged the situation. What I do know is that a new interdimensional crack has opened in Siberia, unleashing a type of creature people have never seen before. You can come with me or you can stay here and fill your journal with more pearls of wisdom."

Jack swallowed, meeting eyes that had watched him with so much warmth last night. They were cold and distant now, and being stared at like this was physically unpleasant. "I never hid that I was sleeping with creatures. I even told you that I might publish a book about it. It's no secret!"

"I didn't think you were serious. I told you last night I will be no one's personal cabinet of curiosities. We don't need to argue about this."

What Jack wouldn't have given to pull Roux close and pet him until all this mess was only a memory. There was no point discussing it any further now, because he couldn't find the right words to change Roux's mind. "So we're ditching JUSTICE for Siberia?"

Roux took a deep breath, and his shoulders sagged. At least he didn't look like he was about to murder Jack anymore.

"We're not ditching it, we're taking a detour. Get some furs in the marketplace. It's cold where we're going."

Jack smiled sheepishly. "Or you could just hug me all the time."

Roux squinted at him. "Be ready in two hours."

Next time on Jack Addison vs. A Whole World of Hot Trouble:

Will Jack and Roux use one another's body heat to combat the freezing air in Siberia?
Is the monster a fire giant about to melt the polar ice caps?
What creature can Jack possibly fuck in Siberia? Yeti?

Jack Addison vs. Foxy Lies

Jack Addison Vs. A Whole World of Hot Trouble #7

K.A. Merikan

"Everyone deserves a chance. It's not his fault his mother was a murdering beast."

After one night of passion, Jack and Roux travel to Siberia to hunt down a mysterious monster that has crawled out of a deep mine shaft and keeps attacking the workers. With Roux regretful about giving in to temptation, the atmosphere between the two venators remains tense, but private matters need to stay in the background when the unknown being proves more deceptive than expected.

Something dangerous lurks in the blizzard, but how can they protect themselves when they don't trust each other? When new truths about Roux are revealed, will Jack be able to man up and become who Roux needs him to be?

Previously on Jack Addison vs. A Whole World of Hot Trouble:

Jack Addison might come from a line of legendary monster hunters and scientists, but real life has taught him that the world isn't anything like he'd been told all his life. After encountering the alluring Nessie during the annual hunt, he's opened up to the idea of dating nonhumans and after years of experimenting, settles his interest on a rival hunter, the cat-like Roux Chat-Bonnes.

After a period of mistrust, Roux learns to appreciate Jack for his good heart and invites him on a joint mission to Transylvania, but his behavior on the way is surprisingly adverse. Jack eventually finds out that Roux's behavior has been affected by hormonal changes brought on by his heat, and the two of them give into temptation and spend a night together. Jack's happiness is short-lived, since Roux denies an interest in pursuing a relationship, after accidentally finding a journal of Jack's sexual conquests.

They agree to still work together on a dangerous job in Siberia. Will Jack be able to prove himself to Roux?

Chapter 1

Jack daydreamed about the warm beaches of Italy and Greece, projecting their image over the endless snow outside. When he and Roux boarded the train in Transylvania, he'd thought it wouldn't be an issue to experience a tough winter once more, since they were always white and cold where he was from. But the Siberian winter was nothing like the coziness of the cold months back home. It was bitingly tough, reaching for them through the tiniest gaps.

Jack was too busy to think about it much at first, fascinated by the different way people dressed out here, by their food, and the fact that they mixed their tea with jam, but the farther east they traveled, the less people there were, until he spent endless hours watching barren landscapes untouched by men.

In the first days of their journey, they'd met other venators heading the same way, but as the snow became thicker, familiar faces were replaced by those of locals. He didn't mind. Many venators were out for their own glory and were difficult to work with, but it was the attitude some displayed toward Roux that made Jack resent the notion of having to travel together.

Sadly, things weren't rosy between Jack and Roux either.

'Civil' would've been the best way to describe the atmosphere between them, but no matter how much they *didn't* talk about what had happened in Transylvania, there was no denying that it had in fact happened. Jack had slept with Roux, loved every second of their closeness, and without his defenses up, Roux had admitted he liked Jack.

So Jack would just trudge on and try to gradually chip at the chat's icy attitude until another opportunity arose to prove his worth as a prospective lover, because now that he'd been inside Roux's tight body, there was no going back. He kept fantasizing about the long tail tightening around his cock, the large, tempting eyes looking at him over Roux's shoulder, about the touch of soft fur on skin.

Somehow, someday, he would capture Roux's heart.

Hopefully, sooner rather than later.

It was dreadfully dark when their train rolled into the Krasnoyarsk station, but despite the icy air assaulting Jack's face from the moment he got off, he was glad to see lights and people.

Roux gasped, and his lips parted, releasing vapor. He stared forward with eyes wide and he was so pretty Jack couldn't take his eyes off.

"Is that a yeti?" Roux whispered, and only then Jack's brain snapped out of his infatuation coma.

A giant in furs stood by the small bar at the platform. Too big to fit through the narrow doors, he accepted a steaming mug through the window. Black, leathery fingers looked like gloves, but when the creature faced Jack and rose to his entire height, one glance at its face was enough to conclude it was not human.

"I-I think so," Jack whispered, wondering if being stared at would annoy the giant, but he couldn't look away, nonetheless.

"A specimen for your memoir?" Roux asked with a smirk.

It was the first time Roux had mentioned the topic since the Transylvania fiasco, and it made Jack's heart skip a beat to hear that Roux was able to find humor in it. Even if Jack was the butt of the joke.

Jack cleared his throat, noticing the glimmer of beads at the trim of the yeti's clothes, and when the creature walked past them, the slenderness of its body was noticeable under the fur. "I think it might be a woman," he said and rubbed his hands together, because they were freezing despite the gloves.

Roux pulled on the hood of his thick jacket. The emblem on the back proudly announced to the world that he was an accomplished venator, yet all Jack could think about was Roux's bare feet freezing in weather he wasn't accustomed to. He'd gladly rub them warm.

"Not your type then. Let's go find the local pactor."

"Are you sure you don't need boots?" Jack asked as they dragged their luggage along the platform.

"I doubt they have my size here. I'm fine. My kind is resilient. We've come from a different dimension, yet managed to thrive here. What's a little snow?" he said, even though his fingers trembled.

Roux was right, but it didn't stop Jack from wishing to protect him from the cold. A stand with postcards caught his attention, and he approached the window of the restaurant to knock on the glass. The young woman inside was wrapped in layers of scarves, and she didn't speak English, but getting the right stamp and a postcard depicting a large local church with onion-shaped domes had been easy enough.

"Just a second. I want to send this to Chad. He collects postcards from me."

Roux squinted at him. "Seriously? He doesn't exactly have hands. I still can't believe you kept that abomination."

Jack flinched, staring back at Roux and tightening his fingers on the pen. "Stop saying that. He's a child. For someone who fights for creature rights, you have very little sympathy for creatures who aren't like you."

Roux huffed and pulled his scarf up over his mouth. "I'm sorry, I just... I don't understand. Why did you keep a tarantoid?"

Jack inhaled sharply. "Because everyone deserves a chance. It's not his fault his mother was a murdering beast."

Roux watched Jack for a long time before rubbing his arm. "You make me sound all too much like that other Addison I know of."

"Then don't be like him."

Jack took a deep breath and focused on the postcard instead of memories of his father and his specist rants. His first instinct was to write *Wish you were here*, but he didn't truly want for Chad to ever experience such adverse conditions, so he used simple greetings instead and tossed the card into the postbox.

The big, soulful eyes were like a grassy plain Jack wished he could lay on in the sunshine. "What do you think will become of him? Of Chad? He won't be like other tarantoids, but won't fit in with the human world either."

Jack sighed and led the way toward the exit from the station. The wind howled in the distance, but they could still hear one another. "He's smart. I'm sure he will fit in with the right creatures. I want him to have a life like any other kid. Develop his talents, find love... it's my job to make this world a place where he can do that."

He'd thought about it before, but saying it out loud and Roux looking up at him in awe made Jack's heart beat faster. Yes, that was what he wanted. That was much more important than being famous or bedding as many different creatures as possible.

"That's sweet, Jack. I will help you with that, you can count on it," Roux said, and even though the topic of their lovemaking was left unmentioned, it still pulled on Jack's heartstrings to hear the declaration of support.

He smiled and squeezed Roux's shoulder. He was getting bitterly emotional when he thought that if Roux agreed to vacation in London, he'd actually get to know Chad, but that perspective was still distant. "Let's find a place to stay first? We don't want to end up stranded in this weather."

Roux nodded, but silence hung in the air. They would be once again facing the issue of sharing a room. Roux wasn't in heat anymore, but things could get awkward. Or steamy and so fantastic they'd forget all about their mission, but Jack was pretty sure the second option was just his wishful thinking.

"So, about sleeping arrangements... I hear lodgings are expensive out here, but I'm fine with it if you want your own room," Jack said as they left the station and entered a broad street.

There weren't many carriages in sight, and people seemed to be walking everywhere in their somber furs and thick boots. The place was an oasis of human culture in the wilderness, and seeing decorated facades after staring at snow and trees for days on end was a revelation. Though the large, monumental structures seemed to be few and far between, with most of the buildings made of wood and surrounded by flimsy fences.

Roux stared at some kind of commotion down the street with a frown. "Let's stay close. We don't know what we might encounter here."

Just as he said that, an inhuman screech echoed through the air, and Roux darted toward the small crowd of people in furs.

Neither of them understood the local language, but as the commotion grew more violent, Jack stormed into a gap made by a group of women who left the gathering in a hurry. Three people were needed to hold down a thrashing man. His feet kicked about clumps of hardened snow, his chest arched, but before Jack could have intervened, fearing that the stranger was struggling for air, he saw the absolute terror on his face. And it wasn't because of the force keeping him in place. He looked into the sky, uttering words of fright and crying out.

A sense of dread overcame Jack when he saw the same fear, even if restrained, in all the faces around him, and when someone touched his arm, he barely kept in a yelp.

But it was only a policewoman. Dressed in furs and a large hat that covered her ears, she had the iron symbol of her role as an officer of law attached to the front of the coat.

"You're not from here, yes?" she asked in a heavily accented yet perfectly understandable English.

Relief flooded Jack's muscles, and he relaxed, letting her pull him away from the gathering and toward Roux, who was also easily identifiable as non-local.

"Are you the local pactor?" Roux asked. "We need to know what's going on if we are to help. This is Jack Addison, the Kraken slayer's son, and I am Roux Chat-Bonnes of the Paris Academy for Interdimensional Matters. Have any other venators arrived yet?"

"I'm Patrycja Popova, a member of the local police. What you see here is not violence. They are trying to help this poor man," Popova said, watching as members of the crowd led the still-struggling man down the street. "They're taking him to church. They say there's demons walking among us now," she said, getting a bit paler.

Jack was too dumbstruck to speak at first. "What?" he asked, briefly glancing at Roux, who appeared similarly dumbfounded.

Popova sighed. "This is a mining town. But the greed of the mine owner pushed things too far. I have not seen it with my own eyes, but people say the miners have drilled their way to Hell. So many of them have been afflicted by this recently. They say voices of the damned scream from the pit day and night. Some of the spirits manage to flee and possess the workers like the one you just saw. It's such a hard time for us all."

Roux cleared his throat, and his whiskers twitched. "We are venators. The local pactor issued an open call for a job here. He believes it's an unknown creature that attacks your people."

Popova shook her head. "A beast nobody's seen," she said, but her expression sobered when she focused on something behind Jack.

He spun around, only to freeze. This time it was not the wind, the snow, nor the bitter cold that chilled him to the bone.

A venator's jacket covered a body that lay on the back of a horse-drawn sled, which stopped right in front of them.

Chapter 2

Jack couldn't believe this shit. They'd dragged their luggage through the snow-covered streets in cold that had his nose feeling like an icicle about to fall off, only to find the Pactor's office shut for the day. And since all the writing on the door was in Russian, they had to rely on the help of a friendly local, who told them that throughout the week, the Pactor held office in various places around the area and was only present in Krasnoyarsk from Monday to Tuesday.

What. *WHAT?*

The same helpful stranger informed them that the dead venator had been Moscow's Mikhail Ivanovich Petrov, and someone—or something—had stripped him of his furs, cut his throat, and then left him to die in the frost. Neither Roux nor Jack knew him or of him, but the fact that he'd died trying to capture the mysterious monster in this remote country still left them somber.

The room they'd rented had two beds, and in the night Jack wished for the heat of Roux's body more than ever before. Their lodgings were warm enough, but the frost still penetrated Jack's dreams, taunting him with howls and visions of walking through a snowscape until his feet turned to ice and crumbled under his own weight.

He was relieved to see light peeking through the wooden blinds in the morning, and rolled out of bed, instantly heading to the pitcher of water left on the mantelpiece. The night terrors had left him sweaty, and he was glad to discover that the proximity of the fire prevented the liquid from cooling beyond a pleasant temperature. The room was chilly, so he shed his sleeping shirt and quickly washed with water poured into a basin. He was about done when a glance toward Roux's bed revealed that one of those large green eyes was open, secretly watching him from the pile of covers.

A part of Jack wished to confront him about it, but Roux's previous reactions to flirting had been adverse, and he didn't feel like dealing with another rejection so early in the morning. So he walked to the wooden wardrobe and chose a fresh change of clothes instead, acutely aware of the green gaze following him.

Why not? He could make a show of it.

He dressed, making sure his muscular back was exposed and tense for Roux's viewing pleasure. If it wasn't for the chill, he might have even gotten a bit over-excited about the idea of Roux lusting for him. All this time, he'd been pining for the skittish chat, but he now knew Roux liked him too. They both knew it, even if it was being left unsaid.

Roux only yawned loudly once Jack was dressed. He stretched in the bed, pretending he'd only just woken up. Sneaky chat.

"Morning," Jack said, preparing a simple breakfast of crackers and canned meat, because he didn't want to waste too much time before exploring the area. Days were not long at this time of the year, and he wanted to make use of all the daylight available.

They sat at the table, and Roux opened himself a can of fish. They'd seen murder and supposed ghost possession since their arrival last night, yet there they were, having breakfast as if they were a couple of friends on vacation. Or a pair of lovers on their honeymoon. Jack rather liked the latter idea.

"Will we really be looking for ghosts?" Roux asked, between one bite and another.

Jack snorted. "I don't believe in ghosts. I once met"—fucked—"this scientist who worked in an asylum, and he said that people can go mad if they believe something very strongly. This might be the case here. It's way more probable that the cries those people hear in the mine are made by a creature."

"Let's explore that first then. I'll rent us a sleigh." Roux patted his mouth with a handkerchief when he was done with the oily fish, and Jack stifled a groan at how cute that looked.

The sleigh came with an additional set of furs, which Jack appreciated, since the sunlight didn't help much in terms of temperature. They'd considered going for the cheaper option of a dog sleigh, but canines acted weird around Roux, and on top of that, none of them knew how to work with a pack like that, so they settled on a horse.

Either way, an hour after breakfast, Jack and Roux were buried in piles of coverings and dashing beyond city limits, into the white tundra.

"I wonder if the mine's still working," Jack said.

Despite his initial worries, he wasn't nervous without people around. Petrov had made the mistake of venturing alone late in the day, but the pale landscape ensured Jack would see any danger from miles away.

He didn't want to move anywhere though, since Roux had cozied up to him so nicely in the sleigh. His warmth was the sweetest torture, and Jack was beginning to wonder whether Roux understood the extent to which his presence affected Jack? Even now, his mind kept serving him images of the two of them stopping the sleigh among the piles of snow and fucking under the furry covers for hours, instead of getting on with the job at hand.

There was something about Roux that made Jack tender inside, even more so than his infatuation with Calix had. He cared for Roux in ways that ran deeper. If Roux never wanted him sexually again, Jack would still desperately crave to remain friends, to be close. To become the kind of man Roux thought of with admiration.

When they arrived at the mine, there were hardly any people left on the surface, beyond a couple of guards who claimed most of the workers had taken leave because of a religious festival. Jack wasn't sure if that was really the case, but he and Roux still investigated the scene, walking the edges of the deep hole created with ingenious technology. He wouldn't call the industrial landscape attractive, but the gold mined here certainly would be turned into beautiful final product.

None of the guards knew any languages beyond their own, since hardly any foreigners lived in the area, but Jack managed to ask about the voices coming from below with a set of gestures. The guards confirmed that this was a real phenomenon, but when Roux and Jack used their Addisons around the mining area, the devices showed no activity. It was perplexing, but without means to communicate with anyone beyond their immediate surroundings and daylight slowly dwindling, they realized it was time to go back to town.

Jack was about to climb into the sleigh when something cold hit him on the back of the head. He pulled out the Gouger and turned in one swift move, ready to take on whatever Siberian monster wanted to eat him alive.

But it was only Roux, who winked at him, scooting with another snowball already in his hand.

No. He would have not.

But he absolutely had.

"Someone's in a playful mood," Jack said, grinning at Roux and pushing his gloved hand into the snow as well. He grabbed a fistful in preparation for battle.

The way Roux's lips revealed his teeth in an honest smile made Jack grin in return. "It wasn't me. Must have been the ghost," he said and threw another snowball at Jack, dodging the one thrown his way.

Jack laughed and this time put more effort into aiming. The snowball knocked Roux's hat off, and the chat was so surprised he fell down.

"Got you!" Jack fell to his knees and rubbed some of the frozen fluff into the top of Roux's head.

Roux meowed wildly, but wasn't fighting half as hard as he could have, instead gathering a pile of snow and pushing it under Jack's scarf. "You will never get me alive!"

Jack chewed on his lip and captured Roux's wrists, pinning him to the ground. "You sure about that, Mr. Chat-Bonnes?" he asked, staring straight at Roux. He would not look away.

Roux's gaze became tender, and to Jack's surprise, he arched off the ground and licked along Jack's cheek with his nubbed tongue, sending a shiver of excitement all the way down Jack's spine.

Jack's brain froze, and Roux pushed Jack over, darting away with a laugh.

"You're so easy to distract, Mr. Addison!"

But when Jack was about to get up, fresh snowflakes melted against his skin.

It was only then that he noticed that it had gotten darker not just due to the time, but also because of the thick clouds gathering above. It really was high time to go.

"You'll answer for your crimes another time," he said, wiping the snow from his clothes and climbing into the sleigh. He wouldn't rub his face dry though, still reveling in the lick that awakened the memories of their night together in Transylvania.

Roux smiled, pushing the hat over his ears. He sat under the covers and awaited Jack as if it were his God-given right to have a servant drive the sleigh for him.

Hell, maybe it was, because Jack itched for an opportunity to impress him.

He buried himself in the furs and snapped the reins, prompting the horse to move. The landscape turned dramatic within minutes, and it was only by sheer luck that the horse seemed to know his way around, because with the swirling snow Jack could see barely anything.

Since speaking was too hard with the wind blowing into their faces, he enjoyed Roux's arm loosely entwined with his, and envisioned a world in which they couldn't find their way back. They would have had to return to the haunted mine for shelter and have to use one another's bodily warmth for comfort. Roux would undress and then one thing would lead to another, since friction also meant heat.

"Jack! There's someone ahead!" Roux yelled over the howling wind, pointing to a lone figure in the snow.

Jack pulled on the reins, making the horse slow down and then come to a halt. The shadow form was barely visible from afar, but when it moved closer to the lantern attached to the front of the sleigh, Jack saw the pretty face of a young man with damp red hair sticking to his cheeks. He was dressed in a smooth, cinnamon-hued fur that dragged over the snow at the bottom, but despite the adverse weather, the stranger didn't seem lost or worried.

He said a word in Russian, touching the side of the sleigh with an ungloved hand. The poor thing had to be freezing!

"We don't speak Russian," Jack said, but the youth offered him a brilliant smile.

"Well, hello!" he said as if he hadn't spent a day away from New York City.

Roux's grip on Jack's arm became tense. "What are you doing out here? Who are you? Do you want to come with us? We're headed to Krasnoyarsk."

Jack didn't know if it was the light playing tricks on him, but the stranger had the most amazing golden eyes. "No, thank you so much for your kindness. In fact, I saw your sleigh and wanted to invite the two of you to my home. You're still far away from safety and a snowstorm is coming." The redhead smiled and put his hand on Jack's.

His touch sent a wave of heat through Jack, even though his hands were bare and should've felt frozen. Was his body naturally hot? Was this also why he wasn't blowing out vapor?

"Your house?"

The youth smiled. "I'm Adam. I work here, and my house is just beyond this hill," he said, gesturing into the white landscape that no longer had any features Jack could recognize. "You are both very welcome," he added, reaching out to grab Roux's hand too.

Roux recoiled and shook his head. "If you're fine, we'll be on our way."

Adam looked up into Jack's eyes. "I would hate for you to miss such an opportunity. I long for a chance to show my hospitality to fellow travellers, and I have a large, warm bed by the fire."

Roux got up and hissed at the pretty temptation wrapped in a ginger package. "Are you trying to seduce my friend in the middle of a snowstorm? What is wrong with you? Can't you see he's not interested?"

Wasn't he? Was this what was going on here? Surely not. Why would a handsome young man venture out into the storm in hope of stopping a passing traveller? It made no sense.

"I mean... we are far away from town, and we might get lost in this weather," Jack said, when the stranger squeezed his hand, his touch making it hard to say no.

"My bed is big enough for the two of you," Adam said with a playful smile, and his slightly pinched features became vulpine. But sexy.

"Jack! You cannot be seriously considering this?"

Jack bit his lip, focused on the sexual adventure presented to him on a silver platter. Why would he not consider it? Was he supposed to stay celibate just because Roux couldn't make up his mind whether he wanted them to be lovers or not? Maybe this was a good time to finally push for answers.

"Why wouldn't I? You were the one to tell me we can work together and nothing else," he said in a tone more biting than he'd intended.

He hated to see the hurt in Roux's eyes, but it was too late to take back his words. In a matter of seconds, Roux's expression hardened. "Do it then! Who am I to stand in the way of your fun?"

Jack exhaled. "Roux, come on. Let's go. I'm sure we'll have a nice evening in good company," he said, rubbing the stranger's arm.

Adam nodded with a smile. "I have delicious food waiting on the table, and more friends for you to spend time with."

Jack didn't know how he felt about Roux going off with Adam's 'other friends', but Roux spoke before Jack could ponder it any further.

"I don't want to go anywhere other than back for Krasnoyarsk!" Roux's voice was getting that hissing undertone which came with his anger. "We're not a couple, I have no reason to keep you. Go on, no hard feelings." He gave the fakest smile Jack had ever seen, but it only caused more frustration.

This was clearly a fit of jealousy, and what kind of right did Roux have to that when *he'd been* the one to reject Jack over and over?

"Fine. I'll see you tomorrow," Jack said and left the sleigh, his fingers already entwined with the stranger's.

Roux stared at him as if he'd been stabbed and still couldn't believe it had happened. "I won't be waiting around when I go out again tomorrow, so make sure you're at the inn in the morning." Without waiting for an answer, he took the reins and urged the horse forward so fast Jack tripped on his way off the sleigh.

Oh well. Adam's arms were there to stop him from falling.

Chapter 3

The tall building emerged from the snow like an oasis in the desert. It didn't look like the castles Jack had seen in Europe, but it was one nevertheless. It reminded Jack of a Japanese pagoda. How did a structure like this end up deep in Siberia? Then again, who was Jack to question people's design choices?

"That's... when you told me you owned a house, this wasn't quite what I imagined," Jack said, pulling the coat closer around him as the two of them approached the giant structure, the only landmark in miles of snow-covered taiga.

Adam grinned and reached out for a red rope, which moved a bell somewhere inside, making it chime. "You expected me to be a pauper? Oh, no, no, no, only the best for my guests."

The door opened, and for a second Jack stood there, staring at a young man so similar to Adam, Jack considered that they could be twins—redheaded, pale, with thin smiley lips and golden eyes.

"Welcome," the man said, making a broad, inviting gesture.

It was so warm inside air vaporized when it escaped, and the man wore only a very long banyan of sorts, with images of flowers embroidered into the fabric.

"Um, hello? Jack said, squeezing the other stranger's warm hand. He flinched when Adam pulled off his fur coat, but he wanted to be a polite guest, so he soon removed his boots too and followed the two men down the corridor where a herby scent perfumed the air. Laughter carried over his head, but whether it came from the floor above or one of the rooms adjacent to the dark hallway—he didn't know.

What he did know however, was that this large home in the middle of the tundra was so well heated he was starting to sweat.

Two pairs of footsteps approached them from ahead. The tap of bare soles against a wooden floor was impossible to miss, even though ignoring socks at this time of the year was somewhat strange.

"A guest! A guest!"

Two voices were like an echo, and when the men revealed themselves as more ginger beauties with features just like Adam's, Jack became increasingly bewildered. These two men were as identical as drops of water, their hair, long and glossy, reached far below their shoulders, and their eyes glinted like gold coins.

"Wow. Your mother must have had a tough time handling so many babies at once," Jack said, squeezing the hands of the newcomers, who herded him farther inside, all excited smiles and soft touches. Was the house even big enough to have a straight corridor of such length? Maybe it only appeared smaller from the outside, because he couldn't spot an end to the hallway.

Adam grinned, and Jack was baffled to see that he too had changed into the Eastern-style outfit, though he couldn't tell when that could have happened. Embroidered with elaborate designs and dark red like blood, it got Jack to stare, but he was distracted when one of Adam's brothers moved a section of the wall. Made of paper on a wooden frame, it was more of a divider, but Jack was enchanted when it revealed food piled on a long, yet exceptionally low table.

Everything Jack could have desired, and more, lay in piles. From steaming steaks to a pie that looked just like the one Jack's grandmother used to make. He stumbled inside with his mouth watering already. How did all this get here? To a castle in the Siberian tundra?

Two more pairs of golden eyes glanced at Jack from behind the feast, and the smiles of the kneeling men widened at the sight of him. They all wore the far-East style garments, and everything was so unusual yet fit so well together, Jack was starting to think he was dreaming.

"Welcome!" they said in unison. They too were like Adam's twins.

"W-what is this?" Jack uttered to Adam, who urged him inside.

"Eat up. We've been waiting for a man like you for so long."

"A man like me?" Jack asked, confused even as Adam ushered him to the table and helped him kneel next to the food. "Another American, you mean?"

Adam sighed and slid his hands over Jack's shoulders as his… friends (?), brothers? sat around the table. "An open-minded man."

Jack looked around, not sure what their meaning was, but the fact that all the gazes glinted his way as if he were a prized stallion that had just won a race had his body heating up. He started eating as soon as Adam filled his plate with the food, and while the flavors were recognizable and pleasant, they also felt quite mild, watered-down almost, but he wanted to be a good guest and complimented the meal.

"How did you all get here? What's your business so far away from home?" he asked when one of the young men shifted closer, and the robe slid down his shoulder, revealing an undergarment of red fur. If that was what they all wore beneath their outer clothes, the lack of pants and bare feet made a bit more sense.

Something furry tickled Jack's nape when one of the men inched even closer. "We've been banished, so we had to come all the way here." He pouted, running his fingers over Jack's knee.

"Banished? Like... from the state?" he asked, suddenly conscious of how vastly he was outnumbered. Was this a gang of outlaws who'd left behind the Western plains and made their way here to escape the noose?

"From our home." The smallest of the men said, hypnotizing Jack with his golden eyes.

"We miss the warmth of a man," Adam whispered and kissed Jack's neck from behind.

They weren't vampires, were they?

Jack laughed, weirded out, no matter how exciting this was. "There's six of you. Might be a bit too much for just me to handle."

Adam laughed, and when he pulled Jack back, pillows appeared under them as if out of nowhere. "Oh, you'll do just fine. As long as... you really are open-minded." He smiled and pulled open the banyan revealing the fur outfit underneath.

Jack did a double take.

It wasn't an outfit--the guy's skin was covered with silky fur. He looked from Adam to his friends, noticing a fat red tail trailing from under one of the robes to swipe the floor. It was so lush, so thick and shiny Jack felt the urge to bury his face in it, but Adam and another of his brothers helped him up and led him away from the table.

Jack had barely eaten anything yet felt so sated from the couple of bites he'd had, as if he'd been dining like a king for an entire week. Just a second ago, he'd been worried about something. What had that been? His mind was too hazy to think straight.

"We have all the time in the world." Adam let out a high-pitched giggle, and when he hugged Jack from behind, his fur pressed against Jack's skin.

When did Jack undress? Did it matter?

What mattered was that there were three more pretty boys waiting for him on a bed of pillows and red furs. He didn't remember how he'd gotten there, but when the young men pulled on his hands, he fell into the sheets, overwhelmed by the sensation of the soft, warm pelt tickling his thighs as Adam moved between his legs, pretty face smiling when his eyes zeroed in on Jack's stiff cock.

There was something Jack was forgetting, somewhere beyond the thin walls that somehow conserved heat.

But he couldn't remember, his mind hazy as if he'd gotten inebriated without drinking.

The ginger fur triggered his memory, but when all nine of the foxy creatures touched him in their nest of pillows, he had a hard time remembering. Thick fox tails rolled around him like fluffy snakes, tongues licking up his neck from both sides.

Maybe he'd died and gone to heaven? The creatures had white bellies, but the fur on their backs was coarser. They smelled of pine and something sweet he couldn't grasp, but it didn't matter when one of them licked down Jack's stomach.

He let out a low groan, pulling one of the identical faces closer and drowning in the pleasure of not knowing and not remembering. Nine pairs of eyes glinted in the dusky light of the bedroom, and as hands with deceptively sharp nails caressed him all over, he started to drown in the sheets until one of the boys stretched along Jack's body so exquisitely he finally felt like moving.

Rolling on top of the beautiful man, Jack pushed his thighs open and moaned when the long tail caressed his knee. He laughed when one of the gloriously furry creatures sucked on his toe, but the one under Jack sniffed him with a frown.

A scowl twisted Jack's face. He had been out and about all day. Maybe they should have started… whatever this was—with a hot bath in a tub for ten, which those wealthy young men surely owned.

"You love another," the creature growled, his face becoming more vulpine as it contorted in a sneer. "He's marked by another!"

All eight heads lifted, eyes pointing at him like daggers. "Another?"

"Another?" Jack uttered, sitting up, his vision hazy at the edges as the nine handsome men focused on him like harpies. Their eyes shone in the dusky light, faces narrow, with pointy noses.

"Someone has marked you. You're of no use to us!" Adam hissed and pushed Jack back to the pillows, but instead of soft down, his naked back met a pile of snow.

There was nothing around him but endless white, all the way to a distant line of trees. No foxy boys, no castle, and his stomach rumbled as if he hadn't had any food at all. He sat butt-naked in the snow, shivering already.

A wolf howled in the distance.

Chapter 4

There was no color to the landscape. No means of recognizing where Krasnoyarsk was. Jack could see no lights, and heard nothing but the wind howling as it clashed with his bare skin. The hardened snow had started melting around Jack's feet already, creating a layer of cold so painful he let out a moan, helplessly stepping in one direction, then another as his brain slowly got back to normal. Even his eyeballs felt as if they were about to freeze.

Once the intoxication-like haze dispersed, he was left with nothing to protect him from the adverse weather, and with a growing sense of despair, because he was positive he'd die here and nobody would even find his body. By the time spring came, his flesh would have been devoured by hungry animals, leaving only bone and no identification.

He'd be lost forever, before leaving his mark on the world.

And he couldn't have that. He was an Addison, the son of a resourceful and resilient family. He had too much to lose to simply give up. He briefly toyed with an idea taken from a fantastical play he'd watched with Drake in London. Its main characters were stuck on an arctic moon and survived by burrowing inside a dead animal, but with no animals in sight, he quickly gave up on that plan and decided to make use of the one resource there was plenty of.

Snow.

Didn't inhabitants of remote areas in the northern hemisphere use it for making shelter? What an ingenious idea in such harsh climate!

With his feet already numb, he wasn't keen on giving his hands the same treatment, but at this rate all his extremities were at risk of falling off, so he pushed his fingers into the snow. It was hard like a meringue with too much sugar, and getting through the crust was so painful that, by the time Jack attempted to form the snow into a block, he uttered a sob of helplessness. Despite the cold, he was feeling oddly warm inside, and that could mean only one thing. He was surely dying.

The snort of a horse made him turn around frantically. He thought it was only a hallucination at first, but when the same noise could be heard again, he waved his hands in the air, even though the snowstorm confused him to the point where he wasn't certain where the sound had come from. "Help! Over here!"

A dark sleigh emerged from the blizzard, and Jack was so desperate to get closer he forced his aching limbs to move.

He couldn't even feel his toes at this point, but the will to live propelled him forward, and he screamed out, heated by sheer desperation. "I'm lost! Please!"

"Jack!" Roux's familiar voice cut through the roaring wind. Jack was so happy to hear him he could've cried. "I'm coming!"

Roux's whip swished through the air, forcing the horse to run faster. When the sleigh finally reached Jack, his teeth rattled so hard he couldn't speak, but the warm fur Roux wrapped around his shoulders brought relief.

Roux pulled him into the seat and started rubbing his arms, with the most caring and desperate expression on his face. Jack had a strange flashback to the time they'd first met and he couldn't yet understand the expressions or the body language of a chat. Now he could read every little twitch of Roux's whiskers, and he longed for their touch on his cheek.

The few minutes spent in the freezing cold had left a toll on Jack, but the heat of Roux's body, the fast massage, and layers of coverings made him feel more secure, even though his teeth still clattered. "You're here, right? This isn't another illusion?" Jack demanded, clutching Roux's wrist.

Roux urged the horse to move through the snow, but dove deeper under the covers. This time, his ears flattened and he wouldn't look into Jack's eyes. "Yes, I'm here. I always am."

"Thank you... I thought I'd die. I thought—" Jack buried his face in Roux's neck and whimpered, absorbing the high heat of the chat's body. His thoughts were still chaotic, but the fact that despite their argument earlier, Roux had chosen to come back for him was already warming him inside out.

Roux sighed as deeply as if the weight of the whole world were on his shoulders, but he didn't avoid Jack's touch. Once they reached the road, Jack spotted the blurry lights of Krasnoyarsk ahead.

"Adam... he... had these eight guys there, but it had to be an illusion, and they all had fox bodies, and pulled me into—"

Roux snapped at him. "I don't want to hear it!"

Jack blinked. "What? Why? That venator they found frozen to death? The miners claiming to see things that can't be there... Adam must be the creature we're looking for!"

Roux grumbled, but his arm felt firm against Jack's back. "That venator hadn't been fucked to death."

This time, heat was definitely back, at least in Jack's face. "They said something strange. They left me when they smelled someone else on me. Told me I was *marked*," he said loudly, so Roux could hear him despite the wind.

Roux shrugged and when he looked away, a snowflake dropped onto his nose in the cutest way. It stayed there for a second before melting. He rubbed his eye and sniffed. "Who would have done that?"

"That's what I'm asking, Roux," Jack said, swallowing as he pushed even closer. "I can only think of one person who'd touched me recently. Why would you do that when you're making it so clear just how much you don't want me?"

Roux's breathing got faster, and he hid his face in his hands. "Because I'm in love with you, idiot!"

Even the snow blown into Jack's face couldn't have cooled the heat of his skin. His heart swelled, and he squeezed Roux's hand harder. "I'm the idiot? You rejected me! You told me it's not gonna happen!"

"Because all you want to do is go around screwing other creatures!" The complaint sounded like a mewl, and when Roux looked at him, fur damper by the minute, his big green eyes were tearing up. "I will not be another notch on your bedpost!"

For fuck's sake.

"But you're not. I've been chasing after you for how many years now? Three? What do you expect me to do? Stay chaste in hope you might one day invite me to your bed after saying no every single time I tried flirting?" Yet despite his annoyance, Jack's heart wouldn't stop beating fast as he replayed the word love in his head.

"I... I find it hard to trust." Roux leaned into Jack under the cover of furs, and Jack couldn't help but accept him for much more than his warmth.

He tightened his hold around Roux and rubbed his face against the furry cheek, which was now damp from the snow. His heart beat faster by the second as the meaning behind their conversation sank deeper into his flesh.

"But you have to. If you want to be with me, you'll need to trust me."

Roux rubbed his fuzzy ear with a whine. "I had this human boyfriend when I was at the Academy, and I was in love with him, and we had sex all the time, even wilder when I was in heat, but then it turned out he was telling all his friends about how things are 'with a chat', as if he didn't even see me as a person with feelings. I was so ashamed he told everyone about our intimacy, as if I was some novelty. No one ever wants me for me."

Jack pushed his hand from under the furs to pet Roux's head. He couldn't imagine anyone treating Roux as only a novelty. He wasn't just an exotic beauty. He was fierce, brave, smart, and loyal, despite his difficult personality. But maybe the other creatures Jack had fucked just for the sake of it had other qualities, too. Maybe he just hadn't seen them? Maybe he never got close enough to learn all there was to know about them?

Was he a bad person?

"That's not true," he said softly.

Roux pressed into Jack's embrace, leaving no room for the chilling wind. "I can't go through that again, I just can't. I'm stupid to fall for men like you, but I can't help it. I can see you want all this adventure with other creatures, and that wouldn't work for me."

Jack exhaled, hugging Roux even more tightly. "I'm sorry you had to go through that. But you know how much I enjoy your company. You make me open up, and we might be so different, but we understand one another. I feel like nobody gets me the way you do," he whispered.

Roux purred and pressed his forehead under Jack's chin. It didn't even matter that he was wet. Soon enough, Jack would take him to the inn, they'd warm by the fire and finally clear up all the misunderstandings.

Roux was in love with him. How amazing, how undeserved, how unimagined. Jack kissed the cold ear as they drove through the outskirts of Krasnoyarsk.

"Are you telling me you won't miss tentacles and centaur cocks?"

Jack could've cried with joy. He squeezed Roux and kissed the wet fur. So he was impulsive, and he liked novelty, but Roux's presence affected him in a way no one else's did. "I'm more interested in those nubs you have," he whispered.

Roux snorted but pulled Jack closer. "You're lucky they're not hooks after all." He licked Jack's cheek, sending hot shivers down his body.

Jack couldn't wait any longer. He trailed gentle kisses along Roux's jaw and finally licked the front of his mouth, practically melting into the warmth of his body. Roux was a challenge, but that also meant Jack would never get bored of being around him. "Only your words can hurt me."

The horse knew exactly where to take them, so Jack focused on Roux and the things they'd do once safely tucked under covers. If Jack's kitty needed safety and reassurance to trust, Jack would happily spend his life making sure Roux got it from him.

The touch of warm pads against his chest made him want to turn around into the snowstorm so that they wouldn't have to face getting out and walking into the inn. He wanted Roux now.

"I take it, you'll warm me up once we're in our room?" Jack asked, nuzzling Roux's cute little nose.

The shy smile he got in return didn't fool Jack. He'd seen Roux writhe and ask for cock. Jack had a sexpot on his hands and wouldn't be letting go of it until they were both sticky.

Their horse stopped in front of the inn, but they didn't get to just hurry upstairs and dive into bed.

"Jack Addison and Roux Chat-Bonnes?" boomed a heavily-accented voice.

Jack groaned, peeking from under the furs when he saw two men staring at him. Both wore similar outfits, which instantly designated them as outsiders. Instead of donning furs, like the locals did, they wore jackets layered under thick cloaks and wide, pleated pants gathered at the knees with wraps that went all the way into their boots. The wide, vaguely bowl-shaped hats and hoods that also covered their shoulders cast shadows on the men's faces, but Jack was stunned to realize that one of them was at least 6'5".

"Yes?" he uttered, covering his body with the fur to spare himself the indignity of strangers seeing him naked.

Chapter 5

This was Jack's worst nightmare. Singled out while naked in a public place, and now sweating into the thick fur Roux had covered him with. Should he excuse himself? Lie that he needed to take a piss? No, that wouldn't work. Everyone would see that he had no shoes on if he left the sleigh.

So he sat in place, buried in the pile of animal skins.

The shorter of the men left the shadows and walked into the area lit by a streetlamp. He was East Asian, in his thirties, and there was a bold white kanji at the front of his cloak, though Jack wouldn't have been himself if he hadn't noticed the spear and sword attached to his back. What did he want with him and Roux?

Not knowing what to do, he pushed his hand out of the fur and raised it in greeting.

"There's no time to explain. We need to hunt down the fox before it can attack anyone else," the man said, and showed off the iron emblem all venators carried on their persons for situations where their identity needed proving. Each depicted the silhouette of a man entangled with a dragon, as a reference to the legendary St. George, as well as the carrier's name and *alma mater*. "I am Namikawa Genta and this is Akito of the Wolf Lake."

Akito choose this moment to emerge from the shadow, and Jack soon realized why he was so tall and broad. Akito, while dressed the same way as Genta, was a giant werewolf. And the werewolves he'd had sampled in Bohemia had nothing on this guy in terms of size.

"I—uh… are they who they're saying they are?" Jack whispered so quietly only Roux could hear.

The green eyes narrowed, but while Roux's whiskers twitched in annoyance, he answered in a low voice. "Can't you see the symbol of the venator academy in Kyoto on their clothes?"

Uh-oh. Jack knew that there were venators in Asia too—because there were venators everywhere—but he never paid much mind to information about creature-related activity in places where he didn't plan working. Would it bite him in the ass now?

"We've never heard of a fox emerging all the way in Siberia," Genta continued, "but we need to capture and kill the beast as soon as possible. The locals have no idea what they're dealing with."

Roux got up, and while he was in the sleigh, he didn't appear that much shorter than the werewolf. "We are ready to do the job. Explain to us all you know about the creature."

Was Jack missing something? He didn't get why a fox, even a rabid one, would require the involvement of four venators. But Roux seemed to know what he was doing, so he didn't reveal his doubts, out of fear of looking like even more of an idiot. He should have paid more attention in school, but it had been so easy not to when none of the teachers were willing to fail the Kraken's son.

"Yeah, I'll just… go to the room real quick," he said, pulling the fur tightly around him as he rose.

Akito's muzzle twitched, and Jack felt the back of his neck heat up. Could a werewolf smell that he didn't have any clothes on? Instead, Akito leaned to Roux and unceremoniously nuzzled his cheek, sniffing loudly.

Roux lost all his professional composure, and pushed at the werewolf with a hiss.

Jack was ready to rise to Roux's defence if necessary, even though he was underdressed and didn't want to confront a werewolf with his cock out. "Do you have to do that? Chats have a big need for personal space!"

Genta ignored Jack's protest. "Why are you barefoot? Oh. Did you *meet* the fox? They will steal everything you've got, the bastardly creatures. And it must be here for the gold."

"I was… stretching my legs. I'll just put on my hunting clothes," Jack mumbled when his mind finally connected the dots. All those pretty boys, and the thick red tails… "Shapeshifters," he uttered, stunned. Just like Nessie. Of course.

Genta approached with a serious expression that made Jack even more self-conscious about his lack of clothes. "They can be. They can appear as male or female, but they can rarely hide their tails. There's only one here, but it's powerful, can create illusions, and appear in more forms. Where did you see it last time?"

Jack pointed to the whiteness consuming the buildings down the street. In this weather, they might not even be able to follow the road beyond the city limits. "Close to the mine."

Akito hummed, and then spoke in an inhumanly low voice. "It must be who possessed the miners. We need to chase it down immediately. The people of this country don't understand the danger they're in."

Jack was fuming. How could he have been so stupid? The fox had messed with his head! "Motherfucker. I'm gonna rip all the fur out of his tail."

Roux nodded. "It's a kitsune. I've read about them. Jack, you need to get dressed, and we have to track this creature fast. Akito should be able to catch its scent if we hurry."

Jack groaned, resuming his walk of shame into the inn. He was still freezing after the time spent completely bare in the blizzard, but there was no chance of Roux losing time to warm him up in this situation.

He wasn't a vengeful guy, but leaving him to die? So not on. The fox… kitsune would pay!

He ran back outside within five minutes, silently mourning the warm fur coat the malevolent creature had stolen from him. Maybe once they captured this vicious monster, he could get it back? This time, he took the Gouger with him, and vowed to never let the legendary sword out of sight.

Akito was far too heavy to board the sleigh, so he walked beside them.

"So… are there many werewolf venators in Japan?" Roux asked, eying Akito suspiciously. Ha. Was he jealous?

"Several," Akito said, breaking into a run to catch up with the sleigh. The blizzard didn't seem to bother him in the slightest.

Genta nodded. "There's nothing scarier for a fox than a werewolf."

Jack, who once again wrapped himself with fur in the hope of retaining at least some warmth, looked at the stranger. "Is there anything else we need to know?"

"Those creatures have been present in Japan for hundreds of years. There's more of them now, and those which are bad, like this one, wreak havoc on people's lives, just for the fun of it. It is fortunate that we have centuries of experience, and know how to deal with them. Unlike the locals here," Genta said, holding on to his hat as they drove against the wind

Akito, who had to jog slower than he could, in order not to overtake the sleigh once they'd left the city, spoke next. "They've only recently ventured beyond the Japanese archipelago. This one traveled on a ship to China. We've been tracking it from there."

Roux frowned, and Jack could just imagine his ears twitching under the woollen hat. "So there's no interdimensional crack around here? Maybe that's why the addison couldn't find anything amiss in the mine."

Genta shook his head. "It's just this one, and it's already affected the lives of so many people. It's a disgrace we let that happen. But maybe in greater numbers, we can entrap it."

Akito let out a yelp and sped up, dropping to all fours and leaving the sleigh behind. The blizzard briefly swallowed him whole, but by the time they reached his kneeling form, he was back on his feet, toothy mouth stretched into a smile. "I can sense him. Follow me!"

Soon enough, they were back at the mine, and this time all the administrative structures were blurred by the onslaught of snow, with only a handful of lamps illuminating the darkness.

Genta nodded. "The foxes do love gold."

Roux jumped into the snow. "But we've been here, and found nothing."

"That's because he was waiting for us outside. Maybe that's where it normally hides," Jack grumbled, forcing himself to leave the warm furs.

The lights at the gate that led straight for the huge opening in the ground were beckoning them from afar, but Akito released a sound that made Genta lean out of the sleigh. "What is it?"

"I smell death."

Great. Just fantastic.

Jack bit his lips, shuddering when he spotted a lone form in the snow, right under a large sign that was partially covered in ice. Roux slowed down, and as they passed by the body, the amount of blood that colored the snow around it proved there was no point in checking for a pulse.

It was one of the guards they'd met earlier.

Roux sighed deeply and sniffed the air. "I think I can sense it as well."

Akito nodded and rushed forward, urging Genta into the darkness beyond the gate, toward the shaft. "It's nearby."

Jack stepped behind the nearby hut in an attempt to escape the punishing wind. While Genta had assured him the kitsune were to blame for all the strange things happening in the area, he still felt uneasy about going down that deep shaft. What if some of the rumors about this being the gateway to hell were true after all?

"Where? How do we kill it?"

Genta pointed at a large tool shed with a snow-covered roof. "You don't, it's too dangerous. Akito is proficient at it. Stay there and wait. Be on the lookout."

Roux groaned. "I've read about kitsune, and according to my textbooks you can kill them the way you would any physical creature. Is that not accurate?"

Akito huffed. "Maybe, but they're tricksters. You have no idea what they can do, so observe and blow this if you spot him." He passed Jack an instrument that resembled a hunting horn.

Jack glared at it, then at the imposing werewolf, who'd dragged him out of the proximity of a warm bed and Roux, for the sole purpose of being a glorified lookout. He was Jack Addison. And he could have dealt with the issue himself if he knew what was going on.

But he also really didn't want to enter the mine, so he accepted his role without arguing. "Will it not hear it?"

Genta shook his head. "No. Only werewolves can hear the sound it makes."

"So... like a dog whistle?" Jack asked, breathing in the frosty scent carried by the air. He was glad he didn't have hair on his face, because the fur around Akito's muzzle had turned into icicles.

Akito growled at him, angered to the point where Genta had to pull him back. "Coming from a man who has the hots for a cat?"

Roux bristled. "A chat."

Jack stared. "What?"

Genta wagged his finger at Jack. "Akita told me you smell of him all over."

Jack shrugged and grabbed Roux's hand, regretful that they were both wearing gloves. "Is that a problem for you? Because it isn't for us. Right, Roux?" he asked, suddenly longing for Roux to confirm his words, not retreat like he had last time, back in Romania.

Roux looked to the snow under their feet, but squeezed Jack's hand and stepped closer. "We will look out for the kitsune."

Genta snorted, but he and Akito soon became blurry figures in the snowstorm. Maybe it was for the better that Jack didn't have to go into that godawful hole. Since the encounter with Chad's mother, he didn't particularly like caves and tunnels.

"You think the other guard is still alive?" Jack asked, somewhat disappointed with Roux's rebuffal. But he didn't want to be too pushy, and led the way to the wooden hut. Still, Roux wouldn't let go of his hand.

"I don't have high hopes. I can't hear any movement around." He took off his hat, revealing the pretty ears. "Nope. Nothing."

Jack opened the hut and sighed when hot air blew into his face. The fireplace buzzed, and he even spotted some food laid out on the table. The two of them had definitely got the longer end of the stick, even if there wasn't much glory in hunkering down in warmth and watching the scenery through cracks in the blinds. For now though, the sight of the flames lighting up Roux's beautiful, smooth fur was much more absorbing than open cans and bread.

"So... uh... you're not ready to be open with other people?" Jack asked, unable to wait until forever for an answer.

Roux's eyes snapped up at him. "What? No. I... I would like that. I just... you surprised me. It's been a while since I've been with anyone. And your father? You're not afraid of him finding out?"

Jack's mouth dried, but he shrugged and approached a samovar, which, as expected, contained deliciously strong tea. He had a sip and squeezed the glass, watching Roux, who peeked outside through the wooden blinds.

"They wouldn't tell him."

Roux stayed silent but then hugged Jack from behind and pressed his head to Jack's shoulder. "This feels so good. I wish we weren't so conscientious, and stayed at the inn."

Jack snorted and put his arms around Roux. He had the loveliest ears, and Jack playfully pulled on one with his lips.

"Right? We're Genta's transport. I think I'd be so much more useful if we were alone at the inn."

Roux's eyes were like two green pools of liquified jade when he stared up at Jack. "Probably. But we're good venators right?" He nudged Jack's nose with his own, which was wet and cold.

Was this really Jack's reality now? Roux finally in his arms? Or was he once again dreaming?

"You're cold," he said, offering the steaming cup. He tightened his grip on Roux and rested his chin on his head, knowing that he wasn't doing what he'd promised Genta and Akito. But there was no one here to judge him if even Roux believed their role ridiculous.

Roux carefully drank from the cup, and watching him gather the liquid on his tongue made Jack realize how much he still had to learn about his...

new boyfriend? His heart fluttered from even thinking about Roux in that context.

Roux pulled out of the hug. "And now I need to very un-romantically, go pee. Back in a second."

Jack scratched the back of his head. "You sure? Maybe I should watch your back?" he asked with a chuckle, leaning against the wall. At this point, he was getting so hot he might remove some of his outer clothes.

"Jack, we're just establishing a relationship. You're not going to watch me pee." Roux chuckled and punched Jack's arm on his way out.

Jack pulled his teeth over his lips and watched him walk out into the punishing snow. It was impossible to describe how badly he wanted to be at the inn. But he wasn't, so he might as well make the best of it.

Waiting for Roux, he removed his coat, gloves, and hat, and rummaged through a cupboard containing supplies. Since the second guard wasn't likely to return, he decided to help himself to some of the food and soon found a good-looking can of sardines for Roux.

Jack was getting antsy when his chat finally came back, stomping loudly to get the snow off his shoes.

He squinted at Jack in a surprisingly seductive fashion, and once the door was closed again, he didn't walk to Jack, he strutted. "They will take forever in that mine shaft. How about we entertain ourselves with shafts of our own?"

Jack almost choked on the tea. "What, now? You naughty chat," he said, and his gaze instantly gravitated down the slender chest that was now covered by a damp fur coat.

"Yes, now. I can't resist you." Roux purred and ran his hands up Jack's neck and to his cheeks. This was a tad unusual for him, but then again Jack had only spent one night with him, so what did he know of Roux's sexual temperament? On the other hand, it was quite unusual for Roux to be so reckless. He wasn't the type of guy who'd be fine getting caught in the act.

"Like you can't resist those?" he asked, grabbing the sardines.

Roux offered him a wide smile, those sexy hips already rocking against Jack, as if he were in heat again. "My favorite!"

They weren't. His favorite ones were from France, and the packaging was completely different. Jack swallowed, convinced Roux's fur was redder than usual. "What was that brand you really enjoyed?"

Roux laughed and lowered his mouth to Jack's neck. "It's fish. I love them all, silly."

Unease danced down Jack's back, but as the soft fur tickled his jaw, he glanced at their shadow on the wall, and saw it.

A thick tail sticking out from under Roux's coat.

His mouth went dry, and he slowly leaned back, his gaze trained on the green eyes that looked deceptively like Roux's. The horn. He still had it attached to his belt.

"How about some tea first?" he asked, but when the kitsune reached out with a hiss, Jack spun it around and flattened it against the wooden wall. He blew the horn before he could consider his own safety.

Chapter 6

"What did you do to Roux? Where is he?" Jack roared, gripping the kitsune's wrists with all his strength. Shapeshifter or not, he had no right to Roux's form. And where was Roux himself? Had he been assaulted and left in the snow?

Was he dead?

Dread clutched at Jack's throat like a spiky collar.

"Where is he!?" He shoved the kitsune against the wall, but the creature chuckled, as if it felt no fear whatsoever.

"Temper, temper. Unless you want that lovely body hurt."

Jack stiffened, lost in the nuance of the kitsune's words. "Is it his? Or are you just impersonating him?" he uttered, but didn't break his hold on the slender wrists. If it was a case of possession, was Roux still there? Aware of what was going on yet locked inside his own body? What a horrific thing to do to another being.

The kitsune smirked with Roux's mouth, turning his head back almost too far for it to be comfortable. "Why don't you smash my head in and find out?"

Jack licked his lips, trying to control his breathing but didn't let go, despite his fingers going numb. If Akito was to be believed, the kitsune was too powerful an enemy for Jack, yet it wasn't going for the kill just yet, instead playing with Jack like a cat with a captured mouse.

He wanted to ask the monster why it was attacking people for no reason, but how could an answer to that question make sense? "Roux, if you're in there, let me know!"

The creature let out a choked sound, and one of Roux's claws bit into Jack's skin, but his face went lax again immediately after that stifled attempt.

Jack couldn't believe the horror of this situation, and flinched when the feline face scowled in an expression that was distinctly vulpine

"He can't do a thing against me, human! If you want him to live, get out of here and never come back!"

Jack bit the inside of his cheek until the tang of blood spread over his tongue. "What about him? I'm not leaving him with you!"

The kitsune opened its mouth, but then its eyes went wide, and it shoved Jack away with a single push, as if he were a scarecrow caught up in a tornado. Jack crashed into the table and fell, with a loaf of bread rolling onto his head, but before the kitsune could have opened the blinds on the other side of the house, the door burst open, and Akito's giant form squeezed inside with a growl worthy of a grizzly bear.

The kitsune hissed, its eyes glowing, limbs tense as if they were about to snap.

"Stop! He's possessed Roux! Don't hurt him!"

But Akito didn't listen and charged at the kitsune. Instead of biting its head off though, he pinned Roux's body to the floor and… licked its face.

And licked it again.

Genta stood in the open doorway with a deep frown, as if the snow blowing past him caused him no discomfort. "Don't worry, Jack. The fox won't be able to stand this for long. They hate werewolves."

Jack let out a panicked chuckle as he scrambled to his feet, nervously watching the twitching tail. "What's he gonna do? Lick him to death?"

Genta shushed Jack with a gesture.

"Enough. Stop," the Kitsune moaned in Roux's voice, and seeing him thrash under the werewolf was a call back that worried Jack and made him deeply uncomfortable.

The werewolf wasn't going to… fuck Roux, was he?

Akito ripped open the front of Roux's coat and licked down Roux's neck, triggering a pang of jealousy that kept Jack on edge.

"Get off, you fleabag!" Roux yelled, uselessly pushing at Akito.

"I'm only letting this go so far!" Jack grabbed his sword, huffing with anger. "This surely can't be the only way!"

But Roux's meow suddenly turned into a yelp, and an elongated, narrow muzzle rose above the familiar face like a ghostly mask. Jack stepped back, shocked to see the vulpine features, which was completely different from Adam's. Smoke filled the air when the kitsune bolted, but it fell flat on its face when Akito grabbed its lush tail. Genta moved with the grace of a ballet dancer and, before Jack could have even thought about attacking, cut the fox's head in a clean swipe of his sword.

Blood gushed from the stump above the kitsune's shoulders, spraying the wall, but also Akito, Gento, and even Roux, who lay still with his hands pressing at his mouth.

Jack knelt by his side and pulled him into his arms, feeling as if they'd been at the brink of an ugly finale, yet had managed to flee death at the very last moment.

"Are you okay? Talk to me!"

Roux coughed, his green eyes dazed. "Jack! Jack! He wanted to kill you! He would have done it with my hands." He could barely catch his breath but still reached out for Jack with the bloodstained paws. The reddish fur was damp on Jack's cheeks, but he leaned into the touch, rubbing his nose against Roux's and hugging him even tighter. He'd been such an idiot. He should have gone out with him, no matter how awkward it would have been.

But at least they were both safe now.

"It's okay. We're okay."

Roux's arms were stronger than they seemed when he embraced Jack's neck. "What if I killed you?" he whispered with a trembling voice. "If we work together, wouldn't this be a constant risk?"

It was such a touching question Jack went silent for a while, just petting Roux's bloodstained fur and looking at the features which were again Roux's own. "Better you than someone else, right?" Jack whispered, pressing a kiss to his lover's angular brow. Holding Roux like this gave him a sense of peace. A sense that his life was finally slotting into place in this half-abandoned goldmine, over a strange creature's dead body.

"Don't joke like that." Roux rubbed his face against Jack's head, effectively massaging the kitsune's blood into him, but Jack was past caring. All he craved was Roux's affection, so getting dirty was hardly a big price to pay.

Genta wrapped the kitsune's head in waxed paper, as if it were meat for his dinner, and then stuffed it into a bag. "We have a long trip ahead of us. Jack, Roux, thank you for your help."

Jack grinned, even though they'd hardly done much to stop the fox. "It's always Jack Addison's pleasure to do his duty. Do we share the reward four ways?" He tried not to snort when he looked at Akito's serious expression, because all he could think was his 'fourway' with werewolves.

"No," Genta said. "We'll be on our way. Do whatever you wish with the rest of the body."

Jack glanced at the nine fluffy tails, which he could now see as clearly as he saw Genta and Akito, and imagined a grand winter coat for Chad.

But no. The concept was a tiny bit too grim.

Jack swallowed, his heart fluttering. The reward for the monster's capture was quite substantial, which meant that Roux wouldn't have to worry about money for a while. For once, Jack was more than happy to share the cash with someone else. Jack squeezed him to his chest once more, wishing they could be alone and speak frankly, with no one to hear.

"I'm sorry. I'll never leave you out of my sight again," he whispered, rubbing his face in the blood-stained fur. He kicked the body when Genta and Akito left.

That was for leaving him alone in the snow.

And he didn't even get his fur coat back.

Roux only spoke once the door shut behind the other venators. "Even when I go pee?"

Jack snorted. If Roux's sense of humor was back, he couldn't have been hurt too badly. He glanced into the soulful green eyes, marveling at the beauty of their narrow pupils as he squeezed the small, furry hands.

"Especially when you pee. I'm always up for watching your pants open."

It was such a freeing experience to openly flirt with the object of his adoration without the constant rebuffal, to see a smile and have his affections reciprocated. He was the luckiest man alive. Taming a chat was hard work, but it had only taken him four years.

"Why do I always fall for the awful ones?" Roux chuckled, and rolled his head over Jack's shoulder.

Jack kissed Roux's soft, furry neck, overcome by the sense of absolute joy. "I won't be awful. I'm all in. I'll be there when you need me. I'll have your back. I promise I'll make you happy."

Roux stilled and took a deep breath. So lovely, so soft, so smart and funny, and everything Jack could ever want. If Roux needed security, Jack would spend his life proving to him that he was safe in this relationship.

"You mean that? We'll make things work?" Roux gave Jack's lips a tiny lick and made him chuckle when he pushed on his forehead with his own until they looked straight into each other's eyes.

"We will. We're like… you know, pieces of a two-piece puzzle," he said, not particularly proud of his metaphor but confident it communicated the right things nevertheless. He wanted Roux. No, he *needed* him.

He was sure Roux would also come around when it came to Chad, and then they could go on adventures together, maybe settle in London one day, be neighbors with Drake. He only hoped there wouldn't be a custody battle over his spider-baby.

"Let's go wash all this blood off and collect our reward." Roux nuzzled Jack once more and smiled.

Oh yes, Jack couldn't wait to undress Roux, wash that blood off him and fuck all night. Roux wanted him just because.

Chapter 7

The heat of the bathing room was a dream come true after leaving behind the cold night air, and the blizzard that had felt more like an onslaught of bullets whenever snowflakes hit bits of bare skin. But now that outer clothing had been shed, and they entered the small space with a buzzing fire and plenty of hot water in a copper tub, Jack could finally relax.

He exhaled, pulling Roux closer as soon as he'd removed his heavy snow boots. "As beautiful as it is around here, I'm never returning in winter."

The bathing room was meant for communal use, but they'd paid for an hour of privacy at Roux's prudish request. Jack didn't mind though, as he was happy to accommodate his kitty. And the reward money they'd accepted made this little extravagance not that big of a deal. They'd earned this, and if he also got to see Roux naked, he'd write this night off as a win-win kind of situation.

"Tell me about it. My pads feel like they're about to fall off," Roux said, but to Jack's dismay, he pulled a wooden divider between the two steaming tubs. Each of those could easily fit both of them, so Jack had assumed they'd be bathing together.

"What are you doing?" he asked, rubbing the dried blood that congealed in the fur on Roux's cheek.

Roux groaned and looked away. "Bathing is very intimate for a chat. Please don't make it harder than it needs to be."

Jack laughed, trying to not let his confusion show too much. "It's an intimate 'act' for everyone. That's the point. Are we not on that... level yet?" he asked while his brain already screamed that it likely meant no sex too.

Roux sighed and took off his shirt, then proceeded to put his forearm into the water. When he pulled it out, the usually fluffy fur stuck to the skin underneath, and Jack couldn't help but burst out with laughter.

"See?" Roux huffed. "This is what I'm saying. I'll look stupid. Better just not."

Wait. No.

He needed to take his laughter back!

"Oh, come on! Every guy looks silly when their hair is wet," Jack said and dunked his head into the hot water. It was a shock to his system, but when he emerged, sending water everywhere, he couldn't miss the twitching of Roux's whiskers. "See?"

Roux ran his hand through Jack's hair, his eyes softening. Having the freedom to touch Roux after so many years of pining for him overwhelmed all of Jack's senses and made him impatient.

"But you have to promise you won't laugh anymore. It's really embarrassing. I usually just comb it, but not with all the blood in my fur, that won't be enough."

Jack stepped closer and settled his hands on Roux's slender hips. When he was growing up, he wouldn't have imagined in his wildest dreams that he'd fall for anything other than a human male. Not in a million years, but Roux had swept him off his feet with that agile tail.

"I promise. We're together now. Why wouldn't we help each other bathe?"

Roux's shy smile was what cloud nine was made of. "I suppose so." He leaned closer and rubbed his dirty fur against Jack's cheek.

Jack breathed in the coppery smell, itching to once again sense the pure scent of fur and pheromones. Roux's whiskers tickled his jaw, and he squeezed him more tightly, smiling when their heartbeats synchronized.

"Finally."

Roux purred, and if that wasn't the purest sound Jack had ever heard, he didn't know what was. He'd love to fall asleep to it with Roux in his arms. "I really thought I'd just be another conquest for you."

He reached to Jack's pants, wanting to unbutton them, but his fingers were thick and short, and he couldn't work it out.

Jack swallowed and squeezed both furry hands before dealing with it himself "I've done some things I'm not proud of, but I promise I'll try to be the guy you deserve," he whispered, ignoring the tension in his chest. Because for all the confidence he had, he was also aware of Roux being gentler, more aware of issues Jack didn't understand. Maybe even smarter. And he deserved someone who would stand by him when it counted.

The deep introspection was cut short the moment Jack reached for Roux's pants and was dumbfounded by a type of buttons he'd never seen before.

Roux shook his head. "They're press studs." He pulled on the two bits of fabric, and the metal fastenings parted with a snap.

Jack chuckled in amazement. "That's clever. Is it a chat thing? Like… a tradition?" he asked, and pressed a kiss to Roux's damp nose. He wasn't even in a hurry to fuck. For some reason, after the long wait, after the tough day, he just wanted to enjoy Roux's company and make him feel comfortable.

Roux wiggled his fingers. "Lots of us have thicker fingers. It can make human fashions tricky. These snap buttons were invented by a chat, but only after we arrived in this world."

The simplicity of this conversation made Jack relax. For once, he could really sense there was no wall between them. He would learn all the little things that mattered to Roux.

"That's such a smart solution. That guy should market this for children! I'd have definitely gotten some for Chad," Jack said, and opened Roux's pants with a decisive tug that made him feel hotter already.

Roux shook his head, but his fingers tensed on Jack's shoulders. "Chad. I still can't believe you're keeping a tarantoid pet."

Jack frowned and removed his undershirt, acutely aware of the way Roux's pupils widened in reaction. But unlike many of his former lovers, Roux didn't just care for Jack's looks and fame. He wanted all of him. "How about we go somewhere hot after this?"

"Hotter than a bath?"

Jack groaned. "No, I mean once we're out of Siberia. I'm so done with snow. I want to treat you to a vacation."

Roux smiled shyly. "I do love to lounge in the sunshine. Even if that makes me a chat stereotype. You spoil me, Jack."

Jack swallowed, running his hands through Roux's fur. "What made you change your mind about me?"

Roux purred and nuzzled Jack's neck. "These pecs."

"No, Roux, I'm serious."

Roux pulled away and tentatively approached the tub of hot water. "You have heart. And courage. When push came to shove, you gave it your all to save that little centaur. Maybe you don't always say the right things, but your heart is in the right place."

So maybe it wasn't anything big, nothing like the grand compliments Calix would sometimes give on his prowess or how popular he was. How Jack was a god among men and that his cock was the biggest Calix had ever seen on a human. Roux looked for a much deeper connection, and being evaluated with such fondness had Jack smiling.

"And you're the smartest person I know. And you make so many sacrifices to show ignorant people who you really are. It's impressive." He smirked and pushed his pants down next. "Also, you saved me from being consumed alive by tarantoid babies. So there's that. Everyone likes a hero."

Roux smiled at him, lowering his eyelids, which made his lush pale lashes stand out more. "I thought you were a shit back then, but I didn't want you to die. Confident guys are my weakness. It annoyed me so much that I was attracted to you, despite your ugly words."

That would explain Roux's snappy behavior in the past. And it did boost Jack's ego to hear that Roux had had to work that hard to contain his attraction for him.

Jack stretched his now-naked body, presenting it to Roux like a chat-approved Popsicle. It was Roux's turn to undress "I was a bit of a shit back then. And you know what changed me?" Jack whispered, cupping Roux's jaw before looking down that slender chest, at the eight nipples peeking out from the short fur.

"The inner need of a man to strive for righteousness?" Roux teased. It couldn't have been a serious question, since they both knew it was Roux who'd spoken his mind about Jack's actions when others wouldn't.

"No," Jack said, and grabbed Roux's belt loops before kneeling in front of him and pulling down the fabric. Heat stabbed his body like a dagger, but he didn't flinch and looked up at Roux's pretty face, even though the chat's privates were right in front of him. "You always told me the truth. You never tried to pander to me. You wouldn't compromise just because you liked me. I had to reevaluate many things to get here."

Roux's tongue darted out to lick his nose, and it had to be the cutest thing anyone had ever seen. "Here, as in with your face in my crotch?" he tried to make a joke out of it, but it came out hoarsely.

Jack smirked and lowered his gaze to the linen underwear that hid his prize. "Among other things? Though I admit I'm curious of how it'll feel in my mouth," he said and rose, wanting to prolong the wait until neither of them could fight the desire that had kept pulling them together throughout the years. He moved closer to the tub.

"Bath first?" Roux slowly put his leg in the tub. If Jack was to make a guess, he'd say the kitty was skittish now that the hormones released during heat weren't there to push him into action. The way he stood now though, with one leg over the edge of the deep bath, offered Jack yet more temptation by presenting the round ass and the long tail so exquisitely he couldn't look away.

It was so perfect. All of Roux was, regardless of how comical he looked when wet.

"I wanna wash you so don't you dare grab that soap," he warned playfully before climbing into the tub too, eager to position himself behind Roux.

It was easy enough to take the spot he wanted when Roux was anxious about the water to the point of it being ridiculous. "Fine, fine, I'm your pet now, after all," Roux grumbled, but didn't actually sound mad.

Jack leaned against the back of the tub and grinned, already rubbing the soap bar as the gloriously warm water thawed his cold body. Roux remained standing, and Jack stole a glance at the pouch that hid his partner's cock and the fuzzy balls he wanted to weigh in his hand. But he started with Roux's thighs, which he first splashed and then soaped up, pretending this wasn't his first time doing this. He'd had hookups with furry creatures, but none of them had felt this intimate. This important.

"I rather enjoy having you as my pet."

Roux ignored Jack's efforts at pretending the touching had anything to do with hygiene and knelt in the water, straddling him. His ginger fur floated under the surface like an underwater current, and Jack couldn't take his eyes off his new *boyfriend*. So graceful, so cute.

"What if it's you who is really the pet?" Roux leaned down and stroked Jack's damp hair.

Jack's breath caught, and he briefly imagined Roux climbing on top of him, and the unusual cock, nubs and all, prodding at his hole. "If I was to be someone's pet, I'd definitely prefer you as my master."

"Then wash the blood off my face, because I hate being dirty."

He sat on Jack's thighs, and the touch of soft balls gave Jack a rush of excitement.

Jack smirked and moved his hands up Roux's belly, and then above the surface, rubbing soap into the chest hair. "Your wish is my command. You deserve to be the King in the Venator card deck."

Roux melted into the touch, and all that Jack needed was violin playing a gentle tune in the background, because his heart soared in ways it hadn't, even during the best moments of his relationship with Calix. He could now see that where Calix had flattered him all the time, appealing to Jack's vanity, Roux's compliments were always honest and told with no other agenda than expressing his feelings.

"You'd be the Joker. Unpredictable."

Jack laughed and carefully washed all the blood and grime from Roux's hands, off his face, head, and cute tufts on his ears. Maybe that was what he should do all the time once he retired? Just take care of Roux, making him feel needed and pampered all day long?

"Am I? Maybe to other people, but you'd know when to play me and how."

A self-satisfied smile spread over Roux's lips. "I could have played you many times if I wanted to. But I don't want to manipulate you into things. I want you to want them." Even though he did look a bit funny with the fur wet and flat, Jack didn't feel like mocking him, even good-naturedly. Getting to know every new facet of his lover only made Jack's attraction grow.

"You succeeded. I'm not the same guy you met the first time," Jack said, carefully removing the soap from the beautiful face. If he ever reached the point where he had an office of his own, he wished to have a portrait of Roux above his fireplace in that room. "And I hope to change your mind about things, too."

"Like what?" Roux slid closer over Jack's thighs so that their chests met, and Jack gasped, because the hard shape prodding at his belly could only be one thing. He inhaled Roux's fresh scent and moved his hands down the lean back until he cupped both of the buttocks, floating short hairs and pert flesh.

"Like... make you accept my son."

Roux snorted against Jack's cheek. "Fine. Everyone has baggage." He ran his claws over Jack's shoulder in the gentlest way, but the gesture still gave Jack a thrill.

"What's yours?" Jack asked, shuddering with pleasure when Roux's hands trailed down his back. A bit more pressure, and he'd be bleeding, but Roux controlled himself perfectly, creating heat with the sense of danger.

Roux licked Jack's ear, rocking his cock against Jack's stomach more intensely. All this time Jack had thought Roux was a prude, yet here he was, as horny as the next guy. The truth was finally out!

"My family I guess. I'd rather focus on the here and now, Jack."

"Your family? Think about mine," Jack said, but he reached to Roux's crotch, keeping up the eye contact to see his lover's reaction.

Roux shivered, and his whiskers twitched. "True. Your dad would lose his shit if he found out you're having illicit relations with a chat."

With his pelt flattened, Roux seemed even more slender than usual, but when Jack touched him, he could sense the strong muscles that allowed chats to move with inhuman grace and agility.

His dad would have disowned him. But maybe, with time, he'd understand. Maybe he would dedicate his time to learning more about other creatures if he saw them from Jack's point of view?

"His head would combust."

Roux rocked hips back and forth, fucking Jack's fist with his cock, which hardened and now fully emerged from its sheath. The nubs peppered all over its surface teased Jack's skin, making him imagine being fucked by this tool. But the way Roux's ass tensed under the touch was just as inviting. When Roux was driven by heat, his insatiable lust left little space for exploration, but now he had the patience to sniff Jack, rub his face against him, and run the soft pads of his palms over Jack's back and shoulders.

Jack smiled at him, leaning in to lick the small lips. The smooth fur felt smooth on his tongue, but when he slid it over the sharp teeth, his dick twitched with excitement. "I don't wanna leave this tub," he said, and squeezed Roux's buttock with his other hand before pushing his fingers closer to the hole.

Roux wrapped his arms tighter around Jack's neck. "Oh, so now you're also a mind reader?" his voice was hoarse, releasing warm breath to tease Jack's ear.

"I love to serve my chat overlord," Jack said, pulling their chests close as he nudged the bare flesh around the entrance to Roux's body. The chat felt so agile in his arms, so unashamedly excited to be here, that Jack wished he could bring him home and finally come clean to the people who were his closest family, yet didn't know the real him.

Roux chuckled, nipping on Jack's ear, but then proceeding to lick... his wet hair, and it was so surprisingly erotic a tremble went all the way down Jack's spine. All of a sudden, he wished to be licked all over by that coarse tongue.

"Serve him with your cock, Jack."

"Oh, yes," he breathed out and frantically looked at the small metal table with bathing supplies. Brushes? Not now. Cologne? Razors? No.

Thick balm.

He grabbed the small jar and bent his head, sucking one of Roux's nipples into his mouth. One dip of a finger, and it was coated. Ready for Roux.

Roux giggled when Jack licked another of his nipples, but that sound turned into a moan when Jack teased his hole with more intent. Roux's tail rose, and the tip made little twitches Jack could see over Roux's shoulder.

No lies, no manipulation, no heat. Just the two of them connecting.

And it was both wonderful, and hot, but most of all—honest. After years of dancing around one another, they were both ready to make the leap.

He shivered when his finger dove in, and the walls of Roux's body tightened around it so wonderfully he wished to feel them on his cock already. "Touch me," he whispered, rubbing his mouth along Roux's jaw.

He didn't need to ask twice. Roux dipped his hand between their bodies and stroked Jack's already hard cock with those gloriously padded fingers. "Like this?" he whispered, squeezing his ass around the fingers and stirring time and time again. If Jack were to have a guess, this kitty was very eager for dick.

And his hand felt so noticeably different to anyone else's that Jack already had fireworks exploding in his skull. "Yes... I don't know where you learned that perfect pressure, but keep going," he said, moving his finger inside

Roux to cover his channel with the balm. He wondered if Roux, who already felt lighter than any human Jack had ever fucked, would be less relaxed without the mating hormones buzzing in his body, but he didn't want his question to feel intrusive and decided to just watch his lover for any signs of discomfort.

"At the Chat Pleasure Academy in Bonnes of course," Roux purred into Jack's ear while one of his hands was worked Jack's dick and the other massaged his shoulder.

"Oh, my God! Really?"

Roux bumped his forehead against Jack's temple. "No, stupid. How do you believe such things? I learned it by slutting around in Paris."

Jack swallowed, not sure if he was jealous or simply annoyed that there was so much Roux still kept hidden from him. "Are you saying you aren't a perfect beacon of virtue? You actually had sex with other people than me and that loser you told me about?"

"Gotta let me keep a bit of mystery, Jack."

It was so hard, though. He wanted to know everything about Roux. Kiss every inch of his fur and devour him whole. Be the one and only for Roux, so any past lovers would become a blur.

But if he wanted to achieve that, Roux had to need him as badly as Jack needed his chat, so he massaged the nub inside Roux, watching his face briefly go slack with pleasure. "I'm so greedy for each of your secrets. You might be in for a fight."

"Oh, I'm up for sparring, Jack. Just not when I want you to fuck me. I like that wide tip on a human cock."

Jack's throat choked up from arousal, and he slid the index finger of his other hand into Roux, gently pulling his hole apart with both. "I want you to sit on my cock."

Roux nodded, biting on his lip, and the teeth sticking out from under it looked so cute Jack could hardly believe that he was even allowed near this lovely, amazing creature. Roux let go of Jack's cock and pushed him a bit deeper into the water. Seeing him so commanding in his need for cock sent sparks of excitement up Jack's dick, but few things could measure up to the arousal of seeing Roux lower himself over Jack's cock with a tiny mewl.

He steadied his prick with one hand and moved the other up and down Roux's chest, caressing the eight nipples with gentle swipes of his fingers. Water splashed his face and entered his ears as his shoulders slid lower down the back of the tub, but Roux's face as he speared himself on Jack's cock remained his sole focus.

Eyes closed, whiskers and lips making little twitches, he was the most beautiful creature that walked the earth, wet fur or not. And this perfect male specimen of a chat had made the choice to ride Jack's cock, not someone else's. He was asking for it, complimenting it. His ass felt so gloriously tight when Roux slowly moved up and down, milking Jack until remaining still became an impossibility. Jack kneaded the muscular buttocks with a groan of satisfaction. The warm air smelled of soap and the nearby fireplace, but he couldn't possibly focus on anything other than the chat in his arms.

Roux was beautiful. Smart. Genuine. Brave.

He was the man Jack had needed in his life all along.

He got breathless when their hips moved faster, splashing water over the edge of the tub whenever they met halfway. Moving his hand all over the soft damp fur, he imagined it rubbing his skin, because it wasn't ugly in any way. Nothing about Roux was, and he wanted his chat to understand as much.

His balls tightened when they both galloped toward release, and Jack grabbed Roux's dick again, tugging on it in tune with his own thrusts.

"Oh, Jack! Yes, that," Roux babbled, squeezing Jack's shoulders, and the pace at which he moved rapidly sped up. Jack would remember that for the future.

He was finally getting to know Roux from this private side hardly anyone knew, and it was such a revelation he couldn't wait for them to explore pleasure together. The nubs pulsed in Jack's hand, and Roux let out desperate meows he must have been holding in before. Roux would be coming soon, and the sounds of his pleasure turned into a hymn in Jack's honor.

Jack grabbed the back of Roux's nape and pulled on it until their tongues met. When the rough spikes on Roux's touched his flesh, Jack came so hard he might have woken the whole inn with his groan. Roux mewled again, fucking Jack's fist to the point of Jack wondering if he'd have blisters tomorrow.

But then Roux's pink cock spurted cum all over Jack's chest and hand.

Time stopped existing when they hugged in the tub, clutching one another as if it was to be their last, not first time. Jack's thoughts raced beyond his control, but they were all about one person.

His beautiful life partner, Roux, who he…

"Loved."

"Hn?" Roux muttered, eventually sliding off Jack's spent cock, yet somehow clinging to Jack's side as if his slinky body was liquid. The dazed, sleepy eyes were so gorgeous with their pale, short lashes. Jack would soon dry Roux with a towel in front of the fireplace and then, if Roux let him, he'd brush him.

Jack licked his lips and looked at the damp fur gathered in streaks of red and white. He felt nervous, but if he wanted honesty from Roux, he needed to offer it in return. "I'm in love with you."

Roux closed his eyes and leaned in to give Jack's lips a lick. "Then I'm the happiest chat on Earth."

Jack exhaled and relaxed in the water, pulling his hand all the way down Roux's back and squeezing the base of his tail. "I'll help you dry. But give me a minute."

This was it. A perfect moment.

Chapter 8

The nubbed cock was as delicious as it was odd. Jack had never encountered a penis like it, but he eventually gave up on trying to compare Roux's dick to anyone else's, and focused on getting well acquainted with it instead.

Salty and hot, it only peeked out of its sheath when Roux was aroused, just as shy as Roux himself, but Jack wouldn't tell him that, unwilling to make his chat hiss at him. So Jack sucked on the warm prick, groaning in pleasure under the thick furs.

Roux's thighs stiffened and relaxed as Jack teased each little nub with his tongue, sucked on the pointy tip, and squeezed the furry balls. The sleigh shook when it hit an bump in the snow, but Jack trusted Roux to not let his focus slip too much. The furs enclosed Jack in pleasant heat that smelled of chat arousal, and he was far too enamoured by his new lover to care about consequences.

It wasn't as if they were doing this in the middle of town. With time to spare before the long train journey back to Moscow, they went on a last sleigh ride through the woods surrounding Krasnoyarsk.

Jack couldn't hear Roux well through the blanket, but he didn't need words to know the swelling of Roux's cock and the little stirs of his hips meant he'd be coming any moment now.

He hollowed his lips around the tasty dick and groaned while teasingly rubbing the furry stomach. Roux wouldn't admit it, but he loved belly rubs, and Jack was more than ready to exploit that to his advantage.

Hot cum splashed his tongue, and he swallowed it all like the greedy slut he was.

This was the best. He already knew their long train journey would be a major sex fest. He could only hope they wouldn't end up kicked out for being too rowdy.

"Just in time..." Roux rasped when Jack peeked out from under the blanket. He'd already come before, so he was relaxed, despite arousal still coursing through his veins. "You really are a *talented* venator," Roux teased. "They should put this skill on your collectible card."

Jack closed all the snaps on Roux's pants, gave the cock one last kiss through the fabric, and finally emerged, shivering when the cold air touched his overheated skin. He pinched Roux's cheek and only then looked ahead, at the city gates. As far as final rides through the countryside went, this one has been very enjoyable.

"Yes. I tame beasts by giving them amazing orgasms."

Roux squinted at him. "It would be funny if it wasn't true."

Jack scowled and put his arms around Roux. "I did it all to become such a fantastic lover for you."

Roux laughed and urged the horse toward the train station. "Oh, yeah, I'm sure that was what you had in mind all along."

"There were no other motivations. Just you and your amazing ass."

Roux wouldn't stop chuckling, for once devoid of tension and constant suspicion about Jack's motives. "You're awful. Why do I like you so much again?"

Maybe because Jack made him smile so much. Or it really was his pretty impressive pecs. Either way, Jack didn't mind.

When they arrived at the station, Jack went to pick up their tickets, while Roux handled the sleigh rental.

Jack was walking on clouds by the time he stepped onto the sidewalk and even waited until his lover disappeared from sight before making his way to the ticket office. A yeti sat in the room made for a person much smaller than him, and communicating with him turned out to be surprisingly easy, despite the yeti being incapable of producing human speech and Jack not knowing Russian. Neither of those issues mattered when they both wanted to understand each other.

He was surprised when the creature handed him an additional parcel along with the tickets, but he only looked at it once he sat on a bench in the waiting room.

He tore the paper, wondering what the package might be, but stiffened with dread when he saw a square box containing his favorite childhood chocolates. These were a special edition, with several people of different genders and races depicted holding hands and smiling. Nothing wrong with the illustration itself, but the slogan beneath it chilled Jack to the bone. It read, Make America Human again! 20% of all proceeds for Bradley 'The Kraken' Addison's cause.

Oh no.

Could he possibly share them with Roux if he ripped off the top of the box? He didn't even know if chats ate chocolate.

He quickly tucked it back into the paper and opened the attached letter, which contained lots of information about Father's crusade. The whole thing made Jack lose all appetite, but it was the last part of the letter that made him stiffer than standing naked in the snow ever could.

"...

I will be in Paris in February, and I want to grasp the rare opportunity to see you. I'm holding a symposium about our cause to bring these necessary ideas to a broader audience in Europe.

I hope you can be the keynote speaker, son.

All my love,

Father."

Oh no!

Next time on *Jack Addison vs. A Whole World of Hot Trouble*:

Where will Jack take Roux on vacation?
Will Jack introduce Roux to his Father?
Are there demon alligators living in the suburbs of Paris?

Jack Addison vs. Catnip Dealers

Jack Addison Vs. A Whole World of Hot Trouble #8

K.A. Merikan

"Catnip is nothing like tea or coffee. It's a drug and should remain illegal."

After finally getting together during their dangerous job in Siberia, Roux and Jack arrive in Paris. On the surface, Jack's life has finally slotted into place, but the necessity of keeping secrets is choking him on the inside.

His father is in town to lead an anti-creature conference, and since he's unaware of his son's interspecies relationship and pro-creature views, he wants Jack to be the keynote speaker. Torn between his love for Roux and his family's expectations, Jack attempts to play both sides and lie his way out of the conundrum.

But when they meet Roux's old flame, a big, sexy chat who knows everyone in Paris, keeping a low profile might not be possible anymore.

Previously on Jack Addison vs. A Whole World of Hot Trouble:

Jack Addison might come from a line of legendary monster hunters and scientists, but real life has taught him that the world isn't anything like he'd been told. After encountering the alluring Nessie during the annual hunt, he's opened up to the idea of dating nonhumans and eventually focuses his interest on fellow hunter, the cat-like Roux Chat-Bonnes.

Following a period of mistrust, Roux warms up to Jack, and they end up spending a night together. In the morning, however, the beautiful chat gives Jack the cold shoulder after discovering a diary of Jack's sexual conquests. Disillusioned, Jack agrees to be Roux's friend, and they travel together after accepting a dangerous job in Siberia.

While out in the wilderness, Jack decides to accept the invitation of Adam, a beautiful man who appears out of nowhere. But the palace-like home Adam leads him to is only an illusion, and soon enough Jack finds himself naked in the punishing cold. Only Roux's timely arrival saves him from freezing to death. Roux finally confesses the depth of his feelings for Jack, who reassures him that this relationship isn't just another notch on his bedpost.

Two Japanese venators appear and reveal that 'Adam' is a kitsune, a shape-shifting monster who they've been tracking for a long time. The kitsune attacks Jack and Roux, who don't have experience dealing with this kind of creature, but the timely arrival of the other venators saves the day.

Content and for the first time certain of one another's feelings, Roux and Jack are about to board a train back west when Jack receives a parcel. Unaware of his son's real opinions, Jack's father invites him to an anti-creature event in Paris. Will Jack be able to hide his head in the sand once more, or will he have to pick a side?

Chapter 1

"Catnip is nothing like tea or coffee. It's a drug and should remain illegal. Of course chats would like to do nothing but chew on it all day, lazing around, but who's gonna pay for their keep? Were this our country, it would have been you and me," Father said, wiping his lips with a napkin.

Jack watched him, busy chewing the tastiest *fillet mignon* he'd probably had in his life, but also one that he couldn't enjoy.

The restaurant was fancy as hell, with crystal chandeliers and giant windows mirrored by glass on the other side of the room. Its walls were decorated with plant motifs and gold paint, but he would have rather have had dinner at a shabby Parisian bistro as long as he didn't have to listen to this nonsense.

But he said nothing and stuffed his face more. He knew for a fact that not all chats used catnip, because Roux had been extremely offended when asked about it.

"Don't they pay taxes too?" Jack said eventually, frowning over his food when that thought hit him.

Father stilled with the glass of red wine in hand, his forehead wrinkling. He was still quite handsome, and the intensity of his life seemed to have kept him youthful, but in this moment, Jack didn't feel at all comfortable about them having similar facial features—something one of the waitresses had commented on earlier.

"As they should. But their little autonomous region gets money for nothing, and plenty of them don't bother to earn enough to pay any tax. Since when are you a defender of hairball-spitters? Living here, you should know by now how useless those creatures are."

Jack cleared his throat, thinking back to Roux's tail swiping across his body earlier. This whole conversation made him deeply uncomfortable, as did the fact that Father had come to France for some kind of anti-creature event, but it was to take place outside of Paris. Maybe it would all blow over.

"I just think we should look at both sides of this argument," he said, feeling cold as he cut off another piece of the meat without looking up from his plate.

Father seemed contemplative. "That is fair, son. You've really grown. There is no way to dismantle their arguments without knowing them first. Back in Florida, I'm fighting for the rights of humans to have their own beaches, separate from the scalies, because the last thing you want when going out for a swim is spotting one of them under you. Gives me the creeps."

"But what is it that they do?" Other than *exist*.

"They scare children out of the water. What are you even asking about? After all your years working in Europe, you should very well know what they do. Speaking of which, I've reserved a spotlight talk for you at the Versailles Symposium on Creature-Human Relations. I'm always so proud to tell people of your work."

Jack was about to swallow the chewed food, but suddenly got nauseous and spat it into a napkin. "What? No, I'm not good at speeches."

His brain was already coursing through stormy waters. So he could just ignore his father's attitude, but there was no way in hell he'd speak against creatures. Not anymore. Not when his lover *and* son were not human.

Father waved it off as if what Jack was saying didn't matter. "Oh, don't be modest, you'll do just fine. You always had a way with words. I just need you to talk about your adventures and the variety of monsters you've slayed to protect humanity. It will be a good opportunity to advertise the new Addison device too. Your sister's designed a version an average person could keep at their home so that they're alerted if an interdimensional crack appears in their area. It's gonna sell like crazy."

Of course. Yet another one of Dad's businesses. Too bad most of them were anti-creature, and promoted ideas Jack's own views no longer aligned with. While his own stance had become increasingly liberal, Father's had radicalised. After Jack actually got to know nonhumans, he found it impossible to see them as anything but people.

When Jack had still lived at home, among other people like himself, and had only seen creatures in sideshows and pictures, he'd believed that was where they belonged. He also used to believe that *everyone* thought this way.

He briefly thought back to the insulting way he'd treated Roux when they'd first met, and shame squeezed his stomach. No wonder his face bore scars as a result of that meeting. "I--I'll see if I can make it," he said, though he already planned to bail on Father. There surely was a very important contract to excuse his absence during the conference.

"Fantastic!" Father beamed at him. "Everyone will want to hear about that kitsune you killed last year."

But before Jack could tell him that it was actually a Japanese venator who'd sealed that deal, Father was already ordering them dessert. Jack wouldn't say no to that.

*

Jack loved Paris, and once Father had retired to his hotel room, he was free to enjoy its atmosphere again.

The conversation left him feeling dull on the inside, and he was torn over feeling such discomfort talking to a person he loved. Father had given him a perfect childhood, all the support Jack had needed, and he was always very giving to members of their community. Back then, it was easy to consider him a good person, but Jack was no longer so sure what to think of his conduct.

He was positive Father would have never randomly attacked a creature who minded their own business, physically or verbally, but he did actively seek separation of nonhumans, and lobbied for laws that kept them in an underprivileged position, banning them from human-established schools and professions of public trust. Keeping them in less developed areas of the country. Keeping them separate from human women and children. He didn't want dialogue, because he was convinced he already understood all there was to know and that creatures would by default lie to people's faces to get what they wanted.

In light of that, no matter how good of a dad he'd been to Jack, and how much he offered to charities, it was increasingly difficult to see him as a decent person.

But out of the hotel restaurant, in the streets lit by gas lamps where creatures could be spotted among humans, it was easy to blend in and forget what his parentage was and what his family had done to keep various species separate.

It took him half an hour to reach the area around Montmartre, and after seeking directions from a policeman, he found the little bistro Roux wanted to meet at. Its outer walls were painted a dark blue, and despite it being a February night, people sat under awnings outside, sharing wine and stories. Most of them were chats, and upon his approach, he couldn't ignore the sense of eyes licking his skin. The warm light inside beckoned him closer, and by the time he crossed the threshold, the unpleasant conversation was almost forgotten.

The restaurant smelled of wine, herbs, with a hint of fish. He looked past a uniformed waitress at the elegant yet simple interior with black and white tiles on the floor and posters of beautiful chat ladies hanging on walls.

He'd been in this chat district of Paris two years ago, when he'd been searching for a chat hookup, but he hadn't actually gathered the courage to enter this bar back then. This time, he'd been invited, yet he still felt like an intruder, and was sure that would remain the case until he found his lover.

Knowing Roux, he was probably wall-flowering somewhere with a cup of milk.-

Jack cocked his head at the sight by the bar. The largest, most muscular chat he'd ever seen stood with his arm around Roux's shoulders. Silver, with stripes like a tiger and a large, flat nose, he didn't even look like the same species as Roux. This chat would never be confused with a female. He didn't even wear a shirt in February! His legs were clad in gray leather pants that emphasized his muscles, and a long, striped tail was teasing Roux's hand, despite Roux swatting it time and time again.

Chapter 2

Jack took a deep breath and forced himself to relax. Roux wasn't the cheating type. He *would,* on the other hand, get angry if Jack went in there and pick a fight with Silver.

Stay classy, Jack. This is surely a misunderstanding.

He approached casually, making sure not to run up to Roux and put his arm over Roux's slender shoulders. He didn't fail to notice that Roux was wearing his new jacket, made of bottle green leather that made his eyes stand out and his fur seem even redder. At the store, he'd mentioned he'd wear it for special occasions, so why was he wearing it on a regular outing to a chat bar? Did he want to attract chats like this one?

"We haven't been introduced," Jack said as calmly as he could, meeting Silver's yellow eyes.

The big chat offered a paw the size of Jack's face. "Tom. Tom Chat-Paris."

Roux smiled and trailed his nose under Jack's jaw, soothing some of his anxiety. "He's an old friend."

Jack squeezed the chat's hand. "Jack Addison. I'm Roux's..."—what. What was he?—"lover."

Tom whistled so loudly other chats looked back at them. "Got yourself a catch, kitty cat. Always thought you'd need another chat with that temperament, yet here we go."

"Stop teasing," Roux got flustered and rubbed his cheek in the cutest way. 'Kitty cat'? What the hell?

Jack briefly wondered if the two knew one another from school, but then remembered that chats used the name of their town of birth as the second part of their surname, and Tom's and Roux's didn't match.

"So, how do you know each other?" So well at that.

Roux waved his hand dismissively. "Long story. Have you heard your dad's in town? Better keep a low profile."

Tom cocked his head. "Who's your dad?"

Did the guy live under a rock?

A tiny chat bartender with metal studs in her ears stood a bit closer, and Jack had no doubt she'd been eavesdropping. But what was he to do?

He cleared his throat and rested his head against Roux's. He couldn't help feeling watched, and as the only human in the bistro, he didn't want to stand out even more. "Yeah, let's just not go to the main tourist attractions, and we likely won't bump into him."

Tom wouldn't let it go though. "So who is your father?"

Jack waited for Roux to come up with an answer to these questions, him being the one to mention Father in the first place after all, but in the end he looked at Tom. "He's an activist. We don't see eye to eye on many issues."

Roux nodded quickly. "He's a specist. But Jack hasn't talked to him in a long time. They're nothing alike."

"Addison. I knew I recalled the name," said the bartender, as if she were part of conversation. "A total creature-hater. And you're fucking his son?"

Roux's fur bristled. "None of your business!"

Jack's chest sank, and he was on the verge of letting go of Roux. He was certain all the chats present were listening. Judging him, but worst of all—judging Roux. "Don't talk to him like that. And stop with your own specist behavior!"

Tom nodded. "Give the guy a break. Who wouldn't fall for Roux?"

The bartender crossed her arms on her chest. "Well, maybe if slutty little chats didn't fuck around with humans, humans would rethink their attitudes. That Addison guy? He's so full of himself. I've read about him in today's newspaper."

Heat exploded in Jack's face. "He's not slutty. What the hell's wrong with you?"

But the bartender just shrugged and sent Roux a sharp glare, as if she wanted to stab him to death with that look alone. "You're nothing but an exotic conquest. He doesn't understand us, and he'll leave you once he meets a suitable female of his own kind."

"Are you speaking from experience?" Jack asked, poisoning the conversation further. Enough was enough.

Tom hummed and shook his head. "How about we just head off to mine? I live nearby, and no one's gonna dip their whiskers in our conversation there."

The bartender hissed. "Yes, how about you just leave."

Roux squeezed Jack's hand, but glanced Tom's way. "Thanks, that really might be for the better."

Jack wasn't sure if he should even look at all the patrons who'd chosen not to join the argument. When he did raise his gaze somewhat, the chat faces expressed a variety of attitudes, but he chose not to engage, and only breathed freely once they were back in the street.

His hand got sweaty and was dampening Roux's fur, but he didn't feel like letting go either. "Why did you mention him?" he asked.

Roux was taken aback. "So that you weren't surprised in case we bumped into him."

Jack pulled Roux close, breathing in the fresh scent of fur without caring that chats weren't as open about liking people of the same gender as humans. He was already going against all rules, so why not this one?

"I just… wish she hadn't spoiled our evening."

But wouldn't it have gone exactly the same at any other chat gathering? As the dominant species, humans saw all bars and cafes as theirs, so no wonder chats were protective of their own sanctuaries and didn't want humans disturbing their peace. Jack wasn't surprised by this, all things considered, but also worried Roux would end up deprived of contact with his own species if they couldn't go out together.

He glanced at Tom, who was leading them down the cobbled street. Would Roux be better off with a man like that? One would have to be blind to not notice Tom's attempts at flirting. He was big, strong, and seemed nice.

Roux kissed Jack's jaw. "Me too. But Tom has a house just around the corner, and we can talk in peace there. Some chats are assholes, just like humans. That's life."

Jack sighed, squeezing Roux's hand more firmly as they passed through an inner yard where a couple of chats hid away from prying eyes on a small bench, and they walked into a staircase, which led them to the top floor.

"Welcome," Tom said when they entered his apartment, and winked at Roux. "Make yourself at home, kitty cat."

A herby aroma hung in the air. The ceilings were quite low and the walls covered with dark-hued wallpapers, which created a cozy atmosphere. It seemed rather large at first glance, and as Tom led them into the living room, which had windows that stretched all the way up from the floor, Jack wondered if he lived here alone.

Or what he did for a living to afford such a house, for that matter.

Chapter 3

"Tom, have you heard of JUSTICE?" Roux asked, seated in an armchair which was more like a gigantic pillow than a conventional chair.

Tom stretched out in another one, comfortable while Jack struggled with the way the filling of the giant fluff bag constantly shifted, forcing him to adjust his position. But he kept his face straight and squeezed his hands on the glass of vodka cream Tom had served them.

Tom grinned, showing off his white canines, and his thick tail swept through the air. "As in criminal justice? Roux, we chats don't always stick to the rules."

Roux huffed and drank more alcohol. "No, no, it's an organization that fights for creature rights and intervenes when harm is being done. You have so many contacts in Paris. I thought it would be great for everyone if you joined."

Tom leaned closer with a grin and grabbed Roux's tail. "Oh? What do I get in return?"

Jack remained silent as anger simmered beneath his skin. So Roux had planned to meet up with Tom in order to discuss JUSTICE, yet had failed to mention it to him? What the hell was up with that?

"He won't hate you completely. That's how it worked with me," Jack said, wanting to stifle Tom's flirting in the bud.

Roux's ears perked up, his attention back on Jack. "You want to actually join us too?"

Tom smirked at Jack from behind Roux. What was the fucker playing at? It was best to ignore him for now, because the last thing Jack needed was another argument with his chat.

"Oh… you know, I don't need to be an official member to help you out," Jack said, meeting Roux's gaze above a wooden coffee table.

Roux's shoulders sagged and pulled Jack's mood with them.

"I get it," Tom said quickly, "Being an *Addison* you might not want to get too involved. But I'll sign up, Roux. You know I'm always up for helping a kitty out." His canines glinted in the predatory smile.

The innuendo was clear, and Jack *would* get to the bottom of it! Right after he murdered Tom Chat-Paris.

Roux took a deep breath and got up. "I don't want to push anyone. It's just that with the symposium in Versailles, we could use the numbers. It's always good to have a list of creatures who are willing to give aid or shelter in times of need. May I… use your restroom?"

Tom snorted. "Of course, silly. It's still on the left behind the bedroom."

Roux was off, but the word *still* rang in Jack's ears like the bells of Notre Dame.

He could sense unspoken animosity hanging in the air and wanted to approach their host, but the shape of the seat made it impossible to do so in a halfway graceful fashion. Red-faced, Jack rolled out of the pillow-chair and walked toward Tom, his heart beating faster when he was confronted by a sly yet level gaze. This fucker was testing him on purpose!

"What's your problem?" Jack whispered.

"You're my problem. The fuck are you doing with my kitty cat, huh? He needs a chat, not a human." Tom rose, and Jack had to begrudgingly acknowledge that Tom did that more gracefully.

Fucking chat flexibility.

The sudden honesty was wood to the fire of Jack's anger, and he stepped closer, balling his hands into fists. "I don't see him chasing after you. He's not interested, so quit calling him 'your kitty', you ignorant, lecherous tomcat!"

But the seeds of doubt had been sown. Maybe Tom *was* right. Maybe the relationship with Jack would rob Roux of the natural contact with his own species? Maybe the compatibility that had brought them together was only skin-deep?

Tom laughed. "Me and Roux go way back. I was there for him when he needed a friend. Funny that you don't seem to know about me. But I'm guessing Roux didn't want to intimidate you. Us chats… well, we can do certain things for each other that humans can't."

"Like what?" Jack growled as insecurity clawed at his brain. He could do whatever Roux might want him to, even lick him clean, if Roux found that pleasurable. He was always so pristine anyway.

"I'm not about to tell you the details of chat sex lives. But when Roux's in heat… well, he needs a lot more than a human dick can give."

Jack's face flushed at the thought of this chat giant on top of Roux.

Did that actually happen? Was Tom *that* kind of friend? After all, Roux had mentioned something about a *slutty* period in Paris.

Jack hated Tom. *Hated* him.

"That's bullshit. If he wanted a chat, there would be plenty to choose from. Maybe he's just not that into you."

"*Everyone*'s into me, Jack. Probably even you. How about we have a threesome and find out who can do Roux better?"

Jack's brain did a backflip. Which one of them did Tom want to fuck? Both? Just Roux? He hated both of those options with a passion. He shoved Tom back without thinking. "Take your dirty paws off my chat!"

Tom spoke through bared teeth, and his tail swung through the air behind him like the metronome of aggression. "I've been gentlemanly so far. If I put my paws on Roux, you'd be just a memory."

The door shutting in the corridor had both of them on high alert.

Jack felt a bead of sweat roll down his back and listened to the soft, beautiful sound of Roux's footsteps. Everything about him was perfection. Jack had courted him for so long, and what... couldn't he just settle into the comfort of knowing they'd be together forever? He'd given up all other lovers, only to be confronted with the fact that he wasn't the only one in their relationship who had options.

"What did I miss?" Roux smiled, oblivious to the war of stares between Jack and Tom.

Tom smiled. "I was just showing Jack my collection of brushes," he pointed do the wall where many colorful brushes hung from hooks, in a display promising a chat hours of pleasure.

Jack's thoughts went to the one old brush Roux used for his hair. He likely hadn't replaced it to save money and help his family, and Jack had been oblivious to the fact that his lover might want a new one. One that had a silver handle and fresh natural bristles.

"They're nice," he said, somewhat flatly, because his brain was preoccupied with the idea of Tom wanting to steal his Roux.

"Oh, you've added quite a few," Roux said with a smile, and ran his pads over the bristles of a red-handled brush in a way that made Jack's blood boil. Were chat brothels filled with such implements? Jack could just imagine Roux spread out on a bed and brushed by several chats while another licked his cock.

Tom chuckled. "You know I'm a fiend for pleasure."

"Yeah, you told me. The threesomes and all that," Jack said in a carefree tone, but felt hot all over when he saw Roux's whiskers twitch.

"What threesomes?" Roux asked, but they were interrupted by an angry rapping at the door.

"Open up! This is the police!"

The smirk that had previously floated over Tom's features dropped. "*Merde.*"

"The police?" Jack asked, already directing his footsteps to the source of the noise. Was there a danger in the neighborhood?

Roux grabbed Jack's sleeve and pulled him close with eyes wide like saucers. "Jack, we need to run. I've got catnip on me."

"You wh—?" But Jack didn't get to finish his question. When someone beat on the door even harder, he followed Roux, ignoring Tom, who was frantically collecting metal tins off shelves. "Where to?"

Chapter 4

Jack's brain still rattled as Roux led him to a tall window. Why the hell did Roux have catnip? He'd told Jack that he didn't use it and always acted so high and mighty about any stimulants.

Roux struggled to open the old window. The wooden shutters wouldn't budge no matter how much he strained his back. "Fuck, fuck, *fuck*! Come on, Jack, help me!"

Jack broke out of his stupor and grabbed the handle, tugging it up with all the strength he had. Something cracked, but the window finally opened, and just as they heard a loud *thud* in the corridor, Roux jumped onto the roof, leading the way toward someone's empty balcony.

Jack made the mistake of looking down. They were in the fourth floor, and seeing people pass in the street below had his head spinning. His legs went soft, and he ended up kneeling the moment the icy breeze pushed him toward the edge. He didn't even see well in the dark, so how was he to follow Roux at such high speed?

He'd fucking die here.

"Jack? Come on, come! I've got you." Roux extended his ginger paw, and while Jack hesitated to give up on stability, he grabbed his lover and let him lead the way.

The air smelled of smoke and the nearby park, but he focused only on Roux's silhouette in front him. As terrifying as it was to walk so high up with nothing to hold them in case of a slip, he trusted Roux. Roux would never knowingly endanger him.

"The roof tiles are slippery, so be careful," Roux said, never letting go of Jack's hand. "I bet that weasel of a bartender tipped them off."

A loud bell resounded through the air, followed by a deafening police siren. Roux hissed, but headed to the tiny balcony at the end of the building.

"This place used to be empty, so let's hope for the best," Roux said, fiddling with the lock on the window as soon as they stood on the tiled floor.

Jack peeked inside, pressing his cheek to the dirty glass. He could discern boxes and furniture covered with fabric, but it was too dark to tell if there was anyone inside.

The lock clicked though, and Roux carefully opened the window, letting out a dusty smell. If Jack's sister were to enter this place, with her allergies, she'd be sneezing constantly.

"We might be safer if we wait things out instead of running." Roux jumped in and coughed when a cloud of dust rose from the floor. He then turned to Jack. "What do you think?"

Jack nodded and slid inside. The floor under his feet felt so much better than the lead roof. "Let's just keep the volume down, and we should be fine," he said, and shut the window.

Roux walked around with confidence, making Jack wish his sight was as good as a chat's. "Can't believe it," he whispered. "It was supposed to be a nice night out." He pulled on a sheet covering a large sofa and shook it to get some of the dust off. He then placed it over the piece of furniture again, clean side up, and sat down. The owner of the apartment wouldn't have been happy about this kind of treatment, but Jack didn't care. If they could afford to keep this place while living somewhere else, they could also afford a bit of clean-up.

His eyes were adjusting to the darkness, and he realized that they were in a fully equipped apartment, complete with artwork hung on walls, and elegant chairs around a large oval dining table.

He sat next to Roux, listening to the distant shouting in French.

"Sorry," he said, squeezing his hands on his knees. "Maybe you'd want me to keep the catnip. It's not like anyone's gonna search me for it."

Roux stilled. He didn't think the catnip topic would just go away, did he?

"Hnn…"

Jack snorted. "What is *that* supposed to mean?"

Roux leaned back on the sofa with a groan. "Makes sense, I guess," he mumbled and pulled out a small tin.

Jack took it off him and put it into his jacket pocket. The silence was becoming eerie when Roux refused to say anything else, so Jack cleared his throat. "I thought you didn't use it."

Roux threw his arms up. "So I do, okay? It's harmless!"

"Okay. I have no opinion," Jack said, watching Roux twitch nervously next to him. "I'm just surprised you lied."

Roux pulled his feet up to the edge of the sofa. "Because it's this big joke that all chats do this. I don't want to be a stereotype, yet, yes, I like it too. You wouldn't understand."

This again. Jack's mouth dropped, and he rested his elbows on his thighs, leaning forward as his mood worsened by the moment. "Sure. What else are you keeping from me because you thought I wouldn't understand? Isn't that specist?"

Roux groaned. "What is this about? I just didn't want you to judge me."

"Because I'm *so* judgmental. Good to know. I bet *Tom* would have understood," Jack said through clenched teeth.

Roux pulled on Jack's hand, watching him closely. "Not because you're judgemental, but because I try... I try to keep a certain image. I guess I'm embarrassed I like catnip just like any other chat, but... are you jealous of Tom? What?"

Jack scowled, rubbing his hands together under Roux's intense scrutiny. He could feel the green gaze already peeling away all the protective layers Jack kept on, even around him. "Because he keeps flirting with you, and you don't tell him off?"

Roux snorted and pulled Jack to the sofa next to him. "He sells me catnip at a discount. He's a dealer, Jack. And always horny for any chat, but that's another matter. I would never go back to him."

There was that word. *"Back"*. The confirmation of Jack's anxieties. Tom was an ex. He hadn't made that up.

Jack chewed on his lip. "That's not what he thinks. And you just told me I won't understand you because I'm not one of you. Which is it then?" he asked, failing to not let his insecurity spill into the question.

He might be Jack Addison, but he was only human.

Roux frowned and cuddled up closer to Jack, pushing his slender shoulders under his arm. "It's Tom who will never understand me. I'm not like other chats. I know that sounds stupid, since I love naps, belly rubs, and catnip, but I've always been different, and never fit in. I went to the venator academy, I like reading, and most of all, I'm... you know, I like men, I'm an anomaly.

"There was a time I was desperate to fit in. After that whole fiasco with my human boyfriend, I had to hide away during heat, it was so embarrassing. One night, Tom was passing in the street by my residence hall. It was a hot night, I had my window open, and he just climbed in. I thought it was romantic at the time. He pulled me into this whole world of wild parties, and catnip, and lots of sex. I thought that this was what I needed, not a human. But I didn't fit in with him and his friends, either.

"I was disillusioned when I found out Tom fucked around whenever he felt like it, and chats like me are rare, so he enjoyed having me by his side. I wasn't happy doing nothing all day, or that I wasn't exactly his boyfriend. Other chats didn't understand it. They thought I was lucky to get a stud chat like Tom to fuck me. I didn't fit in with humans, I didn't fit in with chats, so when I finally dumped Tom, I didn't go out with anyone, and focused on studying.

"Jack, I didn't think anyone would get me. That I would be stuck in permanent limbo between the two species. Until you," Roux whispered, and nuzzled Jack's cheek.

Jack felt as if Roux had cradled his heart and pressed it to his own. "What a dick. He wouldn't see a gem if someone stuck it in his eyeball."

"He still hits on me whenever we meet. His ego can't take the fact that someone might not want to sleep with him." Roux smirked and reached into Jack's pocket for the catnip. "Won't lie, gives me a bit of a thrill to see him pining for me like that. I'm a bad chat."

Jack's lips twitched, and he rubbed Roux's furry hand. He was glad to hear so much reassurance, but Roux still kept secrets from him, and Jack desperately needed to know the truth. "I just worry that being with me will isolate you. You won't be able to go to chat bars without being offended by some dickheads. And you'll miss out on those things you can only do with other chats."

Roux shrugged. "If you haven't noticed, I've traveled on my own most of the time, and I fit in better with the weirdos in JUSTICE than with my fellow chats. It can be hard. I'm 'too human' for chats, but humans only see me as a chat. I'd never fit in at chat bars, and I don't even want to try."

Jack licked his lips, leaning closer, until his mouth touched Roux's cool, tender ear. "But what about the sex things? Won't you miss any of that?"

The ear twitched against Jack's mouth. "What sex things?"

Jack's cheeks were on fire, and he shifted, unable to cope with the discomfort of this conversation. What man enjoyed discussing his shortcomings in the sack? "Tom said there were some things only a chat could do when another one was in heat," he mumbled, staring at the moon outside.

Roux put his head on Jack's shoulder and pushed his shoes off to hug Jack with his legs as well. "I recall your dick being more than up for the task last time. He was just being an asshole. Yeah, you're different, but that's exciting. I really like your hairless body, and the cockhead that's wider at the top."

Jack would hardly have called himself hairless, but compared to a chat, he supposed he was.

Jack hesitated, but in the end pulled Roux close and buried his face in the fluff on his neck. It felt fantastic, and even though some of his previous partners had been even more unusual, perhaps easier to deal with, he wouldn't change Roux for the world. "I want you to be happy. There's only so many people who I can be myself with. But then I'm still who I am, with the family I have," he said, still too ashamed to tell Roux he'd spoken to Father.

"You can't help who your family is. Speaking of being yourself, though..." Roux shook the catnip tin. "I usually only do it by myself, with the door locked. Would you be my safety guard? We'll be stuck here for a while."

Jack grinned, excited to see a chat use catnip. He'd only heard rumors of how the substance worked, but it couldn't be as addictive as some of his professors claimed, because Roux was a very well-functioning chat, and certainly didn't do catnip every single day.

"Go on, we have plenty of time," he said, and pressed a soft kiss to Roux's cheek. His heart galloped with the excitement of seeing yet another barrier break between them, and he was ready for the ride that would follow.

Roux smiled shyly, looking up at Jack with so much affection that even Tom's comments couldn't shake Jack now. "It could get... weird."

Jack snorted and slid his hand under Roux's clothes. "Oh, I'm ready for it."

Roux laughed and took off his jacket, then popped open the small tin. Jack had to lean closer to see, but it had a layer of mesh separating the catnip from a chat's nose, so it didn't stick to Roux's fur when he took a long sniff.

He rubbed the back of Roux's head with his fingertips and was surprised to see his shoulders relax after another hit of the herb. "So... how do you feel?" he asked, watching Roux put the tin back into his pocket.

"It's relaxing. Helped me get through school after that thing when Ivan told everyone about our sex life." Roux leaned more weight on Jack and nudged his ear. "Also gets me horny. I used to lock myself in the room, and have these jerk-off sessions that could last for hours. I would just sit there and lick myself."

Jack's mind stalled, and then lit up like a firework. "L-lick yourself?" he uttered, and his dick twitched, as if Roux's words were a command to rise.

Roux giggled. "Yes, Jack. I can do that. Wanna... see?"

Jack felt like a kid waiting for the candy he'd been promised for good behavior. Jerk-off sessions? Self-fellatio? Jack's mind was blown. "Yes, please," he said, loosening his collar when the cool room suddenly felt warm.

Roux gave him a kiss, but then opened the snaps on his pants with which Jack was very well accustomed by now. "Pull them off, I need a full range... of motion." He burst out laughing, already softer in the way he moved, like a drunk person.

Jack took a deep breath and gently pulled Roux's pants off first, then his underwear. It was still dark, but when Roux shifted his hips, they moved through a ray of moonlight, and Jack spotted the tip of his cock already peeking out of the sheath.

"I'm prepared to be amazed."

Roux's tongue darted to his nose, and he smiled. Seeing him like this would never get old. It was a side of him only Jack knew.

With one foot on the floor, and one on the sofa, Roux folded his body, extending his arms forward. Jack wished there were candles around, because he was dying to see it all in detail, but it wasn't like Roux couldn't repeat this performance in better light.

"Do you want me to do anything, or...?" Breath trembled in Jack's throat, and he slid off the sofa to open the shutters.

When he turned around, his knees weakened at the sight of Roux's slender body bent halfway, and his tongue teasing the tip of his own cock. All the blood from his head drizzled to his dick and balls, making them heavy with arousal.

To make things even sexier, a deep purring filled the room, and with each lick, Roux's cock grew, peeking out of the sheath in all its glory. Jack's head throbbed when he approached just in time to see Roux bend farther and lick his soft, furry balls.

Wow. Just wow.

He didn't even have time to think before his shirt was on the floor. Kneeling by the sofa, mesmerized by the naughty beauty of the act, Jack rubbed the skin behind Roux's ear. Was this how Roux had dealt with his urges for such a long time?

"You're so sexy..."

Roux's tongue felt too sharp on Jack's cock sometimes, but when he caressed himself, this issue didn't exist. Roux was in control, so could easily add more saliva, or lap at his dick more gently.

Roux winked at Jack, leaning into his touch When Jack's gaze settled on his cock and the nubs that got more pronounced with arousal. "And you're a pervert," Roux said between one long lick and another. "Perving on a chat just going about his business."

Jack's breath caught, and he leaned closer, pushing one hand along Roux's chest to roll each of the eight nipples in his fingers. "I am a pervert only when it comes to a certain chat," he whispered, before nipping on the place where Roux's long whiskers grew.

He was wild about all the chat bits of Roux's body. The fur, the whiskers, the nipples, the pads on his hands. Not because he was a chat fetishist, but because they were all parts of Roux. He didn't go around perving on random chats, because Roux was the only one he wanted.

Roux let out a loud purr, nipping on the tip of his own cock with his lips, and Jack could hardly bear how erotic that looked. There was nothing more arousing than a man enjoying himself, and Jack wanted to kiss every bit of that slender, furry body. When Roux's cock was almost entirely out of its sheath, Jack reached between Roux's legs and gently squeezed his balls. His own dick was hard now, and while he wasn't sure what to do about it yet, he was prepared to follow Roux's lead.

Roux giggled and pulled his tongue away from his cock to lap at Jack's cheek. "I love seeing you so horny. I... I've never done this with someone watching. But I fantasized what it would be like to be fucked while I did it."

"Hell yes," Jack said, opening his pants. His dick was practically talking to him at this point, its throbbing like heated whispers of desire.

But... was that an actual request? Because Roux *was* high.

On the other hand, he didn't seem *that* high. Just relaxed and smiley. He'd only taken one sniff.

Thinking became obsolete when Roux rolled around and raised his tail with a low meow. He kneeled on the sofa, and once more folded his body to reach his cock with his little pink tongue. The lusty expression on his face was the last straw for Jack. All his focus was on the white fur at the back of Roux's thighs and the puckered hole between the firm buttocks.

Each time Roux licked along his shaft, the pucker seemed to tighten, the hips stirred, and he let out the sexiest little sounds. Jack frantically searched his jacket and produced his trusty tin of petroleum jelly. As soon as he got some on his fingers, he teased them against Roux's hole, prodding his lover to moan louder.

It was a definite yes, then.

"That's so dirty. Who would have thought? Roux, an upstanding citizen by day, a chat slut by night," he whispered, gently slapping Roux's buttock.

Roux mewled in protest but still choked out a laugh. "It's not my fault I need cock, Jack. It's just nature." He squeezed his hole on Jack's fingers, sucking them into his body in a promise of ecstasy.

He was so relaxed his sphincter yielded to stretching with ease, and Jack let out a raspy laugh before tugging on his own dick. "Whatever you need. I'm at your service."

Roux's eyes glinted, and he slowed down, gliding his tongue up his cock at an agonizing pace. Jack couldn't wait anymore.

He removed his fingers and pushed his prick at the vacant opening, eyes wide so he wouldn't miss a second of this wonderful spectacle. Roux's tail trailed under Jack's jaw, and he moaned at the touch of soft fur, but was already grabbing Roux's hips and pressing his cock in. He imagined Roux licking his own dick, teasing it with that agile tongue. He couldn't see it happen in this position, but his mind played images of that nubby tongue against the red tip on repeat. He wouldn't last long, but hopefully Roux was ready as well.

The shaft pushed inside, disappearing into Roux, and Jack took his time caressing the relaxed back and thighs of his lover. Roux's fur was like silk to the touch, soft and warm, and inviting. The tail kept moving, caressing his neck and tickling his ears as they both voiced their pleasure, already rocking their bodies.

Jack hunched over, reaching into the middle of the ball that was Roux's folded body. The sleek pelt that covered all of him felt soft and was such a contrast with the naked flesh of Roux's cock. He didn't try to squeeze it and just kept his hand still until Roux's damp tongue slid across his fingers.

Roux groaned in pleasure, so inviting, so open to Jack. The air smelled of dust and Roux's fur, and by now, the scent had become an aphrodisiac. In the pale light coming from the streets, blinds created stripes over Roux's body, and despite Jack knowing every inch of his lover by now, there was always something new to marvel at.

He grabbed the fur on Roux's hips and quickened his thrusts to the sound of Roux's moans. His dick delved into the pliant body like it was soft butter, and with his brain unable to take the tension, the fast thrusts built up. He grabbed the base of the tail and let his other hand roam all over the muscular sides of his lover.

Roux shook, his fur bristling, flesh tensing under Jack's touch, and when his hole clamped down on Jack, it became so impossibly narrow Jack couldn't catch his breath. Roux mewled, but he had to be biting on his tongue, because he'd usually be much more vocal.

Jack didn't care about neighbors or the police right now. He wanted to make Roux come and feel his ass throb with heat, milking Jack's cock.

The next thrust toppled Jack over the edge, and he bit on the dusty backrest of the sofa as tremors went through his body in waves. With his face hot and sweaty, as if he'd spent the past hour in a sauna, he curled around Roux, rubbing his cheek against the smooth fur as his dick slid out with a wet slap.

"Oh, Roux... you're definitely *my* kitty."

Roux snorted, breathless, and when Jack slid his hands to Roux's chest, he could feel the fast beat of his heart. "I am."

Jack kissed his nape, but as exhaustion took hold of his body, he moved to lie down on the seat and pulled Roux with him until they cuddled up with limbs entwined and Roux's agile tail curled around Jack's knee.

"You should definitely use catnip more often," Jack said, chuckling as he kissed the cool, thin ear of his lover.

Roux laughed, hugging Jack with his eyes closed. "Hn? Am I not sexual enough with you on a daily basis?"

Jack shrugged and kissed Roux's forehead, letting his lips rest against the smooth fur. "You're always perfect. But I enjoy seeing you so completely relaxed. You aren't like this very often."

Roux sighed, his warm breath tickling Jack. "Because there's so many expectations I'm supposed to meet. I always have to look like the perfect representative of my species."

Jack met his soulful green eyes, and smiled at Roux. "You don't have to be perfect with me. I want you just the way you are."

Roux nuzzled Jack's sweaty cheek. "Jack, would you like to meet my family? They're very rowdy, and loud, and too much, but I'd want them to meet you."

Jack's heart started beating overtime. "Really? You'd like them to know?" he whispered, both joyful that Roux didn't want to hide their relationship, and surprised by it after the reactions they'd gotten at the bistro.

"Of course." Roux stroked Jack's arm. "I plan a future with you. I want to be with you, regardless of what they say. Jack, I'm the first non-human venator in Europe. I might not look like the rebel, but no one can stop me when I want something."

Jack's breath caught, and he pulled Roux closer, suddenly itching for their reality to be different. To live in a world where he could introduce Roux to his own parents and make them understand what a wonderful man his Roux was. But that wasn't going to happen. Ever.

"I'd love to. I'm sure your family's great, or they wouldn't have produced a chat like you."

Roux groaned. "They might not be what you think. And there are a *lot* of them."

"I'm pretty sure they can't be worse than my family, all things considered," Jack said, stretching out on the long sofa. If he were to bring home a human, there would have been no issues, but he couldn't introduce Roux, only to see them reject him. Roux didn't deserve that, and neither did Jack.

Roux just purred, not knowing the turmoil in his lover's head.

What Father didn't know couldn't hurt him.

Chapter 5

The sun woke them up to a beautiful morning in Paris. The apartment didn't have access to running water, so they ended up using public baths nearby. The city was only just waking up, and as more and more people walked the streets, Jack decided it was time for breakfast. They chose to go to a café they'd eaten at several times, and which had excellent options for both chats and humans. It was in another district, but with the weather so fine, instead of catching a metro train, they decided on a brisk walk.

Roux looked beyond handsome in a long emerald scarf to go with his new green jacket. "It's been a few months since Siberia, yet I still feel like there are so many more things to learn about you."

"About me? Really?" Jack asked, somewhat surprised. He knew he was fun to be around, but hardly mysterious. His gaze slid over a store with beauty accessories, and the sight of a collection of brushes meant for chat fur made him seek out the name of the street. Maybe he could surprise Roux with one of those later?

"Yes, you." Roux nudged Jack with his elbow. "For example, why did you decide to stay in Europe? Weren't there enough monsters to slay in America?"

Jack's mouth twitched, and he took hold of Roux's shoulder as they ran across the street. There were many reasons. He liked the way things drastically changed from place to place, or the fact that he didn't have to lie to his father's face quite as often. "I think that most of all it's… that here I'm not quite as much of an Addison as back home, you know? In Europe, people who know of my father are mostly those connected to hunting in some way, and even if his name is known, it doesn't hold nearly as much power. People don't treat me any different from other venators, and I learned to appreciate thaaaa—."

His eyes grew wide when he spotted his own face on a large poster a group of workers were attaching to a billboard. It advertised him as a speaker at the Versailles Symposium on Creature-Human Relations. He pushed on Roux's shoulder, twirling him around so they changed direction.

Roux laughed. "What are you doing? Aren't we going to the bistro? They do that salmon pâté I like."

"Yeah, but I wanted to see that horse first. You know, the one that just went into that alley?" Jack babbled, his brain cooking from the shock.

What. The. Fuck. He had not signed up for this. He only had one option now—take Roux to their hotel room, pack their bags and flee Paris in hope that Roux wouldn't spot his face in connection to the reprehensible event.

Roux cocked his head and he looked around. "What horse?"

Jack's heart pulsed in his throat. Couldn't he just slay monsters and mind his own business? Why did Father have to pull him into this stupid symposium?

"You know what? I wanna be spontaneous. Let's go to the south today. I really wanna meet your parents. We can eat on the train," Jack said, trying to keep his cool while on the lookout for more posters. The stress of it was pushing his blood pressure through the roof.

Roux pushed on Jack's arm. "Jack, I want the pâté."

"Jack Addison?" Someone asked behind them, filling Jack's veins with dread.

Roux huffed and stood aside with his arms crossed. "Go on, Jack, your fans await." This wasn't the first time, or the second, when Jack got stopped by the press, but this time, it could mean life or death. Or rather, Roux or no Roux.

He turned around at a slow pace, like a stereotypical old vampire, only to see several people with notebooks and cameras. Flashlights flickered, but he did his best to appear unmoved as he faced the reporters. "This isn't the right time. I'm on my way to a meeting."

To a train. Roux would eventually forgive him if he couldn't have the pâté.

"Just a few questions, Mr. Addison," pleaded a young reporter with flushed cheeks. "Can you provide any details about your speech at the Versailles Symposium on Creature-Human Relations? We want to inform our readers, give them a glimpse of what's to come."

"Yes," said another reporter. "Many have been following your victories across the continent."

Jack was boiling. He just wanted to run. Turn around and straight up run, but when he turned to face Roux, his lover's fur was bristled and his ears turned back.

Roux cocked his head. His face was saying *what the fuck*, but he cleared his throat and spoke with the most biting politeness. "Oh, Jack, you didn't tell me you were *speaking* at the symposium. So modest!"

Several flashlights reflected in the fiery green of Roux's eyes when Jack spoke. "I forgot to tell you. I'm supposed to talk about my travels and what different creatures one might encounter. And of monsters," he uttered, feeling his clothes dampen from the sweat beading on his body. His brain had no capacity to deal with this.

A woman dressed head to toe in black smiled widely, making notes. "Oh, yes, monsters! The public will want to know all about those."

Roux rolled his eyes. "Monsters. Like tarantoids? Those are particularly horrific, aren't they?"

Jack squirmed under the molten lava of Roux scorn.

"Please let Mr. Addison speak," huffed a man with a bushy moustache.

"No, no," said the journalist in black. "That's no onlooker, that's Roux Chat-Bonnier. Are you friends, Mr. Addison? We like to keep track of such things in Paris."

Jack could barely hear them over the pulsing noise inside his head. Paris spun around him like the inside of a kaleidoscope, and his only wish was to dismiss them.

"We're colleagues. And his name's Roux Chat-*Bonnes*."

"Colleagues," Roux repeated in an ice cold voice before turning to the journalists. "At best. We were just discussing how I don't agree with what the symposium stands for. I am also a member of JUSTICE, the Jolly Union for Sovereignty, Truth and Interdimensional Creature Equality, and I hoped that Mr. Addison and JUSTICE could form some kind of alliance, but after the conversation we have just had, I highly doubt that's going to happen."

Invisible claws stabbed into Jack's chest one after another.

Fuck.

Hell.

"I wouldn't say cooperation is out of the question," he said, gravitating toward Roux on weak legs. He could barely hear the reporters, completely focused on his lover's face while everything else blurred.

"I'm afraid JUSTICE is incompatible with the Addison agenda. Good day, Mr. Addison." Roux turned around, his tail swishing.

Jack wanted to grab his shoulder, but the moment he took half a step toward him, Roux jumped on someone's balcony on the first floor and proceeded to climb up a drainpipe before disappearing on the roof.

Reporters gasped. "Chats are so agile!" a young one said, but they all blurred into a mass of notebooks and cameras.

"Any comment, Mr. Addison?"

Jack had none. None at all.

Next time on Jack Addison vs. A Whole World of Hot Trouble:

Will Jack give up on Roux and join Drake in London?
Does Jack's father have an illicit affair with a vampiress?
Will JUSTICE attack the Symposium?

Jack Addison vs. Doing the Right Thing

Jack Addison Vs. A Whole World of Hot Trouble #9

K.A. Merikan

"Mr. Addison… I'm so sorry to impose, but I was hoping you would sign my venator card?"

Jack thought he had it all: a powerful family ready to offer a helping hand in times of need, success and fame, and the most amazing lover in the person of Roux Chat-Bonnes. Problem is, his family would never accept a nonhuman as Jack's life partner, so for months he was stuck trying to keep his relationship hidden. But when Roux found out Jack had given in to his father and agreed to give a speech at an anti-creature conference, Jack's beloved chat left him.

Ashamed and heartbroken, Jack needs to choose whether he should go against what he believes in and support his Father's cause, or follow his heart and try to win Roux back.

Deep down, Jack knows what's right, but choosing to do the right thing is a whole other matter when it means standing against the world.

Previously on Jack Addison vs. A Whole World of Hot Trouble:

Jack Addison might come from a line of legendary monster hunters and scientists, but real life has taught him that the world isn't anything like he'd been told. After encountering the alluring Nessie during the annual hunt, he's opened up to the idea of dating nonhumans, and eventually focuses his interest on fellow hunter, the catlike Roux Chat-Bonnes.

Following a period of mistrust, Roux warms up to Jack, and they end up spending a night together. In the morning, however, the beautiful chat gives Jack the cold shoulder after discovering a diary of Jack's sexual conquests. Disillusioned, Jack agrees to be Roux's friend, and they travel together after accepting a dangerous job in Siberia. It is there, during a confrontation with a deadly kitsune, that Roux is finally honest about his feelings for Jack, and they decide to become a couple.

Content, and for the first time certain of one another's feelings, Roux and Jack are about to board a train back west when Jack receives a parcel.

Unaware of his son's real opinions, Jack's father has invited him to an anti-creature event in France.

Once they reach Paris, Jack meets up with his father and reluctantly agrees to take part in the symposium to talk about his travels. Disgusted by that, Roux leaves Jack and disappears from sight.

Chapter 1

Jack sat in his opulently decorated room with hastily made notes. How had he even gotten here in the end? He should have ditched the conference being held for an idea he despised and tried to find Roux, but if he made Father look bad by ignoring the keynote speech, their relationship might not survive. He would never spew anti-creature nonsense the way he used to before he discovered the truth, but stories about his travels could hardly do any harm. After his family supporting him for so many years, he owed Father that much

It wasn't a big deal.

So why was his stomach in knots? Even the view of the grand Versailles gardens couldn't lift his mood.

That was pretty clear, no matter how much his mind tried to deny facts. Ditching Roux like this and, trying to hide the truth from him made him a lousy person, and an even lousier partner. The only thing keeping his heart from collapsing was the thought that maybe his stories could shed a different light on creatures and sow the right seeds in at least some minds. Ones that weren't completely hardened yet.

He squeezed the paper as his chest tightened again.

He didn't want to be here, socializing with people who'd likely treat Roux like trash or with polite hostility, at best. He wanted to be at Roux's side, stargazing and walking the narrow streets of Montmartre, cuddling into his warm, fragrant fur.

The knock on the door made him groan. Was it really his time already? He glanced to the tall window. Despite the cold weather outside, the garden beckoned him with promises of freedom.

"Come in..." he groaned without enthusiasm.

A hotel worker in a neat burgundy uniform entered, carrying a tray of food and two glasses of wine. "Good afternoon, Mr. Addison."

Jack offered him a smile, because what was the point of unloading his frustration on anyone but himself? "What is it?"

Cute dimples appeared in the man's cheeks when he smiled. "Mr. Addison... I'm so sorry to impose, but I wanted to treat you, and I was hoping you would sign my venator card?" He put the tray on the bed and fished a little collectible wallet out of his pocket.

Jack's shoulders slumped, and he grabbed a pen from the nightstand before scribbling his name on the back of the card featuring a photo of him holding a whole bundle of necrorats.

He didn't deserve the high stats he had in the Game of Venators.

"Here you go."

"Thank you very much!" The man blew at the ink to make it dry faster, but he didn't seem ready to leave. "About the symposium... I cannot wait to hear you speak, Mr. Addison. I've read so much about you."

Jack's lips tightened. "The reporters exaggerate all stories. I'm just a venator like many others."

The man licked his full lips. "But also... not like many others, right?" His breath quickened, and he brushed his fingers against Jack's, staring into his eyes with a slow-burning fire in his own.

Oh. *OH.*

Jack gave a startled chuckle and looked into the handsome face. "I don't think I understand."

"I thought I could... express my appreciation? I got this job just so I could meet you, Mr. Addison." This time, his fingers drifted to the front of Jack's pants, and feigning ignorance was no longer a possibility.

Jack's body stiffened, and as a flush crept up his neck, all the way to his face, he thought of how tense he was feeling. Sex would have surely provided relief.

But as pretty as this young man was, Jack felt very little toward him, even physically. Five years ago, he'd have jumped on any opportunity for sex with someone decent-looking, but he'd grown up, had much more experience, and the human form felt inexcusably dull in comparison to the softness of fur, the agility of a tail, the depth of green chat eyes.

But if it had been a chat member of staff who'd approached him this way, Jack wouldn't have been up for it either. His thoughts were still with Roux, still full of hope and desperation for him. He'd done enough to betray Roux already.

"I'm afraid I'm already taken," he said, awkwardly spreading his thighs to take a step sideways and escape the touch, which did feel physically arousing.

The guy's shoulders sagged, and for once Jack was happy to hear his father's voice and a knocking on the door. "Are you ready, Jack?"

Father left just enough time for the hotel worker to take a step back. The guy mumbled an awkward goodbye and passed Father as he made his entry.

The heavy brows lowered farther. "Did I come at a bad time?"

Jack cleared his throat. "No. He just cleaned a spill. I'm ready," he said and put on his leather jacket, which had been thoroughly oiled for the occasion.

He supposed most people saw him as a man of success, but whenever Jack glanced into the mirror, all he could see was a coward. Not that long ago, he'd promised Roux he would stand by him, but he'd failed him again and didn't know how to take back his actions, while wading deeper into the mud.

"Two glasses of wine though?" Father smirked.

Jack rubbed his face. "One's for you, dad. To err… celebrate."

Father's eyebrows rose, but he took one of the glasses and patted Jack's back. "I'm so happy to have you here. Your fame will give our cause lots of publicity. I might be the Kraken, but in Europe I'm seen as a bit of a relic. You, on the other hand, are the face of young venators. People look up to you."

Too bad *people* didn't know Jack's thoughts, because he'd been careful to remain neutral whenever he spoke to the press. "I'm sure my stories will be entertaining."

"Not only that!" Father took a sip of wine. "People living in Paris have no idea what their world has become. Your words will surely inspire those present today to dig deeper and seek the truth beyond government propaganda. There are journalists, novelists, and anthropologists present."

Jack frowned. Was he missing something? "What has the world become?"

"We are becoming overrun, Jack. You've seen it yourself. Werewolves murdering human children, Vampires running amok in Romania. It needs to stop."

Jack chuckled. "Dad, when's the last time you've been to Romania? There's nothing amiss going on there. Are there murderers among vampires? Yes, but humans aren't angels either."

Father frowned in a way that had Jack's heart stopping briefly. "I hope that's not the kind of picture you intend to paint in your speech."

Jack shrugged, even though his muscles were already calcifying under the scrutiny of Father's dark gaze. "You asked me to talk about my adventures. That's what I'm going to talk about. I'm not going to pretend all werewolves are out to murder virgins or that gnomes are a danger to society."

"I don't have time for this nonsense. What are you talking about? These *are* dangers to our society, so you better not take this speech in some strange direction."

Jack gritted his teeth and rose, downing his wine in one go. It was sour, but then again his fan wouldn't have 'treated' him to bad wine, so what did he know? "You said it yourself. I am the face of young venators. I am not going to lie in my own name, so if you're afraid my opinion about creatures isn't sufficiently negative, maybe let's call it off."

He didn't dare look at Father, and pretended the tiny bit of liquid still remaining in the glass was the most fascinating thing in the room.

Silence extended for endless seconds.

"This isn't a joke," Father said in a grave voice. "You better give that speech, and you make it good, Jack. I didn't push you through school so that you could go gallivanting all over Europe. You bear the Addison name, and if you want things to stay the way they are, deliver a speech I can be proud of."

Jack found it too hard to form an answer, but he didn't have to. Father left, having barely touched his wine.

Jack's throat tightened when he got nauseous, but he rested his hands on a marble counter and took several deep breaths in an attempt to calm down. A glance at the clock told him it was high time to leave the room, so he drank Father's wine before adjusting his hair and stepping into the corridor with a stiff gait reminiscent of the mummies he'd once seen when he visited the Natural History Museum in London.

It would be fine. He'd just ignore Father's request and keep the content of his speech to anecdotes, sprinkle some of the good and bad throughout, and that would be that. Hopefully, Father would never ask him to make a speech again and keep sending money. Two birds with one stone, really.

He walked down the corridors of the elegant hotel that held so much history, yet today served as home to a conference that would discuss the rights of non-humans without their presence. If Roux saw him now, he'd only feel contempt, angry at himself that he wasted so much time on a human lowlife. If any of his creature friends found out, Jack wouldn't know how to look them in the eye.

Why was it so hard to do the right thing? Did he even know anymore what the 'right thing' was? Maybe the right thing was to leave through the window and never come back? There was no one watching. Maybe Jack could do that?

"Jack!"

Clearly, it wasn't to be.

Jack steadied himself for another confrontation with a misinformed fan, only to spot a familiar face.

"Drake? What are you doing here?" he asked, shocked to see his friend approaching him with a large wheeled table with some empty plates on top.

Drake frowned. "I'm here to ask *you* that question. I came to visit you in Paris, only to see your face on all those posters."

Jack's head was empty, but he still looked back, to make sure they were alone. "I-- Father roped me into this."

"So you're not actually making the speech?"

Jack's throat yearned for more wine, but his focus went in another direction when he saw a black, bristled leg ending in two claws push out from under the long white cloth covering the table.

Tapping in Morse code, it spelled out D-A-D-D-Y.

His heart got so heavy he kneeled and pushed away the fabric, revealing Chad's eight cute black eyes, looking at him with so much admiration he could hardly cope. He pulled Chad into his arms without thinking and petted him through the tiny tuxedo he wore for the occasion.

"Daddy's here. I missed you! Drake, he's grown so much." He glanced at his friend, who stared at him with a somber expression. "Why didn't you tell me you were coming?"

"You're hardly easy to track down. We heard you'd be in Paris, so we wanted to make the trip and surprise you, but then I saw you were doing your dad's event and... err, yeah, here we are."

Chad tapped excitedly that he wanted to see Uncle Roux again and fall asleep in his fur. Jack could empathise with that sentiment, but the baby's excitement only made him feel worse about the whole thing.

"I'm sorry, Chad, but Uncle Roux isn't here. I'm sure he would have made it if he'd known you were coming," he said before gently ushering the kid back under the cloth. It wasn't a safe place for a young tarantoid, and he didn't want to take unnecessary risks. "Be a good boy and stay hidden. We can make a game out of it."

Drake cocked his head. "I don't think Roux would ever come here," he whispered, only making Jack feel worse, but the show had to go on.

Chapter 2

Jack hated the speech before his own. His father's friend and Jack's former professor took his time explaining a bullshit theory about creatures lacking the capacity for higher feelings, and that their family relationships were based on 'collective instinct', and 'the need to procreate' rather than love, in the human sense of the word. Jack knew this wasn't the case, since he would never believe that Chad, not even a chat or vampire but a *tarantoid*, didn't feel love for his adoptive parents. And Roux… Roux was the most compassionate, loving person Jack had ever met.

The bogus claims then continued when the professor presented creature-made art as derivative compared to the art created by humans, as if the idiot hadn't even taken his time to dig that bit deeper. Hadn't he ever heard of *belor*, the body modification technique of nymphs, which involved the person controlling the pigmentation of their own skin to create elaborate patterns? And that was only one of so many unique things various creatures used to enrich their lives with culture and meaning.

By the time the speaker left the stage to a storm of applause, Jack felt physically sick over having to enter the same space as that bigoted idiot.

A storm of clapping followed him up the stairs leading to the podium, as if his presence were the cue for the atmosphere to change from contemplative to more rowdy.

"Show us the Gouger!" someone yelled.

Jack gave a nervous laugh and pulled the sword out of its sheath to hold it up for everyone to see. Maybe the talk wouldn't be so bad after all? Then again, he was no public speaker, and despite having notes, he was already lost over what he wanted to communicate.

"So, um, my name is Jack Addison, and it appears that I'm a famous venator."

The laughter that followed made him feel a tiny bit more confident. Maybe he could play up the village idiot act.

"My experience with creatures and monsters is extensive, despite my age. I'm twenty-four, I've travelled all over Europe, and some of you might have read about my exploits."

"Love you, Jack!" yelled a woman from the crowd, shaking her elaborate hat in the air.

Jack laughed. "Well, you wouldn't be so fond of me if you knew what a swarm of sentient bees did to me once."

The room roared with laughter, but Jack tried to focus on his memories rather than all the ears itching to drink up his words. He was standing in front of a large auditorium, but with the lights focused on him, he couldn't see that many details, and the audience beyond the first couple of rows melted into a dark mass. Maybe that would make this torture easier to survive.

He found himself speaking a lot about Siberia and its breathtaking nature, and while he didn't reveal how little he had to do with the death of the kitsune, he made sure to stress Akito's role in the endeavor. The fact that werewolves were 'useful' in hunting down other creatures seemed to go down well with the audience.

He went on to talk a lot about the lifestyle of a traveling venator and focused on his personal struggles rather than on the monsters, because the public's eagerness to hear about slaying was making him increasingly uncomfortable. He could only hope Chad, who'd stayed behind the stage with Drake, wouldn't take any of it the wrong way. In the eyes of all the people present, Chad would be a threat, a creature to be eliminated before they could even find out what he could do or who he was.

Jack ran out of steam far quicker than he'd intended, so he pretended he'd purposefully left twenty minutes for questions from the audience.

When the lights went on and he spotted a gray head topped with chat ears, his heart might have skipped a beat, and he chose the man to ask a question. But Jack knew this wouldn't go his way the moment he heard the first sentence.

"This is more of an observation than a question," the chat said, ogled by the people around him as if he had grown two heads. "I wanted to say I applaud this symposium. While I don't agree with all theories mentioned, I believe it's right to push for separation. Paris no longer feels like a human city. They are still in the majority, but the crowd in the streets is a mongrel bunch of everything from dog-sized flies to yetis. I'm all for tourism, but things have gotten out of hand. I would also like to address the risk of interbreeding. No hybrids have yet been seen, but I want to keep my species pure, or we will disappear one day, leaving behind a race of mutts."

Jack bit his lip. "Um, thank you for the…er… observation. Has anyone got any questions?"

He was somewhat glad that most of them were quite useless. One man in the front row shared that he'd written a book about the dangers of yet unknown creatures dwelling in people's walls and ranted about no one wanting to publish it, a woman asked Jack to explain what kitsunes were yet again and why werewolves made such good adversaries for them, even though Jack already had, and then another wanted to know what he used to polish the Gouger.

It was a train wreck, but Jack was glad that he didn't have to work his way out of something really uncomfortable.

"I have a question!" yelled a voice from the back. "Where do you stand on sexual relations between humans and other creatures?"

It took Jack two seconds to recognize the voice, but the moment he saw a spot of ginger, his skin covered in cold sweat, veins filling with dread despite the laughter the question caused. He was ice cold when he saw a woman toss a crumpled piece of paper at Roux. But when the impromptu missile hit Roux's head, Jack broke out of the stupor.

"May I ask for order? We're civilized people, and if I see anyone physically attack other attendees, that person will be removed," he said, though once he finished speaking, his head was just as empty as it had been. So he stalled, staring at Roux, who stood in silence at the very back with arms crossed on his chest and chin up high.

He'd come.

He was here.

Jack could dismiss the question, say that it was inappropriate for the nature of the conference, but his heart ached to break out of the confines of his chest and dash at Roux. This was the moment for him to take a stand, regardless of what anyone else said or how much money or fans he'd lose.

And yet his voice wouldn't stay as steady as he would have wished. "I... um, I believe that... I mean, if two—or more!—consenting adults—"

"How do we even judge if a creature is an adult within their own species?" someone yelled.

"I think you answered your own question," Jack told him, feeling as if he was about to go up in flames.

Roux raised his voice. "So it's perfectly fine to *fuck* creatures, as long as you deny them other rights that humans enjoy?"

The cacophony of boos and hissing made Jack's insides ache. Roux was so brave to come here as an outsider and state his opinion in such a bold way, while *he* stood on stage, using up valuable time to be a coward who couldn't even admit he didn't believe in his father's agenda.

"I—" He choked up, cringing when the microphone picked up his breath. But his gaze met Roux's, and for the blink of an eye, it felt as if they were alone. As if there was a whole conversation going on above everyone else's head.

And if he couldn't declare his attachment to one side of the argument presented, Roux would never accept him again. This was a test. One he couldn't blow.

"N-no. I think it's not right to deny creatures any rights humans have," he said, more shaken than he'd been in the clutches of Chad's mother.

He exhaled when murmurs drilled their way into his ears, but words rose in his throat like long-suppressed bile, and he wouldn't hold them in anymore.

"I also *do* think it's okay to have sex with creatures. To love them, and to have relationships with them. I didn't think so in the past, but in years of interacting with a whole variety of other creatures, I've understood this. We're not all the same, we have different needs, since some of us have hands, some paws, some tentacles, and a yeti needs ceilings much taller than humans, but we *can* co-exist.

"And that is why I've applied to join JUSTICE, The Jolly Union for Sovereignty, Truth and Interdimensional Creature Equality. If they will have me, I would much rather spend my career defending others than looking for monsters to slay, no matter how much more glamorous that might seem." Hit last few words didn't echo through the crowd, and blood rushed to his head when he realized someone had cut the power to his microphone. But that would not stop him.

Jack took a deep breath, about to step into the shadows behind the stage, but his thudding heart wouldn't let him. The attendees might as well not exist, because he only saw one person. "I love you, Roux! I'm sorry. About everything," he yelled through hands folded into a tube, over the heads of a crowd so silent he could've heard a pin drop. And then, a collective exhale that powered shouting and boos.

Father rose from his place in the front row, his face dark with a flush, but Jack couldn't go back on his words. Not now. Not ever. But most of all, he didn't want to. Roux didn't smile the same way humans did, but his body language told Jack everything there was to know about his approval.

"You should lose your license, you monster-lover!" shouted the same woman who'd earlier declared her love for Jack. Her face was wrinkled with fury, as if he'd just murdered her new puppy.

Jack grabbed the microphone when it creaked, on again, and dragged it to the back of the stage, surprised to spot Drake behind the curtain, wide-eyed but silently clapping.

"I will not be silent. Most of you, even those who appeared here today in the roles of experts, have hardly had any contact with creatures. You don't know what you're missing. Yes, some are bad, just like some humans can be bad, but humanity can be found in the most unexpected places," he said and stepped toward the curtain, diving under the wheeled table as soon as he saw it.

High on adrenaline, he pulled Chad out, who instantly clutched him with all his legs. The auditorium let out a collective gasp when he emerged, and Jack went tense when he spotted the glint of a blade in the second row.

But *nobody* could stop him now.

"This is Chad, and I'm raising him as if he were my own son."

When voices of disbelief rose, Jack put the microphone close to Chad's leg.

I-M-S-C-A-R-E-D-D-A-D-D-Y, Chad clicked in Morse code, and Jack hugged him to provide some relief. Chad really was getting heavy. Soon enough, he wouldn't be scared of anything.

"It's okay, we'll be out of here soon," he whispered to his boy before looking back at the crowd. "Every venator here has been trained in Morse code, so you know what he's just communicated. Chad is *scared*. He's only four years old! But he is so smart, and *so* interested in the world around him. Maybe if his mother got the same attention, she wouldn't have grown into a beast. I've read about humans who survived alone as children, and they were just as beastly as any other wild creature. If we want to establish good relationships with other species, we need to nurture those who we don't understand, and listen to those we can. We need to seek dialogue and stop seeing them as our inferiors."

But no matter how reasonable this was, the crowd wasn't having it. Some of the people rose, shouting and booing, but their body language was becoming increasingly hostile. Jack had seen enough aggression in his life to recognize it. When a heavy flask flew their way, missing Jack's head by only a couple of inches, he knew it was high time to retreat. He would be fine, but what if someone got their hands on Chad?

Regardless of the need to keep the moral high ground, he had a child to protect. And he'd have disappeared behind the curtain right away if he hadn't spotted Roux gracefully avoiding a punch as he ran toward the stage. Protective feelings flared in Jack, but Roux was an experienced venator, more agile than any of the humans around, and he joined him at the podium, pupils wide and focused only on Jack.

"I came here because I was angry. I wanted to embarrass you, and you… you stupid, wonderful man." Roux gave Jack a hug, unbothered by Chad squirming between them. His eyes were like two pieces of jade, and Jack wanted to wake up to them glinting at him from the pillow every single morning.

Jack considered giving him a kiss, but the auditorium was full of wild beasts, and he carried Chad backstage instead, blinking when they left the bright lights. He turned around to offer Chad to Drake, but Drake wasn't where Jack had last seen him.

Father stood in his place.

Chapter 3

Jack's face throbbed with heat, but he looked straight into Father's eyes. "Like it or not, this is your grandson."

Father's face turned as red as Jack's felt. "You are unbelievable. I will never accept this abomination! Hand over the Gouger. You don't deserve it. I can't believe my own son could have betrayed my trust like this!"

Jack clenched his teeth. Father knew how to hit where it hurt, but Jack wouldn't give him the satisfaction. He passed Chad to Roux, and the little tarantoid clung to him with all eight legs. Jack took the sword off his back, along with its sheath, and held it out to Father with a heavy heart.

"Take it. I don't care. A sword is an object. It doesn't matter the way living beings do, and the fact that you used it to slay a monster doesn't make it anything special. It's just a nice sword."

Father swallowed, his lips shaking. "You're shaming your entire family. You might as well not come back until you straighten up your act."

It hurt like a punch, and Jack wondered whether other members of his family would have been more understanding, actually willing to hear why he'd made the choices he'd made. It no longer mattered. "I used to think you were one of the good guys, but you can't be a good man while wanting to lock away other creatures just because you don't understand them. Or because you don't like them. Or because you believe their presence spoiled your vacation. If you're not willing to see me as my own man, only an extension of you, then you might as well disown me already. I don't need your specist money. And I don't want to be connected to your organization in any shape or form."

"Change your name then. I won't be associated with a chat-fucker!" Father growled.

Jack snorted. "Are you kidding me? I'm not gonna change my name. Let everyone know your son thinks you're wrong."

Roux's paw stroking his arm only made Jack feel more strongly about his decision. For so long he'd been sliding through life, ducking whenever responsibility flew his way, but it was moments like this that made him feel alive. More like himself. The joy he'd felt when he'd saved the centaur, or rescued Laavan the merman from death was incomparable to the glory Father offered.

Roux smiled and lifted his chin. "Well, you could always change your last name to Chat-Bonnes."

Father roared with fury and lowered his body as if he wanted to charge at both Roux and Chad, but Jack stepped in between them.

"If you lay a finger on them I will take out ads in every American newspaper to announce my marriage to a chat!"

Father let out a snake-like hiss and turned without another word, in a hurry to put distance between himself and the son who hadn't turned out the way he wanted.

It was for the better, no matter how heavy Jack's heart felt when he saw the familiar figure disappear from sight.

Jack's shoulders slumped, and he was grateful for the weight of Roux's head. Their eyes met above Chad, but before Jack could have sought refuge in his kitty's arms, Drake burst out from behind the curtain with a large backpack.

"Are you guys insane? We need to get Chad out before someone gets in here! The crowd is furious."

Chad reached out to Drake with four legs and Roux passed the tarantoid to his other dad.

Jack swallowed and grabbed a black curtain obscuring the entrance to a back corridor. He ripped it off and crumpled it in his arms so that it could imitate a tarantoid from afar.

"Roux, go with Drake, take Chad to safety, and I'll distract them! Meet me in the gardens by the Marie Antoinette village" he yelled, and gave Roux a quick kiss.

He ran the other way, only once turning around to make sure Chad was safe on Drake's back.

He'd never felt more virtuous and he *loved* it.

Jack Addison wasn't a scumbag after all.

Chapter 4

Jack breathed out vapor, but he was far enough from the small mob that had formed around him to allow himself a moment of rest. After fleeing the hotel, he climbed the fence surrounding the gardens of Versailles across the street, and since the palace grounds were closed for the night, he took his time, navigating the empty alleys until he found a site map. Away from the grandeur of the formal gardens, the multitude of trees and bushes provided shelter from any guards who might be on patrol. But he'd have to be extremely unlucky to stumble upon one. This place was huge, and staff would walk around with a lamp and could be spotted from afar, anyway.

The cold made him rub his shoulders, but after consulting the map, Jack directed his footsteps toward the hamlet in hopes that Roux would bear good news. Both he and Drake knew how to take care of themselves, but the fact that Jack hadn't seen Chad boarding a train back to Paris had his stomach in knots.

Paws covered Jack's eyes from behind like in a game he often played with Roux. Jack was yet to hear Roux approaching no matter how hard he focused.

"Boo!"

He stiffened, grabbing his lover's hands, and spun around to face him without knowing whether his heart galloped out of love or fright. "There you are!"

Roux sank into him without hesitation. "Chad is safe with Drake and his wife. They're waiting for us at their hotel in Paris, but tomorrow morning we will all be off to London. I don't think we would be safe here for a while."

Jack nodded, mesmerized the way Roux's fur shone in the moonlight as if it had been scattered with glitter. In the perfect silence of this place, with Roux in his arms, Jack felt peaceful, even though he wasn't sure whether the relationship he used to share with his family could ever recover. It was a heavy burden on his heart but still less painful than living a lie.

"Roux, you held Chad."

Roux stilled but then groaned and bumped his head against Jack's shoulder. "I guess I did. He's much lighter than I expected. But also, he is a creature, not a monster. And just a baby. He doesn't deserve hate."

Jack laughed and gave Roux's lips a firm kiss. "Thank you. You'll learn to love him, you'll see. He asked about 'Uncle Roux' earlier," he said, pulling on Roux's hand and heading toward the artificial lake.

"I mean… he's part of you," Roux said with a straight face, but then laughed. Only when they stepped out of the shadows, Jack noticed that his lover's ear was ripped.

Anger was like an itch he couldn't scratch, and he gently touched the fresh wound. "Who did this?"

Roux waved it off with a groan. "This guy, he got me with a piece of broken glass when I was escorting Chad and Drake out. It's nothing."

Jack pulled him into a gentle embrace, overcome with tenderness. "I'm sorry. It's all because of me. I should have just told him no in the first place," he said with a shake of his head.

Roux looked up, stroking Jack's sides. "You should have. But maybe it turned out for the better. You caused quite a riot, Jack Addison. I was very impressed." He purred and gave Jack a kiss.

Jack smiled when the smooth fur rubbed against his cheek. His gaze wandered to the moon, and then the hamlet on the other side of the lake. "I don't think it's safe for us to leave just yet. How about hiding in there?"

Roux nodded and grabbed Jack's hand, leading the way through the garden and to the small old-timey cottage in the middle of it.

"I'd rather wait till morning. Everyone would have had time to cool off by then."

Jack squeezed Roux's hand, his gaze swiping over the bare fruit trees. "I'm not sad. Maybe for Mom. We shall see what she thinks once she finds out."

"Is she... the same as your father?" Roux asked, and when they approached the heavy wooden door, he casually dipped his claw into the lock, fiddling with it until it clicked open.

Jack whistled but hugged Roux as they entered. It was slightly warmer inside, and when Jack's gaze adjusted to the lower light, he spotted that some of the furnishings scattered over the room were still packed with paper and cloth, as if they'd recently been moved here. Wallpaper was only present on one of the walls, and the air smelled faintly of glue. The place was in the middle of a restoration.

Jack exhaled. "She's not as vocal. Maybe not as radical either, but she never argues with him about it."

Roux hugged him as soon as they locked the door. "You did the right thing, though. You can't hide who you are forever. And, to be honest, there's only so long I could respect that. Nobody wants to be a dirty secret."

Jack nodded and kissed the scab that had formed on Roux's injured ear, as they explored the cottage, climbing a narrow staircase. "No. I don't want to hide you. And I won't."

"Was the JUSTICE thing just a gimmick because you were high on your self-righteousness or do you really want to join?"

Jack laughed. "Oh, Roux. I definitely want to join. I can be your human poster boy, if you need one. I'm done keeping a low profile. I want to be your ally and use my platform to promote JUSTICE."

Roux whistled. "Someone's read our pamphlets."

Jack frowned, mildly offended. "Of course I did! It's important to you. And… I also think it's important for everyone. For… you know, peace."

Roux pressed the pads on his paws to Jack's cheek as he kissed him again, gently lapping at his lips. "Peace indeed."

Jack rested his chin on the top of Roux's head, enjoying the soothing temperature of the ears against his skin. In contrast to the lower level of the cottage, the renovation of the room above had been completed. Blue wallpaper featuring a delicate pattern covered the walls, and while there were no paintings or curtains to add the final touch, the space was furnished with a vanity and an elegant, if small, bed with a wooden frame carved into a sleigh-like shape, and a canopy of blue taffeta. This would be the perfect place to lay low, and even if the bedding wasn't warm enough, they had each other to share body heat.

Roux's fur was always so warm. Jack would never forget how amazing Roux's hug had felt after lonely minutes in the Siberian snow. Better than any down-filled comforter, it had been a furry radiator that purred its love at him.

Roux slid his hands up Jack's back. "I wouldn't be able to live with myself if you hadn't made the step you did today."

"What do you mean? You did everything right," Jack whispered, gravitating toward the bed. Adrenaline was pumping in his veins, and that called for a celebratory fuck. Roux had locked the door downstairs, after all.

"Because no matter how angry I was, I would have probably taken you back, but I would have hated myself for it."

Warmth splashed through Jack's chest when the mattress dipped under him. He looked up, rubbing his chin against Roux's breastbone. With his big, expressive eyes and noble profile, his lover was magnificent. Perfect like a statue that belonged as the centerpiece of the nearby garden.

"I know I've broken this promise in the past, but I really want to be the guy you deserve, Roux," Jack whispered, grateful and happy despite his shame.

A small smile played on Roux's lips. "You would have come to grovel with those pretty blue eyes, and I wouldn't have been able to think of a future where I never licked you again. And I'd have said, okay, I'll take you back if you survive my cock." He snorted and stroked Jack's hair.

Jack felt his face flush when Roux's words triggered a spiral of sexual fantasies. Roux was an eager bottom, so Jack had never broached the topic of switching. Not because he was afraid he'd displease Roux by asking for it, but because when it came to sex they always gravitated to their favorite configuration. But now he couldn't stop thinking about that cute red cock pushing at his hole.

"I'm sure it would have hardly been a punishment."

Roux pushed Jack down to the bed and sat in his lap. "The one time I tried it with a human, he panicked and said it was weird. I wouldn't inflict it on you, Jack. I get it. It might not be as compatible with you as your cock is with me."

Jack let out a chuckle, amused by the fact that Roux, who'd witnessed Jack getting boned by four werewolves, thought he wouldn't be up for this challenge. "You're kidding, right? I thought you just weren't interested in topping, kitty," he whispered, his tone dropping instantly when Roux's pupils dilated.

Roux groaned and pulled his nubby tongue up Jack's cheek. "No, I just don't want to cause you pain. It's extremely embarrassing to have a partner change their mind because they think your dick is weird."

Jack grinned at him and reached to the front of Roux's pants, shuddering at the gentle scratch of the damp tongue. "It might come as a surprise, but I love your dick. I love sucking on it, and touching it, and I want to feel it in my ass," he whispered, keeping their gazes locked.

Roux's pupils were so big his eyes became two dark wells into his soul. The deep purr he let out was like nothing Jack had ever heard from his chat. "And you're sure?" But he was already pushing Jack down.

Jack wouldn't have said it out loud, but Roux's cock wasn't particularly large. Perhaps it was, for a chat, but it compared to an average human size, even if its shape was so different. He expected it to cause excitement rather than discomfort.

"Now?" Jack asked, still looking straight at Roux as he rested his hands above his head in submission.

Roux pressed down on his chest with his cute paw-like hands and groaned. "I was just joking, but if you're up for it? Yes, *now*. You're so hot, Jack, it shouldn't be allowed. Ass, thighs, chest, face, dick, I love all of you."

Ohh, yes.

Jack was definitely *up* for that, and these compliments were only making his cock grow faster. "Me too. I love your nubby cock, and I want it to shoot cum deep inside me," he whispered, pushing his hips up with enough strength to lift Roux.

"Then unbutton your stupid pants, or I'm gonna have to rip them open."

Jack made a mental note to get snap fasteners on his clothes so that Roux could undress him with ease, but Roux already sat up on Jack's hips, taking off his jacket and shirt, and revealing his white furry chest.

There went Jack's self-control. Roux's agile, slender body never failed to make his blood boil. He wanted it under him and over him. Inside him and around him. He wanted everything Roux could offer.

Blinded by an onslaught of lust, Jack opened his pants and made awkward attempts at kicking them off without having to move Roux. Warmth was already rubbing its invisible hands up his sides, and he desperately needed to get naked. "What kind of top are you? Are you sweet and gentle? Aggressive and demanding? Will you pinch me?"

"I'll definitely need to make sure I don't scratch you." Roux wouldn't meet Jack's gaze, too focused on the newly exposed chest. "My dick's pretty demanding, though. But you already know that. I've dreamed about this *so* many times. It's feels so good when the nubs are teased." He rose to his knees over Jack's hips. "Turn around."

"You should have said something," Jack rasped but rolled to his stomach, just like Roux had asked. His brain thudded with arousal when he imagined Roux on top of him, with bristled fur and his tail stiff. Would Roux bite his nape like a male cat would his partner? He did know Roux wasn't a *cat*, but his imagination refused to submit. Unlike his body, which was more than eager, and he spread his legs as soon as Roux pulled Jack's pants off.

"It's a sensitive subject." Roux groaned, but he was on top of Jack in seconds and he nuzzled Jack's nape with the wet nose.

"So is my hole," Jack said, glancing at him over his shoulder. He grinned and shook his buttocks in invitation, which only made his dick stir against the expensive taffeta.

Roux laughed and bit on Jack's nape. "Why did I fall for such an idiot?" But his cock was rock hard when it pressed against Jack's buttock.

"I don't know, maybe you like being the smart one," Jack offered, gleefully spreading his legs as anticipation crawled up his spine. He would get to know a chat's cock at last. Roux's cock. What could be better than that? Just thinking of how the nubs had felt on his tongue and how the narrow tip had poked at his throat had him shivering.

Roux pondered that for quite a while, moving his chest against Jack's back. "Maybe I do. You're endearing when you confuse a werehog with a boar."

"And then you can enlighten me," Jack teased, rocking his hips in an attempt to make the tip of Roux's cock push into his crack.

"I mean, chat cocks was one of the first things you asked me about, so it's only fair I enlighten you about that too." Roux pulled the tips of his claws over the sides of Jack's body as he slid lower, licking his way down Jack's spine.

Passion grabbed Jack by the balls, and he uttered a broken sound, arching at the mixture of pain and pleasure. "Show me how you like to fuck," he whispered, longingly rubbing his calf against his lover's fur.

"Well, I do like to get my partner ready and shivering first," Roux said and dipped the lower part of his face between Jack's buttocks. He licked the sensitive skin around Jack's hole, barely adding any pressure. That was for the better, because Roux's tongue *was* coarse.

And because that was its texture, Jack hadn't expected ever getting rimmed. This was a magical night. He'd stood up to his dad and a roomful of creature haters, saved his son, got his boyfriend back, and now his ass would be getting the royal treatment in Marie Antoinette's cabin.

Shivers affected even Jack's deepest muscles, and he moaning helplessly into the bedcover, trapped between wanting more and the fear of this becoming too much somehow. He didn't know how, but the sensation affected him so much he could barely make use of his brain.

The padded hands kneaded his buttocks. "Tell me if it's too much," Roux whispered and the tip of his tongue teased Jack's hole, making him moan and squirm despite the touch being so faint. Was it the anticipation? He wasn't even sure, but Roux was using *lots* of saliva.

How could anything ever be too much with Roux? Jack wished he could consume his lover, and be consumed at the same time. "I just want you to make me your kitty," he growled, rolling his cock over the covers for friction while the damp, nubby tongue teased his opening.

"Never gonna be a kitty, Jack." Roux's hot breath tickled Jack's hole when he snorted, but he was right back at teasing his tongue into Jack's ass. Despite Roux being smaller, his tongue had quite a nice girth as he pushed it past the sphincter.

"Why not?" Jack moaned, pushing back into the lush, furry face. The whiskers were a whole different story, and their touch felt almost like thin, prodding fingers.

"You'd have to grow a lot more fur than you've got," Roux said when he pulled his tongue back and once more lapped at Jack's buttocks, making Jack shiver. His body was a bundle of excitable nerves and wherever Roux touched, sparks flied.

"Oh, come on, you know that I mean," Jack complained and rocked his hips back yet again, his dick getting so hard it was hard to focus on anything else.

Fuck me.

Fuck me with your chat dick, Roux.

His silent plea was answered when Roux languidly pulled away, only to climb on top of Jack. He wasn't heavy. Pleasant as a furry blanket. Roux purred when his cock slipped between Jack's buttocks, already prodding at the throbbing hole with its small tip. The cock broadened closer to the base, but it would slide in so easily.

"You're so... inviting," Roux teased and licked up Jack's ear.

Jack gave a frantic nod and looked up at his lover, raising his feet to rub the furry legs with his heels. "The word's *welcoming*."

Roux chuckled, rocking his cock into Jack's hole. Unlike a human dick, there was no need for pressing the cockhead in first, Roux's erection just pushed on, stretching Jack bit by bit, but he could definitely feel the irregular nubs.

"Yes. Your ass is *very* welcoming, Jack. I can't wait to spend into you."

Jack nodded and pushed back, stabbing himself on his lover's prick, greedy to have all of it inside him.

The nubs felt amazing as they teased Jack's sensitive insides with every movement of the cock. Jack's mind was already clouding. "Please."

Roux groaned into Jack's ear, and his spiky teeth against Jack's scalp were as exciting as they were scary. "Can't promise I'll last long," he said, already panting.

Roux wrapped his arms around Jack's chest, embracing him tightly, and his hips went to work at such a fast pace that Jack yelped and moaned all at once.

He spread his thighs wide when the cock stabbed him hard, delving into him time and time again. The touch of Roux's naked body, warm and fluffy, was such a treat he couldn't promise stamina either. His brain obsessed over Roux's balls and the load they held for him.

"That's... the best dick I've ever had inside me," he uttered, relaxed. It didn't hurt. It wasn't weird. It was *amazing*. The perfect size and fit for him. Unlike some massive thing, like Calix's, this one he could take every single day. The prospect already made him giddy, but it was hard to focus on anything beyond the most immediate future when Roux fucked him with such wild strokes. The way the nubs teased his sphincter with each thrust was bliss, and when they went farther in and massaged his prostate, thinking became an impossibility. How could Roux have had such a perfect pleasure instrument on hand and never before used it?

Roux wouldn't even speak to him anymore, letting out little mewls every now and again as he went all the way in. The last few times Roux pushed into Jack, he made rounded motions, rubbing his soft thighs against Jack's, and the heat between them seared Jack's skin.

"So... full... of cum," Roux mumbled sleepily as he licked the hair at the back of Jack's head.

Jack gave a broken sound, desperate to come while Roux was still inside him, and he raised his hips just enough to fit his hand underneath. "It's so fucking hot inside me," he babbled, jerking off at a frantic pace.

His entire body stiffened when Roux's canines scraped the back of his neck, and he came, thrashing under his lover.

Roux moaned, surely stimulated again when Jack's hole throbbed around him, squeezing his cock as if it didn't want to let it go. Jack never wanted anyone else in his bed but Roux. Their connection was perfect on so many levels. Not only was Roux a fantastic lover, but also accepted Jack with all of his flaws. He cared about Jack. And Chad.

He was it. The One. The End Game.

Minutes passed until Jack was ready to do anything besides breathing, and he moved his head so he could see Roux still laying on top of him. "Satisfied?"

Roux nuzzled Jack's nose and purred. "I've wanted this for a very long time."

Jack chuckled. "Just say the word from now on. We need to make up for lost time, if you catch my drift."

Roux did. He licked Jack's jaw with a happy expression, whiskers twitching, eyes focused on Jack only. "Anytime, Jack."

Jack's eyelids shut as he slowly drowned in the haziness left behind by pleasure.

"Anytime, Roux."

Epilogue

The summer smelled of lavender and milk.

Jack was more than content lying in a large hammock under a tree in the garden behind Roux's family home. The raw fish dish Roux's mom made for him still felt weird on his tongue, but he was starting to value the freshness of traditional chat food and, even more so, the love put into its preparation.

Roux had been right. His family was noisy, all over the place, and far too big for the small house, but none of them seemed bothered that they couldn't afford fancy things or travel. And while the chaos tired him out at times, he appreciated always having someone to talk to. Though privacy was so hard to come by, he was considering building a small hut, just for him and Roux, somewhere at the edge of the village.

Roux had hissed at him when he'd suggested that. As happy as Roux was to visit his family, he didn't want to stay in Bonnes too long. Jack still hoped they could come here for a few weeks every summer. The weather was glorious, with sunshine and a gentle breeze, and the lazy pace of life in chat country brought Jack much needed peace after the painful parting from his own family.

None of his relatives had replied to his letters, which hurt, but he hoped that with time they'd realize he would not budge from the path he'd chosen.

Roux's parents had been perplexed to meet Jack at first and had regarded him with suspicion, but they had come around quickly, happy that a son they thought would forever be a plaything for tomchats had found someone he loved.

Despite initial hostility, even some of the more conservative chats in the village embraced him after Jack fulfilled his promise and had become the first human face of JUSTICE. He didn't think his membership solved anything, but the fact that a venator of his reputation had chosen to speak on behalf of creatures so publically, stirred the conversation at least, and with time it might encourage humans to open up to their nonhuman neighbors.

For now though, Jack was focusing all of his attention on his memoir.

But it wasn't the one he'd planned to publish anonymously. This one would be a very public declaration of his beliefs, stories about the creatures he'd met, and what he'd learned from those interactions. He was already in talks with an American publisher. Father wouldn't be happy about this development, but he would have to understand Jack wasn't doing any of this to spite him.

Jack was a man on a mission.

"We're back!" Roux yelled from afar, and Jack looked up from his notes.

The only tall form approaching through a field of tall grass, Roux, emerged followed by five of his tiny chat siblings and Jack's own son, Chad. He hadn't been sure about bringing the boy here, especially since this was to be Jack's first time meeting Roux's family, but Roux had been adamant that many chats needed to rethink their own attitudes as well, and shouldn't pick and choose what kind of being they accepted into their midst. So here Chad was—a tarantoid as tall as a human ten-year old, frolicking in the grass with baby chats.

Jack put down his notebook and stretched. "Wouldyou care for some food?" he asked, pointing at the unfinished plate as Roux approached, dressed only in linen shorts, which left Jack to marvel at the beauty of his lover's elongated form. He walked with so much grace, coming up to Jack in long strides, shoulders back.

"Oh, yes! I'm dying to eat."

As Chad and the other kids dashed into the back yard, Roux rolled into Jack's hammock. His fur was hot, silky, and smelled of sunshine. What more could a man want from life?

Well, maybe some privacy, because being walked in on by his future mother-in-law wasn't on Jack's agenda. He hugged Roux and inhaled his fresh scent.

"I found a cozy spot by the river," Roux whispered, and Jack knew exactly what this was about. Roux was reading his mind.

He couldn't love him more.

The end

Thank you for reading *Jack Addison vs. a Whole World of Hot Trouble*. If you enjoyed your time with our story, we would really appreciate it if you took a few minutes to leave a review on your favorite platform. It is especially important for us as self-publishing authors, who don't have the backing of an established press.
Not to mention we simply love hearing from readers! :)

Kat&Agnes AKA K.A. Merikan
kamerikan@gmail.com
http://kamerikan.com

NEWSLETTER

If you're interested in our upcoming releases, exclusive deals, extra content, freebies and the like, sign up for our newsletter.

http://kamerikan.com/newsletter

We promise not to spam you, and when you sign up, you can choose one of the following books for FREE. Win-Win!

Road of No Return by K.A. Merikan
Guns n' Boys Book 1 by K.A. Merikan
All Strings Attached by Miss Merikan
The Art of Mutual Pleasure by K.A. Merikan

Please, read the instructions in the welcoming e-mail to receive your free book :)

PATREON

Have you enjoyed reading our books? Want more? Look no further! We now have a Patreon account.

https://www.patreon.com/kamerikan

As a patron, you will have access to flash fiction with characters from our books, early cover reveals, illustrations, crossover fiction, Alternative Universe fiction, swag, cut scenes, posts about our writing process, polls, and lots of other goodies.

We have started the account to support our more niche projects, and if that's what you're into, your help to bring these weird and wonderful stories to life would be appreciated. In return, you'll get lots of perks and fun content. Win-win!

About the author

K.A. Merikan are a team of writers who try not to suck at adulting, with some success. Always eager to explore the murky waters of the weird and wonderful, K.A. Merikan don't follow fixed formulas and want each of their books to be a surprise for those who choose to hop on for the ride.

K.A. Merikan have a few sweeter M/M romances as well, but they specialize in the dark, dirty, and dangerous side of M/M, full of bikers, bad boys, mafiosi, and scorching hot romance.

http:/KAMerikan.com
K.A. Merikan on Goodreads
https://twitter.com/#!/KA_Merikan
https://www.facebook.com/KAMerikan

Other books by K.A. Merikan

Guns n' Boys (single-couple series)
Road of No Return
The Devil's Ride
No Matter What
Red Hot
One Step Too Close
His Favorite Color is Blood
Heart Ripper
Diary of a Teenage Taxidermist
Bare-Knuckle Love
Mr. Jaguar
The Cattery
Werewolves of Chernobyl (written with L.A. Witt)
Break My Shell
Special Needs
The Copper Horse (single-couple trilogy)
Stung
Scavengers (single-couple series)
Crazy Kinky Dirty Love (single-couple series)
The Art of Mutual Pleasure
The Black Sheep and the Rotten Apple
Hipster Brothel

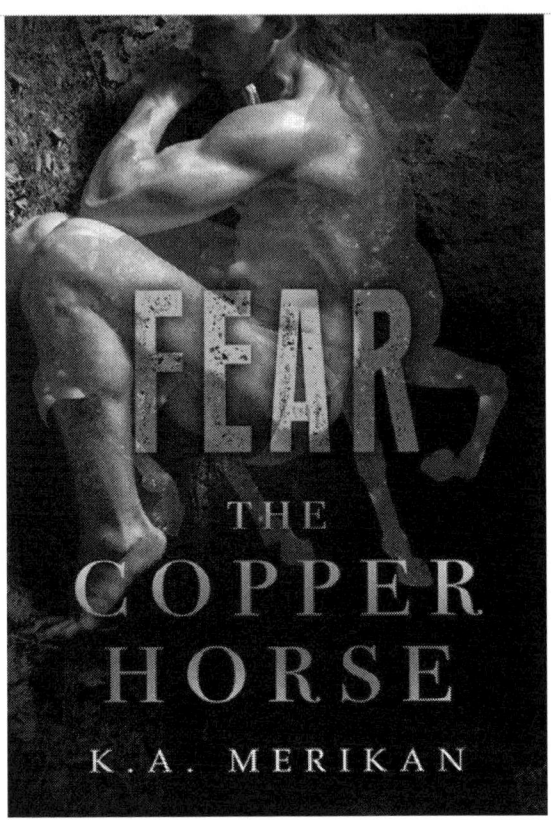

The Copper Horse: Fear
K.A. Merikan

London
1907, twenty years into the zombie Plague

Reuben is a baker living in the slums of London, sharing a room with his father and an extended family of cockroaches. Poor, uneducated, and repressing all his sexual desires, he leads a life of misery, only sometimes sprinkled with gin and a rough tumble in a filthy back alley.

But when he is abducted into Bylondon to be the slave of a wealthy crime family member named Erik Dal, his values are put to the test. His new master is obsessed with all things equestrian, and Reuben soon learns that if he obeys and performs well as Erik's horse, he might just get everything he yearns for: pampering, foods he never even dreamed of, and shameless sex with a demonically handsome young man in leather riding boots.

As Copper, Erik's treasured dun stallion, Reuben must submit to his new master's obscene fancy of possessing another man completely. That is, if he yearns for treats and not the lick of a riding crop. Fake tails, harnesses, and a new haircut to his ginger mane help Reuben transform into Copper, but the fear of losing his dignity in the eyes of society might just prove to be a bigger restraint than any bit, bridle, or handcuffs.

All that for the small price of his freedom. Though at times, Reuben feels it's his soul that Erik is after instead.

Genre: m/m erotic romance, bdsm

Themes: class differences, slavery, steampunk, alternative lifestyle, Victorian, master/servant, captivity, ponyplay, animalization, kink, organized crime, violence

Length: ~95.000 words

The Art of Mutual Pleasure
K.A. Merikan

-The Path to debauchery is strewn with good intentions-

Benjamin Snowley is trapped in a most distressing predicament. He's been feeling poorly and after having recently recovered from influenza, he knows that the fault for his declining health lies in a vice he wouldn't dare mention in polite conversation.

Onanism, self-pollution, masturbation. All names for the same sinful affliction.

For Benjamin, it all started back at school, where he first encountered the immoral Frederick Cory. Ever since then, the man has been plaguing Benjamin's dreams and causing most unnatural urges.

Now is the time for all the infatuation nonsense to stop. With the help of an unorthodox doctor and an indecent proposition to a young stablehand, Benjamin will rid himself of the vile addiction.

But can the experimental treatment be enough to make him forget his feelings for Frederick?

Warning: Contains a clueless young man on a futile quest for chastity and a libertine artist eager to rid him of that goal

Themes: masturbation, historical attitudes to sexuality, medicine, doctor, guilt, unorthodox treatment, master/servant, groom, superstition, moral failure, enemies to lovers

Genre: M/M Regency romantic erotica

Erotic content: explicit language, inappropriate medical examination, cum swallowing, bareback, sex toys, body worship, multiple partners

Length: ~45,000 words

Printed in Great Britain
by Amazon